SERIAL: A Confession

Born in 1950, Jim Lusby is a former Hennessy Award Winner for his short stories and has also written for the stage and radio. He lives in Dublin.

Also by Jim Lusby

CRAZY MAN MICHAEL

MAKING THE CUT

FLASHBACK

KNEELING AT THE ALTAR

A WASTE OF SHAME

SERIAL

SERIAL: A Confession

Jim Lusby

ORION

First published in Great Britain in 2002 by Orion Books
an imprint of The Orion Publishing Group
Orion House, 5 Upper St Martin's Lane, London WC2H 9EA

A CIP catalogue record for this book is available
from the British Library

ISBN (hardback) 0 75285 694 4
ISBN (trade paperback) 0 75285 695 2

Typeset by Deltatype Ltd, Birkenhead, Merseyside
Printed and bound in Great Britain by
Clays Ltd, St Ives plc

To Pauline Förster, who will appreciate,
more than most, the quality of the lies

PART ONE

The Narrative

My father had died unexpectedly.

In the car, squirming uncomfortably on the dampened seat and gasping for breath after running through the heavy rain, I switched on the mobile phone and listened to my sister's voice, recorded two hours earlier, trembling with the news. He's gone, she said simply. Will you be coming down for the funeral? For a long time afterwards, until I was startled by a voice and a knocking on my side window, the network messages droned on in loops, asking if I wanted to save or delete this information, exit or repeat the sequence. I paid no attention to them. I sat staring into the darkness beyond me, through the rain cascading down the windscreen.

Hello! I heard then. It was faint. Like a summons from a distant world. Hello! And then that rapping on the glass to my right.

I turned to look. Outside, her head covered by a plastic rain jacket that she held above her like the wingspan of a bat, leaving her shirt and jeans exposed to the driving rain, a young woman named Mary Corbett stooped, mouthing her concerns against the window. Was I all right? she wondered. Had anything unpleasant happened?

Perhaps she has a bad conscience, I thought. And not without reason. After all, it was she who had brought me to Glencree that winter's night, deep into the heart of the Wicklow Mountains, to deliver a lecture on, of all things, The Trivialization of Death in the Modern Detective Story.

She wasn't responsible for the foul weather, of course. And no one had leaned on me to accept her invitation. But she might have done more to expand or enliven our audience. And who knows? With a livelier crowd, I might have warmed to the topic. As it was, in a cramped and chilly room at the village's Centre for Peace and Reconciliation, surrounded by an exhibition of grim photographs from the religious conflict in Northern Ireland and in no mood to encourage cosy exchanges, I had coldly dissected the genre's faults to eight of its stony-faced aficionados. Of course the detective story trivializes death, I had scoffed. What else can it do? Its conventions insist that a corpse is never a lost human being, mourned by a shattered community of relatives and friends, but always merely a device to start or to keep the plot moving, a cold convenience on a mortuary slab, consisting – depending on the author's research facilities – either entirely of cardboard or entirely of ligaments and abrasions, stomach contents and exit wounds. And this is inevitable. Death, after all, is only significant as a corrupter of what is living. And what the detective story really trivializes is life itself. Think of it. What value can be claimed by a genre where to pause for depth is always fatal to the plot, where people communicate only by a series of inane questions and answers, where the subtlest of stylistic devices is the paraphrase, where the element of surprise is already built into the package and therefore keenly anticipated, where the manipulation of feeling by crude invention leads ultimately to the death of feeling and to its replacement by sentiment, and where the investigator, the reader's only companion, the author's only confidant, is always the same character, always obsessed and alienated, always driven by despair and fuelled by drugs and alcohol, and still far more perceptive than anyone else? Life is cheap in the modern detective story. So cheap that in many cases the only reliable internal guide for distinguishing between the just and the unjust taker of life is the doe-eyed loyalty of the investigator's lover, who constantly directs our moral judgement from between the creases of sweat-stained sheets. You're a good man, Dave, she applauds. You're a good woman, Hetty. As if we wouldn't otherwise know.

The irony.

Lowering my window to Mary Corbett, who had diligently noted all these sour observations on life and death and the crime novel during my contentious lecture and who was now painfully concerned about my welfare, I suddenly decided to share with her the news of my father's unexpected death. His corpse, in effect, became a device to start a dialogue between us. And since she had never met the man, her response was to a cold convenience. I'm sorry, she sympathized.

She wasn't an unattractive young woman, Mary Corbett. Her complexion was a little paler than I usually allow in my fantasies. Her blonde hair was a little thinner and wispier. But her figure was good. Under the wet shirt which, despite the heavy rain, was still unbuttoned at the top, I could see both the outline of her breasts and the soft white flesh below her collarbones. She wore no brassiere. Her nipples were erect from the cold. She had a brown *leather belt, fastened by a silver buckle, around her slim waist. Her hips were full, accentuated by very tight jeans. And I particularly liked the firm curve of her bottom whenever she leaned forward.*

Where do you live, Mary? I asked her.

I was too old to interest or excite her, of course. She was a young student, in her early-twenties. I'm an embittered old man, already pushing fifty, thinning on top and spreading in the middle. But still, although my teeth are decaying and my joints are stiffening, I also know that suffering animates something in the female. A warmth. A protectiveness. It distorts their vision. And the most potent of these stimuli is the news of another's personal loss.

I know all this because in the past I've often used the death of a parent as a storyline to seduce a reluctant woman. Despicable? Of course. But also understandable. Because in this respect – the manipulation of feeling by invention – I suggest that I'm taken after my mother. She too can never be believed. If it had been my mother's voice on the mobile's answering service, for instance, telling me that my father was dead, I would have rigorously checked the story before responding to her news. But it wasn't her, of course. It was my sister. And let me assure you that you can always believe my sister, who has nothing to gain from such fictions.

I live in Enniskerry, Mary told me.

Enniskerry was the nearest town, nine or ten kilometres to the east, and mention of it brought a moment of indecision. It wasn't on the route back to my apartment on the north side of Dublin city, but it was actually closer to my family's home in the south, somewhere I had to pass through to get back home for my father's funeral. So was it worth it, I wondered, returning to my apartment just to pack an overnight bag? After all, it was already past ten-thirty by then.

Are you driving? I asked Mary Corbett.

She shook her head. No.

How are you getting home? I asked.

There's a bus, she said.

Would you mind, I suggested, if I drove you there? I think I'd appreciate a little company right now.

Nursing is irresistible to most women. Nurture is in their nature, so to speak. While the male's aggression inflicts untold carnage on the world, expressing itself in wars and tribal conflicts, rapes and homicidal driving, the female sadly picks up the shattered pieces and lovingly knits them together again, never the assailant but often the victim, driven to violence, in extreme cases, only by the need to protect herself and her children.

Do I exaggerate? Am I being unfair, to either gender?

Within three minutes of accepting my invitation, Mary Corbett had tidied up the loose ends back in the lecture room, pulled on her lightweight rain jacket and was settling into the front passenger seat beside me. She smiled as I started the engine. Turn right, she directed anxiously when we climbed the slight hill to the exit from the centre.

On the road we passed a quartet of dripping aficionados, their heads lowered against the driving rain as they struggled homewards through the wind. Neither of us suggested stopping to rescue them. There are parameters to charity beyond which the gesture is no longer enjoyable.

Because of the dangerous conditions, we drove slowly along the narrow twisting road. At first Mary was quiet. Perhaps she was overawed by the presence of death. Perhaps the poor visibility made her nervous.

Your father, she asked then. What did he do?

I suppose it's still acceptable, even in an age of such diversity as ours, to define members of the older generation solely in terms of a stable occupation. But I have other memories of my father's limitations. He reared chickens in our back garden, I told her.

She may have laughed nervously, although very quietly as well, before she said, That was nice.

No, Mary, I assured her. It wasn't nice at all. In fact, it was intensely embarrassing. Although to appreciate why you'd have to understand the local lifestyle.

Which was what? she wondered.

A road, I said, named after one of the French expressions for the grace of God, but crowded with working people to whom a foreign language and a benevolent deity were equally distant realities. Tiny houses that were too cramped to contain anything larger than the family arguments, with front doorsteps that led directly to the street, but also with enormous back gardens that seemed to stretch away forever from the small yards and into private dreams. And when I was a child, most of those dreams were carried, not on the coxcombs of absurdly strutting chickens, but on the hunched shoulders and bobbing heads of racing greyhounds.

Aren't we always disappointed by our parents? Mary suggested.

On the same road, I said, only seven doors away from us, but still occupying alien territory as far as my father was concerned, because of some

4

bitter feud I could never understand the reasons for, my two uncles kept racing greyhounds. You'd think the relationship between a dog and a twelve-year-old boy was too innocent, wouldn't you, too harmless, to be used as a weapon in a war? And yet, my resourceful mother somehow managed it. From the beginning, she was the one who encouraged my involvement with the greyhounds' arduous training. How was I to know that every hour I spent walking or grooming or feeding an animal was yet another propaganda victory for the forces lined against my father? He himself had nothing to say on the matter. If he experienced my enthusiasm as betrayal, then his resentment was lost among his other silences.

Men, Mary suggested, are not good at expressing their feelings.

Should I have pointed out that women are experts at inventing them? But no. I was wary of digression.

You're right, I agreed. But even in an age of taciturn men, my father was unusually distant. He always ate his meals alone, for instance, separated from the rest of the family, poring over the black, leather-bound album in which he collected Irish stamps or lost in the latest blockbuster he had bought from the second-hand store. He and my mother never spoke to each other, except to argue. A bitter, ongoing dispute. A tense stand-off that frequently, unpredictably, erupted into violence, and that strained our vulnerable nerves. I've always thought of it as an unexploded bomb. Sitting down in its vicinity was unwise. Speaking was particularly dangerous. And to express an opinion or a feeling was inevitably fatal. The only sane thing to do was to minimize the risks. Strangle your emotions, in other words. Pretend to be mute. Bolt your meals and escape as quickly as possible from the house. Do you know what the most efficient form of flight is, Mary? I wondered.

She started slightly. Listening so intently, she hadn't anticipated another question so soon. Flight? she repeated.

The most efficient form, I said again.

She thought about this. I don't know, she admitted then. Travel, I suppose.

I shook my head. No, Mary, I told her. The most efficient form of flight is absorption. My dedication to greyhounds, although rich and enjoyable in itself, was really an escape. This is how I am. I always throw myself into things with such initial vigour, such singular focus, that I quickly become good at them. By thirteen, for instance, I was long past the basics and already master of the scams that colour greyhound racing: holding a dog back by over-feeding it before races and then slimming it down to romp home at generous odds, or rigging a puppy's time trials so that it goes into its first competitive race showing a vital tenth of a second slower than it has actually run. But the downside of flight is that it has its roots in unfaithfulness. And, ultimately, this is where it always returns for inspiration.

I'd intended developing this theme a little further, but the rain was so heavy by then, swirling around our headlights and covering the windscreen, that it was impossible to distinguish either the white markings in the centre of the road or the grass margin to our left. It was probably too dangerous to continue the journey, but for a while, through a series of sharp bends, stopping seemed even more hazardous. There were looming trees on both sides. Occasionally the overhanging branches swayed and flicked against the windows of the car, cracking violently like whips.

I slowed to a crawl. Mary anxiously held her breath. And then, quite suddenly, just as we thought we were past the worst, we came upon another vehicle, stalled in the middle of the road. Its tail lights reared at me, like a monster's eyes. I swerved immediately, struggling not only to avoid it, but also to keep free from the hedges on our right. Somehow I squeezed through the narrow gap. In the rear-view mirror, as I straightened the car again, I caught a glimpse of a young couple standing in the rain in front of their bonnet, arguing violently with each other. And then we'd negotiated another bend and their headlights had disappeared again behind us. As if they'd never existed.

Do you play any sports, Mary? I asked.

I played hockey for my school, she confirmed.

Then you'll understand, I said. Because greyhound racing is like every other sport. It's mostly dedicated preparation. Mostly slog. The long daily walks in all weathers to build up a dog's stamina. The uphill gallops to increase its strength. The careful diet to keep its weight steady. Hard work. Repetitious. And humdrum. And to justify it, you need the intoxication, the forgetfulness, of frequent victory. Perhaps I was already tiring of the grind. Perhaps we hadn't enough success. Perhaps there were wider forces at work.

In the spring of 1968, when I was sixteen years old, when Paris was buckling under student rebellion, when the campaigns for personal liberation and social freedom were advancing everywhere, my uncles handed me a dog to take to the local abattoir. A mild-tempered brindle bitch, she had broken her leg too often to retain the hope of racing and she wasn't considered good enough to breed from. I walked her, past Gallows Hill, and out to the *abattoir, where a fat man in a blood-soaked apron took her from me. And I stood outside, looking in through the open door, while he held a gun to her head and drove a bolt through her brain.*

When I got back, my uncles were no longer at home. They'd also taken the rest of the dogs with them, presumably to spare them the trauma of wondering what I had done to their mate. I stood alone in the empty garden, still holding the dangling lead and collar, and I became irritated by the seedy values at work, by the casual abuse of my own labour and by the callous disregard for my feelings.

Beyond the low hedge that separated us from the neighbouring garden, I noticed the clothes line jerking up and down, as if it was being plucked like a guitar string. I thought a bird had settled on it. Something heavy and macabre, I reckoned, like the grim crows I'd often seen feeding on carrion in the country. But then I remembered that I'd actually removed that clothes line some time before. The house next door had been vacant for almost a year. The old man who'd lived there, a veteran of the War of Independence, had recently died in a nursing home, and one of his last, more surreal requests had been for that length of hemp from his garden to be brought to his bedside.

I walked across and looked over the hedge. The garden on the other side was badly overgrown, although a narrow path had been trodden through the weeds and thistles directly under the clothes line. At one end of this, closest to the house, a woman was pegging sheets to the line. I couldn't see her face. The wind was blowing a sheet against her, almost wrapping it around her. But I could immediately tell from her appearance, not only that she was a stranger, but that she wasn't even Irish. She was American. She had long blonde hair, very light in colour, very fine in texture, that was being lifted from her shoulders by the breeze. She was wearing a yellow T-shirt and blue cut-away denim shorts, a pair of white sneakers but no socks. Her long bare legs and elegant arms were evenly tanned. Glistening. Golden.

She was, quite simply, the most stunning woman I had ever seen.

But she was more than just a mysterious and sexually attractive woman. For me, she also held the promise of everything our grey and ordinary little lives denied us. Mentally, I compared her to my uncles, those massive working men, slaughterers and boners in the nearby bacon factory, with their hob-nailed boots stuck firmly in the conventions of their generation. Those rough bachelors, who made a political statement out of their inability to boil an egg, a manifesto out of their refusal to learn, and whose attention to

7

personal grooming was, at best, restricted. My dour father, already a laughable figure with his derisory fowl and worthless stamps, his cloth cap and unravelled cardigans stained with flour dust from the mills where he worked, declined now to a burden, a liability. More importantly, I measured her against the local women, against their personal sacrifices to the sentence of bearing and raising children, their weariness, their wariness of beauty, their dull, repetitive complaints.

The headlights picked out a road sign indicating a parking area a hundred metres ahead. If anything, the rain was even heavier now than it had been earlier. A fork of lightning suddenly lit up the darkness and, almost simultaneously, a roll of thunder crashed above us. We were at the centre of the storm. And I no longer felt safe.

Would you mind, I asked Mary, if we pulled into the car park for a while? Until the worst of this blows over.

She laughed anxiously. I think you'd better, she agreed.

I turned left at the opening, into a circular clearing that was surfaced with loose gravel. A carved wooden sign told us that we were in Cloon Car Park, one of the halting points along a popular tourist trail that took hillwalkers through the Wicklow Mountains in summer. Beyond the sign, I passed a steel gate, a barbed-wire fence, and then a narrow clearing that led to the approved footpath, which was muddy and waterlogged now, and almost impassable. I parked facing the road and left the engine idling to run the heater in the car. And there we sat, listening to the rain pelting against the bodywork.

Did you ever see her again? Mary asked eventually. Your American.

Yes, I said. Actually I met her on the street the next day. I was returning to school after lunch. She was walking towards me, ambling up the hill, wearing a bright red summer dress and carrying a shopping bag from one of the city's department stores. She seemed to recognize me, although we hadn't greeted each other the previous day. As we talked, she explained that she needed someone to clear and re-seed her garden and she asked if I was interested in the job. I felt uncertain. I simply didn't know what she was suggesting here. My own hopes, of friendship, of romance, perhaps of intimacy, were probably a crude distortion. And what I dreaded most with this sophisticated, educated woman was appearing provincial. I hedged.

I'm studying for exams, I said. They're only two weeks away.

I meant in your vacation, she explained. When you're free.

I don't know . . .

I became awkward, tongued-tied. Suddenly I was aware of my age, my inexperience, the high colour and uncomfortable warmth in my cheeks.

She smiled. But only for herself, I think. Ruefully. My name is Sarah, by the way, she said. Sarah Kleisner.

In the end, I changed my plans that summer. A group of friends, most of them still at school, but some already working in the local bacon factory, had the use of a large caravan that was pitched at a seaside resort, about eight miles south of the city. The idea was to swim, lounge, chat up girls and play football on the beach by day, eat and drink by a camp fire at night. As relaxation after my exams, and as a break from the tension in the house, it would have been ideal. Instead, I stayed at home.

I was bored a great deal, irritated the rest of the time. The heat raised tempers among those still trapped in the city and imprisoned in their overcrowded houses. My parents intensified their eternal conflict. His silence against her garrulity. My father was constantly goaded by noise, by taunts, by sly insults, all meant for him but not directly addressed to him, and all prodding him towards the error of response. My mother, on the other hand, threatened with exhaustion from her own unceasing efforts, and with a fatal collapse into resting for a breath, was infuriated by his stoicism. But above all, with both of them, there was the terrifying sense that even victory would be worthless, or defeat insignificant, a sense that their world was already declining, that life had passed them anyway and that they had fallen too far behind.

It was a fear that was shared by my uncles. Throughout the summer, they argued with the living and the dead. Intolerant of each other and impatient with the dogs, they were also dangerously short-tempered with me. They seemed to forget that I was doing them a favour, that I was working for them without pay.

Late in July, I simply abandoned the greyhounds, walked out of my uncles' front door, took a single step to my right, and rang Sarah Kleisner's doorbell.

Your back garden is still overgrown, I said. And repeated. Until the words finally struck a chord in her memory.

Right, she recalled. The garden. You still want the job of clearing it?
Yes, I said.
When can you start? she asked.
Any time, really, I insisted.
Monday? she suggested. Is Monday okay?
Monday?

Is it too soon?

I had no talent for gardening, no interest in acquiring the skills. My great-grandparents, on my mother's side at least, had once been subsistence farmers, but they clearly hadn't torn their fingertips on stony soil, slaving to establish their children in more profitable occupations, only for their descendants to pervert their torment into a hobby. Under a baking sun, I hacked away crudely at the thistles and nettles and brambles in Sarah's garden, mostly in poor humour. It took me four weeks to clear the space. And since destruction was the limit of my abilities and I was reluctant to admit it, I passed another week just raking over the turned soil.

That Friday afternoon, in mid-August now, I waited anxiously for Sarah to return from her work. Anxiously, because she'd promised to discuss the design and character of the new garden. Usually, she came straight through the house to greet me, still dressed in one of the expensive business suits of which she seemed to have an unlimited wardrobe.

The back door was already wide open that day. Through it, a little after five-thirty, I heard her unlock the street door and close it behind her again after entering. I imagined her picking up the post from where I'd left it that morning on the old mahogany stand in the hallway. There were three local letters, I remember, and one with a New York postmark and an American stamp.

Leaning against the trunk of an apple tree, one of the few surviving features of the old garden, I watched her pass by the large kitchen window. She was absorbed, reading one of the letters. She didn't notice me. Even when she stopped at the window, facing the garden, she didn't look out. Because her head was lowered, her blonde hair kept falling across her eyes and she kept lifting it with her right hand and folding it again behind her ear.

There was only a single sheet of paper in her other hand. Later I discovered its envelope, along with the unopened other letters, on the floor in the front hallway. She seemed to have gathered the entire bundle, but then dropped everything else while reading the first letter. She stared at this single page, or re-read it, for perhaps three or four minutes. And then, quite calmly and deliberately, she folded it and tore it repeatedly into small pieces. I'm not certain where she left the fragments. She moved towards the open back door and possibly threw them on the surface of the old pine table that was placed next to it, but I didn't see her doing this. She may also have burned most of them on the gas cooker or washed them away in the sink.

I expected her to step out, into the narrow yard between the house and the garden, if only to let me know that she was home. She didn't. Perhaps she intended to. A second or two after I lost sight of her through the window, her front doorbell rang. When she answered this, she must have stood for a while in the hallway, talking to the caller, because the draught between the two open doors whipped up the surviving fragments of the torn letter and blew them into the yard and garden, before the back door itself slammed shut. Some of the pieces stuck on the rough stone surface of the yard. Most fluttered into the exposed soil in the garden. None was large enough to contain more than a few hand-written or typewritten characters, meaningless in themselves.

At this stage, some instinctive apprehension made me retreat behind the cover of the apple tree, transforming myself with a single step from participant to spectator. It is, perhaps, the role contemporary western man is now most completely comfortable with, a role which began, for me, with the television coverage that year of both the riots in Paris and the civil rights disturbances in Northern Ireland, and with the death of Sarah Kleisner.

When I saw Sarah again, through the kitchen window, she was backing away, clearly from someone who was advancing on her, and clearly frightened by the approach. I couldn't see who was there. I waited for them to reach the window and reveal themselves. But Sarah stopped. She gestured, at first uncertainly, helplessly, throwing her hands in the air and shrugging her shoulders, but then angrily, pointing her finger aggressively, warning, threatening. It was only when she suddenly swivelled, turning her back on the caller, rejecting any further discussion, that the other, a small unshaven man, finally came into view, stepping forward to lay a hand on her right shoulder.

Instantly recognizing my father, still in his working clothes, with the steel bicycle clips pinning the trouser legs to the tops of his heavy black boots and the soiled cloth cap tugged low on his forehead, I felt as if an abrasive cord was sharply tightened around my stomach, a distinctive band of pain that has stayed with me throughout all the other shocks and traumas of my life.

Naturally, I assumed that he was there because of me. Like Adam cowering from his displeased God in the biblical myth, I desperately tried to shrink out of sight, even though I was already crouched behind the only decent cover in the garden.

I have no idea how much time passed. Perhaps none at all. Perhaps as soon as my father laid his hand on her shoulder, Sarah swung back towards him and struck out, slashing her long nails down his left cheek and leaving him with the trail of scratches that would mark the rest of his life. At the time, he didn't even raise his hand to protect himself or to wipe the blood from his face. He stared at Sarah. He said something to her. As with all their other exchanges, the meaning was lost to me.

When my father turned to leave, I ducked out of sight and waited for him to come to the garden and argue with me. He never appeared. And by the time I risked checking again, I found that Sarah too had vanished.

I stepped out and cautiously approached the back door, watching for any signs of movement inside the house, listening for the sound of voices. I opened the door, still wary. The draught I immediately felt indicated that the street door was still open, and suggested that there was no one left in the house. I stepped in. In the front hallway, the three unopened letters and the envelope with the New York postmark and American stamp all lay on the floor. I picked the last item up. Sarah's name and address were typed on the front. Above them, in the centre of the envelope, the sender's name was pre-printed: Robert Kleisner, Lamson & Luetgerr, Park Avenue, New York.

A relative's letter? Carrying news of some personal loss, some family tragedy?

I put the envelope in the pocket of my jeans. I went through the front door, into the street, and looked up and down. In the distance, descending from Gallows Hill, a man was walking eight greyhounds, guiding four with each hand. Closer to me, outside the entrance gates of the jute factory, a group of young girls were skipping. In the opposite direction, where most of the houses lay, a few labourers were walking or cycling home from work. There was no sign of my father or Sarah.

My father, I learned later, drank with some friends in a local pub until closing time that night. Precisely what time he first entered the pub and with whom would soon become critical questions.

As for Sarah . . .

A little less than five hours after the quarrel with my father, shortly before eleven o'clock, her body was discovered by a courting couple at the foot of the cliff that lay about two kilometres to the north, across the fields at the back of our houses.

The Profile

On a Thursday night in mid-January, at exactly eight o'clock, a middle-aged man named Michael Elwood draws his chair a little closer to the piano in the front room of his house. He's about to play. He coughs self-consciously a number of times. He flexes the muscles in his right hand and then repeats the exercise with his left, totally unaware that the cracking of his bones is setting his companion's teeth on edge. She's Laura Ashwell, a woman of thirty-eight, who works as a cashier in a national bank. And she's sitting directly behind him, out of his vision.

Elwood is extremely nervous. You might think that this recital he has organized, in his own home and for an audience of one, is on too small a scale to carry any pressure with it. But there's a history. As a child, Elwood studied classical music and was considered a talented soloist, before a disaster in some public competition destroyed his confidence. It's almost thirty years since he last risked playing for acceptance and applause. There's also a wider agenda. Elwood intends proposing tonight. In fact, given the strategies this awkward, reclusive man has developed over the years, the performance *is* the marriage proposal.

So naturally, he's hesitant. Shuffling his seating back and forth, he struggles with the memories and the doubts, while desperately trying to keep his tentative hopes in check. Until finally, after returning the chair to its original position, he settles into the first item on his programme.

This is Debussy's étude, *Pour les sonorités opposées.*

His playing is technically correct. It always was, even in childhood. But now, in his mid-forties, it's almost completely stripped of feeling. There's no passion. No emotion, even. No involvement. No more than the rest of his life – he works as a wages clerk for a supermarket chain, he dresses in dark suits and has plain, almost anonymous features – his music retains nothing that is personal or spontaneous.

Even so, it's an expression of love.

Somewhere in the middle of it, however, a youth outside the front window of the house starts calling drunkenly to some mate of his in the distance. 'Yammo! Yammo! Yammo!' The effect is like that of a crazed drummer in the background, repeatedly hammering the same discordant beat from his instrument. 'Yammo! Yammo! Yammo!'

Elwood misses a note. He recovers. He struggles desperately for a while against the interruption. But then, frustrated and angered, he slams his hands on the keys and leaves them there, inactive.

Ironically, the youth on the footpath outside simultaneously falls silent. Not because he's made contact with his friend, but because he's just reinserted his nose in the plastic bag full of glue he's carrying.

'I'm sorry, Laura,' Elwood says tensely, but without turning to look at her.

'Well,' she sympathizes, 'you can hardly expect them to appreciate Chopin in this place, I suppose.'

She means it as a joke, to show that she's more amused than troubled. But . . .

'That was Debussy,' Elwood mutters. 'Was it that bad?'

'What did I say?' she laughs. 'Did I say Chopin? Debussy, of course. And it was delightful.'

Stupid word. She knows it as soon as she says it. Even though she can't see his face, she also knows that Elwood is making an effort to ignore it.

He manages this by changing the subject.

'There's nothing wrong with this place,' he says, although this is a situation he remembers from his own childhood rather than one that still exists. Like most local authority estates in south County Dublin, this one, at the foot of the mountains, about ten kilometres north of Enniskerry, has suffered from drugs and neglect. 'I live here,' he advances as evidence. 'You live here.'

'They live here, too,' Laura Ashwell observes.

'No, no,' Elwood cries impetuously. 'I don't care who lives here. I don't care whether or not they appreciate Debussy, or Chopin, or Ravel. You have certain preferences, certain ideas about how things should be done, but they're for yourself, you can't force them on everyone else. All I ask is the same consideration in return. That's all. But why am I saying this to you? You already agree with me. I should be saying it to the lout in the street outside.'

'Except that he seems to be gone now,' Laura points out.

Elwood listens for a while with a doubtful expression on his tense face. But all he can hear is traffic, far in the distance. He's relieved. Despite the rhetoric, he doesn't want to confront anyone.

'Will we try again?' he suggests.

Laura Ashwell has no particular affection for either Debussy or Chopin. She likes the Rolling Stones and the Doors, and, among contemporary groups, Oasis and Catatonia. She has never mentioned this to Elwood. And now is not the time to start. 'Yes,' she says with apparent eagerness. 'Please.'

But it seems, this evening, as if there's some conspiracy to sabotage Elwood's dreams. All through the preliminaries, while he's clearing his throat and shuttling his chair back and forth, while his fingers, anticipating an interruption, are playing tentative scales, the quietness holds outside. But as soon as he settles seriously into the étude again, someone switches on a ghettoblaster in the street, turns the volume up to an unbearable level and greets the rap tune that blares out of it with a wild yelp.

Elwood crashes his hands on the keys and slams down the lid. His chair topples and crashes to the floor as he rises suddenly.

'Michael!' Laura cries.

'Excuse me for a moment,' he says.

'Now, don't go out there, Michael!'

'It's all right,' he snaps. 'I'm only going to look, that's all.'

He sweeps past her and opens the front door. On the small green opposite the house, there's a group of ten or twelve youths. Fifteen, sixteen year olds. Some are attempting to dance, others are wrestling with each other, a few are stretched on the grass. They're all drunk. When they finally notice Elwood and see that they've disturbed him, they express their delight by shouting obscenities at him and inviting him to do something about it.

Realizing that his appearance has only added to their enjoyment, Elwood turns and goes back inside.

'Cider party,' he says between his teeth.

He goes to the telephone and dials the seven digits of the local Garda station. The line is engaged. His hand shoots out to break the connection and to dial again, but it loses its impetus along the way and drifts off to make a pointless gesture. It's just occurred to him that he doesn't want to call the guards. He has no need of allies, he tells himself, because he has no intention of making or maintaining enemies. Allies, even the ones who are paid for their services, inevitably make counter-claims on your life.

And then Elwood makes a significant connection. It's actually his *girl-friend's* presence that's confused him, he decides. If he was alone he'd just retreat to a back room and read a book until the party exhausted itself. He wouldn't persist with his music. He wouldn't advertise his distress by opening the front door. He wouldn't broadcast it by phoning the guards.

While still brooding on this, he becomes aware that Laura Ashwell is now looking at him quizzically and he realizes that he must be holding the receiver for a long time without doing anything with it.

'My name is Elwood,' he tells the dead instrument, where no one is listening to him. 'I want to complain about a disturbance ...'

Afterwards, while they're waiting for the guards who'll never come, Elwood and Laura Ashwell say nothing to each other. Something distasteful has happened between them. And they both know it. They feel awkward. Apprehensive. They risk nothing. They sit in silence, in separate armchairs, waiting for their separate worlds to fall back into place.

Ten minutes pass. Fifteen. Laura Ashwell starts glancing at her watch. At first it's surreptitious, just to check the time. But it quickly becomes more obvious. It becomes a crude signal.

'I'm sorry, Michael,' she says finally. 'I'll have to get back soon.'

It's a relief, for both of them.

'I'll drive you home,' Elwood offers.

'I can walk, Michael. It's not very far.'

'No, I'll drive.'

Laura Ashwell pays no attention to the catcalls and wolf whistles from the kids opposite as they're leaving the house. She can't be hurt any more than she already is. But the jeering infuriates Elwood. He hurries her away from it, forcing her to walk to the car at a pace she finds uncomfortable in her new dress and new shoes. Both bought especially for this evening, unfortunately. From behind the wheel of his Opel Astra, he hustles her into the passenger seat beside him. And before she can even lock the door or fasten her seat belt, he starts the engine and pulls sharply away from the kerb.

Once they're well out of range, however, midway between their two houses, it occurs to him that he's only in flight. He doesn't want to visit Laura Ashwell's house. Her father, once an active trade unionist but now too old and too disillusioned for anything but preaching, will inevitably lecture him on the causes of delinquency without offering any relief from individual delinquents. But he doesn't want to go home, either, and sit as a prisoner in his own front room. He wants to continue driving, he realizes. He wants to be alone. He's really known this, without admitting it to himself, since pretending to have called the guards. Laura's presence in his life makes him vulnerable. So does the ownership of a piano and the musical pretensions and the need for an audience. He imagines himself driving alone through the darkness, secretly discarding his burdens, until there's nothing left to be protected any more. It's only then, he convinces himself, when he's stripped of them all, that he'll be comfortable again.

He parts from Laura without getting out of the car to walk her to her door. 'I'll have to sort this thing out,' he says vaguely. 'There's no point in arranging anything until I've sorted this out.'

'No,' she agrees, although she knows that they're actually saying goodbye.

While Laura Ashwell goes to her bedroom and puts a record on the turntable of her hi-fi system – it's *Exile on Main Street* by the Rolling Stones, an LP she bought as a twelve year old against the outraged objections of her parents but hasn't played for more than a decade now – Michael Elwood pulls away, leaves the housing estate and turns left at the next major junction, heading into the mountains to the south of the city.

It's 8.45 p.m.

An hour and a quarter later, around ten o'clock according to most witnesses, he walks into Johnnie Fox's pub in Glencullen, a small settlement in the Wicklow Mountains, on the road between Glencree and Enniskerry. This is no more than fifteen kilometres from his starting point. Why has he taken so long to reach it? Although the landscape is wild and breathtaking, it's too dark to go sightseeing. And it's impossible to believe that the driving itself exhilarates him. He's not the type to find abandonment, or himself, on the road. Is he lost? But when he walks through the door of the pub, after leaving his Opel Astra in the car park, he's not agitated in any way. He doesn't ask for directions. He stands inside the door for a few seconds, jingling his car keys and glancing around, and then he sits at an empty table. He leaves his jacket on a chair, reserving the place, and goes to the bar. He orders and pays for a bottle of Budweiser beer and returns to the table.

It's Thursday night. At ten o'clock, the pub is doing good trade, but isn't yet overcrowded. The place is popular with the young. The affluent young. Business professionals. Academics. Students. Tourists. It's a fashionable pub, full of old wood and new money. A middle-aged man, dressed in a dull navy suit and drinking alone, is bound to attract some curiosity. It's a fleeting interest, however. People have their own concerns. And Michael Elwood has no talent for socializing. He lacks any presence. He has no confidence. In fact, whenever he watches people, they get an uncomfortable feeling from it. His eyes are dead. His look is unsettling. It's actually described as dirty, or creepy, by more than one of its victims.

Tonight, Michael Elwood seems particularly interested in a group of young women who are noisily enjoying themselves in a cosy corner of the pub. They're all just a little drunk, in a relaxed sort of way. Their inhibitions are loosened. Two of them, both blondes, are wearing very short skirts. Another is showing a bare midriff, brightened by a massive stud in her belly button. There's a lot of flesh on show. The women are not aware of it, however. It's a girls' night out. They're not interested in men. At least, not until one of them catches Michael Elwood staring at them and draws the attention of the others to this. They all stare back. Elwood blushes and averts his eyes.

In turn, all of this is noticed by a group of young men in the opposite corner, who have been monitoring the women with a view to joining them. They're on the verge of intervening, certainly to rescue the females, perhaps even to batter the pervert. For a few minutes, the mood in the pub is volatile. Nobody else quite knows what the source of the violence in the air is. But it's tangible. Everybody feels it.

And what finally dissipates it again? Nothing in particular. It just fades, like most of these things. More people crowd into the bar, obscuring lines of vision, raising the level of the noise again, and changing the composition of the gathering. The young men's resentment, and the young women's unease, get lost in this new mix. Some of the newcomers take chairs at Michael Elwood's table. They ask him if the spaces are free. He nods without speaking. He nurses his beer.

Over the next thirty minutes, the pub becomes extremely crowded, very noisy and very lively. No one notices Michael Elwood any more, whether he has another drink, whether he moves. He sinks into the mass without trace.

At another table, across the room, there's a man called Gary Gaynor. He's thirty-six years old, but he's sitting with a large group of mates, all of them under twenty-five. They're a football team, and they're relaxing after finishing a training session. He's their player-manager. The younger lads are arguing about girl bands. This is outside the range of Gary's enthusiasms. He's much more interested in a woman he's noticed, who's sitting alone at the bar.

Because Gary is still pretending to be part of the discussion, and because he doesn't want to be rude, he's restricting himself to glancing up every now and again to check on the woman. Afterwards, therefore, his memories of her are like a collection of photographs shown in sequence. The first five are all the same. The woman is sitting at the bar, alone, drinking a gin and tonic and reading from a black folder. She's in her early-thirties, he thinks. She's very attractive. She has thin-framed glasses and auburn – possibly titian – hair, clipped to her head in a bun. She's wearing casual clothes: denim jeans and a purple sweater. The only slight variations in the images concern the position of the woman's head. In most of Gary's memories, her face is averted, turned downwards towards the pages she's reading. In at least one, however, she's looking directly into Gary's eyes, and possibly smiling a little.

It's encouraging. But at this point, someone nudges Gary in the ribs and demands his attention to a joke. He turns away from the bar. He doesn't understand the joke and has to rely on the laughter of the others to convince him that it's finished. He looks back. But now the spot at the bar is empty. Or it's crowded with other people, which is the same thing as far as Gary is concerned. The titian-haired woman is no longer in the frame.

Gary stands up and searches around. And, finally, he sees her. Caught in the centre of the last snapshot he has to offer, she's squeezing through the exit, past a young couple trying to get in, and she's accompanied by a dull little man in a navy suit whose right hand appears to be on her arm.

Oh, well, Gary thinks disconsolately to himself as he slumps back in his seat, they must be on a date. They must have arranged to meet in Johnnie Fox's

The Investigation

My name is Kristina Galetti. I'm twenty-seven years old, of distant Italian descent, 170cm in height, medium build, with black hair and hazel-brown eyes, most frequently seen wearing denim jeans and dark shirts.

You might guess, I was trained as a detective.

I joined the guards straight out of secondary school, when I was eighteen years old. They told me I breezed through the training college. The truth is, I nearly died in there. The guards is a man's world. There are a few institutions still like that. The guards, the army, and the cabinet rooms in government buildings. Women have colonized the newspapers, television, the arts and the social services. Men still rule the physical world, in other words, while women have taken over the emotional and intellectual ones. By and large. That's the way I see it, anyway.

What I mean by the guards being a man's world is that the treatment you get in there is very rough. There are no niceties, no allowances, no respect for softness. Instead you get constant slagging, constant comments about your weight, your shape, your sexuality, your availability, your family or your accent. Anything you might be sensitive about.

In my class in training college there were twenty-five men and four women, so you can imagine the volume of the banter. But you learn to give as good as you get. Or you learn to ignore it. If you don't, you're not going to survive on the streets. Out there, the abuse will simply break you. I know a couple of female guards, for instance, who've had male prisoners masturbate in front of them after an arrest. That's the level of contempt you'll have to deal with.

I must have learned quickly. After a few years in uniform, on the beat in Dublin, I was given plain-clothes work, as an undercover surveillance officer in a unit tackling street crime, and after that I was made a detective garda. Those first couple of weeks back in civvies I was so pleased with myself that I bought a new outfit, a light-coloured trouser suit that I picked up in a sale at Brown Thomas. Two days later it got stained, scuffed and torn during a chase, after a handbag thief slashed a tourist's arm with a Stanley knife and ran into a block of flats to escape. Which is why I'm mostly seen wearing jeans now. Like I said, you learn quickly.

The year I made detective, the force was facing a major crisis. Morale was low. Resources were poor. Political support was non-existent. And the public were losing confidence. We were accused of incompetence. Big-time criminals became so cocky and contemptuous that a drugs gang murdered a crime journalist in broad daylight.

That was one of the two main challenges to our authority at the time. The other was the long list of women who had recently disappeared in Dublin and the neighbouring counties. Fifteen of them in less than ten years. Sixteen-year-old schoolgirls, twenty-year-old students, thirty-year-old secretaries and forty-five-year-old housewives. When you wrote them down, all together like that, and looked at the list, you could understand how it reflected so badly on the professionalism of the force. Ireland is a small country. Its social problems are still manageable. Theoretically, it should be easy enough to police. But none of those missing women was found by the guards. The corpses of three of them were dug out of shallow graves in the Wicklow Mountains, but even these were first discovered by accident, by families out walking or by a workman cutting turf. The investigations into the murders led nowhere. No one was charged. There were no suspects in the frame. The stories made the newspapers and television reports for a few days after the bodies were found, but then dropped out of sight again. As for the twelve other women who were officially listed as missing, no one other than their immediate families seemed to care about them. To be honest, the feeling shared by the various teams investigating the disappearances was that the women had simply taken lovers and legged it abroad. But then, as I'd have to point out, all the members of these investigating teams were men.

You might think that such constant failure would lead to tough questions and harsh criticism of the guards in the media. You'd be wrong. The idea of the crusading crime correspondent was a popular joke within the force. The fact was, the flow of information to most of these correspondents was controlled by the Garda Press Office, so the spin the public always got on the force was the favourable one the guards themselves wanted. We weren't only ineffective, in other words, we were unaccountable as well.

But then, predictably I suppose, a woman with social and political connections finally disappeared. That's how it still is in Ireland. Even as a crime statistic, it's not what you are as an individual that's most important, it's who you know. This young woman, part of a rich set that was into polo, motor racing and yachting, happened to be a relative of a newspaper magnate. For weeks afterwards, the case was never out of the papers. And the media were never off the case. Suddenly, the disappearance of vulnerable young women was a major issue, central to the type of society we wanted to build. The resulting pressure, and the public outcry that followed it, forced the authorities to do something. Their response was a special unit, based in headquarters in Dublin, dedicated to reexamining the files of the unsolved murders and disappearances.

I'll be honest, I didn't know at the time what I'd achieved to merit being picked for this team. I could live with my own uncertainty, of course. The trouble was, nobody else knew either. There were twelve of us initially: an inspector, a sergeant and ten detectives, although only five of that bunch – a wild young fella named Jimmy Coyne, two older men we called The Twins, Sergeant Mullery and myself – were still there at the end.

I was the only woman. I was resented as the token female, dismissed as just a political appointment. The others not only had longer service, they also had much more experience of murder investigations. I felt I had to prove myself at every step.

In the beginning, the inspector in charge of the unit was Carl McCadden. This was a lucky break for me. Because of his record, McCadden was respected by the others. And because he treated female officers as detectives, not as women, the rest had no option but to follow his lead. It gave me the breathing space I needed.

Great things were expected of us. We expected great things of ourselves. Although hanging over our every move was the dread that we were dealing with an extremely clever, extremely resourceful sequential killer, but one who should really have been caught in the early stages.

McCadden, though, had a totally different perspective on this. Once he said to us, 'Probably there is no serial killer. Personally, I don't think there is. Probably the serial killer explanation is just a lazy mental groove, all too easy to slip into these days. Probably there are fifteen separate killers.

Probably the slaughter and depersonalization of women is just a widespread social phenomenon, an extreme expression of a common prejudice. Given the type of world we'd all like to live in, which do you think is the better option? I'm not sure I know the answer to that question. I'm not sure if there is an answer.'

If he was trying to keep our minds open, he definitely succeeded in doing it.

The commissioner, in his much-publicized address to us, had instructed us to search for links between the cases when re-examining the files, links that might have been previously overlooked, because the original investigations were run by different divisions, because information wasn't shared, because there was no central data bank, no computerized comparisons. We did all that. We also sent samples from the various crime scenes for DNA-profiling, a facility that hadn't been available for some of the earlier cases. We re-interviewed witnesses. We trawled through every item of evidence. Almost immediately, we had our first success. Forensic analysis linked a convicted rapist to one of the murdered women. Encouraged, we pushed ourselves harder.

And then, less than a month into the work, McCadden was suddenly transferred to another high-profile case. The daughter of a government minister, fooling around with Satanism and devil worship, had been butchered in a city-centre apartment.

When I heard the news that McCadden's replacement was going to be a woman, Inspector Sharon Taafe, my first reaction was one of relief. An ally, I thought. Or at the very least, someone who wasn't going to downgrade my status within the unit. When I met her, though, I have to admit that what I really felt was envy. For a while, professionalism went right out the window. She was the kind of woman who seemed to have everything: good looks, style, a stunning career, brains, a flat stomach, a healthy family, a genius of a hairdresser, confidence, a devoted husband, the culinary skills of a celebrity chef, and time left over for herself.

I think she was in her late-thirties. She looked a decade younger. What I couldn't believe was that the lads in the unit weren't twice as impressed as I was. Instead they were resentful. They took to calling her Inspector T. Very soon this became Iced Tea, because she was supposed to be frigid, the theory being that any woman who craves power is automatically frigid, while any man who does so has a permanent hard-on. In turn, this was the source of a lot of crude jokes in her presence that she couldn't possibly get. 'Iced tea,' one of the lads would say. 'Now there's something I wouldn't touch, no matter how thirsty I was.' Until I got to thinking would they ever grow up and get some sense? Do boys ever grow up, anyway?

Right from the start, therefore, there were rumblings about the appointment, accusations that it was just a cynical public relations exercise, a knee-jerk reaction to a campaign the feminists were running at the time. As you might expect, Sharon Taafe looked very good in all the newspaper photographs and television footage. Her appointment reflected very nicely, thank you, on the image of the force. She was flavour of the month. With everyone except the people she had to work with.

Probably the worst of her critics on the team was a detective named Tommy Dennison, a big, red-faced country lad, with the build and manners of a rugby forward, who was particularly bitter about women. I had no idea why he was so angry. He'd given me a rough time at the start and we hadn't mixed since then.

I didn't know whether Dennison was right or wrong about the new inspector. I didn't know whether or not she got her appointment purely on merit. She hadn't the same track record as McCadden, for instance, but she was no novice. She'd worked on most of the major murder investigations in Dublin over the previous decade. What I did know was that there were two things weighing against her chances of success with the unit. One, obviously, was the prejudice of the men on the team. The other was her own prejudice.

Let me explain what I mean.

One Thursday morning, late in April last year, news came through to our unit that another body had been found in the Wicklow Mountains. Uniformed officers from Enniskerry were preserving the scene. The Technical Bureau had sent out a scene-of-crime team and the state pathologist was on his way.

I know this is a terrible thing to say, but we viewed this development as an opportunity. Things hadn't been going so well lately for the team. In the six months since Sharon Taafe had taken command, we'd made no significant progress with any of the cases. Along the way, the politicians who'd hitched themselves to our wagon at the beginning, hoping to pick up a few of the law and order votes, had quietly dropped off again. The

Garda Press Office was stuck with us, obviously. They tried to drop us out of the news and out of sight, but the media weren't having that any more. Every other week someone or other ran a story on one of the missing women, usually focusing on the unrelieved plight of the grieving relatives.

The special unit itself had been the commissioner's idea. By definition, therefore, for as long as the commissioner held office, it was a *good* idea. Nothing at all wrong with the strategy and the planning. So the fault had to lie somewhere else. In the *execution* of the commissioner's good idea.

Little by little, the pressure had shifted on to the inspector's shoulders. She seemed to be handling it pretty well. She knew how to massage her image and manipulate the media. But she needed something more substantial. She needed a success. And the chance to get in early on a fresh grave site, before anyone else could foul the evidence, was what she'd been waiting for.

I was asked to accompany her to the scene. Tommy Dennison was ordered to drive. For some reason, probably because Dennison considered driving beneath him, the atmosphere in the car grew tense. I sat in the front passenger seat beside him. The inspector was in the back, not paying him any attention, but studying an Ordnance Survey map of the mountains.

We took the main road south to Enniskerry, which is a picturesque little village with eighteenth-century architecture and a quaint triangle at its centre, popular with tourists and locals as a starting point for exploring the region. But don't be fooled. The mountains beyond it are notoriously treacherous, uninhabited slopes of sinking bog where the weather can quickly turn nasty and leave you trapped, a long way from any help. It doesn't seem to matter who's in power in Ireland, they always have trouble with the Wicklow Mountains. It's bandit country, still untamed in the twenty-first century. One of those abandoned places where it always seems to be wet and wild, bleak and dreary.

And that's the way it was that Thursday morning when Dennison took us further south out of Enniskerry, along a minor road running by the base of Djouce Mountain. His humour got worse with every metre we travelled. And so did his driving. The journey became an ordeal. His right-hand bends threw me against the inside of the passenger door, the left ones swung me in the opposite direction, over the gear lever and almost clutching Dennison himself. I ended up with minor bruising from all this contact, to both my elbows, my right arm and left shoulder.

The inspector in the back, with more room to get flung around in, was probably even more uncomfortable. A couple of kilometres down the potholed road, close to the grave site as far as I could estimate, she finally put her map aside and asked, 'Do you have a problem working for a woman, Dennison?'

I thought he was going to snap. His face reddened. His nostrils flared. The car jerked as his foot hit the accelerator even harder. But he didn't answer.

I wanted to say something to fill the gap. But I found I was too scared and my throat was too dry.

'I said,' the inspector repeated then, 'do you have a problem working for a woman, Dennison?'

He snorted, a quick, dismissive little grunt. 'No more of a problem than I would have working for anyone,' he said.

'I doubt it,' she told him. 'Now slow down, like a good boy, and drive properly.'

I braced myself. Half with dread, half with embarrassment. Her tone was so condescending. But shit, I thought, shouldn't I be clapping my hands and jumping up and down on the seat, applauding a significant strike by the sisterhood? Particularly, I have to admit, as I found Dennison an unpleasant boor, a loudmouth without any common courtesy about him. But, oddly, what I really felt was sympathy. He couldn't answer honestly. It could have gone down on his record as insubordination, depending on how he put it. He wasn't only helpless, he was humiliated as well. Sort of kicked while he was down, I felt. Okay, he deserved the slap on the wrist. He was behaving like a prat. But to have to take the put down with another young woman listening to it, and a colleague at that, was out of order.

In all the confusion, as Dennison somehow cooled himself down and slowed the car, what I suddenly became aware of was not that we were two females and a male, but that we were two detectives and an inspector. It might be the only thing we'd ever share, but Dennison and I were the same rank.

Actually, I don't think the incident would've bothered me so much if the rest of that morning had been different. Or maybe none of us would have behaved as we did if the row hadn't happened. I'm not sure.

Anyway, about three kilometres down the road we hit the traffic. The local guards had set up roadblocks on either side of the approach to the

26

grave site to filter vehicles away on to other routes. It didn't prevent people from parking nearby and walking back to see what all the fuss was about. Death always draws a big crowd. You wouldn't get anywhere near as many people watching a couple having sex as you would looking at a corpse. I find that very weird.

The spectators had gathered on the road, behind the crime-scene tape strung along the wire fencing. I felt their eyes on us as we parked, and still on us as we stepped out of the car and pulled on our rain gear and wellington boots. For some reason, it reminded me of the crowds at film premieres, gaping at the stars as they arrive, although this was a hell of a lot downmarket from the red carpet and the glitzy dresses.

A thick mist was creeping down the side of the mountain. The grey clouds had closed in overhead and a heavy drizzle had started. We squeezed through a gap in the fence, past a uniformed guard, and climbed the mossy slope, up to where we met the second, more privileged ring of spectators. These were the reporters and television crews, all filming and photographing, not only the voyeurs behind them and the investigators in front, but each other as well. The footage would make all the main news bulletins that day, along with a piece to camera by some correspondent who would inevitably use the phrase 'intense media interest', as if they weren't part of it. Something else that always seems a bit weird to me.

Further up the slope, the crime-scene officers had already erected a protective white tent around the grave site. A couple of them, dressed in white boiler suits, were visible outside it. They were talking to a uniformed superintendent, who was obviously in charge, and to a scattered bunch of plain-clothes men. There were no other women at the scene.

Inspector Taafe went to report to the superintendent. We were told to wait for her. She disappeared behind the tent for a while and when we saw her again she was in a boiler suit, like the technical boys, and she was entering through a flap in the tent. I remember thinking to myself that she even looked good in the baggy overalls.

As soon as she was out of sight, Dennison immediately recognized a few mates among the other detectives and went off to chat with them. I couldn't see anyone I knew. So I stood around like a spare wallflower, with my oversized wellies sinking into the bog, giving reassuring little smiles to all the guards who stared at me as they passed me on their business, up and down the mountain. I could tell that they suspected I was an intruder, possibly a cheeky newspaper reporter who'd managed to crash the cordon. But they weren't sure. They all got as far as hesitating as they approached me, but they all passed me without stopping.

I was there for thirty minutes. It felt like a whole day. And it gave me flashbacks to when I was fifteen years old and somehow or other got my addresses mixed up and miserably sipped a Coke at the wrong birthday party for a whole night.

Finally, though, the inspector re-emerged. She peeled off the boiler suit and plastic gloves and gave them to a uniformed guard. She descended towards me, looking irritated.

'Where's Dennison?' she asked.

I gestured vaguely, taking in the pine trees, the streams flowing on either side of us. 'He's around,' I said, 'talking to some of the locals.'

'You can have the pleasure of his driving all to yourself on the way back,' she said. 'I have a conference. I'm travelling with the superintendent.'

'What about the body?' I asked.

She shook her head. 'Nothing of any interest to us there.'

She obviously didn't want to discuss it. She was already moving away from me, on to the next part of her schedule. But I was fairly annoyed myself by now. Half an hour playing handmaiden and not even an explanation at the end of it.

'Why not?' I wondered.

'What?'

'Why *isn't* it of any interest to us?'

She half-turned and looked at me as if I was an idiot. 'Because it's a *man*, Galetti!' she snapped.

It was the way that she said it. For all the respect she gave the victim, it might have been a fox or a rabbit in that grave up there, a fallen tree or a lump of rock, or anything else you might expect to find in a mountain bog. It was a disappointment. Because it was a man.

What came into my head were those old films you still see on television in the afternoons, where the young king is pacing anxiously up and down outside the royal bedroom and this fussy old doctor finally emerges and cues massive celebrations all over the kingdom by announcing, 'It's a boy, sire!'

Things must have moved on, I suppose.

*

When we finally got to view the body – 'Shit,' Dennison suggested, 'we might as well have a look for ourselves after going to all this trouble. I know the lad in charge here' – the crew from the Technical Bureau, under the supervision of the pathologist, had carefully removed the soil from the shallow grave. The earth was in a pile of evidence bags that were stacked in a corner of the tent, waiting to be taken away for analysis. It looked more like an archaeological dig than a crime scene.

The pathologist was Dr Hugh Craig. From what I know of them, which is probably not a lot, I'd say pathologists fall into two types, the cheery and the glum. Craig is gloomy. He's unusually tall, and very thin, so he looks a bit ghoulish, like death itself, when he's bending over a corpse. He's very efficient, apparently, but he never says anything off the record. That can be frustrating for the guards. You don't need conclusions when you're starting an investigation, you need openings. Craig is never relaxed enough with anyone just to discuss the case informally. With him, it's all typed reports and scientific conclusions. If I was honest, I'd have to say, despite his reputation, that I don't think he's very good at his job. He's too serious. Funnily enough, you'd much prefer to work with a character who takes a bit of relish in the challenge. But nobody ever listens to the guards on the ground when they're making these appointments.

We stayed well out of sight, right at the back of the tent, after we were brought in. Dennison had kitted himself out with a very sophisticated face mask. Clever lad. All I had was one of those paper things that keep the dust out of your airways. So for me, the worst of the experience was the smell. Trapped inside the plastic tent, where all it could do was circulate, the rotten air got heavier and heavier, until you felt you were locked inside a garbage bin. Or, since the stench was of putrefying flesh and tissue and organs, inside a fridge that wasn't working and where raw meat had been left to rot.

Because of the number of living bodies working and breathing in the small space, it was also warm and stuffy inside the tent. It was impossible to catch any clean air. I felt my breakfast stirring in my stomach, pushing up my gorge, making it difficult to breathe. And I'd had a careless breakfast that morning. Fried eggs, black pudding, bacon, toast and coffee.

Most of the bodies you deal with in police work, you come across them within hours of their death. You can still see the individual person. Your reaction to them will vary. Sometimes it's as intimate as sadness.

Sometimes it's as callous as relief. It depends on who the victim is. But you respond to them in much the same way as you would when they were alive. With *feeling*.

This was different, because the corpse was so badly decomposed. It was different for me, anyway, since it was the first time I'd experienced it. I'm no expert, but even I could estimate that the body had been in the ground for a long time, months instead of weeks. The face was unrecognizable as that of a human being. Mostly it was skeletal, with deep eye sockets and weirdly grinning teeth and strips of rotting flesh, infested with maggots, clinging to the bones.

What do you do when you're confronted with a sight like that? Do you take a leap, past the notion of the individual, on to the idea that we're all mortal, all human, all destined to end up like this? That's what you're supposed to think, according to the poets you're made to study in school. But I don't think you do that. I didn't, anyway. I'll tell you what I felt, staring at that decomposing corpse. Nothing, apart from my own queasiness. Absolutely nothing. I didn't know this person. I wasn't at all convinced that it actually *was* a person. Looking at it, I couldn't even figure out how they'd decided that it was a man instead of a woman. To me, it was neither.

I spent a while like this, with my head spinning, frightening myself with my own coldness, but once I'd recovered and got back to being a detective again, a number of odd things started to strike me.

In the first place, there were no clothes and no material of any kind in the grave. The man had been stripped and buried naked, without any wrapping or covering. Whether there was clothing discarded or hidden nearby only a detailed search of the area would reveal. Also, there were no signs of any personal belongings the man might've worn, no watches or rings, no chains or medals.

Even apart from this, it was obvious that whoever had buried the corpse had given a great deal of attention to its appearance. Actually, it seemed to me as if the body was arranged to make a point. If you looked at it from a certain angle, you couldn't miss it. It was the posture of a penitent. Here was a man confessing his sins, it occurred to me, at least the way traditional Catholics are supposed to. The victim was kneeling. He'd been buried on his side, to the right. You had to forget that the remains were lying on a flat surface, otherwise you got confused by the image of a sleeper curled up in bed. You had to imagine the kneecaps in contact with the ground, the thigh bones stretching upwards at an angle of about forty-five degrees, the backbone and ribcage upright, the skull slightly tilted upwards, raised to the heavens. The arms were fixed as if joined in prayer. Even spookier, there was something wrapped in protective cellophane or plastic near the hands, positioned as if it was held by the fingers. Something that looked like a prayer book or a missal, although it was impossible to identify it through the soiled plastic.

What I thought of was an execution. The sort of thing you see in war films or in old newsreels from actual wars. Blindfolded, a condemned prisoner kneels and is shot through the back of the head by a revolver. My mind was running along the lines of a gangland killing, drugs wars, an execution after torture. What I was forgetting, I suppose, was that executed men, who might be kneeling before being shot, don't hold on to the pose after falling into their graves. The posture had been staged by whoever buried the man in the mountains.

By then, I couldn't think straight any more, though. I had a bad headache. I was still fighting to keep from puking. And the effort was probably showing. I wanted to leave and get some fresh air, but Dennison was standing directly behind me. I think now that he already knew what was inside that tent when he suggested checking it out. I think he'd gauged the effect it would have on me. And I think he deliberately stood behind me, so that I'd have to face his mockery when I turned to run. I didn't want to give him the satisfaction, so I toughed it out.

He had his bit of a victory in the end, though. When he finally got impatient he leaned forward and whispered in my ear, 'Feeling a bit under the weather, Galetti?'

'I've seen worse,' I bluffed.

And that's when he laughed. 'Your only chance of seeing worse, Galetti,' he said, 'is if you look in the mirror right now.'

It took the investigating team nearly two weeks to identify the body in the mountains. It's an awful long time in any murder enquiry, and more often than not it means that the case is going to be impossible to solve. By the end of the fortnight, the post-mortem results and some of the forensic reports were already in. Not that I read any of them. Our unit had no involvement in the investigation.

There are a few rules to being in the guards and one of the first of them is, you don't make work for yourself. If a file isn't your responsibility, it has no business being on your desk. You do what you have to do with your own cases. If you're told by the Director of Public Prosecutions that you won't get a result in court, you don't kill yourself trying to prove him wrong. You do your best. That's all that's expected of you.

This little homily sounds like it's heading in a certain direction, but it's actually going the opposite way. I broke the rule.

I don't mean I got in on the investigation. It's almost impossible to manage that. But there was a fella I knew stationed in Bray, where the incident room was based. His name was Philip Flynn. A detective garda. He'd asked me to a dinner dance once and I was flattered at the time. I'd say I'd definitely have an interest in him if I wasn't already in a steady relationship. I rang him and suggested meeting for a drink, without mentioning what I really wanted.

I don't know why I did this, particularly. Maybe my nose was out of joint, because of the way the inspector had dismissed the case and treated myself and Dennison. Maybe it was an itch I had to scratch. Maybe I was just annoyed with my boyfriend Fergal, who'd gone down the country on a golfing trip at short notice, and all I wanted was an excuse to meet the other fella. Motives are odd things and funny mixtures.

Anyway. This is what I learned.

According to the state pathologist, the corpse was that of an adult male, probably in early middle age. The time of death he estimated at between four to six months earlier, but the body was too badly decomposed to determine the cause. The victim hadn't been executed, anyway. There were no gunshot wounds to the skull. Or to any other part of the skeleton, for that matter. In addition to this, none of the bones had been fractured or damaged. In other words, the victim hadn't been bludgeoned. He hadn't sustained any serious injuries in a fall or any other accident, and his neck hadn't been broken.

There was one grisly finding, though, that swung things back towards the possibility of a gangland killing, where torture is often a feature. Both the man's ears had been cut off. The pathologist's opinion was that the mutilation had been done with a surgical scalpel or similar instrument. At least this suggestion offered the investigators a few questions to be getting along with. Who had the skills for such a procedure, for instance. Or who had access to the instruments. The ears, or whatever might be left of them by now, were never found. It couldn't be proven, but it was thought they'd been severed elsewhere, at least before the body was placed in the open grave.

As for the position of the corpse, no one else could see the kneeling penitent that had looked so obvious to me. When they analysed the marks in the soil and compared the photographs taken at the various stages of the dig, they decided that the body had been arranged while it was lying in the grave. This had to be done in the twelve hours or so between death and full rigor mortis. But the reasons, they suggested, were either practical – to reduce the size of the grave, for instance – or completely accidental. It hadn't a meaning in itself.

None of the man's clothes were ever found. And nothing else was recovered at the scene to give a clue to the manner of his death, or the reasons for it, or the identity of his killer.

The cellophane wrapping that was lying by his hands was found to contain papers. But it hadn't been made completely waterproof. After four months or more in the bog, parts of the paper were disintegrating. The material had been sent to the forensic science laboratory for restoration and analysis. At the time, nobody knew what was in that package. The best hope was that it was going to help identify the victim, because everything else, from the records of those reported missing to a couple of desperate public appeals, had drawn a blank.

That's how things stood the night I met Philip Flynn.

I was pretty pleased with myself. I'd had a nice evening out. I'd satisfied my curiosity. And I could be mysterious about my movements to the boyfriend who'd come home in bad shape from his golf competition. He'd picked up a heavy cold and looked like death warmed up, but I had no sympathy for him.

'How are you feeling?' I asked.

'Bad,' he said, 'way below par.'

'How was your golf round?'

'Bad,' he said, 'way over par.'

I don't think I'm one of those women who make something feminine out of being thick about sports, but it actually took me a while to sort this out.

Anyway. As far as I was concerned, this ended my interest in the body found on Djouce Mountain. The itch had been scratched. My curiosity had been satisfied. And I assumed that I was finished with the case.

Four days after I met Philip Flynn, early on Wednesday morning – and this was nearly the full two weeks since the discovery of the body – a woman rang the guards in Rathfarnham to report a break-in next door. She'd been out in her garden, she explained, hanging up her washing, when she'd noticed it. The back door of her neighbour's house had been forced and she was sure that the owner was away on holiday.

The station sent out a patrol car. The two uniformed guards checked out the house and found that the woman was right. The wood around the lock on the back door had been shattered, probably with a crowbar. The damage was very recent, because the exposed wood was still dry and clean. Inside, there was a bad smell. It was musty, as if the place hadn't been aired for months, but the stuffiness was mixed with something a lot nastier as well.

The cause of this stench was soon obvious enough. The gougers who'd broken in hadn't satisfied themselves with robbery. They'd wrecked the place. Senseless stuff. Pictures torn off the walls. Carpets slashed with Stanley knives. Even the fuse board ripped apart.

In the front room, an old mahogany piano had been hacked at with a chisel and then used as a message board for obscene graffiti. Its keys and strings had been mangled. Its stool and metal music stand were broken.

Whether it was funk or just sheer contempt, the gurriers who'd broken in had crapped all over the place as well. One of them had wiped himself clean with the music score that had been on the piano. So all over the floor there were these sheets of Debussy's *Pour les sonorités opposées*, smeared with shit.

Upstairs, most of the owner's personal belongings, the things that hadn't been stolen, had been given the same treatment. Vandalized. Shredded. Rubbed in excrement. But enough had survived, when a few of the torn items were pieced together again, to establish the man's identity.

His name was Michael Elwood.

The first thing the guards in Rathfarnham needed to do was to find him, to pass on the bad news about his home. They knew that he wasn't abroad. In the wrecked bedroom, they'd found bits of his torn passport. They asked the neighbour when she'd seen him last and she said that nobody had noticed him for about a month, when he'd painted the doors and windows of the house. There was nothing odd about his being away, she claimed. He was often out of the country for long periods. She thought he worked as an airline steward or was something or other in the travel business.

All this turned out to be pure nonsense.

It's something I've noticed a lot since joining the guards, the way people invent stories to make the facts more acceptable. When you look at abused kids sometimes, when you see the bruising all over their bodies, you think to yourself, how could anyone possibly miss it? But people do miss it. They even invent things to miss it more comfortably. The kid's accident-prone, they say. She falls off bikes. He has that type of skin that bruises easily. They don't even realize they're doing this. They're not lying. They're just seeing the world they want to live in.

Michael Elwood hadn't been working abroad, of course. He hadn't been driving up and down the country on business. He'd been lying in a shallow grave among the woods on Djouce Mountain.

By the time there was no more mystery about it all, when the dental records and DNA analysis had formally identified the body in the mountains as that of Michael Elwood, last seen in the company of an unidentified woman who was also feared dead, the investigating team had established that in the four months since his disappearance, only one person actually missed the man. It wasn't even his girlfriend, Laura Ashwell, who had argued with him on the night of his disappearance. She'd sat around for a week after their strained last date, waiting for the phone call that never came. And then she'd decided that life was too short to spend the rest of it tied to a possessive old father and a timid lover. One morning, without telling anyone, she gathered a few personal things and went to live and work in London, where she found that she was a lot more intelligent, a lot more resourceful and a lot more appreciated than she ever imagined she could be. One of those modern fairy tales. They sometimes happen.

So it turned out that the only one who'd missed Michael Elwood was his supervisor at the supermarket chain where he worked as a wages clerk. But why didn't he report it? 'Look,' the supervisor explained, 'it's not my job to organize people's lives. If an employee doesn't show up, doesn't ring in and won't answer my calls, I've got to get someone else in to do the business.'

When I heard all the details and when I remembered my own indifference at his grave, I thought it was sad, the way Elwood's life had gone. You can't help it, you put yourself in the same position. Who would mourn for you if you were taken? Who would miss you? Would you lie in a wet mountain grave for four months without anyone giving a shit, one way or another? It's a creepy thought.

It scared me so much that I rang Fergal just to hear the sound of his voice. I'd been holding out against him since his golf outing. Things had gone a little cool between us. Holding out for what, I couldn't exactly tell you. I knew that he was the one who felt guilty. I knew this was ridiculous, because I was the one who was at fault. The whole thing was irritating me. So when I scared myself, thinking of dying without a friend, and rang him up, I wanted to say, I'm sorry, I was wrong, I've been an awful pain in the ass . . . Instead, I took the scenic route. You do, don't you?

I said, 'To be honest, Fergal, you're *too* considerate. I think it's a political thing with you. I think you're a victim, in a way. You say to yourself, No, I'll wash the dishes again tonight, women have been doing it for centuries. You know what I mean, don't you? I've taken advantage at times, I have to admit. Who wouldn't? But not any more. I swear . . .'

The poor guy. 'Are you all right, Kris?' he asked. 'What's happened?'

I love him for it. I really do.

I was sunbathing, topless, in the South of France. Not one of the brochure resorts, overrun with British tourists, with their beer bellies, their flaking red skin and their screaming kids. This was a private beach. Secluded. It had clear white sands that were unmarked by anybody else's footprints. Basically, it was the front garden of the palatial home built into the cliff face behind me. You mix with criminals, you sometimes accept their hospitality. That's how it is. Mostly it's confined to a few rounds of drinks in the bars on their patch in Dublin. The odd time, though, you hit something sweeter. I had to clear it with the authorities, of course. The decisive thing is, can they trust you, can you turn the contact to the force's advantage? I knew that the fella who'd invited me over was a big smuggler of cannabis into Ireland. I knew that he was trying to turn my head. And I can't deny that he was good-looking. I'd brought Fergal along, of course. I didn't want him worrying any more. But Fergal had been lured away to the local golf course by the drug baron's henchmen. I was alone on the isolated beach. Expecting a move at any moment from the baron. Wondering what he was really more interested in, my body or my position in the guards. Wondering how far I'd want to go with him. I lay there, topless, soaking in the sun, feeling myself getting more languorous by the second, more yielding, more and more indifferent, the way the Mediterranean climate has that kind of nihilistic effect on you . . .

'Hey, Galetti!' a voice broke in. 'There's someone here to see you.'

I opened my eyes. Standing inside the doorway of the office, soaking wet, with rainwater dripping to the floor from his sodden clothes, was Philip Flynn, the detective stationed out in Bray.

He looked at me suspiciously. 'Were you asleep or something?' he asked.

I pulled my chair closer to the desk. Clear evidence of alertness.

There was no one else in the room at the time. This was the open-plan office shared by the detectives in the unit, but it was lunch hour then and all the others were out.

'No,' I blustered. 'Just thinking.'

He went on staring at me without saying anything, so the atmosphere quickly got strained.

'Is it raining?' I asked stupidly.

That was unbelievable. Okay, it was early-June and the miserable Irish weather might be a reasonable topic of conversation, but Jesus . . .

'Naw,' he said, 'I forgot to take my fucking clothes off when I was having a shower.'

He was really pissed at me. I hadn't contacted him since the night I'd met him for a drink, and I couldn't remember what expectations I'd left him with at the time. I felt bad. All I can say is, it's not my usual style, stringing guys along, playing one against the other.

'Can we go for a coffee?' he asked.

'What's wrong with here?' I wondered.

'I need to talk to you.'

I don't know what I thought might happen at one-thirty on a wet Monday afternoon, but I was jumpy. I took him across the road from the office to a place where the entire front wall of the café was a plate of plain glass. High visibility. It's great when there's nothing on your mind. You can sit back at your table and watch the whole world scuttling by, like on a giant television screen. When you're uneasy, though, as I found out, you feel like a specimen in a laboratory.

We only wanted coffee, but we had to order food as well because of the minimum charge at lunchtime. This put another dinge in Philip's humour, so I offered to pay, even though the reason I hadn't gone for lunch in the first place was that I couldn't afford it.

He didn't touch the food.

'Mary Corbett,' he said.

I gave him plenty of time, but he didn't add anything. 'What of it?' I wondered.

'What do you know about her?' he asked.

I thought this was a particularly stupid question. He should've realized that I knew everything there was to know about Mary Corbett, except her whereabouts. Mary Corbett was the young woman with the powerful connections whose disappearance the previous October had led to the formation of our unit.

'You owe me a favour,' Philip reminded me.

His eyes went cold, remembering the night we'd met when he was interested in me and I was interested in Michael Elwood. I'd hurt him. And he hadn't forgiven me.

As calmly as I could manage it, I told him what we had on Mary Corbett, even though I was certain that he must have known this stuff already.

Mary Corbett was twenty-two years old, an assistant director of a PR agency in Dublin. On 3 October she and her boyfriend, a forty-five-year-old dotcom speculator named Simon Chester, were at a party, near Baltinglass in south Wicklow, thrown by some horsy friends at their stud farm. They drank too much booze and snorted too much coke. When they were apart they bitched about each other to complete strangers. When they were together they fought like cat and dog. Inside the same hour, Mary seems to have screwed a jockey half her size and a stable boy half her age. Simon groped the hostess's thirteen-year-old daughter. When the time came for them to leave, they were so smashed that they couldn't find their own jeep on the front lawn. Everyone pleaded with them to sleep it off. But they weren't exactly a reasonable couple.

They set out across the Wicklow Mountains, heading for Dublin. The driving conditions were terrible, heavy rain and strong winds reducing visibility to practically nothing. Simon was behind the wheel. He took a wrong turn and quickly got lost. Instead of approaching Dublin they ended up heading into the Glen of Imaal artillery range. Simon's efforts to get back out of it weren't impressive. Near the youth hostel at Ballinclear, about halfway between the artillery range and the village of Donard, he had to stop to shift a small tree that had fallen across the road. Mary staggered out of the jeep as well. In front of the bonnet they

38

had another drunken row. This time the insults and the accusations got really poisonous. Simon lost the head. He got back in the jeep and drove off without waiting for Mary.

And that was the last time anyone admitted to seeing Mary Corbett, standing there in her soaking party dress in the middle of a storm on an isolated road in the treacherous Wicklow Mountains.

Simon went back to rescue her. Or thought he went back, anyway. His brain was so fogged and the roads were so unfamiliar that he will never be sure. He thought he was desperately circling the Glen of Imaal, but found himself in the town of Blessington, more than twenty kilometres to the north. Too scared to report it immediately to the guards, he went back to their apartment and waited. But Mary never showed

First time out, Simon's story sounded dodgy to the investigating detectives. And the more he told it, the more unlikely it seemed. For a couple of weeks, Simon himself was the only suspect in the case. They tried to get a confession out of him in the interview rooms. They lifted sackfuls of forensic evidence off him. They even found a bloodstain on the passenger seat of the jeep and established it belonged to Mary Corbett.

I'd say it was a reasonable direction to take, given the circumstances, but it was sheer madness to make it the only one. By the time Simon's high-flying legal team had forced the guards to back off if they weren't going to charge him, all the other trails had gone stone cold.

That's when the media went ballistic, when Mary Corbett's family, who owned bits of newspapers and TV stations all over the place, started to put the pressure on. The accusations were flying like bullets. Garda incompetence. Outdated methods. Poor leaders. Lack of resolve. Laughable resources.

And finally, that's when we got thrown at the problem.

'The élite unit,' Philip said sourly.

'Yeah,' I said. To be honest, I wasn't in the humour for a slanging match. I was starting to wonder where all of this was going. We had to be going somewhere, because Philip could have got this information from a hundred other sources.

'Did ye manage to bring the case on at all?' he asked.

'No,' I admitted.

'But Simon Chester definitely didn't do it?'

'He might have. You'd never know.'

'What do you think?'

'I don't think he did,' I said. 'And neither does anyone else.'

'So it was an opportunistic thing. Someone happened to be passing that way and found the woman stranded in the rain.'

I suppose it was possible that someone might have followed the couple from the party in Baltinglass, even if they had to keep their headlights off. A lot of things were possible. Someone might even have hidden in the back of the jeep. But he was right. The thinking in the unit was, someone who was passing picked her up.

'Well, anyway, Phil,' I said, 'don't tell me you came all the way in from Bray just to sting me for a lunch?'

His big moment. You can always tell the man's big moment. Their chests swell out. I swear.

All those anxious hours in front of *National Geographic*, waiting for the rains to come again to the Serengeti, with a bar of chocolate in my lap, have turned me into a natural scientist.

Phil sat upright on his chair. He took a few folded papers from the inside pocket of his jacket. He put them on the table. 'Read that,' he said.

'What is it?' I asked.

'Read it,' he said.

I picked them up. I opened them out. They were reduced photocopies. Originally they'd been A4 sheets. Now they were two to a page.

My father had died unexpectedly, I started reading. *In the car, squirming uncomfortably on the dampened seat and gasping for breath after running through the heavy rain, I switched on the mobile phone and listened to my sister's voice, recorded two hours earlier, trembling with the news. He's gone, she said simply. Will you be coming down for the funeral?*

'What is it?' I asked Phil again, because I thought he'd written it himself, as a kind of story to impress me. I also thought it sounded fake and I was terrified that he was going to ask for my opinion on it. 'Is it yours?'

He jabbed his finger into the papers. 'Have you read down the first page?'

'I only got a pass in English Literature in the Leaving Cert,' I warned him.

'Have you read the first page?'

'Not all of it. Not yet.'

'Read it,' he insisted.

So I read it. Right through to the end.

I turned to look. Outside, her head covered by a plastic rain jacket that she held above her like the wingspan of a bat, leaving her shirt and jeans exposed to the driving rain, a young woman named Mary Corbett stooped, mouthing her concerns against the window.

I wish I could say that I was terribly excited. Anything but. I was probably more suspicious than anything else. It didn't mean much to me. Not even the bits that were intended to suggest the disappearance of Mary Corbett. All those details had been in the papers at one time or another. They could have come from a hundred different sources.

So, no. I wasn't impressed.

'Who wrote this?' I asked Phil.

His eyes lit up. I realized later that they went like this because he knew that he had me. Maybe someone else would have played with his catch a bit, squeezed a bit more fun out of the situation. He wasn't like that. Or he was too anxious to hook me. He let it go.

'That,' he said, 'was what they found in the cellophane wrapper where your man Michael Elwood was buried out in the mountains.'

And I have to admit, that finally *did* throw me back a bit.

'Michael Elwood wrote this?' I asked.

'There's no proof as to who wrote it,' Phil explained, 'one way or the other. But it was found in his grave.'

'That was five weeks ago,' I said.

'It only came back from the lab a fortnight ago.'

'All right. *Two* weeks ago.'

'And your unit should've *got* it two weeks ago,' he agreed. 'I know for a fact that you didn't. But now you have it. Only you have no idea where it came from or how it got to your unit. Are we clear on that?'

In the beginning, I was certain that I was doing everything by the book. Nothing could be surer. If anyone had said to me, 'Hang on a minute, Kris, you might be a bit out of line there,' I'd have looked at them as if they had two heads and no nose on either. But that's probably the real problem with madness. The way you see it, you're the most reasonable person in the world. You're the rightful queen of Mesopotamia, betrayed by your treacherous sister-in-law, who has you imprisoned in a castle and guarded by soldiers in white coats. Good god, woman, it's your *duty* to escape!

After that lunch with Phil I went back to the office determined to get shut of the photocopies as fast as I could. The thing to do was to put them on the desk of someone who was paid to take that kind of responsibility. If they didn't make a big issue out of it with an internal enquiry, and I couldn't see why they should, I wouldn't have to say where I got them from.

That was the intention. That was the plan. And not a bad plan, either.

But the way things stood, I was out of luck.

I didn't realize it until I went looking for her, but the inspector was absent on sick leave that morning. And the sergeant had just started his annual holidays. There were only the rest of the lads in the unit, and they were the same rank as myself.

I decided to wait for the inspector to return to work. Given the circumstances, that was the sensible thing to do. But I waited three days. Monday. Tuesday. Wednesday. By the end of it, I was starting to get nervous again. I felt like a robber sitting on some very hot property and desperate for the fence to show up and take it off my hands. In that type of situation, the mind starts working overtime. All sorts of mad thoughts go through it. What if this was some kind of test and they had people checking on how I dealt with it? What if there was a deliberate cover-up in Bray and the corrupt guards out there found out I'd got the stuff?

'Are you okay, Kris?' Fergal asked me on Tuesday night. 'Is something bothering you?'

'No,' I said. 'Why should anything be bothering me?'

'You've been dead quiet the last two days,' he said. 'You always go quiet when something's on your mind. Is it me?'

This was eating into my life.

Late on Wednesday afternoon I went for a walk by myself and rang the inspector at her home on my mobile. As soon as she answered it, I felt like a complete wally. She sounded really ill, hoarse and faint, and struggling to put the words together.

'Look,' I said, 'I'm sorry. It's just that I've got a problem at the moment and I'd like to talk to you.'

'I'll be in tomorrow,' she promised. 'If I'm not, you can call out to see me here. You know where I'm living, don't you?'

To be honest, she sounded so bad that I didn't expect to see her in work the next morning. I wasn't surprised when she didn't show up.

By then, without any leadership, the unit had gone sort of slack. There was more dossing than investigating being done. It's only human nature. Nobody was going to make themselves unpopular ordering everybody else around, because nobody had the stripes or the pay packet to make it worth their while. What I'm saying is, I didn't have any difficulty slipping away for a couple of hours around ten on Thursday morning.

The inspector lived in Templeogue, which is one of the more desirable addresses in the city. On a clear day, you can pick out every sheep that's grazing on the Wicklow Mountains to the south, every barbed-wire fence dividing the fields, every little patch of pine trees. It's that close.

She had the kind of manicured front garden that you can't help having mixed feelings about. Shit, you say to yourself, all those perfect borders and dainty shrubs just look unnatural, the handiwork of a control freak. But you don't compare it to your own neglected eden with any pride. I sometimes think that we can't make up our minds whether we want to be straight or wild and that this is what we really need a police force for, so that we don't have to answer that question.

A girl of about sixteen, obviously the inspector's daughter, opened the door to me. She had her mother's beauty, what I'd describe as distinctively Irish good looks, with black hair and soft features and wild brown eyes. But you know what? She talked with an American accent. Not any of the thousands of genuine ones, either. A *television* American accent. If you closed your eyes while she was speaking, you could convince yourself that you were listening to *Roswell High* or *Buffy the Vampire Slayer*.

'That's cool,' she said when I asked to see her mother. 'Mom's resting right now, but you can go right on up.'

I thought she must be alone in the house with her mother. She hadn't dressed yet. She still had on a short cotton night-dress. But I heard giggles from the front room when she went back in there as I was heading for the stairs.

Right then, I started to feel uneasy.

To tell the truth, I'd always been tense about coming to the inspector's house. She was an exceptionally neat woman in her appearance. Never a hair out of place. You tried not to stand beside her too often, because you suffered by comparison. I'd expected her home to have the same character, the kind of place where the toilet is so spotless, all gleaming tiles and sparkling ceramic, that the owners look at you funnily when you ask to use it. You're not actually going to *crap* in there, are you? their expression says.

But what I found was the opposite to what I expected. I won't say the untidiness shocked me. It's not any of my business, how people keep their homes. But it certainly threw me off balance.

The carpet on the stairs hadn't been vacuumed for a few days and it smelled of sour milk, as if someone had spilled a glass and not mopped up properly afterwards. The first of the bedrooms on the landing belonged to the daughter. I suppose like most teenagers' rooms, it was completely disorganized. Nothing remarkable in that, you might say. But next door to it, the mother's room was also a mess. Soiled clothes were scattered on the floor. There were shoes and newspapers and magazines dropped here and there. There were a lot of glasses and coffee mugs, some standing on the furniture, some fallen or thrown to the ground.

The inspector was lying on the double bed, dressed in white pyjamas. She was out cold. She looked bad. Her eyes were puffy and red, possibly from hay fever, probably from crying. Her hair was all tangled. Her skin was blotchy.

But I could see that it wasn't any ordinary illness that had laid her low. It was booze. Pure and simple.

There were whiskey bottles, some of them empty and more on the way to being empty, all over the bedside cabinet and the floor, even in among the bedclothes themselves.

I know that drink is a big problem in the guards. It's the biggest problem in our entire society. Ninety per cent of the crimes you come across, alcohol is involved somewhere or other. And where you have a lot of tension, you have a lot of drinking to cope with it. Young lads in the guards go out and get rat-eyed together when they're off duty. I know all that. I'd just never thought of it as a woman's problem in the force.

There was something else bothering me too as I stood in the doorway looking in at the inspector. It was actually the fact that I *was* standing there, that I'd been allowed to see all this. If I had a problem and a daughter, I said to myself, I think I'd expect my daughter to stand between my problem and the unwanted visitor. I think I'd expect at least that. But what was the point, getting annoyed with a teenager for not protecting her mother? I couldn't do anything about it.

I went back downstairs.

I could hear the giggling from the front room again, along with one of the girls telling a story. 'And he's like, maybe we should meet for coffee sometime? And I'm like, you think coffee turns me on? And he's like, I didn't mean that. And I'm like, you don't want to turn me on?'

The door was a bit open. I looked in before I knocked, because I thought I heard a boy's deeper laugh among all the giggles. I was right. He was sitting on the settee between two of the girls, a lad of about sixteen with a shaven head, and, as far as I could see, he was in a state of intense sexual arousal, staring at the girls in their night-dresses. To be honest, he looked pitiful. Sweating. Red-faced. Fidgety. His frustration was making him clumsy. And the girls, who knew exactly what they were doing, were goading him mercilessly. 'My God, you're so *awkward*, Jerry!'

Well, I had no sympathy for him. Sooner or later, like most men do eventually, he'd have to learn that he can't let his cock do his thinking for him.

I knocked on the door. The inspector's daughter came tripping over to me. 'Hi!'

'Your mother's asleep,' I said.

'Okay.' She shrugged.

'Is your father at work?' I asked.

'*My dad*?' she said. 'Are you *serious*? We haven't seen him since, like, *years*.'

'Do me a favour?' I asked.

'Sure.'

'Don't bother telling your mother that I called. I don't want to disturb her. I'll see her when she gets back to work.'

'Okay.' She shrugged again.

Whatever was going on inside that house, I don't think the daughter kept her word to me. I think she told the inspector that I called and found her drunk, and probably that I went away disgusted. Whether there was a row and it was blurted out in the heat of the moment or whether the girl always intended doing it and only put on that show of indifference for my benefit, I just don't know. But I'm convinced that she told the inspector I was there. I have no proof. I couldn't produce any evidence to back up my claim. Nobody ever mentioned my visit to the house afterwards. But the inspector's attitude to me changed after that morning and there could be no other reason for the change. From then on, I could do nothing to please her. Everything I did, there was something wrong with it.

When she came back to work on Monday morning the next week, she looked her old self again. Healthy. Stylish. Efficient. Except for one thing. She was cold with me. Previously she'd always had time for a chat. Now she was all formal again. 'You and Dennison will take the following interviews, detective,' she'd order. 'Friday, 1500 hours, detective,' she'd tell me precisely.

I wouldn't have minded so much, but I'd been sitting on the narrative found in Michael Elwood's grave for so long by then that I'd started developing theories of my own about it. This is one of the worst things a detective who's part of a unit can get up to with a piece of evidence. It not only takes yourself and the evidence out of context, it gives you illusions about your own abilities as well. But I couldn't help it.

The more I thought about it, for instance, the more certain I became that Elwood was left kneeling in his grave, reading this confession, which he was supposed to have written himself. If that was true, then it meant that there was some connection between his death and the disappearance of Mary Corbett. It was possible that the document suggested not only what had happened to Mary, in other words, but where it had happened and where her body might be found.

On the other hand, the longer I held on to the photocopies, the more worried I became about Phil Flynn's motives in giving them to me in the first place. I hadn't heard from him the past week. I hadn't heard from anyone. And I was obviously getting uptight about it all.

'Can't you talk to me, love?' Fergal pleaded with me on Friday night. 'I'd like to know what's going on.'

'It's not you,' I assured him. And suddenly – for the first time in a whole week, I was horrified to realize – the thought of sex came into my head. 'Let's go to bed,' I suggested quickly.

But Fergal, without really knowing it, had hit the nail on the head. What I desperately needed was someone to talk to openly.

And I don't think I ever got that.

The inspector looked at the photocopies when I offered them to her in her office Monday morning. She didn't take them.

'What's this?' she asked.

'I think it might be evidence in the Mary Corbett case,' I explained. 'Can you read them?'

She still didn't take them. Not from my hands. She forced me to put them down on the desk between us before she picked them up.

The way I'd describe it, I think she read the pages with the *intention* of not being surprised by them. The impression she wanted to give was that she was already familiar with this stuff and, even though she'd been away for a week, I still hadn't gained any ground on her. She read the first few lines of the narrative closely, but then she just glanced through the rest.

Now, for all I knew, maybe she'd already seen the document. She didn't say.

'Where did you get this?' she asked.

'I'm not really free to say,' I explained, 'but the information I have is that these documents were found in Michael Elwood's grave site.'

Anyone in authority can easily be an asshole. It doesn't matter if it's a man or a woman, there's no difference, although there's still a lot more men in power. All they have to do is repeat exactly what you say. 'I slept eight hours last night,' you say. 'You slept eight hours last night,' they repeat. And suddenly, it sounds like the most stupid thing in the world. They're not actually *saying* it's the most stupid thing in the world. They're not saying anything. You're not sure *what* their opinion is, one way or the other. And the uncertainty is a major part of your discomfort.

Well, that's what the inspector did to me that Monday morning.

'You're not really free to say where you found some evidence?' she repeated sarcastically.

'Well, what I mean is, you see ...'

'But your information is that these documents were found in Michael Elwood's grave site.'

'I've been thinking about it,' I said.

'You've been thinking about it.'

'It could be relevant to Mary Corbett's disappearance,' I said, 'and there may be a connection between the two cases.'

'You think it could be relevant to Mary Corbett.'

In the end I got so frustrated that I said something stupid, although I thought I was being clever at the time, because it was a statement the inspector couldn't repeat. I said, 'A lot of people who are concerned about Mary Corbett's disappearance would be interested to read those documents.'

As soon as the words were out of my mouth, I could've bitten my tongue off. One of the first things you learn in the guards is, you don't make threats. You do what you have to do in a situation. Say you walk into a café where a madman is terrifying customers with a golf club, you don't warn him that he'll be in trouble if he doesn't stop. He's already in trouble. You mill in and quieten him with a couple of slaps.

That was the first mistake I made, striking a pose I wouldn't be able to follow through on. The second mistake was the implication that I'd go outside the unit and above her head. That's out of order where we work.

'I'm sorry,' I said quickly. 'I didn't meant anything other than I think it's relevant to the case.'

She didn't comment on this one way or the other, didn't say whether or not she accepted my apology and explanation. She fluttered the pages in her hand. 'If I was you,' she said, 'I'd forget about these, until I come back to you on them. Have you shown them to anyone else?'

'No,' I said.

'Have you told anyone else of their existence?'

'No,' I said again. 'I waited for you to return to work.'

'Good,' she said. 'Let's keep it like that.'

And as far as I was concerned, that's how we left it. She took responsibility for the photocopies. I was out of the picture.

It wasn't the most satisfying outcome. I would've liked to follow through on my own theories and ideas. But there's no way of doing that on your own. That just doesn't happen. You learn to let things go, because otherwise you'd drive yourself mad, thinking about all the unsolved crimes and all the laughing criminals out there

So I let it go. And started to forget about it.

Three days later, my arse was in a sling.

I knew it the minute I walked into the newsagent's on the way to work in the morning and saw the headline in one of the tabloids: GRISLY FIND MAY LEAD TO MARY CORBETT. 'I'm fucked,' I said. And I must have said it out loud, because the old man beside me reaching for his racing paper stopped and looked up at me in disgust.

The tabloid belonged to the news group where Mary Corbett's family had influence. It's not my usual rag, but I bought it that morning. It had one of the photographs of Mary they'd been using to publicize her disappearance. It showed her at a party with a well-known film actor, a minor star who was represented by her agency while he was working on location in Ireland. This was one of the two images they peddled of her, the vivacious confidante of celebrities. The other was that of treasured daughter and friend. From what I knew of her, I don't think either hit the mark.

But anyway.

The tabloid's crime correspondent claimed to have learned of bloodstained papers in the grave of Michael Elwood linking him to the disappearance of Mary Corbett. Although the Garda Press Office had denied the discovery of any such papers, the correspondent could confirm that they existed, because she had seen copies of them. They practically amounted to a confession of abduction and they indicated where Mary Corbett was buried. But the guards had done nothing, the article insisted. Despite the unease of certain detectives on the case, the authorities had ignored this vital evidence. The tabloid could reveal that the remains of Mary Corbett were probably buried in the mountains around Glencree. But no search of this area had ever been undertaken.

It was dynamite, this stuff. Time bombs going off, in four or five different directions, and more of them buried in the ground, waiting for their moment.

I read it while I was still standing on the footpath outside the newsagent's and I got so scared that my legs started trembling. They weren't going to believe me, I decided. When it all came out, and it would have to come out now – about my possession of the photocopies, my interview with the inspector and the bad feeling between us – they weren't going to believe that I didn't leak this stuff to the press. 'These "certain detectives on the case",' they'd accuse me. 'That's a reference to you, isn't it? You're the one who's supposed to be suffering from unease.' The only question they'd have in their minds was, did I get paid for it all as well?

My stomach was sick as I drove into the car park at headquarters. I don't know whether people were looking at me any differently or not as I made my way through the building to our office, but it felt like they were staring. It made my movements awkward and self-conscious.

Inside the office itself, you could only describe the atmosphere as strained. Obviously they'd all heard the news as well. Everybody was keeping their heads down. Nobody was looking at anybody else. You could hear a pin drop in there, it was that quiet. Nine big country lads, normally as crude as schoolboys, and not a peep out of them.

At the other end of the room, the door to the little corridor outside the inspector's office was wide open. I expected a summons immediately. But she wasn't in yet.

I made my way to my desk. I sat down. I pretended to deal with my paperwork, but I was just staring at a page, my mind full of dread.

The inspector came in about twenty minutes later. She stood in the centre of the room, looking around. Nobody looked up at her. She had an announcement to make, she said.

I stiffened, expecting the worst. Shit, I thought, she's going to do it in public.

But she said nothing about the tabloid story. We were joining a search team, she explained. In the Wicklow Mountains. She went through the gear we needed to wear and the equipment we needed to bring. She gave us the rendezvous point. This was the public car park at Cloon, halfway between Glencree and Enniskerry. Finally, she told us what we'd be looking for. The possible grave site of Mary Corbett. And then she left.

The fact that she hadn't addressed me one way or the other did nothing for my nerves. I tried to lose myself in the preparations. And I think I managed not to allow myself too much time for thinking. But as we were leaving headquarters we had to run a bit of a gauntlet by the front gates. Television crews. Photographers. Newspapers reporters. And a small group of noisy protesters. It made us tense again.

The media followed us through the city, out into the mountains and right up to Cloon itself, where they were stopped by the cordon of uniformed guards on duty. We drove on to the little circular car park. I don't think I'd ever been there before, but I remembered all the details from the description in the narrative. The gravel surface. The carved wooden sign. The steel gate. The barbed-wire fence. And the clearing that led to the waymarked walk through the mountains. The circumstances were different, of course. Daylight instead of darkness. A sunny midsummer's day instead of cold and heavy rain.

The place was already crowded with police vehicles and with guards and soldiers, most of them in shirtsleeves because of the heat. They were actually waiting for us. I suppose the inspector must have made the point back in the office, but it was only then that I realized that our unit was co-ordinating this search. She gathered the party together and made her speech, and then we spread out, east and west of the car park, about fifteen metres apart, and headed north through the woods, back over the mountain towards Dublin.

Personally, I think it's one of the saddest sights, a line of police officers searching open ground at walking pace. There can be no happy outcome. Either you fail or you find the body of some unfortunate victim.

We started out at eleven-thirty that morning, under instructions to look for disturbed ground, for suspicious mounds, for the items of clothing that Mary Corbett had been wearing on the night of her disappearance.

In one way, I thought it was a hopeless task. Mary Corbett had disappeared in October, more than eight months earlier. If she was buried on this mountain, the site would have been washed by rain, frozen in ice and overgrown by moss and other vegetation in the meantime. Even with so many eyes, it's very hard to find a concealed body in such a large area. The other murdered women found in the mountains only surfaced because the peat bogs had subsided in dry weather.

On the other hand, though, I wasn't so sure. The more I thought about the account left in Michael Elwood's grave, the more I started stripping it down to its basics. Just a sequence of actions, leaving out all the fancy decoration around them, most of which, in any case, I couldn't remember any more. A man picks up Mary Corbett in the Wicklow Mountains. He drives her towards the village of Enniskerry. But he stops at Cloon Car Park, where Mary Corbett disappears from view. If that was true – I mean, if all those things had happened – then it also seemed to me that the killer, for some weird reasons of their own, actually *wanted* us to find her grave.

Around quarter-past three, nearly four hours after we set out, we got a message over the radio that something likely might have been found. The members of our own unit were told to break off and regroup at this new location, while the others were instructed to keep going.

I checked the map I was carrying and found that I was about two kilometres east of the site. To be honest, I'd completely forgotten about my own troubles by then. But as I set out, walking across the mountain and a bit behind the line of searchers now, I saw a uniformed guard I recognized and remembered that he was stationed in Bray. And then everything suddenly came back to me.

'Is Phil Flynn about?' I asked the guard.

He stopped. 'Didn't you hear?' he said. He stared at me and then looked nervously at the line that was stepping away from him. 'Phil,' he said quickly. 'He's out on sick leave, but he got suspended anyway. It was found out that he was the one leaking the information about that Elwood thing.'

I stood around for a while afterwards, trying to take this in. I suppose it must have been easy enough to trace the photocopies I'd given the inspector. I didn't blame myself for that. Phil knew the risks he was running, I thought to myself, and anyway, I hadn't deliberately shopped him. I still had no idea what he'd wanted me to do with the photocopies or what his reasons for giving them to me were, but I couldn't believe that he'd also leak internal documents to the media. I knew Phil. Maybe in the sense that you know anybody, which is never enough not to be shocked by them, but I still couldn't accept that he'd do anything that stupid, for whatever reason, money, or blackmail, or spite.

I *thought* I knew Phil. I even carried this idea around with me for about a year afterwards, without actually seeing him again, until I bumped into him in a pub one night, long after he'd left the guards and was working for a private security company. I suppose I had too much drink on me, because I asked him straight out what he'd been playing at giving me the photocopies. He looked back at me, just with contempt on his face, and all he said was, 'Go and fuck yourself, Galetti.' Two days later, his wife – or partner, I suppose – rang me at the office, half-hysterical on the phone, screaming at me that I'd already given him one nervous breakdown, and did I want to be responsible for causing another one now.

Breakdown?

It turned out that the first time I'd fluttered my eyelashes at him to get the information on Michael Elwood, Phil, without being aware of it, was in the middle of a nervous breakdown brought on by stress. It turned out that, although I didn't cause it, I certainly became a major feature in this episode, raising his hopes of a meaningful, long-term relationship with my flirting. It also turned out, obviously, that he was plunged into depression when he discovered that I was messing with him. Actually he stalked me for a couple of days while he was out on sick leave. And who knows what was really on his mind when he came into headquarters to see me and stood there in the office, dripping with rain?

All I can say is, I didn't exactly feel proud of myself when finally I learned all this.

Anyway.

On that sunny afternoon in the middle of June I must have stood there on the slope above Cloon, mulling over what I'd just heard about Phil, for a good five or six minutes, until Jimmy Coyne came along and put his arm around my shoulders, thinking I was distressed by the search. We were still among the first members of the unit to reach the site we'd been called to, although the inspector was already there, along with a local superintendent, directing operations.

It looked a nothing location while you were approaching it. The side of a mountain, bisected by a stream, largely covered by pine trees and dotted with rocks and boulders. But one of the searchers had stopped here, drawn by something. Probably the same man or woman had stuck the thin blade of a shovel or spade into the centre of the stream as a probe and then shifted the moist earth sideways to open a gap. The blade struck something hard. A buried stone? A rotted tree trunk? A little temporary dam was built to hold the water. More of the muddy earth was dug away. And more. Until it was discovered that the blade had sliced through rotted flesh and glanced off a bone underneath.

When you were up close, if you could ignore the stench and the strange whiteness of the section of flesh that had been exposed, you could see what had attracted the attention in the first place. The stream seemed to have been slightly diverted from its former course. The surrounding area had been badly flooded in winter and had subsided, except for the mound of the burial site itself. As well as that, a few small rocks had been placed over the site, presumably to hold the loosened soil in place, and if you caught their pattern at a certain angle it actually suggested the shape of a human grave.

A deliberate pointer or pure carelessness? Who knows?

At that stage, there was nothing we could do about it except speculate. And wait.

Wait for the plastic tent to be erected around the site. Wait for the pathologist to arrive and supervise the removal. Wait for the team from the Technical Bureau to take charge of the scene.

Wait.

Until it was ten o'clock and night was closing in and it struck you that you'd contributed nothing, that you could have waited just as efficiently back at the office or at home. But that's the way it goes sometimes. You're almost paralysed by tiredness. And you can't do anything anyway until they've moved the corpse. And it's better to wait in the eye of the storm, at the scene, cordoned off from the media, the politicians, the relatives and the campaigners, all clamouring for quick arrests and instant solutions, progress and movement, or somebody – anybody – doing something, anything.

I suppose everybody knew that the body was that of Mary Corbett, just as everybody had known within days of her disappearance that she was dead, but the formal identification, again from dental records and DNA comparison, still came as a shock to the family and relatives, and to her boyfriend, Simon Chester.

I drew the job of liaising with the parents, so I had to break the news to them. They'd been on our backs, through the media, for more than eight months, going on about our incompetence and our laziness. But all the anger was just drained out of them now. The mother, a small, thin woman in an expensive dress, collapsed in the reception room of their home. The father, more practical, wanted to know if we'd discovered anything that would help identify his daughter's killer. It looked to me as if they'd been rehearsing these responses for months. This is the way the female falls, swooning in a Parisian outfit. This is the way the male stands up, shifting his shoulders inside the jacket of his Italian suit and demanding action.

Maybe I'm being unkind. I don't mean to, particularly. Everybody has their own ways of coping with loss and I just think that this was the style of their set, where the husbands ran business empires and the wives ran dinner parties.

There wasn't much that I was allowed to tell the father. There wasn't much I *could* have told him, really. Even after the autopsy, the cause of his daughter's death was unknown. There were no fractures, no gunshot or stab wounds, no indication of strangulation, no sign that a blunt instrument had been used.

As with Michael Elwood, the victim had been buried naked. No items of clothing had been found in or around the grave site.

There were various theories as to why the grave had become flooded after the burial, all of them to do with the weather and the topography, none of them really conclusive. But because of the wet conditions, the pathologist explained, the body fats had hardened instead of liquefying, giving the corpse that suety white appearance we'd all noticed. To some extent, this process had actually *protected* the internal organs. And there was plenty of alcohol and cocaine in her system, at the time of death.

One of the mortuary assistants, I think a medical student gaining experience of forensic pathology, mentioned over a drink to Dennison that he thought the woman might have died from an overdose of a sedative, the traces of which had since cleared from her system. This couldn't be verified, though, and it never appeared on any of the official reports. Dennison later put it in as a handwritten note on the file. And then we all forgot about it. An oversight we'd end up regretting.

No papers of any kind had been left in the grave. And the body hadn't been arranged to resemble any specific position. It certainly wasn't kneeling. The professionals' opinion was that it had been thrown down, say from shoulder-height, into a grave that was over a metre deep, and then covered where it had fallen. It was lying on its back. The right arm was thrown sideways, away from the trunk. The right knee was slightly bent, facing in the same direction.

As far as the family and the general public were concerned, therefore, there were a lot of differences in the remains of Michael Elwood and Mary Corbett, despite the ghoulish reference to Mary found in Elwood's grave. Given what they knew, they probably decided that the differences outweighed this mysterious connection. But they didn't know everything, of course. For operational reasons, as the Garda Press Office is fond of saying, we'd held back the most significant similarity.

It was this.

Mary Corbett's ears had also been sliced off with a surgeon's scalpel or similar instrument and then presumably kept by her killer for some reason, or some use, that went beyond comprehension.

The day after the pathologist's report and some of the forensic details came in, a Wednesday morning in mid-June, we held a conference in the incident room at headquarters, to analyze what we had and to discuss where we were going. In my experience, there are two types of conference. In the first, everybody pitches everything into the common pool, evidence and hunches, doubts and theories, and everybody takes responsibility for whatever comes out of it again. In the other, somebody talks and nobody else listens. This one, at a crucial stage in the investigation and a crucial stage in the development of the unit, was definitely one of the latter.

Dennison and the rest of the lads just sat there with their arms folded, saying nothing, wearing those expressions that challenged, 'Right, show us how good you are then,' and 'Right, let's see how well you do without us.' The inspector, a superintendent with operational control of special units and a sergeant from the Technical Bureau, sat looking back at them.

Even before it got started, it never had a hope of going anywhere. And the superintendent already knew it. He sat apart from the inspector. I'm just an observer here, his attitude said. I don't have an active role. If this thing doesn't get off the ground, it's not my fault. I'm not the one who's going down with it.

In this atmosphere, the inspector stood up to take the session. A month earlier she might've carried it, but now her confidence was going. You could see it in her appearance. She'd worked hard in front of the dressing-table mirror that morning, but it's impossible to conceal the signs of stress. Her muscles were tense. Her manner was abrupt. Her voice was sharp. All the little symptoms that make-up can't disguise, no matter what miracles the advertisers claim for it.

If ever she'd needed the unit to throw its weight behind her, it was now. But she'd already been judged and resented as a woman, and she hadn't made up any ground on that position. Like I said before, it was her own contempt for men as much as the prejudice of the lads that damaged her.

It didn't matter that I could fill in the reasons for her attitude now. Her husband had left her, I was pretty certain. Probably because of that, she had her problems with the booze and with a resentful teenage daughter. Sometimes, though, understanding doesn't really add anything to your sympathy.

So we all nursed our own little concerns that morning, even though the inspector's theme was the one that was uppermost in everybody's mind. Was there a connection between the murders of Michael Elwood and Mary Corbett?

'There's something I need to clarify,' she started off. 'It's about the printed pages found in Michael Elwood's grave. From the beginning, we considered the possibility that Elwood's killer wanted to direct us to the grave of Mary Corbett as well. That's why the decision was taken not to distribute the printed pages, and not to make them available to this unit. It's also why the decision was taken not immediately to search the area around Cloon, where Mary Corbett's grave was found. It was hoped that the killer would become impatient and further show his hand. The leaking of the papers to the media made this strategy redundant.'

She paused.

I looked around. All the arms were still folded. All the lips were still tightly closed. How much did they know? I wondered. Did anyone, apart from the inspector, realize that I'd been given photocopies of these papers before they turned up in the media? If they did, they had nothing to say about it.

In any case, I wasn't convinced by the inspector's stated reason for not releasing details of the papers found in the grave, and I don't think anyone else was either. There was an obvious problem with it. If someone wanted to guide us to the grave of Mary Corbett by leaving directions in Michael Elwood's grave, how could they be certain that Elwood's grave would be found first? How could they be certain that his grave would be found at all?

The fact is an anonymous telephone caller to the Garda confidential line had given us the location of Elwood's grave, claiming that they'd stumbled on it while out hunting in the mountains. The informant was recorded as a female and it was presumed that she was involved in some minor criminal activity and wanted to conceal her identity.

Well, maybe.

But by that stage I didn't believe in any uninvolved anonymous caller. I didn't believe that Phil Flynn had leaked confidential files to the media.

What did I believe?

When I came to write them down, I decided that there were three possibilities.

In the first of them, there was no real connection between the murders of Michael Elwood and Mary Corbett. The killer of Elwood, months after the disappearance of Mary Corbett, played a little black joke with the narrative in the grave. At the very least, this left the amputation of the ears unexplained, except as coincidence. And it was impossible to accept it as that.

The second theory was a bit more plausible. According to this, it was Michael Elwood who had abducted and killed Mary Corbett, and his murder, duplicating hers, had been carried out as revenge, complete with a graveside confession. Actually we chased this theory for a while, so I can tell you there's no point wasting any more time on it. Michael Elwood was at a recital in the National Concert Hall with his girlfriend, Laura Ashwell, on the night Mary Corbett disappeared. They stayed late at Laura's house afterwards, caring for her father who was ill at the time.

All this left the only possibility that I could actually believe in, namely that the same person killed both Michael Elwood and Mary Corbett. I believed that Elwood had been buried to be found and that the narrative left in his grave had been written to be widely read. I believed that his killer, frustrated at how long the body was taking to surface, finally lost patience and actually pointed the guards in the right direction and then, annoyed by the subsequent censorship, sent a copy of the narrative to a journalist.

There were nights after I'd decided this when I pored over books, reading about killers who had interjected themselves into the investigation, and trying to understand the odd compulsions that drove them to it.

There were nights as well when I sat in front of the television, watching tapes of the news footage of the discovery of Michael Elwood's grave. I was looking for the killer among the spectators. It was the sort of thing the murderer would do, I thought. After letting us know where the body was, why not come along to see how we handled the dig and reacted to the papers inside?

I didn't know who or what I was searching for, though. In fact, I wasn't even sure what *gender* I was looking for. But when I said this, I was laughed at.

It happened at that crime-scene conference, when the inspector, worn down by the lack of co-operation, started to wind things up. 'Well,' she said, 'we'll obviously investigate all the other possibilities, but I think there's general acceptance at all levels that the same man killed both Michael Elwood and Mary Corbett.'

The last thing she must have expected was a challenge. The last thing she needed, I suppose, at that stage anyway, was debate.

'How do we know it was a man?' I asked.

She stared at me. Maybe she'd already settled on how to deal with any of my questions. Maybe she was too tired to come up with anything of her own. 'How do we know it's a man?' she repeated.

'It's an assumption,' I said. 'Which is okay, if it's recognized as that. But there's no evidence. The only thing that suggests it's a man is that narrative found in the grave. Nothing else. I know there's confusion about this, given the night she had at the party, but it seems that Mary Corbett wasn't raped. On the other hand, Michael Elwood was last seen leaving Johnnie Fox's pub with a woman. She hasn't been traced.'

'You know the feeling on that. She may have been killed as well, and buried elsewhere.'

'But she still hasn't been *traced*,' I said. 'We don't know who she was. And a woman apparently rang to tell us where Michael Elwood's grave was. Maybe it was the same woman.'

'Maybe that woman at Johnnie Fox's was a fucking transvestite, Galetti,' Dennison put in.

Out of the blue. He hadn't opened his mouth until then.

'Maybe,' I said. 'But given your understanding of women, Dennison, would you be able to tell the difference?'

This started a row, I have to admit. But since the row got us precisely nowhere, and the point I was trying to make got lost in the middle of it, there's no point going into any of it.

In the weeks after that conference, the thing you noticed most was how often the superintendent kept dropping into our offices, checking on our progress. The brass were worried. And they obviously had the inspector on a rope that was getting shorter and shorter by the day. Bad enough to have so many unsolved missing persons on our files. But the mountains had just given us two bodies and we still had no leads.

We couldn't find the woman who had left Johnnie Fox's with Michael Elwood. We couldn't find Elwood's car, the Opel Astra that he'd driven up there after dropping Laura Ashwell home. The media were making a meal of it. And the superintendent was getting desperate.

'This idea of yours,' he said to me one morning. 'Do you really think the murderer could be a woman?'

I went back and interviewed Gary Gaynor, the football manager who'd noticed Michael Elwood leaving the pub that night. The guy had a wife and four kids, so the more you forced him to recall eyeing up a woman in a pub, the less he remembered being really interested in her.

'It was just a casual thing,' he claimed. 'You know, the way someone catches your eye like that.'

'You said originally that she had a strong build,' I reminded him.

'Did I?' he asked. 'I can't remember. I wouldn't say she was skin and bone, anyway.'

For three weeks, from late-June to mid-July, reinforced by detectives drafted in from other units and swollen to ten times our original size, the team pressed the investigation into the deaths of Michael Elwood and Mary Corbett.

Our efforts led nowhere.

You can't blame the failure on anyone involved. The fact that the inspector was disliked, for instance, was largely irrelevant and had no bearing on anybody's work. We gave it our best shot. It wasn't good enough. And that was soul-destroying. To know that you've checked and double-checked everything and still come up with nothing is really dispiriting. You have no hope left, because you have nothing left to pin your hopes on. Everything is played out.

When you have no hope, all you can do is face defeat. People have different ways of doing that. What we did was, we sat there, waiting for the inspector to be transferred and replaced.

PART TWO

The Narrative

I have, perhaps, a responsibility to quiet men. It's a sense that alerts me to their presence. I hear their silence.

In the crowded pub, sitting at the bar on a high stool and pretending to read my lecture notes, I watched him slope through the entrance and knew immediately that he was weighed down with a sadness he would find almost impossible to share. Almost. He was a small man. And he was quite unattractive. He looked middle-aged in a style that has already dated. He was balding, for instance, but instead of shaving his head and making a virtue out of the obvious in the modern way, he vainly attempted to conceal the problem by growing some wisps of hair longer than the others in an effort to cover the gap. He wore brown trousers and a bottle-green jumper, both of a type and colour available only from cramped shops that persist in calling themselves establishments and from geriatrics who advertise themselves as haberdashers. Despite the fact that it was March, and mild, and that he must have driven up to this pub high in the Dublin mountains, he also wore a glass-green oilskin jacket.

He used the jacket to reserve a vacant table by draping it over the back of one of the chairs. He came to the bar, quite close to me, ordered a Budweiser beer and took this back to the table. He smelled, I thought, of old wood, of unventilated interiors. I watched him for a time, in case a fretting companion was dragged in behind him, like an afterbirth. He would inspire such attachment, I thought, somewhere in his life. But not there, and not that night. He was alone.

A group of lightly dressed girls, high-pitched on drink, imagined that they caught him staring at their bodies and embarrassed him by staring back. It's a modern anomaly that we are all trained as spectators but forbidden to practise in public. In fact, the man was unaware of the women until they forced him to blush. His eyes were fixed, and vacant, only because he was contemplating his own future.

Shortly afterwards I took my gin and tonic from the bar counter, folded my lecture notes in my other hand, slipped from the stool and walked slowly towards his table. I was aware of several pairs of eyes following my movements. These were the eyes of those loud males who had already noticed me – an unaccompanied woman, sitting alone at the bar – and who had grown more boisterous as the evening advanced in an effort to seduce my attention. They never seem to learn that this type of display has the opposite of the intended effect. The loud man bores the entire world with his crude story and keeps nothing in reserve for the intimacy of conversation. By contrast, the man sitting quietly alone has an irresistible mystery about him.

I stopped at the table where the quiet man sat. Excuse me, I said.

He looked up.

I'm in a little trouble, I added quickly, before he had time to harden his resistance. The fact is, I've been abandoned up here. My ex-husband has driven off in the car. The barman is calling for a taxi, but says it may take a long time. Would you mind if I sat with you while waiting? You understand, don't you? A woman alone here . . .

The silent man, particularly one as old-fashioned as this, has a highly developed sense of chivalry. He never asks to be bothered by strangers, of course. When he is, his first reaction is extreme irritation at the intrusion. The last thing he is capable of is the complication of involvement and his scowling is merely the earliest of his defence mechanisms. But the long years of being alone by himself have also left the silent man with severe handicaps. He doesn't know how to get rid of people who are even mildly persistent. He has never acquired the gestures and vocabulary necessary for this. In extreme situations, he will sometimes retreat into the absurd pretence that he is deaf, or blind, or otherwise incapacitated. But mostly he will flounder. And while floundering, perversely, he becomes burdened with guilt, which quickly solidifies into a sense of duty.

I know all this because my father was a silent man. A man who preferred, by and large, the company of dumb animals to the chatter of humans. The chickens he reared in our back garden. The dogs he kept. The caged songbirds he bred. All creatures whose own vocabularies were so limited that they allowed him to respond to them with a narrow range of sounds. Sounds that communicated, but that were hardly words. They lacked the inherent ambiguity of language, an absence that made my father's life more straightforward, but also poorer.

Perhaps he felt like a monarch in his own garden, because those sounds of his always meant exactly what he intended them to mean. With us, his wife and children, he was withdrawn, taciturn. There were stories that he came alive outside the home, that in the pub, for instance, under the loosening inspiration of alcohol, he was the life and soul of the place, entertaining friends and strangers alike with wit and anecdotes. They were mere legends. I never witnessed such animation, and I never met anyone who did.

It's worth noting, before we leave my father's creatures, that the double meaning of the word dumb in the English language, while it may be unfortunate, is also significant. But it's only one example from a pattern that testifies, in ordinary speech, to a dread of silence. As silent as the grave. The sound of silence. Speechless. Death, alienation and incapacity. If silence isn't feared as threatening in itself or as a destructive weapon used by others, then it's presented as a symptom of inadequacy.

Was my father a sinister man? A primitive man?

I know that he was impossible to reach. I know that, as his silence grew more profound, my mother's voice grew shriller and her inventions became more colourful. She would suddenly announce, for instance, an expected visit from rich American relatives who were not only on holiday in the country, but also bearing gifts for each of us impoverished children. She would somehow scrape together enough money to buy some delicacies to serve them with their tea. On a Sunday morning, after mass, she would dress us all in our cleanest clothes and have us wait, past midday, through the entire afternoon, and into early-evening, when she would finally collapse in tears and accuse my father of alienating the strangers. They won't come, she would wail. Why should they? They could never have any comfort with you here. They said that to me. Exhausted, hungry, and empty with disappointment, we would join in the crying. How were we to know that the rich American relatives, far from being unreliable, did not even exist? Did my father know? And if he did, why did he seem unmoved by our hatred?

I have no idea which of my parents was mad. What I mean is this. Was my father like Murke, the young radio producer in Heinrich Böll's short story, who takes the small sections of soundless tape home with him whenever he has to cut inadvertent pauses from contributors' radio talks, splices them together and then plays back the silent tape for his own comfort? A man, in other words, who has found a clean alternative to verbal pollution. Or was my mother like Scheherazade in the Arabian Nights, weaving narratives as a strategy for survival?

Perhaps, in themselves, both are tenable. Perhaps it's only in the disputed *wastelands between lies and silence, if you're forced to struggle for survival there, that you'll sustain any serious damage. In our own home, we lived as refugees when we were children. Nine, ten, eleven year olds, we sat in a tense household, our nerves at breaking point, waiting for the next violent quarrel between our parents. A tension we endured for so long that we finally learned that the only escape from it was to destroy our own nervous systems. Insensibility or breakdown. Those were our choices. And we chose to become hardened. We learned to mimic statues, since the smallest sound or movement could trigger a ferocious argument. And we also grew the hearts of statues. Denied any spontaneous expression, our feelings withered and died. Like plants without light.*

One morning in spring, my uncles handed me a greyhound to take to the local abattoir. A mild-tempered brindle bitch, she had broken her leg too often to retain the hope of racing and she wasn't considered good enough to breed from. I walked her past Gallows Hill and out to the abattoir, where a fat man in a blood-soaked apron took her from me. And as I stood beside him while he held a gun to her head and shot a bolt through her brain, I felt . . . indifferent, I suggest. Impassive. Curious, perhaps. But that's something else, outside the range of feelings. And yet, when it was all over, when the dog was stretched on the ground and its blood was seeping on to the concrete from the head wound, I took a boning knife from the scabbard hanging around the fat man's waist, I stooped, and I sliced off the pointed brindle ears of the dead greyhound. I don't know why I did this. I understand that I was trying to save her from either the silence or the chatter of the damned. But the question is, why should I care, either way, when I was so unmoved by her death?

Beside me, once he'd recovered from the shock, the fat man sweatily did his sums. Adding together the novelty of a girl training greyhounds, the coolness of my response to violence and the forbidden pleasures of mutilation, he suddenly found his hand on my breast, with my heart beating rapidly underneath. In reality, the fat man was rather repulsive. But I felt a strange excitement that morning, the intensity of which, I believe, had as much to do with the long suppression of my voice at home as with the still warm and dripping ears that I held in my left palm.

Under his blood-soaked apron, past the metal buttons on the crotch of his blue overalls, I found the fat man's erection, as his own hand dropped away from my breast and dived under the skirt of my school uniform to fumble with my knickers. I came on his plump fingers as soon as they penetrated me.

But it wasn't enough. It only increased my appetite. And yet, the frenzy almost faded disastrously. For a moment, as he worried whether I still held the boning knife or not, the fat man's cock went limp in my hand. But his desire soon overcame his fear again. I can't say that my furious manipulations helped. I was still sexually inexperienced. But I suspect that the greyhound's ears, still warm and oozing lubricating blood, and which had somehow become participants in the stimulation, considerably added to his excitement.

Beyond a certain point, of course, I was no longer physically capable of dominating the situation. I didn't mind. The fat man tore my knickers away. He lifted me up and laid me on the edge of his wooden table, with my legs high in the air, my bare bottom slipping in the blood of slaughtered animals. When I reached out to steady myself, my hand grasped offal, intestines, livers and kidneys. The fat man had dropped his overalls, but never removed his apron. He lifted it to expose himself and then let it down, so that, intentionally or otherwise, it covered my face when he took me. I felt his paunch settling heavily over my own stomach. I thought of it as a whale, or a dolphin, or some other viscous, earless mammal, working its smooth body against my clitoris. This was what made me come again. As for his cock slipping in and out of me, I hardly felt it. I know it was plump and sturdy, like his fingers, if not especially long, but the truth is, I hardly felt it.

When it was all over, when he was dressed again and I had cleaned myself as best I could, the fat man handed me the lead and empty leather collar from the dead greyhound and said hoarsely, Don't tell anyone.

Don't tell anyone.

I have a particular interest in narratives, I explained to the quiet man sitting at the table in Johnnie Fox's pub, and in the artifices of narrators. His second question to me, after asking my name – My own is Elwood, he told me, Michael Elwood – concerned the lecture notes I was still carrying in my hand.

Having spent the first sixteen years of my life with tautened nerves, the experience has left me with a bad digestion, a fondness for flight as the first solution and an inability to share my feelings, fatally combined with a mastery of artifice. Needless to say, after a false trail or two in my late-teens, an illusion or two that needed to be punctured in my twenties, I have, of course, beached myself in the English Literature department of a major university, divorced, and alienated from my own two kids.

They're sections of a paper on the role of the narrator in crime fiction, I explained. Do you read crime fiction, Michael?

He was a timid man, eager not to offend, since offence invariably brings entanglements, but for a moment a flicker of disdain passed over his features. No, he said.

I was surprised. I had imagined him sitting in front of an open fire on winter evenings, enjoying tea and sweet biscuits, while immersed in the classics of the golden age, Allingham and Christie, Sayers and Berkeley. Perhaps I treat the genre with too much seriousness, of course, offering it a significance it hardly deserves. But one should treat every pursuit with the utmost seriousness. Absorption, after all, is the most efficient form of flight. For me, escape was once defined by greyhounds. Now literature fills that role. Lost in the text of a novel, linking metaphor to metaphor, elision to elision, I form a circular seal that excludes the messiness of life.

So, yes, I was disappointed by Michael's ignorance of crime fiction. I had hoped to get his views on the crisis of confidence among contemporary narrators, those poor creatures crippled by the weight of technical information, who, in an effort to convince us of their authenticity, swear that they have consulted experts in the fields of forensic anthropology, drug abuse, environmental disasters and psychological profiling. I had hoped to share with him my admiration for Doctor Watson in the Sherlock Holmes stories, still, in my opinion, the most skilfully used narrator of them all. I was a whetstone for his mind, Watson explains in 'The Adventure of the Creeping Man', which, like all the other stories in the series, also contains the obligatory question from Holmes: What do you make of it, Watson? We already know, of course, that Watson will make far less of it, whatever it happens to be, than Holmes himself. And yet, Watson is a professional man, well-educated, very intelligent, extremely resourceful and remarkably brave. This is why I had hoped to confide in Michael my intense irritation at Hollywood. When it got its hands on the Sherlock Holmes stories and made a series of films in the 1940s, Nigel Bruce played Watson as a buffoon, slow on the uptake, always putting his foot in it and unable to handle a revolver without endangering the lives of everyone except the villain – a crude characterization entirely missing the point that it is only by comparison with a competent intelligence that both the brilliance of Holmes and the genius of his criminal adversaries can be fully savoured. But, as I said, I was disappointed.

As Michael finished his Budweiser beer, I drank the last of my gin and tonic and looked at my watch.

I'd better check on that taxi, I said.

Where are you going? he asked.

It's not actually very far, I admitted. Close to Roundwood, south of Enniskerry.

I could drop you there, he offered. Unless you prefer to wait for the taxi.

But it's out of your way, I protested. You must be heading back towards the city.

Sometimes, he said, I think it's the responsibility of those with transport to look after those without.

His car, a light blue Astra, was parked at the side of the pub. When we left, there was only one couple sitting on the benches outside. The night was cool by then, but they were warmed by passion, and by each other, and they paid us no attention.

We turned south after leaving the car park, descending from Glencullen Mountain and crossing the border on the way, from Dublin into County Wicklow. We didn't actually drive to the village of Enniskerry. Michael took a shorter route, along the narrow lanes through the lowlands to the west of the village, until we rejoined the main road to Roundwood and started climbing again, into Djouce Mountain.

He was an intense driver, and even quieter behind a steering wheel than elsewhere. Outside a single topic, I doubt if conversation would have been possible. But the silent man, particularly one as old-fashioned as this, has a highly developed sense of chivalry and the contest between the knight and death is surely inevitable in the western tradition.

We buried my father this morning, I said. We were on our way back from the funeral when we stopped in Johnnie Fox's for a drink.

Unable to ignore this unexpected confidence, Michael slowed even further to consider his response, switching on his full headlights as he did so and illuminating a startled rabbit in the grass margin to our left. I'm sorry, he sympathized. Was he elderly?

He was eighty, I said.

It must have been an impressive funeral, then, he suggested.

No, Michael, I said, it wasn't. Apart from myself, my ex-husband and two children, and my sister, there was no one younger than seventy there. And they all came to that windswept country graveyard only to console my mother, none to pay their last respects to my father. They hated him. He had once been accepted as a harmless oddity, a lover of domestic fowl and worthless stamps, an error which made their subsequent hatred all the more intense. The cruellest irony, however, is that my mother doesn't even miss him, or perhaps only as one misses a once-familiar object around the house, and she certainly did not need any consoling. Her performance at the funeral, mimicking grief, wove a pretence through the ceremony, an entire narrative of love and loss that was, like any art, profoundly unnecessary. It didn't seem to matter to her that her audience was small or that its members were largely deaf. A natural story-teller, with all that this description implies, she still had the ears, and the sympathy, of her contemporaries. My father lay in his coffin, mute, embarked on the last of his many silences, no longer able to challenge her account of the world.

But then, her methods of enlisting support had invariably been far more sophisticated than his. She was utterly dishonest, of course, but she always looked you straight in the eye. Did you know that Charles Dickens, writing about the plain-clothes detectives in the newly reformed Metropolitan Police Force, once said of them admiringly, 'They all can, and they all do, look full at whomsoever they speak to'? The implication being, of course, that they were therefore frank, upright and truthful. But, Michael, I said, if humans had tails, some would undoubtedly wag them while preparing to bite you. We're liars, really. For our own purposes we mislead each other, not only by words, but by gestures, by facial expressions, even by postures. But perhaps we enjoy misleading ourselves most of all. Or perhaps we would go mad if we couldn't believe in the existence of trust. For once every four years or so, hordes of well-dressed men and women descend on the rest of us with outrageous promises. They look us steadily in the eye. They shake our hands vigorously. And you'll never catch one of them lounging or slinking about. They're called politicians, they control a large part of our lives, and they're voted into power by the rest of us.

Car headlights suddenly flashed from behind us and a horn sounded angrily, shattering both the narrative and the darkness at the same time. Absorbed by the story, Michael had slowed to a crawl and drifted into the centre of the narrow road, leaving no space for anything to overtake him. Like all nervous drivers, he became tense when under pressure and spiralled towards panic. Instead of merely pulling over and allowing his tormentor to pass, he seemed to freeze with fear, his hands gripping the steering wheel more desperately as the car behind him weaved and swerved, first on the outside, then on the inside, probing for a gap to exploit.

There were, I knew, a number of parking bays along this route, small clearings set into the woods or mountains where visitors left their cars to ramble the area on foot. I waited for a sign indicating the next one. Perhaps, I said then, it might be better if we stopped here for a while.

This almost precipitated an accident. Michael didn't answer. But when we reached the clearing, he pulled to the right without indicating, just as the driver behind, infuriated at being blocked, surged to overtake on the same side. We avoided a collision by mere centimetres. And I doubt if Michael was even aware of the near miss. He braked gently inside the parking area. When we stopped, facing the shadowy pine trees on the lower slope of Djouce Mountain, he left the engine idling and the headlights on. He drew a deep breath. But it seemed unrelated to the terrors on the road.

Why did his neighbours hate your father? he asked.

When I look back on my childhood, Michael, I said, I realize now that it was really a period of suppressed life, of things that existed but were never mentioned, of dark hints and furtive codes, of realities denied by being ignored or locked away, out of sight.

And yet, it was also a time of great change. The traditional industries were dying. The factories were closing. First the flour mills where my father worked. Followed by the jute factory, the iron foundry and the steel plant. And finally even the bacon factory where my uncles sweated, boning the carcasses of pigs. A way of life was passing. My father was already a dated figure, in his cloth cap and unravelled cardigans stained with flour dust. And when I think of my uncles, a decade younger than him, I remember uncouth men. Between the obsessive polishing of their footwear, a neurosis that concerned Irish mothers of the period, and the brushing of their slicked-back hair, an image copied from Elvis Presley, their neglected bodies were largely untroubled by hygiene. They were all fearful, all timidly traditional, untouched by the openness that was gradually flowering elsewhere.

For us, the teenagers of the period, our role models lay elsewhere. We had no investment in continuity. Our inspiration was America, which for us meant only the personal freedoms of San Francisco, the sexual energy of the Doors, and the political radicalism of the Vietnam War protests. And it was from this world, I was certain, that the stranger who turned up one summer in the vacant house beside my uncles, a young American woman named Sarah Kleisner, had come to us.

The city had an eerie feel to it that summer. It played no role in the global unrest that brought riots to Paris, demonstrations to London, flowers in the gun barrels at Berkeley University, and yet its life and character were fundamentally altered. Almost everyone between the ages of sixteen and twenty-five was drawn away at some stage, to distant battles, to rock festivals, to political campaigns. There seemed to be days when the city was occupied only by grubby-faced kids in short pants playing marbles on the hot concrete streets and old men and women watching them enviously from shaded doorways, days when the only sound was the buzzing of flies and wasps.

By the end of it, when the rains of early-autumn came, the young American woman lay dead, sprawled at the foot of the cliff about two kilometres to the north, across the fields at the back of our house, her body disfigured by the fall, but not so badly as to conceal the stab wounds that had killed her before her descent. A week later, when they came to search our house and found, at the bottom of the locked chest of drawers in my parents' bedroom, under my father's black leather-bound stamp album, the boning knife that had ended Sarah Kleisner's life, I wondered who had betrayed us. My father was in the garden, feeding maize to his chickens, the peak of his cloth cap shielding his eyes from the weak September sun. He seemed unmoved by his arrest, a factor that later told against him. He said nothing. As they brought him, handcuffed, through the house he looked at me and smiled faintly. Outside, torn equally between hostility to my father and sympathy for my mother, a huge crowd had gathered. The police were few, a uniformed sergeant and two plain-clothes detectives. When the crowd surged forward to attack my father, throwing stones and sticks and insults, the officers struggled to keep their prisoner. In fact, they had to retreat to the house again and call for assistance.

I couldn't understand the crowd's anger, or their hatred. Shock, of course, might well have been expected. Incredulity, perhaps. Even disgust. But why such hatred? The woman was a stranger. What investment did the community have in her survival? If she represented – for us, at least, the corruptible young – the rebellious energy of America, surely her removal should have been at least a neutral matter for our parents? Relief, say, balanced by regret. So, yes. Why, indeed, did the neighbours hate my father?

I met my husband in America, Michael. While I was studying for my PhD in New York we discovered that we shared a fondness for the arid peace that textual criticism brings. What relevance has that? you wonder. None, perhaps. Except to admit that I came to America to search for the Doors, for San Francisco and for the anti-war movement, and that I found a husband instead, and to reveal that while I was there I also found, after a brief search, the office suite on Park Avenue owned by Lamson & Luetgerr. The last time I saw Sarah she had received a letter from this address, apparently written by a Robert Kleisner, who was perhaps a relative. I had expected an attorney's office. Not only because the form of the name suggested it or because Park Avenue is crowded with prestigious law firms, but because the letter had so *deeply distressed Sarah that she tore it into tiny fragments and scattered them to the wind after reading it.*

Lamson & Luetgerr, however, turned out to be a film production company, although who Lamson and Luetgerr themselves were and what precise roles they played in the enterprise still remain a mystery to me. The firm seemed to be dominated by Kleisners. In a vast conference room, I was coldly interviewed by Sarah's father and by her two brothers, Edward and Robert. The father was a thin, cold-blooded creature, a shrunken frame behind a huge desk, and carrying a pair of light-rimmed spectacles on the bridge of his nose as if they were a heavy burden. Edward was in his early-fifties then, a big man who was careless in his dress and in his appearance and who had sparse blond hair, a red face and flailing arms. Robert, a few years younger, had his father's frail physique. His thin spidery hands were forever worrying at something. A button, perhaps, a pencil, or a folded sheet of typing paper.

They would tell me nothing about Sarah, not even why she'd come to Ireland at that time. They distrusted my interest and suspected my motives. In particular, they would not accept that I had been close to Sarah. Why should they, when she had clearly confided nothing to me about her family?

You may suggest, Michael, that her silence might be open to another interpretation. And you may be right. Silence is always open to many interpretations. Her reluctance to talk about her family might suggest her estrangement from it, her desire to escape it, or perhaps even a secret about it she needed to conceal. I managed to confirm, for instance, that it was Robert who had written that final, troublesome letter to her. He was interested to hear that she had received it, but he refused to tell me any of its contents. The day before he posted it, however, as I subsequently discovered from other sources, Robert, after decades of unhealthy celibacy that had been a major worry to friends and relatives, had stunned his family by announcing his intention to marry, after a short engagement, a politician's titian-haired daughter. And surely it was this momentous news that he had communicated to his sister. It could be nothing else. But why should Sarah, imagining her brother lost between the welcoming thighs of another woman, react as if the letter was a rejection, as if the development was a bitter personal loss? I draw my own conclusions, Michael, but I will not share them.

Certainly my father had his doubts about the young American woman who had come to live among us. One morning, as I was preparing to go to work in Sarah's garden, clearing it of the weeds that had overtaken it, he said to me softly, She's no good, you know. When I mentioned this to the detectives and lawyers after his arrest, encouraging them to probe it in their investigations, they considered it of no importance. They failed to understand. And how could they prosecute or defend when they could not understand? My father said so little, and so begrudgingly, that when he did speak, voluntarily at least, it invariably had a profound meaning for him. I knew, for instance, even from this brief expression, that he already had an abnormal interest in Sarah Kleisner. It was a view confirmed after his arrest, when numerous witnesses – neighbours of his, workmates, fellow bird enthusiasts and dog owners, tradesmen and shopkeepers – all came hurriedly forward to testify that he had enquired obsessively about the American woman's habits and movements, tastes and interests.

And the more despicable the revelations about my father, the deeper grew the communal sympathy for my mother. Instead of denying the nightmare, of course, she colourfully embroidered it, and thereby sustained it. She cast herself as the passive heroine in a tragedy. Isn't this how it always is? her posture suggested. The man lusts after younger flesh while the woman ruins her beauty rearing children. These are the immutable roles assigned to us by fate.

When I think of her, Michael, I always wonder what attraction, what passion, first impelled her towards my father. It must have been strong. He was poor, from a labouring tradition. She was rich, from a family of prosperous landowners. In material terms, she gave up everything for him. Her family, fiercely opposing the match, eventually made her an outcast. And yet, by the time I was old enough to notice such things, the passion had withered. And the attraction, too. There was nothing left but regret. And the regret was so intense that it had turned into a tendency to deny what had happened, into a desire to conceal a fatal mistake. Into silence on one side. And lies on the other.

Over my father's coffin at the funeral this morning, Michael, I asked my mother if she really believed that he had killed Sarah Kleisner all those years ago. Do you know what she answered me? I have his stamp album for you, she said. The one with the black leather cover. He wanted you to have it.

The Profile

At eleven o'clock on a Tuesday morning late in July, in the tranquil valley of Glendalough in south County Wicklow, a woman is standing in the entrance hall of a rambling Victorian house. The house is Moytura, called after the site of a decisive battle in Celtic mythology. It belongs to a prominent local family. Its owner, Timothy Lowry, not only founded a thriving import business but also served as a government minister in numerous cabinets. He's long retired, however, and the family's only son, Daniel, has inherited both the business and the parliamentary seat, although his party is currently in opposition.

The woman's name is Karen Stokes. She's thirty-four years old, dark-haired, deeply tanned from a recent holiday in Greece and quite formally dressed in a dark suit and white blouse. Although she works as a journalist for a national daily newspaper, she's not here in pursuit of a story. On the contrary, she estimates that she must have spent more than half her childhood in this house and its gardens. Her own home, a more modest house in the nearby village of Laragh, she remembers as being dull and cramped by comparison with Moytura. There was little source of energy there, she recalls. Her father – Timothy Lowry's election agent and trusted lieutenant – was much older than anyone else she knew, already in his late-fifties, for instance, when she was only ten years old. Her mother was far too unhappy to be lively. And she herself was an only child. The Lowrys, by contrast, had two daughters and a son around her own age. Their windows looked out on the upper lake in Glendalough. Their house was often crowded for extravagant parties and was always alive with fierce political argument.

As she waits in the entrance hall, and wonders why the family has replaced the old portraits that hung there with a set of oriental paintings, a call comes through on Karen Stokes's mobile phone. She doesn't actually hear the tone for the first few seconds. Even when she becomes aware of it, she thinks it's the house telephone. Her mind is tuned to another time, long before cellular phones were in use.

Eventually, however, the noise drags her back to the present. And inevitably, because of the noise and colour of her memories, to a sense of faded power. Around her, the old house is so silent now that she can hear the rustling of her own clothes as she shifts on her feet. It has the hushed feel of a hospital ward in the dead of night, an atmosphere that's suddenly sharpened by an old man's dry coughing that starts in some distant corner and then echoes interminably through the empty rooms.

She lifts the mobile from her bag. As she turns while punching the keypad to take the call, she notices a figure moving along the balcony above her. Its the Lowrys' only son, Daniel. Seeing her, he hesitates a little, and then comes towards her. He descends the way he always moved, she thinks. Gracefully. But aloof. Even as a child, he was always tall and erect. Self-contained. As if he was holding himself against the liveliness of the house. She smiles ruefully, half at the real figure as he slips quietly past her, half at the memory of the stilted boy she almost married.

Karen Stokes's call is from a junkie named Billy Traynor, an informant she's been tracking for a week. He claims to have a scoop on some corrupt politician's involvement with a drugs gang, but he's uncertain about · risking his neck for the amount of money the newspaper is offering. At first, there's just a rasping on the other end of the line. It seems menacing and deliberate, but actually it's neither. In fact, Traynor's breathing is so pained that it eventually makes him sound more vulnerable than threatening.

'I, ah, I made up me mind to see you,' he says hoarsely then. 'Tonight. All right? I got that thing for you ...'

By the time Karen Stokes has wrapped up arrangements for this meeting, the middle-aged nurse who's replaced one of the secretaries on the Lowry family staff is also standing inside the entrance hall. The nurse doesn't speak. She raises a finger to signal. Karen Stokes follows her, along a wide corridor and into the small library, conscious of the clacking her leather shoes are making against the wooden floor and of the fact that the nurse's chunky bare legs disappear into silent white tennis shoes.

Timothy Lowry is sitting in a wheelchair inside the library, looking mournfully through the window at the lake beyond. Karen Stokes feels guilty as soon as she sees him. She hasn't visited for a long time. And the old man is clearly dying. But in many ways, this guilt of hers is so old and so stale by now that she knows exactly how to deal with it.

It is, in fact, almost a decade old. Six months after she broke off her engagement to Daniel, Timothy Lowry suffered the first of his strokes. The marriage of herself and Daniel had been one of the very few certainties in everybody's life and its collapse had probably fractured much more than an old man's health.

She hurries across now and crouches beside Timothy Lowry to kiss his forehead. He embraces her, his right arm around her shoulder, while gesturing with his left at the tray on a side table.

'I can't join you, though,' he complains. 'They won't give me any coffee. It's a stimulant, they say. Here I am, trapped in a bloody cage with my brain seizing up, and they're worried about stimulation. Did I keep you long?'

She sits in an armchair and pours herself a coffee. 'I was looking at the new paintings in the hallway,' she says. 'Why did you take away the portraits?'

'Bloody portraits!' the old man swears. 'Everybody looks as if they think they're immortal in them. And they're all dead now.'

He gestures around the library. In the spaces between the shelves, the wooden panels are covered with framed black and white photographs. Most are from the 1970s and 80s, the heyday of his political career. Most show him greeting other politicians, national and international, all of them now long deposed or forgotten or passed away.

Karen Stokes stays for an hour, talking to the old man. It's less than she should, she feels. But it's also thirty minutes more than she can actually afford. She's running late. She needs to get back to Dublin in time for lunch with her fiancé. She's slightly irritated, therefore, to find Daniel Lowry waiting for her by her car afterwards. He thanks her for coming down to visit his father and confides that the old man will probably not last beyond the summer. As he talks, he runs his right hand wearily over his face, pinching his closed eyes with his thumb and forefinger, not wanting to show his emotions. There is still awkwardness between them. She suspects that he has never really recovered from her rejection of him ten years ago. He hasn't married. It's a disadvantage for a male politician in a rural community, and one that's finally beginning to show in the polls. And instead of sharing his feelings, he's started to take refuge in formality. Another handicap for a politician, in any constituency.

It's way past noon before Karen Stokes gets away from Glendalough, and there's twenty minutes out of their lunchtime before she sits down with her fiancé, Richard Howard, in Thornton's restaurant in Dublin.

Howard is a television producer. He can't match Daniel Lowry for either breeding or height. He's not much taller than Karen herself, his complexion is tanned, his dark hair is too wiry to train properly and his features have the rough strength of generations of farm labourers. But he's also dynamic and extrovert. He seems to know everyone, and be known, and liked, in return. He belongs to the present, Karen Stokes feels. He's fully alive.

By the time the main courses are served, she's finally shaken the mustiness of the old house and the old life at Glendalough out of her system and is enjoying herself. Warmed by the wine, and by her responsiveness, Howard mischievously suggests slipping back to their apartment for an hour after lunch. She has a couple of problems with this idea, attractive as it is. Sex on a full stomach has never really appealed to her. And even more of a deterrent, she has a lengthy article to file for the morning edition of her newspaper.

So this is where she goes for the afternoon when lunch is over, back to her office in central Dublin. In a room beside her, a colleague is working on a major article covering the recent murders in the Wicklow Mountains, a story that has dropped out of the front pages, and out of sight, the last few weeks. The editor, under pressure from the proprietor, is interested in reviving it. But this isn't Karen Stokes's beat. She's more into Dublin's gangland, the feuds, the turf wars, the huge profits from imported drugs, the reported links to legitimate business and a high-profile politician.

It's almost eight o'clock that evening before she finally files her copy. Afterwards she rings Richard Howard to let him know that it's going to be even later still before she gets back to their apartment, because it's just occurred to her that she forgot to tell him that she has an interview lined up that evening. At eight o'clock, she switches on her desk phone's answering machine, packs her mobile in her bag, and drives from the newspaper's offices to a run-down shopping complex on the south of the city. Billy Traynor, apparently desperate enough now to run the risk, has agreed to meet her here at a diner – its own description of itself – a long way from the prying eyes on his usual patch.

She has no problems finding the seedy diner. Its lurid neon sign, glittering in the heavy rain that's started falling, shouts at her as soon as she turns into the almost deserted car park. She takes an inconspicuous space between a couple of white transit vans.

She's already late, of course, by the time she steps inside the diner and is worried that she may have missed the rendezvous. She stands for a while, taking in the long narrow interior, the plastic fittings, the imitation leather, the strong smell of over-used cooking oil. Five or six loners straddle stools at the counter to her left. The booths to her right, along the street window, are mostly full of either dour or squabbling families. She can't see Billy Traynor. She walks the length of the diner, slowly checking the booths. As she passes one, a gaunt figure dressed in an army surplus jacket and camouflage fatigues struggles up and puts out a trembling arm to block her path.

His hair is two-tone now, the roots growing black again under the parts he's bleached. His cheeks are skeletal and his eyes are sunken in their bruised sockets. When he sucks in air, it croaks past his throat and rasps through his lungs. And he coughs. Constantly. Helplessly.

As Karen Stokes sits opposite him and glances down at the meal he's eating – eggs and bacon, french fries and coffee – he manages a weak laugh. 'I don't really have any money,' he admits. 'I can't pay for this. But I thought you wouldn't mind, you know, standing me some grub.'

Karen Stokes shrugs and orders a coffee from a sullen waitress. Suddenly she's aware that she hasn't changed her clothes since dressing up to visit Timothy Lowry in Glendalough that morning and she feels uncomfortably out of place in her expensive suit. Because of this, she also begins to feel vulnerable. She needs to get out quickly, she decides. She needs to establish whether Traynor has anything significant or not.

She leans forward. But suddenly the sullen waitress delivers the coffee and sulks away again after scratching the additional item on the bill.

Karen Stokes stirs in milk, but doesn't taste the brew. It looks undrinkable. She asks, 'What have you got for me, Billy?'

Traynor eats a little of his meal, remembers that he's hungry, and then settles into clearing his plate, gesturing with his knife for her to wait for him. 'Was your aul' fella lucky, by any chance?' he asks then.

'In what way?' she wonders.

'My aul' fella had one of them trades technology took over,' Traynor explains. 'All he ever had was his hands. He was out of a job before I was old enough to go to school.'

'Is this relevant to what you're going to tell me, Billy?' Karen Stokes enquires.

'Depends on what you've got for me,' he hedges.

'What I've got, Billy,' she tells him, 'is ten minutes to figure out whether or not you're worth listening to. That's all I've got.'

Fifteen minutes later she's out of the diner again, not much wiser, but with another name, another contact, and another rendezvous for another night. Billy Traynor, she's just discovered, is only a go-between, working for a fee. The real informant is far more careful. Although probably not as clever as he thinks, if he's relying on a junkie to keep his secrets.

The two transit vans have left by now and her black Mondeo sits exposed in the centre of the empty car park, drawing attention to itself. There doesn't seem to be anyone about, though. It's still raining heavily, so it's not a night for lounging or prowling.

She steps from the footpath and walks across the open ground towards her car, conscious again of the noise her shoes are making, this time on the uneven concrete, in the stillness of the night. The light fades as she moves away from the diner. The darkness closes around her. She starts to walk faster, and then tries to slow down again when she realizes that her footsteps are betraying her fear.

She doesn't know why she's so nervous tonight. She's been in these situations many times before. But she *senses* something menacing.

She already has her keys prepared as she approaches the car. She's about to immobilize the electronic alarm and release the central locking when she catches a noise behind her. She looks back. A heavy middle-aged man in a green and red jacket and dark blue jeans is walking from the diner, heading straight for her. It's his speed, his determination, that worries her. He's only fifteen metres away when she turns and he immediately makes eye contact with her. Just for an instant. But there seems to be recognition in that instant. And the fear of being recognized himself. His head goes down. His right hand is raised quickly, to cover his features, to pull the peak of the baseball cap he's wearing over his plump, bearded face.

Karen Stokes senses danger. She tries to open the door of her car. She fumbles. The keys slip from her wet hand and clatter to the ground. The man is so close now that she can smell the rain from his clothes and his stale sweat rising through it. She tenses. He's almost upon her, level with her . . .

And then he's gone again.

He's brushing past her, his sharp movement creating a gust of wind that lifts her long dark hair and makes the rain feel cooler on her face.

As she relaxes, and as her breathing slows and quietens, finally she hears the sound that must have deterred him. It's the tapping of a cane or a walking stick on the concrete. The rhythm is slow and a little laboured. In the darkness, it takes her a while to locate its source, but when she does she laughs aloud, with release of tension. The intruder is an old man, shuffling across the car park.

The Investigation

What's always surprised me since joining the guards is the way unexpected things can influence an investigation, the way somebody's attitude can decide the whole focus of a case.

The ordinary punter thinks that when a crime is reported or discovered and guards go to the scene, they follow the clues they find there and arrive at the solution, maybe after a few red herrings and a couple of ad breaks. That's the logical way of looking at things. That's the mentality of the person who believes that because only one thing happened, then only one explanation is possible. But the job is not like that at all. Most of the time you either know very quickly who did what, because you're dealing with those people all the time, or you're relying on talk from informers. But for the rest, particularly the more serious crimes like murder, where there's still an element of mystery and you have no idea who's responsible, what's much more important is the prejudices of the investigators.

People brought up on TV crime dramas might find that hard to accept. But say a woman smothers her four-month-old infant. Say they're discovered together, the dead infant and the grieving mother, and the pathologist, because mothers are only protective in his belief system, writes down Sudden Infant Death Syndrome or Reyes Syndrome as the cause of death. There's no investigation. There's not even suspicion. This actually happened, in America, in the 1970s. It actually happened eight times with the same woman. Eight little babies asphyxiated before anyone even said, 'Hey, hang on a minute.' Eight!

One of the other examples you're taught about in training is the Bamber case in England in 1985, where police were called to the scene of a murder, followed by the suicide of the 'killer', and spent months building up evidence to support this explanation, until a pair of amateur detectives pointed out that someone else must have killed both victims since the gun supposedly used by the suicide had been locked away in a cabinet *after her death.*

The point being made is that you don't go looking for clues to prove a theory. But like every abstract rule it doesn't really mean much to you, except as an abstract rule. You have to go out and make the mistakes before you learn. Experience counts for a lot. But even that's shouted down by prejudice at times.

I know it's hard to understand, but the fact is, it was a whole month before the disappearance of Karen Stokes was passed to our unit. Looking back on it now, I can see the stupidity of it all. The authorities set up a specialist unit to look into the disappearance of women – and the first woman who disappears after its formation is not even referred to that unit. But it seemed perfectly reasonable at the time. I saw nothing wrong with the initial investigation. And I've never met anyone who did.

Because Karen Stokes was a crime journalist and hot on the trail of a sensational story, naturally it was assumed that she'd been taken out by someone who thought they would have a lot fewer problems without her being around. Nobody ever questioned this assumption. All the media coverage at the time – and it was intense, saturated stuff – was built on this assumption.

One of the main reasons no one questioned it, of course, was that it had happened before. You remember? Big-time criminals became so cocky and contemptuous that a drugs gang murdered a crime journalist in broad daylight. It was thought the criminals had learned from that. This time they struck at night and left no body for forensic examination. Naturally, the Garda authorities were determined to learn as well. They weren't going to repeat any of the mistakes made in that first investigation.

So they made another mistake instead.

The resources thrown at the case were absolutely huge. A lot of it was driven by the media as well as by concern for the force's reputation. The same newspaper who championed Mary Corbett's case also employed Karen Stokes as a journalist. But they weren't the only ones to put in the overtime. Just as guards will work extra hard if one our own is brought down, so people in the media have a personal interest in catching the killer of a journalist. That's fine. It's understandable. Except it bent the investigation in one direction only and everything else suffered.

For instance, all the new detectives who'd been drafted into our unit were taken away again. At a time when we probably needed reinforcements most, we were back to our original strength.

In an odd way, though, the whole thing also saved Inspector Taafe's job. The brass were on the verge of replacing her. They had a man lined up, a superintendent with a lot of experience of murder enquiries. But instead, he was seconded to the task force that was ploughing through Dublin's gangland for the missing journalist.

By then, I had no doubt in my own mind any more that the inspector was actually inefficient. The way I'd decided it, she only *looked* up to the job. When the pressure was on, she couldn't deliver. But once the pressure was off again, looking was good enough again. She was helped by the fact that we were now forgotten about. Along with Michael Elwood and Mary Corbett, I have to say. Human attention is an awful funny thing. What's horrifying and unbearable today can be pushed into the background tomorrow. Maybe we were always like this, down through the ages. Maybe we only ever jumped from one sensation to another. I think myself, though, that the dominance of television has made us worse, although we probably invented TV for that reason anyway.

I have to admit, however, that this month, when the rest of the country worried about Karen Stokes, was one of the best I'd had for a long time. I know it's a terrible thing to say, but it was like a holiday. We had nothing to do in the unit. Over the previous few weeks, once we'd done everything we could and hit all the brick walls, it was only our conscience that made us feel bad. But now that there was no pressure any more, there was no conscience either. You don't get obsessive about cases in the guards. That's a myth. Most guards will honestly put in their shift and leave it behind them once they're out the station door, apart from dramatizing it all to each other in the pub. Maybe only the ones definitely going for promotion would do that bit more. Most of us are not self-driven. Me, I took my annual leave, rebuilt all the old bridges with my boyfriend and generally had a ball.

We all kept an eye on the investigation into Karen Stokes's disappearance, but this was from a distance, mostly through station gossip or coverage in the media, and as something that wasn't involving us. What was most interesting for me personally was the image created of the victim. I suppose it was really the way the writers wanted to see themselves, since they were all crime correspondents as well. She was depicted as fearless, dedicated to the truth, passionate about the fabric of society, and a wonderful daughter. The gougers she tried to expose, on the other hand, were portrayed as the scum of the earth, ravaging poor communities with heroin and smack, hooking even their own kids on hard drugs, cold and ruthless and rich.

The junkie she'd met in the southside restaurant, Billy Traynor, was very quickly identified and lifted. They put him through the wringer and he broke down almost immediately. Junkies always spill everything very easily. Through him they found the fella who'd wanted to talk to Karen Stokes, a bag man with one of the big city gangs, and it was when he decided to enter the witness protection programme that the fall-out became massive. It was so sensational that what was lost for a time was any concern for the original victim. A whole chain of legitimate business people, including a building contractor and a hotel owner, were implicated in laundering the drugs money. A prominent politician was named as a director of the companies involved. The government had to face a number of edgy motions of confidence. Someone even remarked that the institutions of the state itself were threatened. The picture got so big that everyone forgot the human loss.

Karen Stokes's fiancé, the television producer Richard Howard, got confused between making and reporting the news. I don't know him personally. I'm sure he must have been a decent fella before all this, but he looked messed up to me. He reminded me of the participants in those Reality TV shows. He couldn't just have natural emotions, he had to have them big enough for the camera to pick up and admire. I'm not saying he was faking any of it, but that's the way we live our lives now, with an eye on performing all the time, and I think it cheapens things.

To complicate the story even more, Timothy Lowry, the elder statesman who was touted as such a formative influence in Karen's life, died two weeks after her disappearance. He was dying anyway, apparently, but again he was presented as another casualty of the drugs war.

Every little distortion like that kept the investigation flying along the wrong track. And there was nobody to cry halt because nobody wanted to be caught on the wrong foot in the war against drugs and everybody tried to take what they could out of the situation. The politicians and the media had to be seen as leading the general public, just as the Serious Crimes Squad and the Criminal Assets Bureau ending up leading the guards.

But none of it led to the discovery of Karen Stokes or her car.

They traced and interviewed everyone who was in the restaurant that night. They located the drivers of the two transit vans Karen Stokes had parked between when she arrived. The big man who'd passed her in the car park after she left Billy Traynor turned out to be an innocent local. He was Henry Mullan, a fork-lift driver in a food processing factory, living in a housing estate nearby and taking a short cut home across the car park.

Of them all, Mullan was the witness our unit returned to most often when we were finally given the case. We hadn't much else, to be honest. There was one CCTV camera in the area, but it was covering the entrance to a furniture warehouse close to the restaurant and not the relevant section of the car park.

'I barely even noticed the woman, to be honest,' Henry Mullan told us. 'It was pissing rain and I had my head down. All I wanted to do was get in out of it. I nearly bumped into her. I only saw her at the last minute and swerved to avoid her. I think she'd dropped her keys. I kept going. I didn't bother her or anything. There was an old man I passed coming in the opposite direction. I didn't pay much attention to him, either. I don't think he was local. He didn't greet me or anything.'

'Did you hear the car starting up behind you?' we wondered.

Mullan shook his head. 'No, I can't say I remember that.'

'Did you get a look at the old man's face?' we asked.

'He had a soft hat on,' Mullan remembered. 'And he was holding it down with one hand. He had a walking stick in the other. The walking stick was in the right hand. Anyway, his arm was covering his face, the way he was holding the hat. I couldn't see what he looked like.'

This was nothing. But to be fair to Mullan, it was the same nothing he'd given the early investigators and the same nothing he'd been repeating ever since.

Our interview with Henry Mullan took place more than a month after the disappearance of the journalist. Four weeks to the day after Karen Stokes had vanished, on a Tuesday late in August, a man walking his dog in the woods below Sorrel Hill in the Wicklow Mountains had stumbled on a buried corpse that turned out to be the body of the missing journalist.

Because we knew almost immediately that her killer was the same one who'd taken Michael Elwood and Mary Corbett and because it looked as if the discovery was carefully planned, someone said that the time lapse of a month had to be highly significant. Humans are very susceptible to anniversaries and very suspicious about dates. I'm not. I even forget my boyfriend's birthday. I actually thought it was just a coincidence. It wasn't as if we were anonymously tipped off, as we were with Michael Elwood, or given written directions, as we were with Mary Corbett. It was a dog, after all, who'd sniffed out and dug up the body. I accepted the reasoning behind the anniversary theory – which was, that the killer used the time between a murder and the discovery of the corpse to stalk their next victim and only released information about the grave site when they were ready to kill again – but I thought they needed longer than a month for this. Actually, I thought the early discovery of Karen Stokes's body was the first real break we'd got in the hunt and the first real setback the killer had suffered. But nobody seemed to agree with me.

In another sense, apart from its early discovery by the dog, we also had a lucky break with the site of Karen Stokes's grave.

It might be hard to accept, given the positive spin on police work that the media usually generates – most of it orchestrated by the force's press office, I have to say – but one of the biggest obstacles to an efficient investigation is the guards themselves. We still have no centralized database on computer here in Ireland, so unless a crime is really high-profile, one district wouldn't have a clue what another is up to. Even then there are rivalries between units, rivalries between areas, and rivalries between individual superintendents, who all have one eye on the next promotion and the other on how the competition is shaping up against them. I'm sure every job is the same, but it fouls up criminal investigations. I've no doubt, for instance, that the crime scene at Karen Stokes's grave would have been contaminated, from our unit's point of view, except for a coincidence no one could have predicted. It just happened that one of the first senior officers on the scene was the superintendent who had been earmarked to replace Inspector Taafe. He was already familiar with the files on Michael Elwood and Mary Corbett. The minute he arrived at the grave site, he knew immediately that this murder had nothing to do with gangland executions and everything to do with the earlier killings. He had a bit of a struggle apparently, but he managed to keep the Serious Crimes Squad from going anywhere near the scene, at least until our own unit had been notified.

I remember sitting in the office that Tuesday afternoon, re-checking witness statements, when the telephone rang. Dennison lifted the receiver. You could tell he was listening to a superior officer giving orders from the expression on his face, a mixture of concentration and irritation. Nobody could have known it then, but when he passed the call into the inspector's office it marked the end of our idle holiday. We heard the news from her about five minutes later. The body of Karen Stokes had been discovered in the Wicklow Mountains and there were similarities between her grave and the burials of Michael Elwood and Mary Corbett. It's hard to imagine the effect this announcement had on us. We were stunned. The development was so unexpected, so unpredictable, that we couldn't come to terms with it very quickly. We were too puzzled.

It was in this confused state that we just dropped everything we were doing and set out. This time I volunteered to drive the lead car, not only because Dennison and the inspector were still niggling at each other, but because when you're going somewhere, carrying a bit of hope with you, it's better to keep your mind occupied with something else. I think it was in everybody's thoughts as we travelled south out of the city that this journey was becoming too familiar by now, even though the route was a little different this time. The other grave sites had been in central and east Wicklow. This was in the mountains to the west of the county. We took the carriageway to the village of Blessington and then crossed Pollaphuca Reservoir by Blessington Bridge. The narrow roads after that were full of tourist signs, for megalithic tombs and cairns and standing stones, the sort of things we all go and look at without having the faintest idea what they were really used for. One of the roads, a cul-de-sac, cut straight into the mountain, climbing sharply before it ran out of steam and ended in a dirt track at the base of Sorrel Hill. This was the one we were directed along by the uniformed guard on point duty at the junction. Looking out at the crowds already gathered at the junction, I asked permission to photograph or film them. I wanted to compare the shots with the news footage I already had of the crowds at the other sites, on the off chance that it might throw up a match among the faces. The inspector refused my request. Fair enough. She was eager to press on and get to the scene. But I suppose I would have thought more of her decision if she'd had some ideas of her own to offer.

We parked on the dirt track at the end of the road, along with all the other official vehicles. Sorrel Hill rose straight ahead of us. We didn't need to climb it, luckily. Our destination was to the left, through the woods on the lower slopes of the hill. There was a track, popular with walkers, zigzagging through these woods, stretching from the banks of the reservoir in the west right across to the eastern section of the road that ringed the mountain, a distance of about four kilometres. I suppose the killer of Karen Stokes, when they were burying the body, had been pretty confident that the site wouldn't be found until they wanted it to be. It was deep into the woods, more than a kilometre from both the track and the nearest stretch of road. You could see from the vegetation and the condition of the trees in the surrounding area, not to mention the absence of any litter, that nobody ever came here. It was a good spot for concealment. The killer had obviously given it a lot of thought. But no one can think of everything, of course.

It was late in the afternoon when our unit reached the site. By then, the excavation of the body, under the supervision of the pathologist, had been completed, the preliminary examination was finished and the scene-of-crime officers from the Technical Bureau were well advanced in their work, collecting samples for analysis. The pathologist had given instructions to remove the victim for a full post-mortem, but the superintendent had insisted on leaving the body in place, along with the cellophane-wrapped papers lying beside it, until we got there. As far as I was concerned, that was our real break. It wasn't so much what any of us saw at the site that mattered. The crime-scene photographs would have offered the same evidence. It was more the different reactions of people on the spot and the way they worked with and against each other.

For a start, it was obvious that the body of Karen Stokes wasn't as badly decomposed as the previous two had been. After a month in the ground, of course, it wasn't pretty, either. The skin had blistered. The eyeballs had liquefied. The internal organs and cavities had burst. Maggots had eaten into much of the flesh. The stench from the escaping gases, again partially trapped inside a protective white tent, was nauseating. But what I found myself reacting to first wasn't the decay or the smell, it was the gaping hole where one of the ears should have been. The head was in profile, showing only the left side of the face. It was impossible to tell just by looking whether the other ear had been amputated as well, but nobody had any doubt about it.

In many ways, I found the sight of Karen Stokes's naked body a lot more disturbing than the other two corpses. It was even more upsetting than gaping at Michael Elwood while struggling to hold back the vomit.

The reason was simple. Despite the decay, you could still see the individual person you'd been looking for. The body was only halfway on its journey, from the lively woman who had been Karen Stokes to the dry bones that would make the skeleton, and I found it distressing, although I hadn't known the woman personally, to be able to look back and forth like that.

It took a while for my head to clear. But even when it did, all sorts of weird thoughts went through it. I'd already noticed, for instance, that the arrangement of the naked body was the same here as it had been with Michael Elwood. It was lying on its side. The upper part, including the torso and the head, was erect, but the legs were bent at the hips and again at the knees. The arms might have been joined in prayer in front of the chest, but to me they seemed, again, as if they were supposed to be holding those papers or pages that were wrapped in cellophane. I tried to remember if the other bodies had been buried facing west like this one. Had the heads been to the north, the feet to the south? Could there be any importance to that? The idea hadn't occurred to me before. But I just couldn't recall the details from the earlier graves. And that's what made my head spin again. All I was certain of was that the arrangement had significance. It told a story. It made a point.

'She looks like she's sleeping,' the inspector's voice broke into my thoughts.

The noise was faint. It felt like it was coming to me from a long distance away. I could easily have ignored it. But it had a terrible effect on me. There we were inside that stifling tent, myself and the inspector, Dennison and the superintendent, all in our white overalls and masks and our protective footwear, looking less human than the unfortunate corpse we were examining. Maybe I was still annoyed from earlier, when the inspector had refused my request to photograph the spectators on the road. Maybe I was frustrated. It had certainly flashed through my mind that we were about to go through the motions of another investigation, and get nowhere all over again. And I knew that this was undoubtedly an opportunity. I was pretty certain now that the killer hadn't wanted this grave site discovered so early, maybe not even until the rains of winter had come. Apart from the fact that the corpse was more preserved, there was also a greater likelihood of lifting trace evidence from both the body itself and the surrounding area. Already the officers from the Technical Bureau had cordoned off areas where they'd found impressions of footprints. So I suppose I was frustrated. To me, there are very few things more annoying than having to put up with sloppy work because someone in authority is inefficient.

'She looks like she's sleeping,' the inspector said.

I couldn't help it. It just snapped out of me. 'She's *kneeling*!' I snarled.

It wasn't what was said, it was the way that I said it. Through my teeth. Making it obvious that I thought the inspector was a complete fool. Everybody looked at me. Maybe it was fortunate we all had masks on, since no one could see anyone else's expression and react to that. And there was always the chance that my outburst had been distorted by the mask, come out in a way that I hadn't intended. Apparently I got the benefit of the doubt. Nobody said anything. Not then, anyway.

Outside, though, the superintendent hung back after the inspector had stormed away and took the chance to ask me what I'd meant. I told him. He wasn't wildly impressed, I could see that. He didn't really look the type who was easily impressed: a calm, white-haired man who'd probably already experienced too much in his career to get excited about theories. To tell the truth, I hadn't expected anyone to start presenting me with bouquets. What pleased me, though, was that he accepted it as a possibility, an avenue to be explored. One of the hundreds of little ideas that crop up in the course of an investigation and that usually come to nothing, but that shouldn't be ignored if you're going to be meticulous.

I was so pleased that I pushed my luck with the superintendent. I said, 'I have an idea, because the bodies are arranged so carefully and because there are so many messages, that the killer might be tempted to keep an eye on how we're responding to it all. They might be in the crowd of spectators at the scene. I wanted to photograph them earlier, when we were driving here.'

But he saw through me on that one. 'You might be right,' he agreed. 'But you'd better clear it with your inspector. I can't give you the necessary permission.'

I'll put my cards on the table here. From everybody's point of view, the logical thing to do at this stage would have been to replace the inspector with the superintendent, expand the unit and give it the same resources that had been thrown at Dublin's gangland for the previous month. The high-powered investigation into the death of Karen Stokes could continue. All that needed to be shifted was the focus.

But the more dealings you have with state institutions, the more you realize that there are more important things than logic to them. There are more important things than efficiency, even. A lot was happening behind the scenes. I heard rumours that the inspector was threatening to start a case for sexual harassment and constructive dismissal against the commissioner if she was transferred. There couldn't be any substance to the case. It was all bluff on her part. But that didn't matter. At the time, an academic had just published a doctoral thesis on sexual harassment in the army, listing complaints of attempted rape, sexual assault and daily verbal abuse of women soldiers. It had thrown the government into a minor panic. I don't doubt that most of the accusations were true. It happens in the guards as well. These places, they're a man's world, like I said before, and a lot of fellas still can't deal with a simple no without lashing out. But things are never simple. Nothing in life is straight down the middle. Some people use the genuine grievances of others to get benefits for themselves that they're not entitled to. And governments always seem more worried about accusations of sexual harassment than they are about the miserable percentage of women working in the top jobs. Of course, you actually have to do something long-term and imaginative to deal with the second problem, while making the right noises about dignity and respect will still rake you in the votes.

I honestly believe that Inspector Taafe put a lot more effort into fighting to save her job than she did into doing it. You'd think the two should be related, wouldn't you? But not in the modern world, they're not. In the modern world, fellas running companies that lose millions for their small shareholders get rewarded with huge performance bonuses at the end of the financial year.

Early in September – I have to say as an *excuse* for appearing to do something, as far as the rest of us were concerned – the inspector started to get obsessed with the papers found in the graves of Michael Elwood and Karen Stokes. It wasn't that the rest of us couldn't see the connections she kept emphasizing. These were obvious. But she made them even more obvious by distributing a chart for our use:

	Mary Corbett	Michael Elwood	Karen Stokes
Gender:	Female	Male	Female
Age:	22	45	34
Trait:	Abandoned	Quiet	?
Last Seen By:	Unknown attacker after Simon Chester, her boyfriend	Unidentified woman in her 30s	44-year-old labourer Henry Mullan or unidentified old man
Grave Site:	Mountains above Cloon Car Park	Woods below Djouce Mountain	Woods to the north of Sorrel Hill
Narrative in Grave:	None	*My father had died unexpectedly. In the car, squirming uncomfortably on the dampened seat and gasping for breath after running through the heavy rain, I switched on the mobile phone and listened to my sister's voice, recorded two hours earlier, trembling with the news*	*I have, perhaps, a responsibility to quiet men. It's a sense that alerts me to their presence. I hear their silence. In the crowded pub, sitting at the bar on a high stool and pretending to read my lecture notes, I watched him slope through the entrance and knew immediately that he was weighed down with a sadness he would find almost impossible to share.*

Narrator:	None	50-year-old male (Michael Elwood?)	Female, apparently in her thirties, although the internal evidence from her recollections suggests an older woman, possibly 50 (Karen Stokes?)
Narrator's Victim:	None	An abandoned female in her early-twenties (Mary Corbett?)	A quiet middle-aged man (Michael Elwood?)

This was fine, as far as it went. But the real problems started once the forensic science laboratory confirmed that they could offer us no leads on the papers found in Karen Stokes's grave. After that the inspector decided to concentrate on what she called 'the internal evidence' of the narratives. She roped in a variety of experts to help her out on this. Experts on literature from the university departments. Experts on style from communication studios. Experts on character analysis from the psychiatric professions. All a complete waste of time and resources, I thought. Obviously, if you read a personal letter written by someone to a friend, you can have a fair stab at guessing the writer's age, interests, relationships and habits. But there's one crucial difference. The writer of the letter isn't pretending to be someone else, isn't trying to conceal some things and distort other things, isn't trying to use a fake style, and isn't playing a game with the reader that only they know the rules of.

In fairness, though, with time moving on and in the absence of any clear leads from forensics, *everyone* in the unit seemed to get hooked on one particular aspect of the case. With the inspector, it was the narratives, as I've said. With Dennison, on the other hand, it was the ears. With myself, it was the confusion of genders, not only among the victims, but among the last people to *see* the victims as well, and of course among the narrators of the accounts found in the graves.

I'm not saying we didn't do the legwork. We went back over the ground covered by the original investigating team and interviewed everyone again.

We renewed the efforts to trace the old man who had crossed the car park at the time that Karen Stokes was last seen alive. Because it seemed likely that the killer had stalked the victim, we meticulously filled in the details of Karen Stokes's life for the month prior to her death. Some of this had already been done, but with the emphasis on her job as a journalist and on her criminal contacts. Now we focused on her personal life. I think it was Jimmy Coyne who suggested that the killer probably followed Karen Stokes that day. Since she passed twice through County Wicklow, on her way to and from Glendalough, the killer might even have randomly picked out and trailed her. This idea struck everyone as a real possibility and gave us hope for a while. We identified and contacted hundreds of people who had been on the relevant routes at the appropriate times, asking if they'd noticed anything suspicious. We even established a number of definite sightings of Karen Stokes.

All in all, then, I have to say that our day-to-day work was tremendous. It couldn't be faulted. But what was missing was any decisive co-ordination, any genuine bit of inspiration, from the officer in command. Or failing that, any new opening from the forensic and pathology reports.

We'd hoped for so much. But the state pathologist came straight out after the autopsy and said that if he'd been called to this fatality in ordinary circumstances, where there was no prior suggestion of a crime, he would have given the cause of death as heart failure. What can you do? You have a woman who's been abducted and probably ritually buried after enduring God knows what, and your pathologist tells you she had heart failure. When we told him bluntly that we weren't accepting this, we found again that he wasn't a man to speculate. I know Dr Craig was fairly new to the job and still laying claim to it. I suppose he wasn't going to risk making a guess, because there was an equal chance he'd make a big mistake instead of a big breakthrough. But to be honest, we found him hopeless. He wasn't up to the demands of the job.

There's a story to everything, of course. And the story to Craig was that his appointment had been hurried and, as is the way of these things, political. The old man who'd previously filled the office throughout a colourful career, Dr Powlson, had finally fallen foul of the mandarins in the Department of Justice and three weeks after he was sensationally sacked his assistant retired, claiming ill-health, leaving an opening for a fairly bright, but utterly dependable young thing. I learned all this when some of the older lads, admittedly over a few pints, started fondly remembering Dr Powlson's antics and others repeated rumours about the appointment of a new assistant pathologist. But while we mourned the old messiah and waited for the latest one, we had to make do with what we had, which was Craig's report.

Basically, despite the better condition of the corpse, it was the same as with the other two. Karen Stokes was already dead when she was buried, as there were no signs of suffocation. She hadn't been sexually assaulted. The vaginal, anal and oral swabs provided no evidence of penetration. There were no external or internal injuries consistent with an attack. Examination of the body fluids showed no trace of poisons, only the food she had eaten that last day and the wine, vodka and coffee she'd had to drink. It was suggested that the ears had been sliced off with a dissecting knife or a scalpel, again pointing to the possible involvement of someone with at least basic medical knowledge. And that was it, once you'd broken down all the technical jargon.

As for the forensic analysis of the various specimens taken at the scene, we got the results back day by day, and every day we watched our options reducing a little more. Karen Stokes had been buried naked and no item of clothing was found in or near the grave. So in the end it came down to a natural fibre discovered in the grave site, a single human hair found on Karen Stokes's body but not belonging to her, a single animal hair also found on the body, and one faint impression of a footprint in the dry ground close to the grave. The fibre was cashmere and couldn't be matched to any of the clothes Karen Stokes was wearing on the day of her death, or to any she and her partner owned. Intriguingly, the animal turned out to be a greyhound, brindle in colour and fairly advanced in years. For my own reasons, though, I was more interested in the strand of human hair and in the faint impression. They both belonged to women. That was a cast-iron certainty in the case of the hair – it was dyed blonde, the laboratory told us, originally black and from the head of a woman who was probably in her thirties – and it was a safe bet with the footprint, which was too small and narrow for an adult male.

I seized on this stuff. I was still the only one *seriously* questioning the assumption that a man had killed all three of our victims. I accepted that there was more than just thick prejudice driving the assumption of the others. However you feel about women being nurturers and not being given to violence except in self-defence, it's hard to think of them overpowering victims and lugging their bodies through dense woodland for burial. But it's not *impossible* to think that. It's not an impossible job for a woman. That was my point. And I felt my point was supported by this new forensic evidence. But by then, the gender thing had been identified and dismissed as just the irritating bee in my own particular bonnet. The hair probably belonged to some female acquaintance of Karen Stokes, they said. The print was too old and probably made by another owner of another stray dog. They had an explanation for everything. And every time I stood up to argue any different, the response was, Oh, here we go, lads! Galetti and her Adam and Eve theory again!

I'm not saying I was victimized. Or not particularly, anyway. We were all at it in the unit, putting one another down. I remember sitting there watching Dennison getting ready to say something and thinking, Christ, not the fucking ears again! I remember having to put up with the inspector rambling on about the narratives found in the graves, listening to her searching for clues to the author's identity in the images and going on about the psychological experts she'd consulted, and all the time screaming inside my head that the things were so obviously make up that she might as well have been looking for a signature on one of the trees in the Wicklow Mountains.

We were a shambles, to be honest.

Whatever about the inspector and the various pressures on her, I couldn't understand what was going on with Dennison at that time. He was getting more and more aggressive. He was confused and angry all the time. Any mention of gender by me was guaranteed to drive him mad. You'd think with his fury against women that he'd be delighted by my analysis. Just the opposite. Like a mad bully having a tantrum, he'd stand there on the floor of the office with a big red face on him, shouting me down. I suppose he might have been attacking the inspector through me. Another woman, as he saw it. Hare-brained. And useless. After the argument he'd quieten down and drift into his latest thoughts about ears and a sort of weird silence would fall on the rest of us. He sounded unbalanced. I mean, he talked for ten minutes one morning about, I think, Crazy Horse's vision before the battle of Little Big Horn, in which the old Indian chief saw cavalry soldiers without ears riding towards his camp. Can you imagine it? And can you imagine the inspector responding to it with her latest theory extracted from her latest analysis of the narratives?

This was the bizarre world we were trying to work in.

You think of investigations being plodding, and they *are* most of the time, but this was genuinely surreal. After a while we went into conferences in the incident room the way kids go into virtual reality games. Full of enthusiasm. But not in the real world.

There are two things I'd say about our separate obsessions at that time. The first is, that they were all coming out of despair, out of the knowledge that we had no genuine leads or evidence. And the second, that they were all converging on the psychological profile.

In major police enquiries these days, once the traditional methods have been exhausted – the house-to-house questionnaires, the list of suspects drawn up and investigated, the forensic evidence examined – the tendency is to reach for a psychological profile of the offender. Once you understand this, I think you can make better sense of all the apparent madness going on at the time. The inspector, for instance, was only trying to imagine the author of the narratives. Dennison was curious about the personality of a criminal who cut off ears. And I was wondering if a woman could kill and mutilate so often and with so little remorse. More and more we took to saying, this might fit the profile. Or, this doesn't seem to fit the profile. The funny thing was, we didn't *have* a profile. Even funnier, we wouldn't admit that we *wanted* to have a profile.

Guards are very suspicious of academics who have no experience of police work. Guards are very hostile to anyone from outside the force. It's a closed world. Interference isn't welcomed. Outsiders are resented. I'd say, the only possible way we'd entertain an outsider was if we could manage to blame them for everything that was going wrong. And I suppose that was how the unit got ready to welcome the forensic psychologist when the inspector finally called one in.

It didn't help that she was a woman.

Her name was Michelle Condon and she was attached to the psychology department at University College Dublin. She was young, no older than myself anyway, and she looked very nervous. I can't say I blame her. An audience of male detectives is one of the most intimidating a woman can stand in front of. It's sceptical. It's unimpressed. It's dismissive. It's unco-operative. It's impatient. And it's sexist. As audiences go, it has to be one of the toughest and the least responsive. Worse than a bunch of schoolkids who don't want to be locked in the classroom.

During her introduction, when she was trying to explain her methods to us, she kept looking for support to the inspector, who'd worked with her over the previous two weeks on the case summaries and autopsy and forensic reports. This was a bad mistake. I remember thinking that any psychologist who couldn't see the divisions in our unit mustn't have been the brightest in her class. To make things worse, whenever her eyes shifted away from the inspector, back to the main audience, they settled on me. That didn't go unnoticed, either. Nothing does among a group of guards. And it created an unnecessary split along gender lines.

As far as I could understand from her introduction, she seemed to be working in reverse, at least when you compared her method to normal police procedure. We're trained to keep an open mind on the identity of culprits until the evidence is conclusive. We have to do this because it duplicates the procedure in court – innocent until proven guilty – and you won't get a conviction only with suspicion. In practice, of course, at some crime scenes you can immediately see the hand of certain criminals already known to you. This, I think, is what the psychologist was trying to explain to us. Even if you *don't* know the identity of a killer, you can still recognise their hand. Or signature, as she put it.

It was a pity that no one was really listening to her, although things improved a bit after she cut short the introduction and turned off the lights. What she presented to us then, going through it step by step with the help of an overhead projector, was the following preliminary psychological profile of the killer we were hunting.

Age. Although no energy was expended in subduing or killing the victims, the strength required subsequently to move them to and from vehicles and to the grave sites indicates that the offender is in good physical condition and probably relatively young. On the other hand, the complex planning involved in the execution of the crimes excludes a youth or teenager. The killer is a car owner and an experienced driver. The killer is therefore mature, but not elderly, and most likely to be aged between thirty and forty years, which is generally the age range of the victims also.

Sex. Although there was no sexual assault on any of the victims and therefore no seminal discharge or other trace evidence to confirm gender, the degree of strength required for the tasks indicates a male offender.

Intelligence. The killer is of extremely high intelligence. I cannot stress this strongly enough. The level of organization required for stalking, abducting, killing and burying the victims in these cases is very demanding. The fact that so little trace evidence was gathered from any of the scenes reinforces this point. In my view, therefore, it would be a waste of Garda time interviewing suspects of average or below average intelligence.

Education. Probably educated to university level. The killer displays a knowledge of forensic pathology and criminology consistent with wide reading and a probable access to research facilities, if not a formal qualification in these or related fields. Combined with the high level of intelligence mentioned above, it suggests that investigators should be looking for someone of high academic achievement.

Family. I suspect that the killer is single and living alone. Unless engaged in an itinerant employment, such as a tradesman or sales executive – and this is unlikely – the killer would be unable to sustain the levels of movement required by the crimes without alerting anyone living with them. The killer was almost certainly driving alone when they picked up the first victim, Mary Corbett, and is likely to have been alone while stalking the subsequent victims and examining possible grave sites. The killer seems sociable and gregarious and undoubtedly has the ability to put strangers at ease. But this charm is entirely on the surface. The killer has few if any real attachments and may have a volatile personality inconsistent with sustaining any long-term relationship. The killer may have a history of family or interpersonal problems that previously came to the attention of the Garda or social services.

Residence. The killings and burials display a great familiarity with vast areas of County Wicklow. The killer lives in or near the county and frequently checks out possible sites and victims within it. The killer may have been born in the county, but is now living close by, most probably in Dublin city to the north or an isolated rural location to the south. Anonymity would be an important feature of either dwelling. Taking into account the previous points on education and intelligence, the killer may own an apartment in an up-market city area or a restored cottage or farmhouse in a remote rural location. I'm inclined towards the latter, which would offer the killer a useful surface personality as an eccentric academic or artist, and because I think the killer is most comfortable living away from normal human communities. The crimes exhibit an extremely strong desire on the part of the killer totally to control the environment. This would lead to obvious frustration in an ordinary community. Such a tendency towards control will also be apparent in the killer's home and possessions, which will all be tidy to the point of neurosis.

Vehicle. The killer clearly does a lot of travelling. The vehicle, therefore, must be extremely reliable, and is probably new, less than a year old, although with surprising distances on the clock for its age and the apparent lifestyle of its owner. The killer may trade in for a new model on an annual basis, and if so will have a contact with a local car dealer. This is one of the few close contacts the killer will have to maintain for practical purposes. It is a contact the killer will resent, but cannot escape from. The vehicle will not draw attention to itself. It will, therefore, most likely be a mid-range family saloon of a dark or dull colour and will fit without notice into the chosen environment of the killer. Like the killer's home, it will be meticulously clean and well-kept.

Employment. I do not believe that the killer is currently working, because I find it difficult to accept that they are able to sustain the level of pretence that a full-time job would involve. The killer may have taken early retirement from an academic position or some other teaching occupation.

Psychosexual history. This cannot be known from the evidence of the crimes themselves. It seems probable that the creation, placement and discovery of the narratives reportedly found in the graves may supply the killer, in the absence of actual sex, with a major psychological gain. They are essential, in ways that can only be guessed at, to the completion of the crime and to the gratification of the killer. They may even be the reason why the killer abducts and murders.

Nobody wanted to admit it, but after that presentation our unit started using the profile as our main guideline. I think we'd expected a really boring lecture, full of dead jargon and totally irrelevant theories about the human mind, and we were surprised at how practical it all turned out to be. The fact that it opened up new avenues in a stalled investigation was welcome. But the fact that it gave us a chance to blame someone else if things went wrong was what really guaranteed our support. 'Ah, well,' we could say afterwards, 'they're not our usual methods and we always had reservations about them.'

Personally, the only thing that I was disappointed about in the profile was the issue of gender. I'd gone in to the presentation hoping to have my view that a woman could be involved in the murders confirmed. Instead I found a complete rejection of the idea. I did notice, of course, that after the entry on sex, none of the nouns or pronouns had a gender at all. I wanted to raise this when the psychologist asked for questions afterwards, but I have to admit that I funked it. I knew that all the fellas would just moan and go on and on about it. And why bring it down on myself again? If there had been other questions and a bit of debate I probably would've put my hand up, but the only one who said anything afterwards was Dennison and he tightened everybody up with his attitude.

I know that Michelle Condon was very disappointed with our response and with the way the session just petered out without anyone other than the inspector even thanking her. But that was our style. We couldn't admit we needed help from outside, although you'd never guess it next morning when everyone in the unit was scrambling to claim some section of the profile as their own. Some of the fellas were eager to check out the possibility that the killer was an academic. Some got hooked into the possible history of family problems. Others wanted to trawl through the lists of convicted offenders again, except with a new filter this time. I'd always thought that the entry on vehicles was going to be the most interesting and luckily that's what I ended up with.

The inspector, in fairness to her, swung some extra resources our way and we all got additional staff to help. I got three uniformed guards, young fellas not long out of training college, but excited about the work and eager to get going. And as one of them said, it's absolutely amazing, the amount of illegal activity going on in the country at any one time. A few months earlier, during the foot-and-mouth crisis, the culling of sheep in one county had turned up two animals receiving government subsidies for every one that actually existed. We came across something similar. We were asking car dealers for details of sales over the last two years, looking for vehicles that might have been offered for trade-in with unusual distances or unusual wear for the age of the car. No matter how much we tried to assure them that all information was strictly for a murder enquiry, they always gave a knowing look that said, 'Yeah, but you'll keep it on file and somebody else will use it against us.'

It was tough going. And of course, once we got over that hurdle and started getting some co-operation, it was something else entirely trying to make sense of the huge mass of detail we collected. Eventually I was given a computer and the necessary software to manage the data. It sounded like a quick solution to my problem, until I realized that I had to transfer all the stuff from paper to the hard disk before the system could do anything for me.

That's what I was working at in the office one October evening, drawing down a list of car owners I wanted to interview over the coming week. I wasn't officially on overtime. I'd arranged to meet Fergal in town to go to a film and there wasn't any point driving home and back in again.

Most of the lads had already knocked off, drifting home or to the pub. The inspector had hurried off about six, saying that if her daughter called in or phoned then to tell her the package was waiting on the inspector's desk for her. Eventually, there was only Dennison and myself left.

Now Dennison, if anything, was even weirder by then than he had been. He'd gone completely in on himself. One of the lads said that he had a totally irrational reaction to the fact that the psychologist hadn't mentioned anything about ears in her profile. I couldn't really believe this, although Dennison *had* raised the issue after the presentation. He'd been sullen and aggressive about it, though, and his attitude had made Michelle Condon unsure and very nervous. As best she could, she explained that she hadn't included any reference to the severed ears because it was an act she couldn't understand the meaning of. The motive was private to the killer and it didn't help to guess about it.

'Where there's mutilation in serial killings,' she said, 'it's almost always connected to sexual sadism, something which obviously doesn't apply here. Some serial killers take trophies from the scene. Sometimes these trophies are body parts. Some use them afterwards to re-enact the crime or to act out deviant sexual fantasies.'

'What about the dog's ears being cut off in that story left in the last grave?' Dennison asked.

'I'm aware of the narratives, of course,' the psychologist told him, 'but as I did not have access to the texts, I cannot comment on that question.'

'That's fucking helpful,' Dennison sneered.

He sat down after that, but you could see that he wasn't satisfied. In the weeks after the presentation he got quieter and quieter, driven more and more in on himself. He was drinking a lot, I heard from the rest of the lads. But he was doing it by himself, not in any sociable way. Obviously there was something wrong with him. But he wouldn't tell anyone what it was.

I didn't fancy being alone with him that evening. I thought he was on the verge of breaking and I didn't trust him. But I wasn't going to run from him, either. It's one of the first things put up to you as a female guard, that when the going gets tough, will you be able to hold your ground? Because if you can't, you're no good to anyone. It's not just a personal thing. As you soon find out, the whole credibility of any police force depends on it holding its ground.

We didn't talk that evening after the others were gone. We sat there in this strange atmosphere, me clacking at the keyboard, him scratching something on a writing pad.

About six-thirty I heard a commotion out in the corridor and then the inspector's daughter burst into the office, followed by a young uniformed guard who was trying to stop her. When I told him who she was and that her visit was expected, he got a bit mad and asked her why she hadn't just told him that instead of making him chase her. She gave him a haughty look that said he should consider himself lucky to be given the chance to run after her.

She liked provoking men, Ms Taafe did. That was exactly the thought I had at the time. Maybe it was just the natural envy of a fairly plain-looking girl, because the young guard had clearly had his head turned by the daughter's attractiveness in a way that I couldn't manage and actually went off smiling about his troubles.

Any other day my bad thought would've stayed the niggling little thing it really was and died off the way bad thoughts usually do. Not that evening, though.

'Your mother left a package for you on her desk,' I told the girl.

I didn't know her first name at the time. It was Nicole, I learned later.

'Cool,' she said in her affected American way, and I remember telling myself not to be too hard on her, that she was only a kid.

I don't know how long she was in her mother's office. I went back to work and forgot about her. Next thing I knew, Dennison was looming in front of my desk, tapping at his watch. I could see that he was het up. His face was bright red and he was sweating.

'She's in there an awful long time,' he said.

'You know kids,' I said. 'She's probably on the phone.'

'She shouldn't be in there at all,' he went on. 'There are confidential files in there.'

I was going to tell him that it wasn't our problem, that the girl had the inspector's permission. I didn't get a chance. Dennison turned and stormed away. I thought he was going back to his desk. But he kept on past it, through the door at the end, into the little corridor that linked the inspector's office to ours. If I'd been thinking I would have followed him. Instead I ignored him. Or *tried* to ignore him. He was getting on my nerves.

Since that evening, I've gone over in my mind a thousand times exactly what happened and what I experienced, and I always come up with the same sequence. I noticed nothing until the door at the end of the office was opened again. I heard nothing until then. I didn't hear any scream. I didn't hear any scuffle. I heard the door opening. I looked up. The inspector's daughter was standing just inside the office. I couldn't say that she looked roughed up, but her hair was tossed and the blouse she was wearing was definitely torn around the left pocket. She didn't seem to be wearing a bra and most of her breast was visible.

That's as much as I could take in.

She stared at me for a second, and then she burst into tears and ran, still crying, past my desk and out of the office the way she'd come in.

I was too stunned to follow her. It happened too quickly. Anyway, before I could even move, Dennison strolled back from the inspector's office. And *strolled* was what he did. He was relaxed. And he was casual. As if nothing in the wide world had happened. He had a sheet of paper in his hand and he seemed to be absorbed in reading it. He glanced up and headed straight for my desk.

Before I could ask him what the hell was going on, he put the page down in front of me and said, 'You'll be interested in this, Galetti.'

I looked at it. It was a copy of the psychological profile Michelle Condon had drawn up. We'd been working with it on the unit for nearly a month by then. That's what I said to him. 'Are you all right, Dennison?' I asked

'For fuck's sake!' he said. 'Look, will you!'

He jabbed one of his big fingers down. It landed on the section between *Age* and *Intelligence* in the profile. More than that I couldn't figure out at first. I actually had to move his finger to see the text. And then I read:

Sex. There was no sexual assault on any of the victims and therefore no seminal discharge or other trace evidence to confirm gender. Although the degree of strength required for the tasks indicates a male offender, there are several other factors – that very absence of a sexual element, for instance, along with the absence of physical assault on the victims and the ease with which two women in already threatening situations and a reclusive man were lured to their deaths without being physically subdued – which suggest a *female* perpetrator. I'm simply uncertain.

For a week I did nothing, either about the likelihood that an assault had occurred in the office or about the possibility that the inspector had doctored the psychological profile.

They say that the stranger you most often meet in police work is yourself and what I've noticed since becoming a detective is that I'm cautious. I'm slow to take the initiative, but then doggedly persistent once I get going. Maybe that's why they made me one in the first place. I'm not sure if it's a good thing, though. I'm not decisive or imaginative enough. I want to think things through before taking any action and that's not always the best way to get results.

What kept coming into my mind, for instance, was why Dennison, of all people, should draw my attention to a cover-up. He was the one who'd always scoffed at my idea that a woman might be involved in the murders. And now he was volunteering evidence that I might have been right all along? You could say that he wanted to undermine the inspector. But he could have done that more effectively by telling any of the other lads on the unit. He didn't. He only told me.

Why did people keep passing dubious documents to me? Were they all as disturbed and as dangerous as Phil Flynn had been? Had Dennison, for instance, decided that this was the one thing that might distract my attention from the incident with the inspector's daughter. A sort of pay-off, if you like. 'Here,' he was saying, 'have this. Now you owe me. So stay quiet about what you saw.'

Maybe I'm overly suspicious. Maybe you have to be in the guards. But what I wondered was, did Dennison already have a copy of the second profile and only pretend to find it then? Was the thing even genuine at all? Was *anything* genuine? From what I'd seen in the office that evening, all the signs pointed to some attempted or actual sexual assault, but you couldn't afford to leave out of the picture that the inspector's daughter was a clever, manipulative kid, well aware of how to use her body.

I'm not saying that she deliberately provoked a situation. It's not a simple thing, one way or the other. We all use our bodies at times to have a particular effect on other people. It's only natural. But where it goes over the line from normal behaviour into a kind of harassment or provocation in itself I just don't know. Most people will tell you that a girl behaving like the inspector's daughter is flirting with trouble, but it can be a tough call for a teenager who is desperate for approval and confused about how to get it. The bottom line? For me, the adult in the situation is always the responsible one. But on the other hand . . . The fact is, the girl could have rearranged her hair *and* her clothes in the short corridor between the offices, out of sight of both Dennison and myself. If she'd already learned that the desirable woman is one of the most powerful images in our society, she'd probably also learned that the image of woman as a victim is just as powerful in another way. And I keep repeating, I didn't hear anything.

In the days afterwards I tried to recreate the conditions of that evening, with only myself in the main office and one of the lads volunteering to move around inside the inspector's, without knowing why I wanted him to do it. It wasn't very conclusive. I could hear him when he called out, but not otherwise.

I never said anything about the incident to Dennison. He didn't mention it to me. In fact, *nobody* said a word. And while nobody wanted to make an issue of it, I figured it wasn't my business to make the running with it.

I felt different about the two drafts of the profile, though. That I took personally. But to be honest, since I had only Dennison's word that the second draft was genuine, I didn't know what to do about it.

I spent a week at the normal routine, interviewing car owners. Nothing came of that first trawl. I had to make sure to do the job properly and not let my attitude affect the work, but all the time, underneath the surface, I was chewing on my annoyance. Finally, I made up my mind. I rang the psychology department at University College Dublin and asked for Michelle Condon.

She remembered me and was only too delighted, as she put it, to discuss the profile and find out if it had been any use, but also surprised it wasn't the inspector who'd called. Apart from giving the impression that I was deputizing, I didn't have to do anywhere near as much lying as I thought I might. The psychologist's enthusiasm did it for me.

I drove out to the campus at Belfield that afternoon. Michelle Condon had a tiny office crowded with books and scripts. It felt like a changing room in a really cheap clothes shop. It was *that* cramped.

There was the usual awkwardness and small talk before we got down to business. She apologized for the lack of space. I hoped I wasn't keeping her from lectures. That sort of thing. She said then that she was anxious to hear about the response to the profile. I told her the truth, that we were following a lot of the lines she'd sketched. She was pleased with that. When I added that there were a few things I needed to clarify, she was only too eager to oblige. She was so eager, actually, that she didn't even wait for the questions.

'I've given it a lot of thought and a lot of study since,' she said. 'It was only a preliminary profile, after all, and I expected to be asked for a more detailed analysis. What I'd like to add now is this. Whoever is responsible for these killings is clearly obsessive about control. Ultimately, they want to have control over the life and death of others. That's their thrill, the sense of power that this dominance gives them. But they not only want to control the *victim's* destiny, it also seems to me that they seek to control the subsequent investigation. A tremendous amount of planning and organization is displayed at the grave sites, and presumably, since they've never been located, at the abduction and crime scenes as well. This is not someone who kills randomly, as the opportunity arises. This is someone who carefully selects victims, scenes and sites, spending months in the process.

'Now, all the research data shows that this type of serial killer, because they derive their satisfaction from the exercise of their power, will torture their victims before death, usually for some sexual gratification. But the bodies here exhibit no signs of ill treatment. Quite the contrary. I find this baffling.

'There's another conundrum. All serial offenders, as I'm sure you know, display a *modus operandi* peculiar to them. In serial *killers*, the method of capture, the method of killing, the manner of the burial and the type of victim selected, will show a remarkable level of consistency. If we look at the three killings here, however, we see puzzling variations. We don't know the cause of death or the method of abduction. We do know that all the victims were buried in shallow graves in the mountains, two in

108

very similar postures and accompanied by written material – the texts of which I still haven't seen, incidentally, a point I'll return to. What's most remarkable, though, is the dissimilarities between the types of *victim*: a twenty-two-year-old female businesswoman, a middle-aged male clerk and a thirty-four-year old female journalist.

'Taking all of these factors into account, it seems to me now that the killer is driven by inner compulsions, but also has an extraordinary measure of control over the working out of these compulsions. I've come to the conclusion, actually, that the killer may be intimately familiar with the same research data on serial killers that I've just outlined to you and may have the ability coldly to apply this learning. A more virulent *strain* of killer, in a way. The homicidal equivalent of a superbug, immune to the antidotes that destroyed its predecessors. Do you understand what I mean?'

I didn't particularly, not at the rate she was going. In fact, I was starting to panic a little. 'Why are you convinced that the killer is a male?' I asked.

I know now that I shouldn't have interrupted her. She was flowing along nicely and probably would have come to the point all by herself. But I was anxious. I was frightened of losing touch. This was the reason I'd come, after all, to get an answer to that question. For the last few minutes I'd only been half-listening, while waiting for an opening.

She jotted something on the pad in front of her. I thought she was recording the question to come back to, but it must have been a reminder to herself of the next point she'd intended making. 'Have you read the alternative draft of my preliminary profile?' she wondered.

The correct answer to this, as it turned out, was, 'Yes, I have read the alternative draft.' But who would have thought that a brazen confession was the ticket? I didn't.

'What alternative draft?' I asked innocently.

She was sharp, I'll give her that. She was also cautious. I learned later that this was her first major outing as a forensic psychologist. Her professor, away in California at a convention, had passed the commission on to her. She was determined not to make any wrong moves.

As soon as she sniffed trouble, she clammed up. Her whole face and body closed down, for all the world like a computer screen that had frozen. She said, 'You gave me the impression on the telephone that the inspector had sent you.'

'I don't think I did,' I bluffed. 'I said I was following a line of enquiry you could help me with.'

'What you are doing is unprofessional,' she told me then. 'You're placing me in an invidious position.'

Shit, I thought. I'm in trouble here. *Unprofessional. Invidious.* All the best-sounding words make the thickest glue to get bogged down in.

I told her my situation. I explained about Dennison and Nicole and why I couldn't go to the inspector for confirmation. Just as she was insisting that she didn't want to get involved in our office politics, and *particularly* didn't want to get embroiled in a court case, I produced the profile Dennison had given me.

'You've already said that you did an alternative profile,' I pointed out. 'I'm not asking you for additional information, I'm only asking you to clarify something. So just answer one straight question for me. Is this the alternative profile or is it just a fake?'

She looked at it. She took it. She read it. 'It's the profile I wrote,' she confirmed.

'So whose decision was it to go with the other one?' I asked.

'That's two questions,' she said.

So it was.

When you're just a foot soldier, a minor part of a large-scale investigation – and we had more than a hundred officers again in our unit – you often have no clear idea of the bigger picture. You're stuck with details. People who know you're working on a particular case sometimes come up to you in pubs and try to get information out of you in a roundabout way. They don't understand that at that time you mightn't know any more than they do. You're at the bottom. You're not expected to spend your time cultivating an overview. You're expected to go from door to door, witness to witness, piece of paper to piece to paper, collecting evidence that somebody else will fit into a pattern. It's like a beehive or an ant colony.

The only exception to all of this is that you're relying on the regular conferences, when the main detectives on the case come together to pool their findings, to give you some idea of what you're a part of.

One Friday morning in mid-November we all trooped into the incident room for one of these conferences. We sat down at the oval table we had. On the walls around us were the photographs, the witness statements, the maps and the rest of the material relating to the three bodies that had been found. The mood wasn't anything special, neither up nor down. This was routine as far as everyone was concerned. Nothing significant was expected.

We chatted away while waiting for the inspector. She was ten minutes late. This was very unlike her. She was a very particular woman in relation to all aspects of the job.

I suppose the delay was deliberate on her part because it had the effect of making the rest of us uneasy and very quiet when she did arrive. She stood at the head of the table, looking down at us. She said nothing for a good while. And this made us even more uneasy. You could start to sense now that something was in the air. Fellas who'd been lounging in their chairs sat up straighter. A bit of a laugh from somewhere died off into the quietness. All the hands on top of the table went still, not fiddling with paper clips or anything any more.

'For the past few months,' the inspector said then, 'in laboratories here and in England a number of scientists and psychologists have been examining the documents found in the graves of Michael Elwood and Karen Stokes. I've already passed on to you a few of the earlier findings. Now I need to bring you up to date.

'Firstly, forensic analysis has yielded very little of practical use. Whoever handled the material was extremely careful not to leave any trace evidence. No fingerprints were found, but a number of *glove* prints were successfully lifted. Two different pairs of gloves were used for the two narratives. Both were leather, but the creases and marks generated by use were different. Both were slightly smaller than average size. The owner was predominantly right-handed.

'The paper itself is standard A4 copier sheets. The make and model of the printer, along with the type and release date of the computer software used, have all been identified. None of this, which may be vital in securing a conviction in court when we do have an accused, will in itself point towards a suspect. Neither, I believe, will the psychological analyses of the narratives found in the graves. I do believe, however, that these point somewhere else which is just as vital. I believe that they point to the killer's next victim.

'I believe that the killer's next victim will be an old man, probably living alone in an isolated part of the Wicklow or south Dublin Mountains.

'Because of this, I'm convinced that I was wrong about something. I've always assumed that the woman who left Johnnie Fox's pub with Michael Elwood was also murdered and is buried somewhere in the mountains. I now think that you need to question this assumption.

'There's no evidence for the following, but let's take as a starting point the idea that a middle-aged man abducted and murdered Mary Corbett, as is suggested in the first of the narratives. Michael Elwood was a middle-aged man. Again there's only circumstantial evidence to support this, but let's say that he was lured to his death by the woman in Johnnie Fox's. Then a woman, approximately thirty years old, will be the next victim. Karen Stokes was thirty-four. The last person seen with her, as far as we know, and if we maintain the elimination of Henry Mullan as a suspect, was an unidentified old man. If we assume that *he* killed her, then it follows that an old man will be the next victim.

'Some weeks ago, I requested resources to locate and visit elderly men resident in County Wicklow and south County Dublin. Yesterday I was told that my request had been refused. It was felt that I was taking the investigation in the wrong direction, that I had become obsessed by a figure capable of changing shapes, a "master of disguise", as the assistant commissioner put it, "straight out of science fiction or a child's video game". It was also suggested that I was falling into the trap of confusing the world of the narratives with the world of the killer. On an operational level, it was decided that the resources I had requested were out of the question.

'I was left with the impression that I had no alternative but to accept the recommended transfer from this unit. I do have an alternative. This afternoon I tendered my resignation from the Garda Síochána, with immediate effect.

'My file on the narratives found in the graves of Michael Elwood and Karen Stokes now becomes the responsibility of Sergeant Mullery. I wish you well in your continued efforts.'

And then she turned and walked away.

You know all those films and television dramas, where the previously unpopular squad leader shows personal integrity in a principled fight against bureaucracy and all the foot soldiers organize a mini-revolt in support, after which they all march on together to make the world a better place?

Forget it.

Nobody moved or said a word.

We were too stunned.

PART THREE

The Narrative

The old are exempt from suspicion. Past seventy, with our wasted muscle and blunted incisors, our creaking joints and slow brains, we are considered too frail to pose a physical threat. Our energies and emotions lie buried somewhere in the past, our interest in the future is tenuous, and we have neither the passion nor the motive to drive us to crime.

Like all such popular beliefs, this one also can become a useful weapon.

The dark-haired young woman stranded in the car park in the urban wasteland that night was already alert long before I approached her. She was hardly nervous. When she searched around for possible trouble, she did so aggressively, conveying the message that she was capable of dealing with it. A rolling barrel of lard in a crimson baseball cap, waddling a little behind her as if he was stalking and ready to pounce, had inadvertently heightened her senses. At first I cursed the fool. But for the adaptable, young or old, even the spoiling clumsiness of others may present an opportunity. Once the oaf had passed the young woman, completely unaware of the unnerving effect he had had on her, I was then able to enter her world only as an aspect of the relief she experienced.

Appearances are deceptive, according to a self-important old caution. But they are only deceptive within the right context. And timing is crucial. For all her education and ability, the young woman's head was crowded with myths. Everything in her upbringing informed her that, in the situation in which she found herself, the sight of an old man was welcome. The figure was fatherly. He evoked images of her own childhood. And nothing is so comforting in danger as the memory of the childhood we thought we had.

The resilience of childhood folklore, and the reduced impact of later events on the individual mind, continues to absorb me.

Some time before that Saturday night, but still fresh in the memory, a father in a southern Irish town shot dead his six-year-old daughter after being on the run with her for almost two years. A little earlier, of course, a woman in America had drowned her five children in the bath while her husband was at work. Curiously, the man killed himself after his act of filicide and the woman telephoned the police. Perhaps the father knew in advance that he would be demonized, just as the mother knew that she would be treated as mentally ill. Our worlds are so deeply rooted in our childhoods that the certainties formed there may be undisturbed even by subsequent experience.

The young woman in the deserted car park had clearly had an untroubled childhood. In her case also it was obvious to me that her heart was softened towards old men at that moment. She felt close to them and grateful to them. More importantly, she also felt guilty about them and saddened by their plight. When she saw me ambling towards her, my walking stick in one hand, the empty dog lead in the other, she immediately categorized me as harmless and crouched to retrieve her keys from where she'd dropped them on the concrete.

The tight black skirt of her business suit slipped up her thighs with the movement and was pulled tight and smooth around her firm bottom. For a moment, as I imagined the moist delights just underneath the rough material, life stirred again in my old loins. I held the dog leash to my nose and sniffed the leather. Instantly, I was back in my own childhood, or youth, when I was sixteen years old and my uncles handed me a greyhound to take to the local abattoir. A mild-tempered brindle bitch, she had broken her leg too often to retain the hope of racing and she wasn't considered good enough to breed from.

I stood outside the abattoir, looking in through the open door, while a fat man in a blood-soaked apron held a gun to the bitch's head and drove a bolt through her brain. When the fat man came back he handed me the empty lead and leather collar, along with the dog's left ear, which he had sliced off and which was still dripping with blood. In our district at that time, we stamped the inner ears of racing greyhounds as a means of identification. When a dog was put down, the ear, with its indelible stamp, had to be returned to the authorities governing the sport.

As I carried the equipment home afterwards, I felt a ghost tugging on the empty collar. When I got back, my uncles were no longer in the house. I stood alone in the back garden, still holding the dangling lead and collar and the severed ear. Beyond the hedge our new neighbour, a young American woman named Sarah Kleisner, was hanging washing on her line. It was summer, the middle of August. For weeks her sun-tanned body and transparent clothes had driven me wild. Now she was dressed only in a man's red shirt. Her feet and legs were bare. Every time she raised her arms to peg an item on the line, the curved tail of the shirt lifted to reveal her naked bottom. Every time she stooped to pick something else from the basket, she presented herself fully to me.

Terrified that my uncles' sudden return would disturb me, equally frightened that the woman would finish hanging her clothes before I was satisfied, I took my cock through the unzipped fly of my jeans and started stroking it, unaware at first that I still held the greyhound's severed ear in the same hand, but gradually conscious of an enhanced sensation from the peculiar softness of the short fur and the smooth firmness of the organ's membrane. Perhaps the American woman was aware of what I was doing. Perhaps she heard my moaning. She stooped once and held the posture for several seconds, her legs slightly apart. And that's when I came, my white sperm mingling with the drying blood and seeping into the dog's inner ear.

By the time my uncles came back, I had washed both myself and the ear. I thought I had left no trace of my pleasure. But I was ignorant then. I was careless. And it was only their inability to interpret the signs or imagine my act that saved me. What kind of fool are you? they demanded. You've got the bitch's blood all over your own trousers! I have never forgotten that embarrassing error. Ever since, I have been extremely wary. Neurotic, perhaps

Such were my memories as I approached the young woman in the car park. I must confess, I was gloriously tumescent inside my clothes. And this unexpected revival almost confused me. I became suddenly undecided about which image of age to play on. Weakness or strength? Tragedy or resilience? The old as helpless or the old as cheerfully defiant? I had to remind myself on several occasions that she was already alert and defensive, and that the image of weakness was therefore the most appropriate.

I said, I seem to have made a fool of myself.

It's a mistake to think that women in danger seek only protection and look always to the strength of the male for it. The illusion of superiority offered by the sight of an old man in difficulty is a far more potent erosion of their defences.

Can I help you? she offered.

I held up my leash and empty collar. I've lost my dog, I said. I'm sure it's already gone home by now. It's far more sensible than I am, and equipped *with far better radar. But in searching for it, you see, I've managed to get myself lost. Could you point me in the direction of Old Bawn?*

She seemed slightly amused. Who wouldn't? She looked around, searching for orientation. I waited on her guidance.

You've drifted a long way, she said.

Oh, dear, I muttered.

What's essential in relationships is knowing the correct button to press with an individual at the appropriate time. Most crucial of all is the understanding of an immutable law, that what makes us most human also makes us most vulnerable. The most decent of people are the likeliest victims. The most heartless evade capture for longest. From a time now lost in the narratives of history, we humans have buried our dead and cared for our aged. It's what originally distinguished us from our brutish competitors and we will never relinquish it. In other words, I knew before she did that the young woman would offer to drive me to whatever street and house number I cared to name. And also, that the offer would make us intimates. My name is Karen, by the way, she confided. Just as I knew that she wouldn't look at me too closely afterwards. We're warned as children not to stare at others, an absurd caution that makes us stupid and defenceless if it is heeded too seriously. From an early age, the most obedient of us substitute desirable images for the reality we're forbidden to examine. And humans are simply too good, for their own good, at inventing desirable images. What Karen saw was not myself. It was the image in her mind of an anxious old man at odds with the difficult world of motorways and shopping centres that had replaced the country footpaths of his youth.

As if I had suddenly become an invalid, she insisted on fastening and adjusting my seat belt when I sat beside her in her car. She had long and delicate fingers. Their attention was soothing. Almost seductive.

Searching for something to restore the mood I needed, I noticed a number of paperbacks under the glove compartment and lying on the rear seat. Most of them were recently published exposés of Dublin's gangland, one of which was even written by Karen herself. I picked up a few and read the blurbs on the covers.

They all seem to rely on a particularly narrow view of the criminal, I remarked.

Karen laughed lightly. Perhaps she hadn't heard properly, or didn't understand what I was referring to. Perhaps she was preoccupied with finding the way. We still hadn't left the housing complex around the shopping centre. In any case, she wasn't ready to respond yet. I waited, until we were clear of the narrow roads and out on the carriageway.

Bertolt Brecht, I said then, once asked what the crime of robbing a bank was compared to the crime of founding one.

Now she glanced at me with a new interest. Here was the perfect combination in a male for an intelligent young woman to relax with: a decrepit body and a vigorous mind.

Are you a writer? she asked.

I ignored this rather dangerous question. Don't you think that we use the word somewhat too promiscuously these days? I suggested instead.

What word? she wondered.

Criminal, I explained. In ordinary conversation. In the newspapers. On radio and television. We use it as a noun. As an adjective. As a filter on the world. The criminal underworld. Criminal elements. Convicted criminal. Even career criminal. And whenever we use it, what we casually mean is a man in a balaclava wielding a baseball bat and attacking our home, where we felt perfectly safe until his arrival. In the darkness of our nightmares, the criminal is always male, always masked and anonymous, although recognizably from certain deprived areas of our cities, and always lunging with a weapon – a baseball bat, a blood-filled syringe, a Stanley blade. And he always comes from outside to threaten our security. If you're working in crime fiction – my own particular interest as an academic – you either accept this image as the better part of the whole truth, or its crudeness will make you queasy. Accepting it, as so many do, you will naturally place your reader in the comfortable position of spectator. You will cater for the nerves rather than the brain. You will provide a vicarious thrill, a satisfying assurance that justice will be done. You'll offer resolutions at the end of your story, solutions to the problems posed. You'll leave the world a better, a safer, and a more comprehensible place. Don't you think, in this limited notion of criminality as a threat from outside, that we can distinctly see the remnants of a religious perspective that experiences evil as an external force and that prays for protection against it?

Although I was talking generally, I was thinking specifically of my father. He had died the previous week and we had buried him, resentfully it seemed to me, in the family plot. In particular, I was thinking of him during his trial for the murder of Sarah Kleisner, the young American woman who had come to live in the house next door to my uncles'. Throughout the trial, you see, he had refused to change his style of dress. His lawyer pleaded with him to wear a suit, that Victorian image of respectability and rectitude, that lie that has corrupted the world. He refused. He remained in his working clothes, his heavy trousers and hob-nailed boots and unravelling cardigan, all still stained with flour dust from the mill where he had worked before its closure.

Perhaps, at last, this was a statement from him. Fundamentally he was a labourer, a working man, and he was not going to pretend otherwise. How was he to know that the world was changing, even as he sat in court, from a landscape where men sweated to a room where they watched the images of others sweating? Television, destined to be the only reality in our new world, had just begun to colonize our lives. How was he to know that this change would become an integral part of his trial and that his decision to look like the man he really was would ultimately condemn him?

Do I admire his stubbornness and steadfastness? His silence? His integrity? His refusal to concede? No one else did at the time. The crowd was hostile to him inside the court. His former friends and neighbours, all now dressed as his accusers, the men in dark suits and the women in their Sunday dresses . . .

Sunday.

I looked at the clock on the dashboard of Karen's car, remembering that it was Saturday night. There were five minutes left to midnight.

Did I admire my father and his old-fashioned faith in the physical world? Or did I prefer my mother's universe of shifting inventions, which was much more likely to adapt and prosper in the virtual new world that was coming towards us?

Even out of the remnants of her life, the ragged pieces that were left to her after my father's arrest, my mother magically created stories that attracted sympathy to her. She defended my father to the last. You might think that throwing her lot in with the baying crowd would have generated more admiration for her. But this is to underestimate the depth of my mother's understanding of the effect of artifice on a thirsting audience. They admired her loyalty. Heroic! they called it. And they pitied her plight. Tragic! they said. And her explanations for my father's predicament, her proposed defences, were all so outlandish, so preposterous, that everyone feared that her mind was cracking under the strain. She suggested that the boning knife found in the locked drawer under my father's stamp album had been put there by another. The key to the chest of drawers was missing, she pointed out. Find the key and you'll find the murderer, she claimed. She insisted that witnesses must be mistaken about the times they'd given. My father had been seen going into Sarah Kleisner's house in the early evening and not seen again until he arrived at a public house later that night, at eleven-forty. But my mother seemed to remember him coming home at midnight. He had woken her with his noisy entrance. And he surely couldn't have stayed only twenty minutes in the pub.

As her audience listened, so their sympathy deepened, not for my accused father, but for her. How could they know that she did not believe a word she was saying? How could they know that she had calculated precisely the effect of each invention; that while she was appearing to defend my father she was actually condemning him? And, most astonishing of all, simultaneously enhancing her own reputation.

Had she stayed within her own privileged family rather than abandoning it for youthful love of my father, I believe her abilities would have found a worthier stage. Had she been born a generation later, it might not have mattered that she married a working man. Although her talents, of course, were never quite wasted. They have since passed on to me.

A silver Jaguar, driven by one shaven-headed youth and crowded with five others in the passenger seats, hurtled past us at more than twice the speed limit in the outside lane of the carriageway and then cut across our bonnet to overtake the next car on the inside. Stolen, I thought. An observation almost instantly confirmed by the screech of sirens behind us from the police in pursuit. The chase was a distraction. Absorbed by it, we made an error and ended up taking the wrong route. Instead of turning off for Old Bawn, we continued along the carriageway, heading south towards the village of Blessington . . .

Our interests are rooted in our personal experience, I said to Karen. And no doubt my passion for crime fiction can be illuminated, let us say, by the fact that my father was tried for murder when I was a boy of sixteen. For years afterwards the hatred his plight provoked among his own people continued to baffle me. I thought perhaps that it might be something rooted in old feuds or jealousies that had thrived long before I was born, something to do with my mother, who was a stranger brought into the community as a young bride. But I could never unearth any memories of these.

He was a respected man before his arrest. Not particularly loved or liked, but genuinely respected. His role as a labourer was a valued one. And yet it was this very image of the working man that provoked the deepest hatred during his trial. The longer he remained in his ragged working clothes in the dock, never speaking, not even to plead in answer to the charges, the more extraordinary the spectacle grew in the public gallery, where his neighbours had plunged themselves into debt with moneylenders in order to dress like the middle-class.

Vital matters were obscured by this trivial display. What Sarah Kleisner was doing in Ireland, for instance, was never revealed at the trial. Nothing at all about her, apart from the physical facts, was considered to have any relevance. There seemed to have been a pact between prosecution and defence to consider her only as a corpse. Such secrecy breeds curiosity.

Are you repelled by the practice of incest, Karen? Or are you one of those who understands that society's taboo, imposed to keep deformities from the genes, is no longer relevant in this age of mass contraception and personal emptiness? Sarah had a brother named Robert. His letter to her, on the day of her death, revealing his unexpected decision to marry, drove her into such a rage that she tore the pages into small fragments and scattered them to the wind. Was this information relevant to my father's trial? Perhaps not. Nobody knew about Sarah's intimacy with her brother. And this was clearly not the guilty secret that my father's neighbours were concealing under their expensive new clothes.

For years, as I've said, I was baffled. And it wasn't until quite recently, when I was involved with the Irish Film Board in discussions on a proposed script for, of all things, a crime drama, and an official asked if I was related to the man who had killed Sarah Kleisner, that I finally learned the truth. Sarah was in Ireland to produce a series of documentaries on the country, one of which profiled the close-knit traditional urban community she had come to live among. A community that was already disintegrating, of course, because of the closure of its industries, the unemployment of its adult males, the departure of its unfettered young for San Francisco or Nepal. A community that assisted in its own death, so that its young could prosper. The first society in history to undertake this terminal act of altruism.

Consider it, Karen. Our parents sacrificed themselves to keep us in school, and then recoiled from the knowledge we brought home, pitifully dragging the old superstitions around with them for protection. This was what ultimately made us strangers to our parents, and made our parents incomprehensible to us. Not sex or drugs, rock and roll or radical politics. But knowledge. And above all, the awareness that the new types of media, and television in particular, also created a new reality.

My father's neighbours had an inkling of this, but only in the way that a child knows a car will transport it if someone else can do the driving. This was what inflamed their hatred of my father. Sarah Kleisner's death had not only deprived them of revenue, not only of fresh meaning in a rapidly changing world, but also of immortality. They were eager to embrace television, believing that the images it created of them working would somehow compensate for the actual work they'd lost, that its images of them living would somehow make their lives more real. An error repeated by millions subsequently, Karen. We reinvent ourselves as mere shadows of things we abandoned to become images. We destroy whole life forms and then build theme parks to admire an imitation of what we killed. We are most comfortable as spectators at our own dissolution. And that was the beginning of this process, when I was sixteen years old and Sarah Kleisner came to live among us and observe us with a producer's eye.

Whenever I notice the ubiquity of cameras these days – in the surveillance that intrudes on our public spaces, in the lens thrust in the faces of those dying from famine or disaster, in the camcorders the tourists bring to record holidays they can't otherwise experience – I always think of my father's doomed effort to hold back the tide, his refusal to change his clothes for an audience, his silence, perhaps his murder of Sarah Kleisner. I think of his definitive collection of Irish stamps, which he mounted in a black, leather-bound album. An alternative view of the world. Each beautifully coloured stamp was really an effort to freeze a moment and to hold it against inevitable change. There, that's the end of it now, he would declare each December, after adding in the last issue of the year, usually a Christmas stamp depicting the Madonna and Child or the Holy Family. As if no more stamps would be issued and January would never come. As if things could always remain the same. And, yes, I can still see the final complete page of his album, from the sixteenth-century manuscript and prehistoric kerbstone at the top to the Holy Family by Giorgione at the bottom – the last, ironically, preceded by a sprinting greyhound, a stamp issued to commemorate the golden jubilee of greyhound track racing in Ireland.

I think too that his earlier struggles against my mother, pitching his silence against her garrulity, may well have been the first skirmishes in this war against lies. What difference was there between my mother's persuasive but empty inventions and the persuasive but empty inventions of television? She too created an imaginary world and obliged others to live in it. It is not only that the camera always lies. This is too trite an observation. It is not only that the portrait, the profile, the narrative and the story, all dehumanize.

The subtlest tragedy of all is that we ourselves begin to lie as soon as we step in front of a camera. And this was the extraordinary effect my mother had on her own audience. They wanted to see themselves as she saw them.

But perhaps we all live in a virtual world these days, Karen. Or most of us, in any case. In our unwillingness to believe that anything is real unless it appears on a screen, in our eagerness to turn ourselves into mere images – from the exhibitionists on game shows to the fools waving at a passing camera during a football match they supposedly came to watch – haven't we all come to inhabit a mere soap opera? And who is the god of this new universe? The producer? Or the slayer of the producer? The producer offers life to the characters. The slayer takes it away. Is it a crime to extinguish a mere image? I don't think so. Wasn't it Sartre who wrote that humans look absurd and dispensable if viewed from a great height? Or perhaps it was Saint Exupéry in his aircraft. I can't remember. The point is, television now achieves the same effect at a level which is accessible to all. It makes all of life absurd and dispensable. The burning bodies falling out of bombed buildings are neither stuntmen in a film nor refugees in a war. They are mere images.

And yet, before the death of Sarah Kleisner, our community, like so many others at the time, was capable of a different direction. Consider the ownership of greyhounds, for instance, surely an extraordinary purchase in times of hardship, surely a singular commitment of time and resources. And yet the greyhound, of course, was really an investment, not only in the future, but in a different kind of future. Owned, trained, housed and groomed by the one man, it offered the illusion of total mastery. And on race nights, for thirty intense seconds around an oval track, while its owner watched from the stand, there was a hectic drama of the ordinary man's own creating, to which he had contributed an essential ingredient. Almost uniquely, greyhound racing seemed to offer no distinctions between spectator and participant.

Greyhounds no longer feature in what is left of that community, of course.

After my father's funeral last week, I went back to the old haunts of my childhood and I stood again for a few minutes in my uncles' back garden, looking once more over the hedge, into the neighbouring garden where I first saw Sarah Kleisner all those years ago. Other than my memories, nothing of that world had survived. My uncles were long since dead. Around me, the extensive dog kennels they built were all in ruins. The roofs had caved in. The brick walls had crumbled. The debris was overgrown with weeds ...

On the dashboard of Karen's car, as we entered the village of Blessington, the clock flicked onwards to midnight. It was Sunday again.

The traffic was light. And very few were walking the streets. We turned left, crossing the reservoir at Blessington Bridge. On the other side there was a parking bay for visitors, close to a spectacular viewpoint and a boating dock. I advised against stopping here. The more popular locations are always rather spoiled for me. I suggested briefly turning south and then swinging east along the deserted cul-de-sac that led to the base of Sorrel Hill.

The strange thing, I said to Karen then, is how grimly we cling to keepsakes from the old world that we killed off so long ago. In the western world, no other day carries as heavy, as ambivalent and as complex a burden as Sunday. It is the best of days, the day of the sun, source of light and life, and therefore an object of worship. It is the Sunday of life, as Hegel wrote, which levels everything and rejects everything bad. Unfortunately, as well as being the best of days, Sunday is also the worst of days, not devoted to life and light, but condemned to darkness and death. There is a gloom for me attendant upon a Sunday, Charles Lamb once wrote. A glum note that has been struck time and again by observers ever since.

But perhaps Sunday is only the day on which what we know as normality is temporarily suspended. The Sunday driver, for instance, is not really a driver at all, but more a bizarre fugitive from public transport, gripped for a day by a deadly delusion of independence. So what we do on Sunday should not, perhaps, define us for the rest of the week. Don't you agree?

The Profile

It's morning. Breakfast and the other sombre rituals of the dark house have been endured, and Jacob and Matthew are ready for school.

'Mind, boys!' Down the stairs, beyond the gates and along the gravel path which they walk, their mother's soft lament pursues them. 'Be home early, boys!'

'Hurry!' Jacob urges. As he strides, his shoes bite hastily into the gravel and his head is turned to the ground, not so much against the wind blowing in from the sea, as away from the colours which tempt the corners of his eyes.

'Look . . .' Matthew invites, lingering by a hedge to disturb his brother.

Jacob merely quickens his retreat.

But Matthew, not yet broken by the tyranny of fear, is in revolt against the cramped gloom of their lives. Alone in his bedroom, he invents entire landscapes of freedom. Once, shivering with desire, he takes an old boat from its moorings and spends the day exploring a small island in the bay. Whether from spite or jealousy or righteousness, his brother informs, and this small service to their mother has elevated the elder to be his brother's keeper. From such conflicts their dislike of one another grows into fear and into a sullen, unspoken hatred.

When they return from school each day they find their mother locked in the same posture as they left her in the morning, as if only their presence can animate her. Only now, after an excess of nervous fingering about each of them, will she rise and put on her black clothes.

Loneliness has made her rituals odd. Coming into the room where the brothers do their homework in the afternoon, she always pauses and peers into corners for flies thrashing in a spider's web. She has become obsessed with the plight of animals and insects at their extremities. For a time her interest fastens on a stray mongrel who has been nosing about the house, a lean bitch whose coat is pressed against its bones from the rain, and who is starving and cannot hide it, not only in the taut flesh where the stomach caves but in the savage hunger of its eyes.

'Ah,' Mrs Rushford moans. She notices that only violence will drive the bitch away, only food attract it, and that tenderness has no power in its basic world. All day she pries on the mongrel through a slit in her bedroom curtains and only the knowledge that her sympathy will dissolve as the animal fattens forbids her taking it in.

But in the hours of darkness, Mrs Rushford turns to her children.

'Boys,' she calls one night.

Some foreign sweetness in her voice makes Matthew shiver, but Jacob dutifully dries the ink from the nib and puts away his pen and squeezes closer to her.

'Christmas is almost upon us,' Mrs Rushford sighs.

'Twelve days, Mother.' Precision, as always, is Jacob's indulgence.

'Yes. And the school examinations, boys. Isn't that right? Ah, how I would like to keep for myself the little prize I have bought for the boy with the highest marks at Christmas. How I would like to keep it for myself. Yes.'

All December, as she imagines their work to be a hungry striving for her praise, she is almost happy, because she enjoys the power of setting things in motion against each other. Finally, almost reluctantly, she approaches the great climax on Christmas Eve, spreading the two report cards on the table in front of her and indicating with a persistent return to her shawl that it is from there the secret will reveal itself.

Despite himself, Matthew is alive with curiosity. Even with hope. But when his mother has finished talking, and when the Bible with the red cover has passed from her hands into his brother's keeping, he forces a spasm of bitterness away from expression. It isn't defeat that sours him. It's the hollow trickery of a gift which could have no meaning for him even if he had won. He moves away from the dark figures, who are bent over the Book of Life in a sickly harmony, and from the chill of his bedroom, sixty years later, helplessly ill and dying himself now, he recalls the snow that fell that year, troubling the winter birds with its mask, and he listens again to their frantic chirping as they perch and burrow and as they rise again in a flutter of wings with only water dripping from their beaks.

Sixty years later.

It's not the memory that the old man wants to embrace. And yet, it won't let go of him.

He lies on his bed, locked inside his freezing cottage in the heart of the Wicklow Mountains, and he searches desperately for something else to cling to for survival, some source of warmth, some fondness, some token that will offer him strength. But he's as unable to summon brightness from his past as he is to feed himself. And he hasn't eaten now for almost two whole days.

He describes what has happened to him as a turn. He thinks of it as a weakness that came over him. But what the old man has actually suffered is a stroke. Three weeks have passed since the first attack, two days since the second. He hasn't seen a doctor yet. Because he lives in the isolated cottage on Trooperstown Hill, and because he has alienated his few neighbours over the years, no one is aware of his illness. He's not certain if he has any surviving relatives. But he knows that he has no surviving friends.

As he drifts in and out of consciousness, his dreams and his memories become almost identical, recreating the events of a single weekend from the winter of 1956, when he was still young, still in his twenties, still full of potential.

'Angela?' he calls out repeatedly.

He's feverish. Drenched in his own sweat, he tosses and turns in his soaking pyjamas, back and forth beneath the sodden bedclothes. But no matter where he twists, he always sees the same bright face.

'Angela?' he cries.

She's a student nurse, the youngest daughter of his first landlady in the city after he's left home, a lively, dark-headed girl of nineteen, a few years younger than himself.

'Mr Rushford' she calls him.

She is standing in the hallway outside his room, rapping her knuckles on his door. 'Mr Rushford?'

The door creaks as he opens it. Although he's dressed in an overcoat and it's early in the afternoon, he looks as if he has just woken from sleep.

'I heard a noise, Mr Rushford,' the girl explains. 'I didn't know whether it was you or not.' She has a habit of mimicking her mother's phrases and then mischievously undermining them. 'Is it?' she asks.

'Yes,' he confirms with absurd dryness. 'It's me. I've just come in.'

'You're home very early,' she probes. And when he doesn't respond to this, she offers her own apprehensions. 'You're not sick, are you? You're not coming down with something?'

'Well, yes,' he says wearily. 'A slight chill, actually.'

'Can I get you something?' the girl offers.

'It's nothing serious,' he snaps, defeating her intention, whatever that might be. 'Thank you.'

When he stands alone again behind the safety of the door, he hears her steps reluctantly descending the stairs and he knows that the siege, for the moment at least, is lifted. But he also feels oppressed, as if the room has just been emptied of a crowd. He becomes aware that his overcoat is heavy with rain and that his shoes and the ends of his trousers are steaming. He's cold and he feels a strong, uneasy desire for sleep. It's already getting dark in the room and the bulb throws only a dim light when he clicks the switch.

Searching his pockets, as he always does before removing a coat, he comes across the damp ball of the telegram, wedged into a tear in the lining. He takes it out and smooths the paper on the surface of the table.

MOTHER DEPARTED, it reads. YOU'LL COME I EXPECT

Jacob hasn't signed his name, but the short, ordered manner, the hints of a happier world and of his own threatened morality, are all unmistakably his. Economy is Jacob's genius, and he has a monk's intolerance of waste, whether it finds its form in sentiment or pleasure.

Matthew sits down in the grey light of the room and thinks, for the first time in months and in a dull state between drowsiness and pain, over the years of his childhood with Jacob and with the woman who has died. 'Mind, boys.' Out of the past, like the forms of a nightmare solidifying into life, their voices call to him again. 'Mind, boys.' Down the stairs, beyond the gate and along whatever road he takes, his mother's warning pursues him. 'Be home early, boys.' 'Hurry,' Jacob urges. 'Christmas is almost upon us.' 'Twelve days, Mother.' 'And the school examinations, boys. Isn't that right?'

Memories.

He brings them with him when he leaves, only to bring them back again when he recoils.

Now he has returned for the first time, and even here, across the neat abyss of the grave, her legacy reaches out to hurt him.

Against the black coat, against the grey drizzle and the sombre mood of the burial, like a clot of blood fixed on a coal, the red cover seems incongruous. Jacob hugs the Bible to his stomach, crossing the leather with his pale fingers and finding the attitude of death so familiar to his hands. His bowed head might be staring at the book, recalling its consolations.

The priest doesn't speak while he sprinkles the coffin, but his arm rises and casts with the rhythm of silent prayer. The holy water is lost somewhere in the heavy rain.

It's a sparse and chilling memorial.

Later, on the brow of the hill above the graveyard, Jacob and Matthew halt after the funeral, and since neither of them can hold the other's eyes, they look behind them along the valleys in the grass where they've climbed. In a while they grow restless and shift the grass and the stones beneath them with their shoes. Words will have to cover the open scars of their meeting.

'You'll stay at home?' Matthew asks.

'Yes,' Jacob says. 'I have the place to myself now.'

He infuses the words with his resigned optimism, but Matthew knows too well the dark ghosts which people emptiness. Virtues can be created from the most barren of lives. But not joy.

He says nothing, though, and they are silent for a while, the rain and the terror of some breach in their old distance driving them towards where they wouldn't choose to go, back to Dublin or to the sombre house where their childhood grew cold too early.

'Are you staying,' Jacob asks, 'for the night?'

Matthew shakes his head and looks at his watch.

'You don't believe?' Jacob asks then. 'You don't believe in the Faith?'

'No.'

'It's a pity. I think sometimes . . .' Jacob begins. He looks down at the Bible which is still in his hands and then holds it out, as a child reluctantly offers his world to be shared by another. 'I think at times . . . but perhaps you would like to read the Book. Give it a chance, do you know. Perhaps . . .'

Compassion shifts within Matthew, but he wishes he could see his brother's eyes. The disorder in Jacob's language is close to the chaos of tears, but what lies behind it . . . what lies behind it he can never penetrate.

'You may return it at any time, do you know,' Jacob continues.

'Perhaps in the spring, when the weather improves, you might bring it down. Perhaps in the spring . . .'

Jacob looks up at last. The eyes are inscrutable, an almost polite enquiry defending their meaning.

When Matthew turns and leaves, does Jacob watch him descending the hill? Does he listen until the noise of his brother's shoes biting into the gravel path is not real any more, but only the echoes of memory sounding in his mind? Does he turn too after a while and go back to their mother's grave, pursuing the dead?

'Were you down the country, Mr Rushford?' the girl asks him.

Impatient for his return, she stops him in the hallway of her mother's house.

'Were you down the country, Mr Rushford?'

Matthew stares at her. He wonders if she has entered his room while he's been away, if her slim fingers have probed in his secrets, if her brown eyes have read his brother's telegram, left on the table inside. For the second time that day, he feels the soft invitation to surrender attracting, and then repelling him. He opens his lips to speak, but tightens them again.

Confession, he thinks, standing in the hall with the draughts whipping his ankles, confession is like ecstasy or a heavy meal, a momentary joy, and then the hours, perhaps the years of discomfort afterwards.

'No,' he answers the landlady's daughter. 'No.'

What does she do when he turns away from her and climbs the stairs to his room? Does she feel a tear on her cheek?

As he undresses and lies down to sleep, he deliberately excludes her from his thoughts.

And yet, when he opens his eyes again, she is standing by his bed.

'Angela?' he calls.

The woman who looks back at him seems older, however, and appears to have different-coloured hair. A stranger. And yet, vaguely recognizable.

Confused, the old man waits for his sight to clear. When it does, she is still staring down at him. He waits then for the fog to lift from his mind. And she still stands there. Still smiles down at him.

Frightened, the old man tries to rise in his bed. He looks anxiously around his cottage. But nothing seems to have been taken. And there is no one else inside. Only the woman.

He sighs and lies back on the damp pillows, already exhausted from his efforts.

And then, as she moves to rearrange his pillows, he suddenly remembers. A few days earlier, when he had his second attack, while walking along the road to the village, the woman stopped her car and gave him a lift back to the cottage.

He can't remember asking her to return, however. He wonders why she has. And indeed, how she has managed to get in.

'Are you a nurse?' he asks her weakly.

The Investigation

We heard later that Inspector Taafe had joined the private sector on the *Monday morning* after her resignation from the force. One of her brothers-in-law, a former assistant commissioner, owned a security firm at the top end of the market, advising banks and multinationals, and he recruited from his old contacts in the guards and the army. There was a drain on higher ranks from the state sector at the time anyway, and like they used to say about emigration to the United States, it was the brightest ones who seemed to have left.

It was obvious that the inspector had been planning her move for a long while, and probably only the timing of it was changed by events. Her salary was about fifty per cent better in her new job and she had a company car, along with a lot of other perks. As one of the lads said, it was a terrible price to have to pay for failure.

In the way that those who are left have to get on with it and make the best of it, we managed to see her departure as evidence of a long-standing lack of commitment on her part. She wasn't putting the work in, we told each other, because she already knew that she was leaving. There were too many like that. And the job was better off without them.

But still, you couldn't help dreaming about what you could do with her new pay and conditions. And you couldn't help envying her for being in the position to treat crime only as a danger to her employer, a threat she had to deflect, rather than an incurable social problem. In the private sector, the fact that the criminal is going somewhere else after you've knocked him sideways is none of your business. The little old lady in the corner shop with the blood-filled syringe held to her neck? It's none of your business. Unless you own the shop. In the guards you do what you can. In the private sector you do what you're paid to. There's a big difference. But it would only become obvious if *everybody* did what they were paid to do.

During your first year in the guards, when you go in all idealistic and then see the devastation crime wreaks on people's lives, you're inclined to take it personally. But you soon learn the hard truth that nothing you do individually is going to make much difference. You have to block off your emotions. To save yourself, you have to be hard. After a while, it can badly affect your personality and your private life. That's the real attraction of the private sector, I think. Your emotions are not involved and you can keep them for those that want them.

The reason we heard so much so quickly about the inspector's new career was because Dennison was suspended on full pay in late-November, pending an investigation into the alleged assault on the inspector's teenage daughter. Not that anyone told us this at the time. Dennison's desk was just empty one morning. We assumed that he was on sick leave. Even when his work was passed to someone else, we thought he'd extended his leave, and it was only when one of the other lads finally rang him that we found out the truth. I think detectives from another unit investigating the alleged assault had called to his flat and just told him not to bother showing up for work.

Whatever your opinion of Dennison, the treatment of him was typically sneaky and insensitive. As soon as there's a whiff of bad publicity about you, the authorities don't want to know you any more. You're on your own. You hear stories about uniformed lads defending themselves from attack in the streets and then having to face assault charges from the gougers responsible, with no support at all from their superiors. Things like that contribute to the disillusion and bad morale in the force.

What had happened with Dennison was that the inspector had threatened a civil action. Nothing had been done about her original complaint, and while she was still a member of the force, she had to keep going through the official channels. The minute she was out, though, she had lawyers crawling all over the case.

You might wonder what all this had to do with the hunt for a killer who left stories for the guards that might or might not be the stories of his own life, but I would have thought the answer was pretty obvious. One more obstacle, that's what it was. One more distraction. One more source of disruption. Otherwise, it had no relevance at all.

There was a possible exception at one time.

Among the items found in the clear-out of the inspector's desk was a paper by another psychologist she'd consulted about the narratives from the graves. The thing about this man that distinguished him from all the others was that he described himself as a narrative psychologist. His view was that we all, to some extent, create the stories of our own lives. Which is fairly obvious if you think about it, since the one thing everyone can tell you, even the most uneducated criminal, is their own life story. Whether the details are true or false is beside the point. If you're convinced that you were abandoned as a child, then that will influence your actions and how you deal with people.

It was suggested by the psychologist that the writer of the narratives left in the graves was probably aware of these theories. So the narratives themselves were either an exercise in mockery, as he put it, or a deliberate attempt to blur the real story left by the crimes, or probably both together.

I found the essay tough going and I didn't understand some of the technical language, but I also thought that it was interesting. I remember thinking that it could have changed things if it had been discovered earlier, and that it still might change things. But this man was never consulted by the unit again. I know why, too. It sounded as if he was just in the business of offering excuses and alibis for criminals. 'You're currently torturing rival drug pushers?' as Jimmy Coyne put it. 'You must have had a difficult childhood, then.' But probably even worse than that, his theories flew in the face of standard police procedure, which is to understand the crime, not the criminal.

So many things like that got lost in the mess we were stuck in at the time. I was in the middle of interviewing car owners in north County Wicklow, for instance, when I was told to drop everything and present myself as a witness to the alleged assault by Dennison. It pissed me off. I told the investigating officers the same as I'd told everyone else. From what I saw, I couldn't tell whether Dennison made a move on the girl or whether the girl faked it. They wouldn't leave it at that. They grilled me on it for a couple of days, checking and double checking everything. By the time it was finished, I was too tired and too annoyed to do my own job properly.

But that wasn't the end of it for me. Not by a long shot. Before they made any decision on whether or not to charge Dennison, I met him one morning on the street. He claimed he was surprised to bump into me, but I'm convinced that he must have been watching and following me, waiting for his opportunity.

He looked worse than I had ever seen him before. His eyes were dog tired and staring all the time and they were completely blackened around the sockets. The complexion on his cheeks was really unhealthy, a high flush that looked almost like a rash. His movements were nervous and jerky. And his clothes hadn't been cared for.

He suggested going for a coffee. I didn't fancy it. It sounded to me as if it could get too complicated. But I hadn't the heart to turn him down.

I said, 'If we can make it quick, because I'm meeting Fergal in about twenty minutes.'

We ended up in an odd place off Grafton Street in the city centre, an expensive joint that served very good coffee. What I mean by odd is that it was Dennison's choice and I thought it a strange one for him. The tables were crowded together. Apart from the fact that there was very little room between them to squeeze in and out, you could hear almost everything going on at any of the neighbouring tables.

Actually, at first I thought this was a good thing, because it would help to keep the conversation trivial. But in between the time we ordered and the time the waitress brought the coffees, Dennison broke down. Literally. He just lost it. He had his elbows on the table and his head in his hands. He was looking down. I thought he was just fiddling with the napkin and the cutlery. But suddenly his shoulders started shaking. He drew a breath through his nose and when it came back out he was crying. I couldn't believe it. I still couldn't see his eyes, but I watched the tears dropping off his cheeks and falling into the red napkin underneath, where they started spreading through the tissue.

For a while things went horribly quiet at the tables around us. People tried not to be too obvious about looking and listening, but their curiosity was only natural. Across the aisle there were two fellas dressed in black, both of them with closely cropped hair and polo necks, who were staring more openly.

I hadn't a clue what to do. Maybe I'm as bad as all the rest who think that boys don't cry and I suppose I would have been better equipped to deal with a woman in that condition, but *anyone* crying in public, even children, I find upsetting. To make it worse, the waitress arrived with the coffee and stood there, totally at a loss because Dennison was slumped over the area where she wanted to put the cups and plates. Everything seemed to freeze for God knows how long. 'Put it on my side,' I said finally. So I ended up with two coffees and two Danish pastries.

Strong emotions ruin your appetite, though. Have you ever noticed that? You don't have taste buds any more until everything is resolved, and then you're ravenous. Anyway, it seemed sort of heartless to sip coffee and chew pastries with a distraught man at your table.

He took a long time about it and the coffees went cold during the wait, but Dennison finally managed to pull himself together enough to tell his story. You don't always believe other people's stories in the guards, of course, and I was fresh from that psychologist's report on the narratives, but like I said earlier, sometimes it doesn't matter whether the details are true or false, what the person believes will explain their behaviour.

The basic facts were clear enough. Ten years earlier Dennison had married a country girl from his own parish. When he was transferred, they came to live in Dublin. They had two sons, one aged eight now, the other six. Three years ago, for whatever reasons, Dennison and his wife divorced. His wife was given custody of the kids. She went back down to the country afterwards, so obviously Dennison had limited access to his boys. Again for one reason or another, he had seen less and less of them over the past year.

That's as far as the facts went.

I'm not going to speculate on the ins and outs of Dennison's relationship with his wife. Any guard will tell you that the worst thing to be called out to is what is known as a domestic, a family dispute. The emotions are so entangled that it's impossible to get at the truth. To put it in a way that psychologists might have, one narrative completely contradicts the other, even though the two people have been living together for years.

For all I know, the woman could have been depressed because she wanted to be home in the country among her own people and the pressures of city life really did have her verging on being a nutcase, like Dennison described her. But for all I know, Dennison, like a lot of male guards, could have been sleeping around, taking up with every bit of skirt that threw itself at a uniform. I just don't know.

What *was* obvious to me, though, was that Dennison loved his sons. This wasn't just an act. I know it's easy to fake devotion, with the tear in the eye and the photograph in the wallet, but in Dennison's case the feelings were backed up by all those boring statistics that proud parents carry around with them and that have the rest of us grinding our teeth. He could tell you every game they'd played in their under-age Gaelic

Football teams, every goal they'd prevented, every point they'd scored. He could tell you the details of their school reports, their successes, their disappointments, their hopes. He could list all the Playstation games they owned and the ones they'd grown tired of and didn't play any more.

Listening to him, I started to understand his behaviour over the last year or so, his anger, his turning in on himself, his drinking and his despair, and most of all his dislike of women and the campaign he waged against us. Listening to him, I even started to like him a little bit.

It was typical of him, though, that he didn't pick up on this shift in my feelings. He was too eaten up by resentment, which I'm not saying wasn't justified, considering the lengths he had to go to just to keep in contact with his own kids.

We might have reached the point of agreement, but just as I was softening towards him, and just as he was cooling his anger, I found myself part of a political meeting instead of the intimate conversation I thought I was in. The two fellas in black from the other table suddenly appeared on either side of Dennison and, without a by-your-leave, sat down on the vacant chairs. I was too taken aback to ask them what they were doing.

They were very intense, the two of them. Very concerned. They laid their hands on Dennison's shoulders to console him. They addressed him by his first name. 'Take it easy, Tommy,' they said. Then it dawned on me. This meeting had been pre-arranged. I'd been set up in a way. And it annoyed me.

Now, it obviously didn't negate everything that had gone before, Dennison's tears and his genuine love for his boys, but I'd have to say that it definitely coloured my attitude to it. It made all those personal things political, as I said. I sat back in my chair. I wasn't conscious of doing it, but I was obviously withdrawing, putting a distance between myself and the other three.

Dennison introduced the two newcomers. They were from some organization he said the name of, but which I didn't catch or can't remember. I don't know whether they came with the intention of converting or recruiting me, but they were very eager to get their message across. One talked about the injustices of a judicial system that automatically granted the custody of children to the mother, regardless of her competence. The other talked about the prejudices of a society dominated by what he called 'negative feminist values'. And they were both full of aggressive questions. Did I know that fathers were always presented in court custody battles as potentially violent rather than loving, as in need of psychological assessment before access could be granted, as monsters that couldn't be trusted with their own children? Did I know that most boys would never have a male primary teacher, that their values were subjected to derision by women from an early age, that the education system as a whole derides masculinity?

'This is about getting justice for Tommy,' one said. 'But it's about more than Tommy. It's about justice for all men.'

'Tommy explained how you championed the notion that women too can be violent,' the other added. 'And I'm sure, that like us, you find the current victimization of men abhorrent.'

I was feeling a little overwhelmed. I tried to interrupt a number of times, but their fervour kept carrying everything before it. 'Hang on a minute,' I managed finally. 'I have a question for Dennison.'

'What is it?' one of the fellas in black asked.

'It's for Dennison,' I insisted.

He looked up at me. What I saw on his crumpled face was despair. I wondered if he'd gone to these people looking for help and advice and found their big agendas and political rhetoric dwarfing his own pain, and I felt for him again.

'Why did you give me the second draft of that profile?' I asked him. 'You know the one I'm talking about. We never got on. You'd always rubbished my work.'

'If I could prove that the bitch was concealing evidence,' he said, 'I could discredit her. They weren't going to believe it from me, though. You were the one for that.'

It made sense, in a warped kind of way.

I wanted to go at that stage, before we got round to the dangerous topic of what evidence I might be giving against him, but even though I insisted that I was already late for my boyfriend, I had trouble getting out, since I was trapped on the inside of the table. I called the waitress for the bill and used her as cover.

As I was leaving, I remember thinking to myself that I might be in for a long campaign from Dennison and his mates, but three days later the authorities charged Dennison with assault and after that we couldn't meet except through his legal team.

*

Dennison's arrest and release on bail got a small paragraph in a few of the papers. Even though he was named, it was never mentioned that he was part of the unit investigating the Wicklow Mountain murders or that his alleged victim was his own commander's teenage daughter. It was always done in such a way as to ignore the connections. DUBLIN GARDA CHARGED WITH ASSAULT. That sort of thing. Nothing special.

What had happened was this. The media gunslingers that led the posse out of town in hot pursuit of the drugs baron who'd killed their colleague Karen Stokes had gone quiet and obedient again, now that it was obvious they'd made complete fools of themselves. After a couple of sharp reminders that they were supposed to be reporting and not leading investigations, they were eating out of the hands of the Garda Press Office once more. The vast majority of these correspondents had no other steady source of material anyway, so they were stuck.

The galling thing for us was reading the upbeat headlines every day, when we were actually bogged down and getting nowhere. MINISTER COMMITS NEW RESOURCES TO ELITE UNITS, we were told. NEW DIRECTION IN MURDER INVESTIGATIONS, we were promised. And finally, NEW HEAD FOR SPECIAL GARDA UNIT.

This appointment was finalized two weeks after the inspector's resignation. I don't know what took them so long and I don't know on what basis they make these decisions, but the man we all expected to be working for, the superintendent who'd been groomed for it, wasn't given the job. This sounds unbelievable, but it's true. I think he'd gone to America as part of a liaison group working with the FBI on international terrorism.

Instead, we got Superintendent Gerry Mullane.

To read about him in the papers you'd think his father was Sherlock Holmes and his mother V. I. Warshawski. You couldn't deny that he'd had a great career so far. A Dublin man born and bred, he'd pulled himself out of his working-class background and up through the ranks at a steady rate of knots over the years. Everywhere he'd gone, he got results. Most things he'd put his hand to had been a success. The only problem was, all his previous experience was confined to dealing with paramilitaries and political extremists.

I still didn't know that much about serial killers. What I did understand, though, is that their motives are always private, and peculiar to themselves. The motives of terrorists and revolutionaries are out there for everyone to see. The motives of serial murderers are hidden, even from the people trying to track them down.

Superintendent Mullane was a tough, no-nonsense sort of fella. He probably had a tough, no-nonsense sort of philosophy on life. He gave a hundred per cent commitment, and he demanded the same from his staff. But I'm not sure that he had a clue how to deal with the files on the Wicklow Mountains murders. He was out of his depth with the psychological reports and the profiles and the rambling communications from the killer. I don't think he ever got away from his old habits of mind. The narratives found in the graves were like political manifestos to him. Their author had to be *saying* something. Their meaning had to be somewhere on the surface, had to be something basic, like it is with all political manifestos. I think that's how he genuinely felt about the material.

Because nothing in his career had prepared him for all this confusion and all these conflicting signs, his instinct was to simplify. But, as the days went by, you could see that he was getting more and more frustrated, because the material just wouldn't reduce itself. The type of man he was, though, he still had to bring a plan of action to our first conference with him. Admitting that he was lost was out of the question. And just discussing the case wasn't good enough. So he presented us with his plan.

He probably didn't understand our reaction, but when he announced that he'd got approval to locate and check on elderly people who were living alone in the mountain regions where the three bodies were found – the very issue the inspector had resigned on after she was refused the same request – we all just groaned cynically. I mean, you get used to the idiocies of a bureaucracy in any state job, but sometimes the madness still manages to surprise you. I think the superintendent suspected that we were complaining about the extra workload. In the initial stages, he hurried to explain, the operation wasn't going to involve us, except as co-ordinators. The local Garda stations in the various areas would be responsible for house-to-house enquiries. If anything suspicious turned up, we'd be called in to take it from there.

I don't think the superintendent took this course of action because he believed in the inspector's theory that there was a predictable pattern to the murders and the narratives. I think he was deeply uncomfortable with all the psychological stuff and probably considered it a waste of time. He made his move out of desperation. There was nothing else to do. The only alternative was sitting around and coming up with even more theories.

I asked if we were still working to the psychological profile supplied by Michelle Condon, and if so, which of the two drafts we were supposed to be using. 'What are the differences?' he wondered. When I told him that they were exactly the same, except that one suggested a male offender and the other wasn't sure about the gender, he told me to prepare a report on the feasibility of a female being responsible for the murders.

'What about the enquiries into vehicle transactions?' I asked.

'Leave that aside for the moment,' he said. 'It doesn't seem to be going anywhere, does it?'

One of the other lads, trawling through lists of university graduates on the suggestion of the original profile, wanted to know if he should continue looking just at males, go back over everything to include females, or wait for my report to come in?

It opened a can of worms, because it suddenly showed the awful dangers of what we'd been doing while we were relying on the first profile. The people who draw up these things don't claim that they're infallible, or even exhaustive. Like anybody else, they're going to make their successes known, but you won't hear too much from them about all the ones that were way off the mark. What had made it so dangerous for us wasn't the inadequacy of the report. It was our own desperation, our failure to come up with any other leads, our total reliance on the parameters of the first profile. We'd been considering only males. Now, if we were going to include women as well, everything that had been done before would have to be repeated. Considering we hadn't actually *got* anywhere, and were even less likely to succeed second time round, this was soul-destroying.

Personally, I thought the job I'd been given was a waste of time. It *sounded* important. The unit hadn't openly addressed the possibility of a female killer before. Put like this, it even sounded like what I'd been agitating for all along. It also sounded decisive. 'Have a report on my desk!' Actually, it was the opposite. It was the oldest time-waster in the book. Instead of making a decision, you make a report. Then you have to decide whether to adopt the report or not. And by the time you've sent it back for clarification, hopefully you'll have moved on to another job and the report will be someone else's responsibility.

Why not just keep an open mind about the gender of the killer? I thought. No matter how brilliant my report was going to be, that was the best recommendation it was going to come up with, anyway. I also resented being taken off what I was doing, which I considered much more likely to turn up something significant.

And I was right.

I mean, at the end of all my research and consultations, I could tell you that a Marriage and Relationship Counselling Services Report issued the previous June had come to the conclusion that women are more likely than men to inflict violence on their domestic partners and that in the letters columns of the newspapers this report had been welcomed by the male correspondents and rejected by the female ones. I could tell you that women have maimed, killed, robbed, burgled, infected with AIDS, carjacked and committed arson in surprising numbers over the last two decades. I could tell you that the women who did these things were mothers, housewives, students, daughters, workers, company directors and beauty queens. I could tell you that the much-loved theory that women commit violence only out of self-protection and after years of abuse is true in less than half reported cases. On the other hand, I could also tell you that of the 587 homicides in Ireland during the period 1972–91, 545 of them were committed by men and 42 by women.

What difference did it make, other than opening my eyes a little?

'What's the story, Galetti?' the fellas on the unit kept asking me. 'Are we looking for a man or a woman?'

The guards sent out to check on vulnerable old people living in the Wicklow Mountains were under instructions not to frighten anyone with warnings. They were to present the visit as a normal call, part of a new scheme to keep the force in close contact with the public. They were to sit down and have a chat, and a cup of tea if necessary, and quietly suss out if there had been any strangers in the area, any signs of unusual activity, anything suspicious at all.

There was a particular reason why this low-key approach might work without setting off any alarm bells. One of the odd things about the murders we were investigating was that the series of killings hadn't created a panic anywhere. Usually, a cluster of violent deaths in a rural area, quiet and peaceful beforehand, will have the residents terrified. They'll start putting extra locks on their doors and windows, start escorting their children everywhere and start watching for outsiders.

Usually, the murder of lone women like Mary Corbett and Karen Stokes will spark off a frenzy in the tabloids about the predatory serial killer living in our midst.

None of this had happened. Partly because most of the details linking the cases hadn't been released. Partly because journalists were on the back foot after their excesses on the Karen Stokes case. But mostly, I think, because only the *bodies* had been found in the Wicklow Mountains. The *killings* could have happened anywhere. That's the way people think. It won't happen to me. Not on my own doorstep.

The most obvious members of the force to check on the old people in the county were the community guards, since they were already involved in that kind of outreach work. John Driscoll, who was stationed in Wicklow town, was one of these. He admitted later that in the beginning, when he was setting down his list of people to call on, he decided to push an old man named Matthew Rushford to the back of the queue. He needn't have admitted this. A list is a list. *Somebody* has to be at the bottom of it. But once he told us, we wanted to know why.

For days afterwards he wouldn't explain properly. He sat on the green settee in the front room of his little semi-detached house in Wicklow, slumped forward, just shaking his head. I don't think he ever recovered from the guilt he felt. He had a wife and a young family, three kids, all of them under six years old. I don't know how he'd got on with them before that, obviously, but he pushed them away from him afterwards, not knowing how to deal with their concern for him. I remember his wife, a lovely-looking blonde woman, in the kitchen of their house one afternoon, bent over the sink, her body shaking with the way she was crying, and their eldest girl – the way kids do when they can't understand something in adults – just standing there staring at her. Overnight, the woman had found herself with a different husband. The fella who'd been funny and confident, who played Gaelic football for the county and soccer for one of the top amateur teams, who went off to work happily every day, that fella was gone, maybe never to return. In his place, as she put it, she had her own father all over again. A difficult man, out of reach, and probably clinically depressed. He wouldn't even go for counselling at first, no doubt convinced that he could deal with the problem himself, and it wasn't until his superior ordered him to do it that he took it up. I can't imagine it did him much good. They never managed to get out of him why he deliberately placed Matthew Rushford at the bottom of the list.

Anyway.

When John Driscoll finally did get round to visiting the old man, on a morning in mid-December, he went there with another guard, who had a summons to serve in the same area. Matthew Rushford had a cottage and a small bit of land in a place called Trooperstown Hill, which is about twelve kilometres inland from the coastal town of Wicklow and much further south than any of the locations where the other bodies were found. The minor roads that criss-cross Trooperstown Hill are all well dotted with houses and they pass through a couple of villages, including Trooperstown itself. But the cottage was set about a kilometre back from one of these roads, at the end of an overgrown dirt track, with woodland behind it and on either side.

The front door was locked and the curtains were closed on the windows when John Driscoll and his mate drove up. It was raining, a real miserable pig of a day, and it was dark as dusk, even though it was still the middle of the morning. One of the gutters was broken on the roof of the cottage and the rainwater was splashing down, a little to the side of the front door. You couldn't stand there knocking without getting drenched.

There was no answer. They thought the old man might be still asleep. He'd hardly be out anywhere in weather like that. So they decided to finish their other bits of business and drop back later. They asked along the road and in the village if anyone had seen Matthew Rushford around. Nobody had. Nobody was surprised by that either, though. The old man kept to himself. So it was only when the two guards learned in Laragh that Rushford hadn't collected his last old-age pension allowance at the post office there that they got concerned.

They went straight back to the cottage. The door was still locked. And the curtains hadn't been moved in the windows. This was a bad sign. If the old man had been asleep, he would have been woken by the earlier knocking and at least disturbed the curtains to look out. Probably, he would have opened thcm. The two guards went round the sides and the back, checking everything. There was no sign of a break-in, nothing particularly suspicious. Even so, they took it on themselves to force an entry after failing again to get any response to knocking on the doors and windows.

They got in through the back door, which didn't give them much resistance anyway. Inside, they found the cottage empty. There was no one there at all, either in the smaller room that was used for sleeping or in the larger one that served as the kitchen and the living room and everything else. Funnily enough, the front door had been locked from the inside, the back door from the outside.

The old man could have gone off to stay with relatives for Christmas, of course. He wouldn't have felt it necessary to let anyone else know. And it would explain why he'd missed collecting his pension. But John Driscoll had been in this cottage before. Although there were no signs that any disturbance had taken place and as far as he could see nothing was missing, not even the one item of any value, an antique fire screen, he was convinced that someone else had had the run of the place lately. The interior was too clean. It was gleaming. All the surfaces had been scrubbed. All the clutter had been tidied away. You might think that some over-enthusiastic relative or neighbour had got carried away with themselves, but not if you already knew that the old man was very particular about anyone touching his stuff. If he'd been able to, he wouldn't have allowed it.

The two guards decided to radio local detectives for their opinion. And the detectives immediately contacted us. So from the time John Driscoll and his mate stepped back out of the rear door, the cottage and surrounded area were treated as a crime scene that had to be preserved.

We interviewed John Driscoll as soon as we got there. He was already getting uneasy by that stage, bothered by his vague, mysterious sense of guilt, and some of his answers were almost evasive, but we agreed with him that the signs were suspicious. Within an hour we had a crew from the Technical Bureau at the scene. They couldn't find any evidence of a crime. In fact, because of the way everything had been so thoroughly vacuumed and washed and polished, they couldn't find anything much at first. But like the rest of us, they thought all the sparkle was a dead give-away. It was too efficient to be real. Nothing obvious, such as blood, ever turned up, and the vacuum cleaner that had been used was never found, but gradually, in little crevices here and there, or on curtain material and on the edge of the ash pile where a fire had been lit in the grate, the technicians lifted a substantial number of human hairs, animal hairs and clothing fibres. They took these away for analysis, along with the old man's clothes and the few items from the cupboards in the kitchen area.

Until the forensic reports came in, the disappearance of Matthew Rushford was officially treated as a missing persons case. Because of the circumstances, though, we obviously put a lot more resources into it than into a normal alert. We interviewed everyone in the surrounding area. They didn't want to know, particularly. The old man wasn't liked. He was reclusive and bad-tempered. There were stories that he'd killed or maimed some mountain sheep that had wandered on to his bit of land to graze, and even though we never found any proof of these accusations, they gave an indication of how deep people's resentment was. To the kids in the neighbourhood he was the bogeyman, so dangerous that he might eat you, but only after doing all the other unmentionable things.

Evil has to have a face, I suppose. But we always seem to get the features wrong. Good has to have a face too, of course. It was only two weeks to Christmas at that time and people were building up to it. Every house you went into had its Christmas tree in the front room, its flashing lights in the window, its decorations and its excited kids. Nobody wanted the festival spoiled with talk about old men, unless they had a white beard and dressed in red and drove an old sleigh that was powered by reindeers. Could you blame them? From our point of view, yes. But in any society at any given time, the guard's point of view is only a nuisance for people going about their business.

We got one break. A little man with a list of convictions as long as your arm for breaking and entering came into Wicklow Garda Station of his own accord with a tale so odd that they passed it on to us. I never met Robbie Finn. Apparently he was a weaselly little fella and the sort it wasn't wise to turn your back on. A very unlikely hero. I read the transcripts of the interviews two lads on the unit had with him.

According to Finn, on the first Monday in December, past eleven at night, he pulled off the road, into the dense woods that stretched for about two kilometres behind Matthew Rushford's cottage. God knows what he was doing there. He could have been hunting illegally or burying or retrieving stolen goods, but he might have been cutting down small Christmas trees for the black market. 'Would it be all right if I said I just stopped for a piss?' he wondered. He could have stopped to masturbate, for all we cared about it. Whatever he was doing, in any case, he noticed another car through the trees. This was when he'd already walked some distance into the woods. Anyone in a car would have to make a big effort to get to the spot. It was so dark, he couldn't see the make or the model. He thought it might be a family saloon from its shape. What he did see was someone walking around it. He didn't fancy any company, of course, so he turned around and left. He was certain, however, that the figure was a woman. 'Unless it was a man with two small footballs under his shirt,' he said. He didn't go back to that particular spot again, but he was confident that he could identify it in daylight with a little bit of help. And that's exactly what he did.

The day after the Technical Bureau organized a fingertip search and lifted further samples from this site in the woods, the early results came through from the laboratory on the hairs found in Matthew Rushford's cottage. Most of the human hairs obviously belonged to the old man himself. But the analysis of the rest excited us. Under microscopic examination, they had been revealed as identical to the hair retrieved from the grave of Karen Stokes. The lab had another, more complex and reliable process to get through, called neutron activation analysis, which identified fourteen different elements in each hair. They were also hopeful that a section of the root on one of the hairs from the cottage would provide live cell tissue for DNA analysis. But pending the results of these tests, we could assume that the same young woman who had the unknown link to the grave of Karen Stokes had also been in Matthew Rushford's cottage. And judging by the animal hairs found in the cottage – they were also identical to the single specimen found in the grave – we could equally assume that she owned or lived close to a greyhound.

It was this information that forced the superintendent to upgrade the case from missing persons to a murder enquiry. Given what we had, with news of a mysterious car lurking in the woods, we knew that the old man, or his body, might be anywhere in the vast areas covered by the Wicklow Mountains. Nevertheless, we decided to organize a detailed search of the woods, from the back door of the cottage to the site where Robbie Finn had spotted the car and the woman. It was the most likely location for a nearby grave. And even if we didn't find a body, there was always the chance of discovering further evidence.

Early on Tuesday morning, exactly a week before Christmas Day, as dark grey clouds closed in over us and a heavy drizzle started to fall, we set out from the back of the cottage to sweep the woods. We had a few dog teams with us, animals trained in search and rescue, and we had the use of a new radar unit for penetrating the ground that the commissioner was eager to try out. Most of the going was downhill, because the house was almost on the peak of Trooperstown Hill. This wasn't really an advantage. It's actually more difficult to go slowly downwards, because you have to keep working your leg muscles all the time to control your descent. For a while, as the trees sheltered us from the rain, the conditions weren't so bad. But as the water got too heavy for the branches to hold and started dripping down on top of us, it became very unpleasant. Things went quiet for a time afterwards, as people got more sodden and depressed. Nobody was talking any more. You couldn't even hear the handlers encouraging the dogs. You heard the drip of the rainwater falling on the vegetation. You heard the squelch of your own boots in the soggy ground. You got used to the quietness, and felt yourself sinking deeper and deeper into it.

And then, suddenly, there was total chaos. People started shouting. The dogs started barking. The handlers started whistling to restrain them.

It was over to my right. Not very far, I estimated, although I couldn't see anything clearly through the rain and the mist and the trees. I seemed to be the nearest detective from our unit. I asked the two uniforms on either side of me to come in a bit and close the gap when I left, and then I started running across towards the noise.

It was immediately obvious what had excited everybody.

What they were now standing around and pointing to wasn't a two- or three-month-old site, overgrown with vegetation and almost invisible, like the others had been. This was a freshly dug and fairly shallow grave. Some effort had been made to conceal it with fallen branches and by redirecting a nearby creeper, but the mound of newly turned soil, loosened even more by the recent rain, couldn't be missed or mistaken. To mark it even more clearly, one of the dogs had burrowed excitedly at the base before its handler arrived and had uncovered a badly blistered and discoloured human foot.

I stayed there all day this time, from the discovery of the grave to the removal of the corpse, sometimes helping, sometimes only watching, as the body was carefully exhumed. I wasn't aware of being wet and cold, even though I came out of it with a chill that I couldn't shake off until after Christmas. I knew that this one was different. Even with my limited experience and the fact that I understood very little about pathology, I could see that this body had been recently buried. We were told later that the estimated time of death was fourteen to seventeen days previously, but we were already working off an assumption identical to that before the autopsy was finished.

For the first time, we felt as if we could reach out and touch the killer. We were close to them at last. This wasn't another case of trailing months behind events, when all we had was a badly decomposed corpse and not even the faintest shadow of the killer other than the ones they deliberately left for us in those mocking narratives. All the rest of the cases had left us grasping at thin air, at something so elusive that we couldn't even imagine its shape, whether it was man or woman, young or old. But now we could sense a physical presence. We could sense a woman moving around the cottage and cleaning it up. We could imagine the car parked in the woods below the hill and the physical journey from there to the back door of the cottage, the same physical journey we had retraced and experienced ourselves. We could imagine the hurried digging of a new grave. Our quarry was tangible. Not a ghost any longer. But human. And therefore within reach.

That's why so many of us from the unit stayed at the grave site all that day, first outside in the rain, and then under the shelter of the large tent that was erected. I'd say that there weren't any of us by then whose lives hadn't been changed by this investigation and this long hunt. I know that I suggested earlier that most guards don't carry the work home with them. And we don't. But you can't go into a job – *any* job, I don't care what it is – and face your own failure day after day, face your own inability to do that job properly, day after day, for more than a year now, and that failure not have a terrible effect on you. I think we were all so low by then that the experience had brought us together. Or at least, had prepared us for coming together. I think there was a feeling among us, particularly among the ones who'd been there from the start, that outsiders couldn't understand what we were going through.

We agreed on three things, those of us who stood there in the rain while waiting for the pathologist and the crew from the Technical Bureau to arrive. We assumed that the body in the fresh grave was that of Matthew Rushford and we assumed that it had been buried with another narrative. We were right on both these counts, as it turned out. But then, that didn't take a genius to predict. The third thing we decided was that we would find the woman who had left her hairs behind her in the old man's cottage. It didn't matter what the killer's narratives suggested or what eyewitnesses thought they saw, the physical evidence proved that a woman had been in that cottage and we would find her. If that meant going back over all the work that been done already, but this time looking

for a woman, then we would do that. If we couldn't do it in official time –
in other words if the superintendent disagreed with our assessment and
wanted to take the investigation in a different direction – we'd still get it
done, somehow or other.

I was asked by the sergeant for an update on the report I was doing
into the feasibility of a female killer. I gave everyone my findings up to
that point, explaining that, by and large, the whole shooting gallery
refused to believe that women could be vicious, self-interested killers –
police forces, the media, fiction writers and psychologists – but that the
evidence proved the opposite.

'I'm sorry, Galetti,' the sergeant told me, 'but we passed that barrier
five hours ago. We're looking for a woman.'

And I didn't mind. If anything, I was glad.

You could say that at last someone seemed to have taken charge, at last
we had a leader in Sergeant Mullery, but I honestly believe that without
us coming together like we did no one could have led us anywhere. I also
believe that it was only in that moment, standing in the rain on the side
of a mountain in Wicklow, that we finally gave ourselves any real chance
of finding the killer.

In the early stages of the exhumation of Matthew Rushford, we were all
baffled by the condition of the exposed parts of the naked corpse. To us,
it seemed an awful lot more blistered and inflamed in some areas than
you'd expect from a body that was only three weeks at most in the
ground, and then a lot harder and yellower in other areas than we'd ever
seen in a corpse before. But we also knew that there are too many
variables influencing decomposition, like soil and temperature and
moisture on the one hand, and age and health and cause of death on the
other. Questions can be a distraction in the early stages of a medical
examination. So we didn't ask. The pathologist – a tight man with his
opinions anyway, as we knew – didn't volunteer anything. And it wasn't
until the genitals and the head were uncovered that the truth dawned on
us.

For once, the fact that both the corpse's ears had been sliced off didn't
draw the first of the outraged comments. Everyone noticed the
mutilation, of course. But everyone responded first to the other piece of
savagery. There was no hair left on the old man's body.

Human hair won't decay, even when it falls out. It outlasts everything

151

except the skeleton and the only foolproof way of destroying it is with fire or acid. In this case, Matthew Rushford's hair had been burned. We were told later that it seemed to have been done with a blowtorch, which someone had methodically worked along the surface of the body from the feet upwards. It hadn't been done inside the cottage, obviously. There were no signs of burning or smoke damage in there. They reckoned it had probably been done in the open, on some sort of base that was then disposed of somewhere else.

We were also told that the old man was still alive while his lower legs were being burnt, but that he seemed to have died by the time the torch was applied to his knees and beyond. At first, this sounded like someone trying to be too clever, but it was obvious enough once it was explained. A living body reacts to burning with inflammation and blistering. A corpse doesn't. The skin of a corpse becomes hard and yellowish under flames.

It was further suggested by the pathologist that the old man's heart might have given out under the shock and the trauma. No other definitive cause of death could be established.

Needless to say, we weren't inclined to accept that suggestion. For a start, none of the other victims had been burned, and therefore the same explanation couldn't be applied to *their* deaths. Probably more importantly, there was no evidence that Matthew Rushford had been assaulted or restrained, no contusions to suggest that he had been knocked out or tied down. 'He was already dying,' we said, '*before* the burning started. So what was killing him?' I think Dr Craig, the pathologist, got professionally offended by our persistence and by the implication that something was being missed by the medical team. He got more stubborn instead of more co-operative. He went through the official reports with us again and again. The toxicological analysis of the blood. No poisons. No drugs, other than alcohol, and that in small quantities. The analysis of the stomach contents: porridge, milk, vodka, tea, bread, butter.

'I will not speculate,' Craig said prissily. 'I'm a scientist. Like you, I'm interested only in facts. And the fact is, I do not know what the cause of death is. If I do not know what the cause of death is, I will not risk misdirecting the investigation with a guess.'

A row started when the sergeant suggested that maybe we should get someone who *did* know. 'This isn't a four-month corpse too badly decomposed to work with,' he pointed out. 'This man was killed two weeks ago.' The way he spoke his mind didn't endear him to the authorities and landed him in particular trouble with the superintendent, who was a stickler for internal discipline. But it made him very popular with us.

When we were discussing it among ourselves afterwards, we came to the conclusion that Matthew Rushford must have been already unconscious and on the point of death when the blowtorch was lit. You'd have to accept, therefore, that the killer *thought* the old man was dead, was surprised to discover that he wasn't, and probably waited until there was no more doubt before scorching the rest of the body. The burning hadn't been done as torture, in other words, for the twisted pleasure of the murderer. It had been done for the same reasons that the inside of the cottage had been vacuumed and scrubbed and polished. The killer could feel us closing in. In much the same way as we were coming across glimpses of the murderer, they could also catch sight of us. We were that close. All the burning and cleaning had been done to destroy evidence that they knew we would otherwise find.

There was a touch of panic about this, we felt. It didn't fit with the pattern of the other killings. In previous cases we'd been lagging a whole lap behind, so to speak, finding things only when we were told to find them, reading only what the killer wanted us to read, running around in hopeless circles. Now, the killer was no longer totally in control. Things weren't going to script any more. They were slipping away and falling apart. And since absolute power, as all the psychologists kept reminding us, was the killer's main thrill and major motive, the loss of it was going to force them into even more mistakes.

Horrific as the burning of Matthew Rushford's body was, therefore, we took some encouragement from it. It actually improved our attitude to a lot of things. To the narratives, for instance. Another one was found in the old man's grave, of course, close to the joined hands of the corpse, which again had been arranged in a kneeling position. It was cleverly wrapped in cellophane. It was cleverly free from all trace evidence. The same widely available paper, printer and software had been used to produce the document.

The old are exempt from suspicion, this one told us. *Past seventy, with our wasted muscle and blunted incisors, our creaking joints and slow brains, we are considered too frail to pose a physical threat. Our energies and emotions lie buried somewhere in the past, our interest in the future is tenuous, and we have neither the passion nor the motive to drive us to crime . . .*

What were we supposed to imagine while reading this? That Matthew Rushford had lured Karen Stokes to her death and was executed for it by some other little god, who would end up dead in the next grave we found, waving another confession at us? Were we supposed to imagine that there wasn't just one killer, but a kind of daisy chain of killers and victims?

It was obviously ridiculous.

Before, we might have been hesitant about saying that. I don't mind admitting it, we were probably scared of the narratives, the same way a kid in school doesn't know how to go about giving an honest reaction to a poem the teachers say is famous. You're not taught to have opinions and how to back them up. You're taught to play it safe. Parrot the experts. Parrot your superiors.

And that, I think, is how we'd felt about the narratives before. Intimidated.

So.

Had we finally grown up and grown out of that sense of inferiority? Well . . .

Two days after copies of the Rushford narrative were released by the laboratory and we'd all had a decent chance to study it, the superintendent called a conference in the incident room. He had another psychologist with him. 'Are they like personal trainers?' Jimmy Coyne asked. 'Do you get one of your own when you reach the rank of inspector?' This man was attached to the Central Mental Hospital, where the criminally insane are held as prisoners. And he had a point to make about the narratives.

'If we read all three of them in sequence,' he said, 'disregarding the contexts in which they were found, we can't fail to notice that, for all the apparent contradictions, the underlying story has a progressive structure. In other words, the writer already has a particular dénouement in mind . . .'

After about five minutes listening to this, when it was obvious that it was heading towards another profile of the killer – which was exactly what we *didn't* need at the time – the sergeant stood up. I think he deliberately played it a bit dumb at the beginning. He had a very pronounced rural accent, untouched by more than fifteen years living in the city, and he made the most of its roughness. 'When you say that the story has a progressive structure,' he asked, 'do you mean, like a cliff-hanger? Is it that sort of thing'

'Something like that,' the psychologist agreed.

'How interested would you be in seeing the next episode?' the sergeant wondered.

'Immensely, of course.'

'Well,' the sergeant said, 'it's going to cost you another human life to get your hands on the next instalment. Are you *that* interested? And if you are, could you pick the person whose life you want to exchange for it?'

The psychologist was taken aback – he'd been asked in to lecture us on his own brilliance, after all, not to get involved in an argument about human sacrifice – but then he recovered a bit and gave the sergeant one of those I'm-not-sure-I-appreciate-your-attitude sort of looks. You get them from experts all the time, whenever you question what they're saying. 'You're missing the point,' he said.

'No, I'm not,' the sergeant told him. 'I'm interested in catching this fucker. I'm not interested in seeing the next instalment of the narrative, or in finding out what happens to all the characters in the narratives. You know why? Because the only way I'm going to see the next narrative is if I find it in a mountain grave beside the corpse of some other poor innocent with their ears sliced off.'

'You're still missing the point,' the psychologist insisted.

I don't think the sergeant had any intention of getting the psychologist's point, whatever it was. He had too many of his own he wanted to get across. 'Look,' he said. 'All the experts will tell you there's one thing that distinguishes violent criminals. They don't treat their victims as human beings like themselves. The victims are objects to them. Playthings. Instruments. If I'm not mistaken, the American killer Ted Bundy, who was responsible for murdering nearly forty women, called his victims potted plants. Am I right? Apart from *actually* harming people, what could be colder than making them characters in a story? They're objects. Playthings. The writer's instruments. The potted plants.

'I have another point to make. We're looking for a twisted fucker here, someone who cuts off corpses' ears and makes God knows what use of them afterwards. To us, this is a monster that needs to be locked away. How come this monster can convince a stranded young woman to get in their car in the middle of nowhere, persuade a reclusive man to drive them way off his route, persuade a hard-bitten journalist to give them a lift and persuade a bad-tempered old man to invite them into his home? How come they can do all that?

'Every psychologist you read will give you the same answers. The sociopathic serial killer is very plausible, great at lying, the best in the world at manipulating other people's feelings, grand at seeming charming and harmless. We all think we'd see through the sociopathic killer, don't we? We wouldn't be fooled. We're the hunters. We're the experts. If our killer came up to us and invited us into their parlour, we'd spot the danger straight away. So we like to think, anyway. And yet, here we are, treating the killer's *written* stories the same way the victims treated the *spoken* stories, looking for things to believe in them, looking for sense and patterns. Anyone looking for things to believe in those narratives is as much a victim as the poor people who looked for things to believe in the killer's stories on the road, although anyone taken in by the narratives is obviously not going to die from their mistake. That's what this killer is telling us, that we're all a bunch of naive suckers. Why else do something as daft as leave stories with corpses? And anyone looking to find out what happens in the next instalment of these narratives is as cold-hearted as the killer, although they're never going to actually murder anyone. That's what I think, anyway.

'So let's stop trying to look at things the way the killer wants us to look at them. That's what we've been trying to do for too long. I think you're the third psychologist who's actually talked to us and probably the thirtieth whose theories we've studied. For a change, let's look at things instead from an investigator's point of view. It might be strange to say it, but I think we've got away from that. Guards are happier with hard evidence. Now that we've got some, let's use it. We have evidence linking an unidentified woman to two of the murders. We'll find that woman. The sooner all resources are dedicated to that, the sooner we'll find her. I'm not saying there isn't a role in any investigation for all the rest, the psychological profile and the like, but when it comes down to it all this is just speculation. The profile might or might not be accurate. It might or might not be going in the right direction. But hard evidence is fact. And it's the facts that'll lead us to the killer.'

Nobody had ever heard the sergeant talk for so long or with so much feeling. I don't think it had much influence on the superintendent, though, because shortly after that conference, which ended in chaos, he had half the unit searching for links between the details of the last narrative and real events outside it. The model he kept encouraging us with was the Unabomber case in America, which he'd studied while on a course there with the FBI. Ted Kaczynski, a recluse with a dislike of the technological society, sent parcel bombs to academics and airline executives over a period of seventeen years and had only been caught when the political manifesto he insisted on having published in the papers gave clues to his identity.

I couldn't see the parallels, to be honest. Maybe in the extreme methods used to avoid detection, because the Unabomber had scraped labels from batteries and used equipment that was long out of production, but not in the writings themselves. Kaczynski was politically motivated. His main theme was that freedom and dignity are more important than prosperity or physical comfort. He had a *message*.

There was no chance of the narratives from the Wicklow Mountains killer ending up in Irish newspapers, of course. For one thing, publicity wasn't an issue with the killer. But the superintendent gambled on the text throwing up hints about the murderer's life experiences that could then be stitched together into a biography.

We actually thought we were on to something at one stage, when one of the lads confirmed that the stamps described in the Rushford narrative – the ones depicting artefacts from the National Library, the greyhound and the Holy Family – had all been issued by the Post Office, in that order, in 1977. We checked through every murder investigation for that year, every violent death, every reported assault on non-nationals, but there wasn't anything in the files that resembled the death of the American woman. Someone else then pointed out that we were in the wrong year. 1977 was the last *complete* year in the stamp album, so the father must have been arrested and the crime must have happened in the summer of 1978. And then a third objected that the international events described – the riots in Paris and at Berkeley University – had happened exactly a decade earlier, in 1968. We checked both. And still found nothing.

Eventually the sergeant complained that this chasing of ghosts and shadows was a waste of resources, and was probably what the killer was hoping for. The sergeant was all for tossing the narratives into the bin at this stage, he was so frustrated by them. He said that the superintendent's approach was only the other side of the same coin that the psychologists kept trying to palm off on us. Either the narratives had an *internal* meaning that was going to lead you into the killer's mind, or the narratives had an *external* meaning that was going to lead you into the killer's life.

'But they have no meaning at all!' the sergeant insisted. 'And the only way they're going to lead you is by the nose!'

I didn't enjoy my festive season that year. I took a few days off around Christmas and went across to Galway with Fergal, but my mood was down and I found it hard to lift myself. And then I did exactly the same for the New Year, spoiling a trip to London that we'd been planning for a long time. There was too much on my mind. Normally, I can let it go. But not this time.

For one thing, the unit had two funerals to attend over the holiday, one on either side of Christmas Day.

The first was that of Matthew Rushford, which took place on a windswept day in the village of Laragh, close to his cottage. Standing together in the rain a week earlier at the grave site his killer had picked for him, we had decided to attend the old man's proper funeral when the body was released and the arrangements made. Not just to send a representative, as we did with the previous victims, but to go in strength, as a unit. This had become important to us.

Not that there were too many there to witness our new resolve. The Garda Press Office had publicly asked for relatives of the old man to come forward, but none had appeared. He'd had one brother, it turned out, a man named Jacob, who had joined a religious order in late-middle age after a career as a court clerk, but he had died almost a decade earlier. A few of the neighbours and the sheep farmer whose land was next to the old man's plot turned up to pay their respects. The priest, obviously. And the new community guard filling in for John Driscoll, who was still on sick leave. And that was it. Early in the afternoon, with the light already fading and the wind not only whipping our clothes and hats away, but carrying across to us the sound of children practising their Christmas carols in the nearby church hall.

The television stations didn't even send out a camera between them, not like the massive coverage they'd given the funerals of Mary Corbett and Karen Stokes. Television scheduling is a funny science and I suppose news footage of an old man whose ears had been sliced off with a surgical instrument and whose skin had been burned with a blowtorch would put a bit of a dinge in your enjoyment of *Miracle on 34th Street*, of *White Christmas*, and probably even of *Seven*, where Brad Pitt and Morgan Freeman chase a serial killer who murders to the pattern of the seven deadly sins.

That was our first funeral. And it was rough enough. But our second time in a graveyard over the holiday season was to bury one of our own.

I think that in the growth of every group there's always a point that's particularly crucial. Under pressure, it either cracks and begins to show its faults, or it bonds together. And how it reacts to its first casualty is probably the most decisive moment of all.

Friday morning, three days after Christmas Day, four of the five of us who had agreed to come in and knock our heads together for an informal session were already in the office, waiting for the last. Myself, Sergeant Mullery and The Twins. With one exception, the surviving members of the original unit that had been formed almost fifteen months earlier. Only Jimmy Coyne was missing.

When Jimmy did arrive, it was immediately obvious that nothing pleasant had delayed him. He wasn't his usual chirpy self. No bad jokes or slagging from him that morning. No dubious seasonal one-liners. He was glum.

He stood in the centre of the office, where we could all see him clearly. 'I have a bit of bad news for everyone,' he said. 'Tommy Dennison killed himself last night.'

I don't think you ever take the full impact when you hear the news of someone's death, unless they've been very close to you. With the sickly, you're already prepared. With the others, the bigger-than-life characters like Dennison, with his enormous strength and enormous anger, it doesn't really sink in for a while.

Apparently, Dennison shot himself with a semi-automatic pistol, holding the barrel under his chin while squeezing the trigger. He hadn't left any note behind. Just a silence it was hard to associate with such a loud man. He hadn't done it anywhere that was likely to make a point, either, since he'd ended his life in the flat he was renting. Generally, he'd given no indication at all that his state of mind was so desperate. Some of the lads had kept in touch with him. A few had been out drinking with him over Christmas. He claimed that he was confident about beating the charge of sexual assault against him, and there was no reason to believe that he was just putting a brave face on it. Probably, the separation from his kids over the holiday period had pushed him over the brink – Christmas is a bad time for the lonely – but we all knew that the long, soul-destroying investigation into the Wicklow Mountains murders was what had brought him to the edge.

He was our first casualty. And as I said before, the whole credibility of any police force depends on its holding its ground. You have to do something definite about it when one of your own goes down.

Because of the autopsy, there was a slight delay in releasing the body and Dennison's funeral didn't take place until the following Monday, which was New Year's Eve. Even though it was down near his birthplace in County Tipperary, about 150 kilometres south of Dublin, the entire unit attended, and I don't think there were any of us who didn't have to change our holiday plans to make it.

Poor Dennison. Throughout the ceremony I kept going back in my mind over all the run-ins he'd had with the inspector and myself, from the time he nearly killed us driving furiously through the mountains to the grave site of Michael Elwood to the last time we'd met, in the café off Grafton Street in Dublin. It would have been nice to fight with him again.

I saw his wife and two boys at the graveside. It's a funny thing, but you always have a flattering picture of people you've heard about but don't know. You think of them as attractive. You never imagine them as bow-legged and snub-nosed, for instance. It must be because all our mental pictures come from television these days, and normality is hardly ever seen on the box. Dennison's wife was actually squat and overweight, and only a complete conversion to political correctness would keep you from noticing that she was ugly too. His two boys didn't look like sportsmen, either. They had their mother's stocky build and they were carrying too much fat. I don't doubt that they were as talented as Dennison said, but they weren't fit. I wondered if this was another bone of contention between the parents.

Looking at the family at the graveside I was struck by something very sad, because it seemed to me as if the two boys were frightened of showing their loss. Their mother was more bitter than grieving. She didn't allow the boys any room for mourning. She even stood well back from the open grave, as if she was keeping her distance. And she said some odd things to a number of people who were offering their condolences, including some of our own group. 'Couldn't he have waited until the holidays were over?' she said. 'No. He had to go and spoil Christmas for everyone.' It wasn't fitting. And it angered the sergeant so much that he organized an unscheduled tribute, lining us up at the graveside to salute our colleague.

The pair of activists from the café in Grafton Street, the last time I'd met Dennison, were also at the burial. Funnily enough, although they were dressed completely in black in the café, now they weren't. While everyone else was in mourning, they wore brown. They kept staring at me throughout the funeral, a look that said I could have done more to save Dennison. It didn't bother me. I knew that it wasn't the assault charge that had driven him to suicide. Whether he had done it or not – and only the inspector's daughter would ever know the answer to that now – he couldn't have been convicted on the available evidence. He knew that as well as I did.

We didn't go with the family to the wake afterwards. We picked a pub of our own and sent Dennison off in the time-honoured Irish tradition, by getting completely sozzled. For all his faults, he was one of our own. This was the first time I drank heavily with the rest of the fellas. I won't say it was just the drink, because I know there was a lot of other stuff going on, but from that time I never had any problems on the unit. I was accepted. I think it was appreciated that, for all my disagreements with Dennison, I went out of my way to pay my last respects to him. If I stood by Dennison, the others felt that I could be trusted to stand by them too.

Bingeing is not something I'd like to do too often, though. Apart from the ferocious hangover the next day, I forgot to let Fergal know how late I was going to be getting back to Dublin and he was absolutely furious when the worry eventually wore off him. You can only stretch a considerate man so far. We didn't talk for the best part of five days. We flew to London, toured it, and flew back again, all without communicating. I'm stubborn enough, but there isn't anything as stubborn as a genuinely attentive fella who finally decides that he's been taken advantage of. Eventually, I had to apologize.

I'm sure a lot of nonsense was talked in the pub in Tipperary when we were all drunk, a lot of rosy memories of Dennison, a lot of wild pledges to nail the Wicklow Mountains killer, a lot of gooey sentiment. But there's good nonsense and bad nonsense, and this was the better kind, harmless in itself and helpful in creating the camaraderie any group needs to carry out a difficult job. And something unexpected came out of it.

Late in the evening, I just couldn't take any more pints of Guinness. I was already drunk and now the sheer volume of the stout was giving me trouble. It was too heavy on my stomach. When I hit shorts, I like vodka better than anything else. Gin has a sweetish scent on my nose and whiskey doesn't agree with my system. I ordered a vodka and white lemonade. But when it came and was placed on the table in front of me, I found that I couldn't drink it. I couldn't even pour the mixer in on the alcohol. I just stared at it, and I felt sick. The mind obviously works in funny ways, even when you think booze has closed it down, because what I'd remembered, even though it took a long while to rise to a conscious level, was that vodka had been listed in the autopsy report on Matthew Rushford's corpse as being among the stomach contents. He'd had vodka as his last alcoholic drink on earth. Not a tipple usually associated with old men in the Irish countryside. Whiskey is more their thing. But still, there are always exceptions. And on cold winter days in the mountains, one would give as much warmth and comfort as the other.

But even after getting this explanation away, my brain was still struggling to reach something else. I knew there was more. I just couldn't seem to get hold of it at all. I went quiet. I dropped out of the general conversation. I closed off all the noise around me. And then it occurred to me. Karen Stokes also had vodka in her bloodstream and stomach. And didn't Mary Corbett or Michael Elwood show traces of it, too?

I looked around at all the laughing, drunken faces at our table. They were all blurred. And there were far too many of them. Two sergeants. Three Jimmy Coynes. I staggered to my feet. I waved my arms. 'Wait!' I said. 'Wait! I have something to say!' They all fell silent. They stared at me with that intense concentration drunks need to do the simplest of tasks. Someone shouted encouragement. I couldn't tell who it was. But I knew that I wouldn't manage to say what was on my mind. I was too drunk. And there was no point even starting. I think I said, 'I love you all!' before collapsing back on the seat. There was a huge roar of appreciation. Lots of hugs. And lots of kisses.

Through the rest of the binge – I switched to gin and tonic – through the journey home on the bus we'd hired, through the argument with Fergal and the pig of a hangover the next day, I kept a small section of my throbbing brain free to hold the thought. As soon as I got back to the office after the holiday, I checked my memories of the autopsy reports. Matthew Rushford, Karen Stokes and Mary Corbett all had traces of vodka in their bloodstreams. Michael Elwood's body was too badly decomposed.

I mentioned this to the sergeant.

'One of them came from a late-night party, Kris,' he said. 'One had lunch in a licensed restaurant that day. One had a liver already diseased from too much alcohol. But you might have a point. It should be easy to check. We have witnesses. Except for the old man.'

'That's the thing,' I said. 'I checked the inventory of the stuff taken from the cottage. Three empty whiskey bottles. But no vodka.'

The only person I knew of who was in any way acquainted with the old man's habits was John Driscoll, and he was still on sick leave. He talked to me in the same room I'd interviewed him in before, and he still had the same hunted look about him. He got very agitated at first when I asked him what Matthew Rushford usually drank and only calmed down when I explained why I needed the information. Maybe there was a clue there to whatever was eating the man. But I didn't have time to follow it.

'He drank whiskey,' Driscoll said.

'What kind?' I asked. I knew already from the inventory, but I wanted to test Driscoll's accuracy.

'Only Irish.'

'Only?' I repeated. 'Was he particular?'

'Very.'

'Did he ever drink vodka?'

'Never, no,' Driscoll insisted. 'From what I know of him, anyway. I couldn't be a hundred per cent certain, but I'd be very surprised.'

I wasn't aware of it when I was leaving Driscoll's house, of course, but the other lads sent out by the sergeant had reached the same conclusions about the earlier victims. None of them was known to favour vodka. And none of them had been seen drinking it during their final hours. Mary Corbett drank rum and bottled lager and snorted cocaine at the party. Karen Stokes had only wine with her lunch and no alcohol afterwards. And just for the record, Michael Elwood had nothing to drink while Laura Ashwell was in his house and only a single Budweiser beer in Johnnie Fox's.

It was their killer who carried the vodka.

As far as it went, this finding was significant. The trouble with it was that vodka won't kill you. Not in those quantities, anyway. And no poisons had been found in the bloodstreams of the victims that might have been mixed with it.

So why did the killer carry and dispense vodka?

PART FOUR

The Narrative

Between Trooperstown Hill and Laragh, where the road bridges the Avonmore River, there is a parking bay and picnic site for tourists. This is where the old man had stopped that early-December morning. When I pulled in to offer him a lift, I assumed that he was resting. I was wrong. The old man was seriously ill, and more or less incapable of advancing by himself. But my error would have been insignificant if I hadn't compounded it with another.

I've had a bit of a turn, girl, he said to me. I'm not too steady on my feet. Maybe you could take me back to my cottage.

I should have closed the car door and driven on, leaving someone more deserving than myself to endure his sullen thanks for rescuing him. Instead, I waited for him to slump into the passenger seat before I turned in the parking bay and headed back along the disintegrating narrow road I'd just travelled. I've wondered since about the reasons for my decision. Why, when my intention was to appear merely kind, did I submit to the demands of appearing charitable? You may argue that to distinguish between the two is to quibble. I disagree. The illusion of charity demands a much greater and more complex effort than the illusion of kindness. I drove the old man to the door of his ramshackle cottage on the peak of Trooperstown Hill, for instance. I helped him indoors and stayed with him until he was sleeping. In the process I became confused, uncertain whether he was part of my illusion or I was part of his.

Are you a nurse? he kept asking me.

Perhaps I was. I had no desire to be. Nursing, after all, is not only the most exhausting of the professions, it is also the most futile. Contrast the vigour and the drive of those dedicated to profit and pleasure, for instance, with the weariness of the nurse, although both are overworked. Isn't this why members of the medical profession are permanently haunted by a look of *despair? Not because they lose so many of the good, as their publicity agents claim, but because they save so many who are useless.*

It was, therefore, a strange period for me, this time of confusion, of change, of shedding one skin before another had grown. A vulnerable time. There is a point, of course, beyond which structure merely disintegrates. Longevity is not, in itself, a virtue, and of all the absurd prohibitions in our softened world, that against suicide is the most ridiculous. For no matter how obsessively we force it into minor detours, nature always reasserts herself.

When I was a girl, I said to the old man – his name was Matthew, he told me grudgingly – when I was a girl, twelve or thirteen years old, I went to my uncles' house one evening to pick red- and blackcurrants from the fruit bushes that overwhelmed their garden, and I found instead that the plants had just been brutally uprooted, found the bushes withering, the berries already rotting, and their corpses strewn around the fresh foundations of what would eventually become extensive dog kennels and paddocks. As a woman, after my father's funeral last week, I stood again in that garden for the first time in many years. The kennels were nothing but ruins. Their roofs had caved in. The brickwork was crumbling and the debris was overgrown with thistles and nettles. But among the weeds, if you looked very closely, you could see the tangle of an old redcurrant bush, resiliently reclaiming the ground that had been taken from it all those years ago.

The old man didn't respond. Perhaps he hadn't heard. Perhaps he had seen through my illusion of a world. Perhaps he had no desire to enter it.

Are you a nurse? he persisted in asking me.

I searched for distractions. Knowing that it is only on the point of death, faced with the ultimate neat ending, that most of us finally appreciate that lies may well be the vital source of life, I told him stories. Openings that were full of promise. Developments that were full of interest.

Many readers of my classic manual, C Is For Anarchism, I said, and indeed many admirers of my work as a garda inspector, have kindly asked me about my childhood. May I say at once that I was schooled by the Irish Christian Brothers. Two things they taught me well: how to locate, penetrate and mould the souls of others by chastizing their flesh, and how to write beautiful letters. My calligraphy is not only the real source of my self-respect, but also the key to my personal philosophy.

Are you a nurse? the old man asked.

They brought him in by military convoy, I said, inside an army ambulance escorted by jeeps and motorcycle outriders. Armed soldiers sprang from the jeeps and stood on guard while they wheeled his stretcher from the ambulance and into the hospital. He was taken immediately for surgery. Once, as we hurried through the corridors, he seemed to regain consciousness for a moment and said, The enemy is at the gate, and laughed afterwards. Six hours after his admission, he was taken to intensive care. His condition remained critical throughout the night.

Are you a nurse? the old man asked.

My Uncle Charles, I said desperately, my Uncle Charles, whose mission was to save the world and who always wore four cardigans of varying colours, once escaped from the local psychiatric hospital and wandered into a meeting called to agitate for the legalization of cannabis.

Are you a nurse?

One evening, however, feeling better or more despairing, the old man asked for the whiskey he kept in the kitchen cupboard and afterwards, in his cups, with his humour improved and his tongue loosened, he rambled over the imagined memories of his youth.

It was only then that I realized how distracted I was, how careless I had been. How could I have forgotten that nothing is more comforting in distress than the memory of the talents we think we had? I moved immediately to regain the initiative. I had already noticed the coats of arms, hand-painted on a variety of materials, scattered around the cottage and I knew, from reading his personal papers, that the old man had worked as an heraldic artist, painting family armorials for American tourists, who were not entitled to bear them and did not understand their meaning, but who had the money to do whatever they liked with history. Except erase it, perhaps.

Six hundred years ago, I said to the old man, when wars were fought by knights so completely protected by suits of armour that it would have been impossible to identify who they were without the distinctive markings on their shields, your predecessors, the heralds who could quickly identify, record and depict these markings, were invaluable in battle. They were the favourites of royalty and their services were rewarded with expensive gifts. They acted as ambassadors to princes and as war reporters to the general population.

In the world of surfaces and images that we now inhabit, those with the ability to make things always consider themselves vastly inferior to those who merely market them. In other words, the old man's appreciation of himself deepened with every titbit I fed him, his self-esteem generated not by his own talent but by my description of it.

Did I enjoy this insubstantial power I wielded? I doubt it. But in so far as the old man had become my father, a remnant of a lost world, and I had turned into my own mother, as every woman does, I was absorbed by it. Perhaps that was sufficient. All the vast majority of us really desire, after all, are the comforts of escape.

Do you realize, I asked the old man, that you and your fellow heraldic artists are among the very few who can understand precisely why St Patrick drove the snakes from Ireland and why Cinderella ended up wearing her impractical glass slippers?

I'm not quite sure he appreciated this slight change of texture. He seemed apprehensive. Perhaps he feared that I was going to quiz him, aware as he was that his own ignorance would expose him.

This chaffing relationship, when the stories we launch catch an unexpected current and drift back, edging too close to the life we want to escape, has always been an irritant. As my mother once discovered, it is the great problem with invention. Inherent. Unavoidable.

It must, for instance, be one of the more amusing ironies of our educational system that Robert Louis Stevenson's essay 'An Apology For Idlers' was often compulsory reading for students. If you look back on your own education, Stevenson writes, I'm sure it will not be the full, vivid, instructive hours of truantry that you regret; you would rather cancel some lacklustre periods between sleep and waking in the class. Anyone attempting to follow his advice was treated as a delinquent, of course. Although we're obliged to study the stuff as a subject, in other words, it's not really meant to be taken seriously. No more than the Russian Zamyatin's contention that literature can only be produced by madmen, heretics, rebels and sceptics.

One poses, of course. One imitates the liberal gestures. But deep down I have always believed that the education authorities were right. All the vast majority of us desire are the comforts of escape. Absorption in the trivial. In the self-contained. A crime novel. A stamp album. A soap opera. And the curiously arid peace I have found while losing myself in the text of a poem or a novel, linking metaphor to metaphor, elision to elision, forming a circular seal that excludes the messiness of life. My mother, with her endless reinventions, her constantly shifting universe and fluid dislocations, stood in the meagre ranks of the enemy, shoulder to shoulder with Stevenson and Zamyatin.

But when you come to think of it, Matthew, I said to the old man, who really wants to know that in ancient Ireland, as in many ancient cultures, the snake was a symbol of fertility? Who wants to know that on March the seventeenth each year, at the carnivals in honour of St Patrick, we celebrate the emasculation of the lusty old gods and rejoice in their replacement with papier-mâché substitutes? Who really wants to know that in the original French version of the fairy tale, Cinderella's slippers were vair, a fur used to trim robes in the middle ages and as a background on heraldic shields, that this was wrongly transcribed as verre and so wrongly translated as glass, thus explaining why the poor girl was forced to waltz until midnight in footwear that must have been killing her? The man committed to the truth, Matthew, is a man dedicated to unravelling the entire weave of history, starting with that single stitch he wants to correct. My father, sitting silently in the dock in his ragged working clothes, declined the challenge by refusing to respond to the charge of murder against him.

The truth may be impossible, Matthew. But silence is not the alternative. Silence is unbearable. It's inhuman. Murke's girlfriend, while having her silence recorded on tape, breaks down and cries out that it's immoral. We imagine creation as a bang and even Armageddon as explosions. Never as silence. Murderer! they cried at my father from the public gallery in court. As they had accused him at his earlier arrest, gathering in a mob outside our house. Now, into the gap between the reading of the charge and the thud of the judge's gavel, they jumped immediately, in case my father's silence might be heard. Murderer! they cried.

We isolate the hero and the villain, so that we do not have to share in their tragic fate. It is the great weakness of our civilization. It is only when one tires of the insistent individual in our culture that one finally sees this. The cult of the hero is debilitating. Achilles, Antigone and Arthur. Cú Chulainn. Prometheus. And Holmes, of course. Just as the complementary cult of the villain is debilitating. Paris, Creon and Mordred. Maeve. Pandora. And Moriarty, of course. Think about it, Matthew. When other cultures attack our own, they measure the scale of their success by the number of dead they leave behind. When we cry out for retribution, we search for the mastermind behind the plot. The individual bandit. We round up posses to hunt down this elusive outlaw. We draw up posters of his likeness. We corner him in a gulch ten thousand kilometres away. And when he dies in the shoot-out with our hero, we blow the smoke from the barrels of our pistols and imagine ourselves safe again, imagine that order has been restored. Our enemies laugh at our naive lack of understanding, our imminent decline. The outlaw never existed. He was only an image created *by our enemies to satisfy our need for villains. We have failed to grasp that it is not the individual who alters history, but numbers. And struggle as I might, Matthew, I haven't fully embraced this insight myself, a tardiness you may yet find unfortunate.*

As for the official case against my father, although it hardly needed to be stunning, considering that no defence was offered by the accused, it also operated on a primitive level. The fact that the murder weapon was found in one of his locked chests was considered decisive. The fact that no one could account for his movements between the time he was seen entering Sarah Kleisner's house and the time he arrived at the pub that night, combined with the fact that he would not account for them himself, added to the fact that he had publicly denounced the young woman . . . And so on.

Throughout it all, however, no mention was made of the only fact with any real significance. Sarah Kleisner, with her distinctively American proportions and character, her glowing skin and gleaming teeth, her full lips, her bare legs and cleavage, her nakedness under transparent summer dresses . . . Sarah Kleisner was a sexually disruptive influence on our narrow world. Men sweated in her presence, tongue-tied with desire, and afterwards held her image in their minds as they rammed their cocks with more than usual ferocity through the opened legs of their wives or through the more accommodating circle formed by their own thumb and fingers. Women envied and resented her.

Wasn't this a more plausible reason for her murder than the xenophobia advanced as my father's motive? Wasn't it possible that whoever killed her had had their sexual advances rejected beforehand? The idea was never introduced at the trial. Not because of the prosecution's incompetence or the defence's caution. It was suppressed simply to avoid making the rest of us complicit. That is the most essential purpose of a trial, Matthew. To deny that we are all complicit. To define the criminal as a threat from outside. My father, once admired as a solid working man, could no longer be allowed to represent his community. Could no longer be allowed to represent his time, even. The slimy darkness of his crime was hinted at – an attractive young woman, the prosecutor said repeatedly, vulnerable, and living alone in a foreign country – but this was always accompanied by the suggestion that such sordid perversions belonged to the barbarity of the past, that they had no place in the fresh new dawn awakening our country, heralded at the closing of that decade by the dominance of the most open, the most accessible of all media, television.

Oh, the ironies, Matthew. Not so much that my entire childhood, grotesquely warped by these recent converts to the light, had really been a period of suppressed life, of things that existed but were never mentioned, of dark hints and furtive codes, of realities denied by being ignored or locked away. More that the haste with which they wanted to leave the better parts of their lives behind was laughable. They were hurrying towards death, flicking through the last few pages of their story at a frantic pace, understanding nothing except their own eagerness to get to the end. For all the world as if they were reading a crime novel.

My father was a sacrifice to the new gods. His trial was a ceremony. I looked around the courtroom while it was in progress. His accusing neighbours. My shape-changing mother. My uncles. I remembered watching them, my uncouth uncles, less than two months earlier, energetically grooming a greyhound's coat, toning its muscles with oils and hand massage, their caresses all the more vigorous, all the more urgent, because their minds were not on the job, because their blood was overheated, because they were staring through a gap in the hedge at Sarah Kleisner in the neighbouring garden. She was weeding one of her borders, on her hands and knees, rocking back and forth as she tugged and uprooted, wearing only a light floral dress that the wind lifted on occasions over her naked bottom. I remembered, later that same summer evening, that one of the dogs sniffed a bitch in heat and became excited. I remembered my uncle savagely flicking with his walking stick at the dog's exposed penis, until the pain drove that sensitive organ back into its sheath. What was my uncle doing, except brutalizing his own desire? Who was he at that moment, other than St Patrick, wielding his crosier to drive the snakes from Ireland? Couldn't either of my uncles have murdered Sarah Kleisner? Or both together, perhaps?

For a moment here, for the first time since the innocence of early childhood, I found myself approaching the extraordinary possibility that my mother could be believed. I had to remind myself that her protestations of my father's innocence were only an act, an artifice whose primary function, as with any fiction, was not to uncover the truth, but to strike and hold a pose. And yet, in a strange way, her fantasies changed our world. For to publicly imagine a future, Matthew, is to help to bring it about in some way that wouldn't otherwise be possible. Would Macbeth have risked the murder of his king without the seductive certainty of the prophecy from the three witches? Would those who fought to bring communism into being, those who fought to sustain and structure it, and those who fought to give it permanence, all have risked it without the seductive certainties of the prophecies of Marx and Engels? The future exists only for humans. And yet, of course, the future doesn't exist at all.

Do I mean, when I say that my mother's fantasies changed our world, that my father was unexpectedly acquitted? I do not. My father was convicted of the murder of Sarah Kleisner and sentenced to life imprisonment. He served twenty-two years of this sentence and died a fortnight ago, a mere six months after his release on parole. Those of his neighbours who had vilified him, poor shadows, came to his funeral only out of respect for my mother.

What I mean is something else.

From the moment I first saw Sarah Kleisner, in the garden next to my uncles' house, when I was sixteen years old, I was aware of an intense, unsettling attraction. I noticed her body, her small breasts and firm hips and long slender legs, barely covered that day in a light blouse and skirt, in a way that was different from my response to other women. She was beautiful. And yet, I wasn't envious. I was excited. Do you have a boyfriend? she asked me afterwards. I didn't, as it happened. And I hadn't been comfortable about it, until then.

I had no idea how old Sarah was when I first saw her. And I couldn't tell you how long I stood there watching her. She must have been conscious of my interest. I met her on the street the following day. I was returning to school after lunch and she was walking towards me, ambling up the hill. Beyond her I could see a school friend of mine, Peggy Deane, leaning against the railings outside her house, waiting for me to reach her. On the opposite pathway, two local women stood in an open doorway, gossiping. A coalman, his face and clothes blackened with dust, was cycling past on the road. I experienced them all, these familiar figures in the landscape, as clumsy intruders. Perhaps I slowed as I approached, trying to think of something natural to say, trying to summon the self-control to deliver it calmly. We stopped on the footpath, facing each other. I'd anticipated awkwardness, that awful spluttering rhythm of probe and monosyllable that still marked our engagement with adults. But she transcended this smoothly. I need someone to clear and reseed my garden, she said. Would you do it for me?

Can I tell you, Matthew, that the most significant thing about our subsequent relationship was that she laughed at me only once? She didn't laugh at my crude efforts at gardening. She didn't laugh when I followed her admission that she had no interest in men with an immediate declaration that I shared her lack of enthusiasm. She didn't laugh as I lay on her bed, tense and unresponsive, while she vainly tried to arouse me during our first, stilted sexual encounter. And she didn't laugh at my clumsy attempts to satisfy her with my tongue and fingers. This is why I stayed on in the dead city during that fateful summer of 1968. To reward her patience. To explore a world that was without politics or violence.

I wasn't so naive, or so absorbed, that I considered myself immune. But I thought that the danger would come – not from the men, who couldn't imagine an alternative to rutting – but from the local women, with their weariness, their wariness of beauty and love. Those who are most denied pleasure in life also have the keenest appetite for scandal.

The fact is, when I first heard the rumour, from my closest friend in school, Peggy Deane, I thought it was a joke. Is your father really having an affair with that American woman? Peggy asked. The one you work for in her garden. I wasn't even shocked. I was amused. The notion was absurd. The images it evoked were comical. I refused to take it seriously.

Perhaps I was already too smug by then, too content. But I should have known that such an improbable rumour could not have been invented by schoolgirls, whose bitchiness thrives on credibility. The fact that it had reached Peggy meant that it must have seeped downwards. It was therefore widespread. And, I gradually came to believe, must have some basis in reality, no matter how tenuous.

In the days afterwards, the fear that Sarah had taken a male lover began to torment me. And sexual jealousy, although it distorts the senses, also heightens them. I noticed that Sarah was indeed more preoccupied than she had been, more distant, less attentive. Something was distracting her. When I asked what it was, she claimed that she was worried about her brother in New York. I didn't believe her. I decided to spy on her. But she seemed to be aware that I was watching her and managed to elude me on several occasions. Perhaps she was clever. Perhaps I was merely inept. My surveillance was inconclusive. And yet, the circumstantial evidence accumulated. And amazingly, it still involved my father. The pair of them seemed to disappear simultaneously. While I was out looking for Sarah, my mother, or my sister, was also searching for my father. He was seen a number of times retreating furtively from her house, once a little after midnight. And he lied. Not by word. His silence was absolute. But by appearance. By routine. He dressed, for instance, to drink in the pub on Saturday night, as he always had. But he didn't go there. And no one could tell where he went. Was it possible? Had my comical father, with his derisory fowl and worthless stamps, his cloth cap and unravelled cardigans stained with flour dust from the mills, somehow become a central character in an overheated soap opera?

Finally, I could bear it no longer. One Friday early in September, before I went to school in the morning, I stopped Sarah in the street while she was on her way to work and I asked her crudely if she was fucking my father. And this, Matthew, was the only time she ever laughed at me. Her laughter was loud, and seemed contemptuous. Hearing it, the crowded street fell silent. A labourer, cycling to work, twisted to look back, his front wheel wobbling furiously as his movement dragged the handlebars sideways, before he regained his balance and pedalled on. Others stared. And then they too started to laugh, imagining that they knew precisely why I was accusing the American and precisely why she was scoffing at me.

I had no answer. Either to my question, or to the laughter. Sarah slipped away from me without otherwise responding. I nursed my anger through the day and when I came home from school that afternoon and my uncles handed me a greyhound to take to the local abattoir, I knew, precisely, what I wanted to do. I wanted to sever the dog's ears and bring them back to lay on the pillows in Sarah's bed. I wanted to steal a boning knife from the fat man in the blood-soaked apron who owned the abattoir. And I, too, wanted to be sexually unfaithful, and also with the most unlikely of lovers.

I went to the abattoir in my school uniform, knowing that the fat man had a lecher's fondness for schoolgirls. When I came back to Sarah's garden, no longer a virgin, my clothes were stained with blood, some of which at least was my own, and I carried the boning knife and the greyhound's ears. I waited for Sarah to return from her work. A little after six o'clock, I heard her unlock the street door and close it again behind her after entering. Through the large kitchen window I watched her reading her letters. It was only when she suddenly swivelled from these, looking sharply upwards after turning, that I realized that she wasn't alone and that her companion, a small unshaven man, finally came into view, stepping forward to lay a hand on her right shoulder. Instantly recognizing my father, still in his working clothes, I felt as if an abrasive cord was sharply tightened around my stomach. Unaware of me, they argued for a while – a lovers' quarrel, I was convinced – until Sarah stepped back and struck out, slashing her long nails down his left cheek and leaving him with a trail of scratches that would mark him the rest of his life. When he left shortly afterwards, Sarah tore one of her letters into tiny fragments and then rushed into the garden, no doubt to

176

recover herself, to breathe fresh air, perhaps to soothe her troubled nerves with exercise.

She was horrified to find me there. Staring at my bloodied clothes and at the greyhound's severed ears, she suddenly lost control, screaming at me to leave her alone and running away from me, down the length of the garden and over the uneven stone wall at its end. I followed her across the fields at the back of our houses, to the edge of the cliff that lay about two kilometres to the north, where I finally managed to catch up with her and stop her.

What, she demanded angrily, is your problem?

Did Americans use this expression at that time? I'm not sure. The meaning, however, was identical.

You laughed at me, I told her.

She threw her hands in the air. One of her blonde hairs, I remember, detached itself from her fingers and fluttered over the side of the cliff.

You're fucking mad, she said. You, your old man and your mother. You're all fucking mad.

It's true that I had pledged to restrain myself unless she laughed at me again. And it's true that she didn't laugh. She threw her hands in the air. A gesture of despair. So perhaps I meant to beat her only with the greyhound's ears, which I thought I held in my right hand. Instead, I found the boning knife plunging into her breast. A number of times, I have to admit. Quite a number.

What I will emphasize is that, when I left her, she was lying on the grass, five metres or so from the edge of the cliff. How did she fall to the bottom? And how did her blood come to stain my father's clothes? That it was Sarah's blood was proven by the tests they carried out. Did my father find her as she lay injured? Did they embrace? Did she recoil from his attentions? Did she throw herself from the cliff? Or did he finish the job by pushing her? Only he would ever know the answers to these questions and he would carry them to the grave with him.

Even in an age of taciturn men, my father was unusually silent. In the following days, if he noticed the boning knife, which I'd cleaned and placed under the stamp album in his chest of drawers, he never said anything about this either. It's true that he kept the drawer closed, but the lock was old-fashioned and easy to pick. When the police questioned me, I told them about my visit to the abattoir. I explained that I had stolen the boning knife, but then, frightened by what I had done, I had admitted the theft to my father and given him the knife to return to the fat man in the abattoir. I still believed, you see, that my father and Sarah had been lovers. The police never tested the blood on my uniform, satisfied that it could only belong to greyhounds and other animals. I wasn't called as a witness at the trial. They had enough without me. And my father never contradicted my story about the knife. That, too, he took to the grave with him.

Would he have talked if I had made it to his deathbed before he died? Perhaps not. He was awkward to the last, my mother reported. The only thing he ever said was that he wanted you to have that old stamp album. This seems significant, doesn't it? It seems a calculated gesture, pregnant with meaning. But you have to remember that it may not be true. He may never have said any such thing. There was no independent witness to corroborate it. And it may only be another invention of my mother's.

Which leads us to the greatest irony of all, Matthew. Only an idealist would call it cruel. It would be naive to do so. But it's surely the greatest. The rumour that my awkward father, with his cloth cap and unravelled cardigan, was immersed in a torrid sexual affair with a young American woman, the rumour that provoked my jealousy and that led to Sarah's violent death, was started by my own mother. I'm only telling you, she confided to an outraged neighbour on a warm July evening in that summer of 1968, because I can't bear the cross all by myself and I have to tell someone, but my eldest girl, who was weeding the garden up there, is after seeing the two of them going at it like animals. Isn't that a terrible thing for a young girl to have to see her own father doing? God help the poor child. Don't breathe a word of it to anyone, Biddy.

This was a story, above all other stories, that simply had to be true. This was a story, above all other stories, that simply had to be believed. For what woman would sacrifice her own daughter merely to discredit her husband? Women, particularly mothers, are nurturing and vulnerable, never the assailant but often the victim, driven to violence, in extreme cases, only by the need to protect themselves and their children. Isn't that so?

I'll spare you the mind-numbing stages of the minute investigation that eventually led me back to the source of the story about my father's infidelity and only repeat, admiringly, that we were all mere characters in my mother's nightmares. My father in particular, perhaps, since he chased and pestered Sarah Kleisner only because he was convinced that Sarah herself had started the rumours that were ruining his life, or, if she hadn't, that only she had the power to quash them. We will all disappear, of course, when my mother finally dies. Perhaps not immediately. No more than the dream that *was communism collapsed the moment its creators died. No more than the reign of Macbeth disintegrated as soon as its prophets, the three witches, melted into thin air. But when illness finally strikes my mother, she will lose everything to it, including her natural gift for narrative. A compulsive storyteller, she will still talk. But confined to her bed, with no new sights to nourish her descriptions and no new experiences to vary her tales, her stories will become repetitious, redundant, irrelevant, tedious. And then we will all surely fade as we drift further and further from our only source of light. All our complexities will be behind us. And we will be left to flick impatiently through the last thin chapters of our lives to a disappointing dénouement.*

After my father's funeral, when I was helping to put his things in order, I came across the black, leather-bound stamp album my mother claimed he wanted me to have. It was still buried in the bottom drawer of the old-fashioned chest, but now under an untidy pile of the crime novels that he was so addicted to. These were the ones he had been reading after his release from prison, when, confined to bed, with his hen houses long levelled in the back garden, his songbirds and terriers long dead and their cages and kennels thrown out, his stamp album frozen on a fateful year from the past, all he had left was his love for the simplicities of the detective story. But the extraordinary thing about these books was that each of them had the last twenty pages torn out. When I asked my mother why this was so, she began to cry and claimed that she had bought them second-hand and had been duped. I found it impossible to believe her. I think she tore them out herself. I think my father must have started each story avidly, flicking eagerly through the pages and wallowing in the horrors the characters were enduring, until he came to the end of the book and discovered that it was not the end of the novel. There are pages missing, he must have complained. What difference? my mother must have asked. But what happens? he must have demanded. I want to know what happens. What does it matter to you? she must have goaded him.

And when you come to think about it, Matthew . . .

What did it matter to him?

The Profile

In driving snow, near the peak of Corriebracks in the east Wicklow Mountains, a woman is tacking tarpaulin to the exposed foundations of a small outhouse next to her cottage. It's Sunday afternoon, a little after three o'clock, hardly more than a month into the new year. For days the weather has been harsh, covering the mountains in snow and making the narrow exit routes almost impassable. The temperature has hardly risen above zero during daylight, plunging to minus eight at times by night.

Although the woman is well clothed, in a fleece-lined jacket, heavy jeans, snow boots and a hunter's cap, she feels cold because she's tired and because her energy levels are low. She's been working since early morning. She's cleaned and tidied the interior of the white-washed cottage. She's checked and re-pinned the protective covering over the vegetable plot in the rear garden. She's fed and walked the greyhound that's kennelled behind the house and she's changed its bedding. She's polished and vacuumed the cars that are kept in the barn, although two of the three haven't been used since she last did these chores, a few days ago. Now she's re-fastening the tarpaulin that the wind has lifted from a corner of the exposed foundations.

The woman's name is Margaret Malone, a thirty-four-year-old dental nurse. And she's working so continuously and so hard on one of her days off because she's unhappy.

She's stopped only once since breakfast, to prepare lunch for herself and to eat it. Apart from that, she's avoided the pitfalls of rest. The inevitable memories. The resentment. The useless regrets. But even the work itself sometimes taunts her with her loneliness. When she strikes a nail or a length of wood with the hammer, the noise reverberates around the silent mountain. And there's never any answer. The nearest house is more than two kilometres away, on a minor road that leads into the village of Donard. What worries her most, though, is the thought that it will be dark in about an hour. Then she will have to go indoors. She wonders how she'll kill the time. Television, possibly? Housework?

Behind her, at the strip of fencing between the cottage gable and a corner of the barn, the greyhound suddenly starts barking furiously. Distracted from her thoughts, the woman glances across at the dog and sees immediately that it hasn't been disturbed by anything trivial. She stops hammering and listens. And finally, she too hears the noise of a car slowly climbing the steep track to her cottage. Not recognizing the sound of the engine, she stands up, tells the dog to quieten, and waits.

The car is a silver Mercedes. It edges out of the pine woods at Blackpits below her and approaches cautiously. When it reaches the cottage, it has trouble parking. Unable to find traction on the snow-covered slope, it slips backwards for a while, its engine roaring uselessly, before the handbrake is pulled. When the driver finally switches off the ignition and gets out, he stands there, leaning on the open door and waving vigorously across at the woman.

He's Patrick Kelly, a shopkeeper from Donard. The woman knows him, mostly from her visits to the town of Carlow, thirty kilometres to the south, but also because Kelly has invited her on dates a number of times. He's young enough, only a year or two older than herself, and he's wealthy and charming, but she's always refused. Not only because he's married, with two small children, but because she's frightened of her own partner's reaction.

'How are you, Margaret?' he calls across in his strong country accent. 'Is himself in?'

She shakes her head. 'No.'

'Do you know when he'll be back, at all?' Kelly asks.

'He's away,' Margaret Malone tells him. 'He left on Friday. I don't know when he's returning.'

'Damn,' Kelly swears. 'I wanted to ask him about greyhounds. I'm thinking of buying a few pups. He said he might know a few breeders.'

'When were you talking to him?' she asks.

'What?'

'When did he tell you that about the greyhounds?'

'Oh,' Kelly blusters, 'a while ago . . .'

The woman stares at him, loosely swinging the hammer in her right hand. She doesn't respond. Although he's not aware of it, her mood is bitter and vengeful. She wants to tell him that he's wasting his time, that 'himself' is really a fraud and knows as much about breeding greyhounds as he does about breeding koala bears. It should be obvious to anyone with eyes in their head, she thinks, that the people who own the dog behind her are anything but experts. The brindle bitch is so old that its whiskers are grey. If it ever raced, it must have been nearly a decade ago.

She opens her mouth, about to tell Kelly that he's either a liar or a credulous fool, but he suddenly changes the subject before she can start. And with it, just as abruptly, he alters her mood as well.

'Have you done something different with your hair, Margaret?' he asks.

Very little of her hair is visible under the hunting cap she's wearing. If she wants to blunt the obvious flirtatiousness in the query, she can simply ignore the question. But the fact that he notices her appearance pleases her. She's eager to be flattered, of course, after the day's drudgery, but his attention, and the implied compliment, make her feel warm and appreciated again.

So her next gesture is wholly calculated. She takes off the hunting cap and shakes her hair loose for him to admire.

It's not merely a change of style she's asking him to applaud, it's a whole new image. Weeks earlier, snowflakes settling in her hair would have stayed visible until they melted. But not any more. Back then, her hair was jet black and rather long. Now it curls inwards before it reaches her shoulders, and it's blonde.

'What do you think?' she asks.

Kelly whistles. He's surprised. But he's also excited. An experienced man, he thinks he understands the meaning of Margaret Malone's display. In a public place, in the company of others, it might be no more than a safe tease, a mild encouragement to explore a little further. But since she's alone at an isolated cottage, he's willing to gamble that it's a sexual invitation.

Kelly is not dressed for being outdoors in harsh weather. He's wearing a charcoal grey suit and black leather shoes. He's been leaning on the door of his car because he wants to keep the weight off his standing right foot, preventing it from sinking into the snow, while leaving his left leg still inside the Mercedes. He looks across the snow-covered ground between himself and Margaret Malone and sees no path, no clearing, where his footwear and the ends of his trousers are going to be saved. But he doesn't hesitate. He steps fully out of the car, swings the door shut and walks over to her.

He has never seen her like this before, because now she's actually posing for him while she waits. Every other time they met, on the streets of Carlow, she was either cautious or abrupt. Of course she always had the old tyrant with her, he remembers, or if not with her, then hovering around her somewhere, keeping his possessive eye on her, eavesdropping on every little intimacy, fouling the mood. When the cat's away, he thinks.

As he reaches her, because he *is* an experienced man, he does the consistent thing. He strokes her hair. He takes its fine strands between his fingers and his thumb and appreciates the texture, allowing the back of his hand gently to caress her warm cheeks at the same time. When she turns to him, their faces are so close that their lips are almost touching. She darts her tongue from between her teeth and runs it across her mouth to moisten the lips. He raises his left hand, intending to place it behind her head to draw her closer. But he slips it under her hair and around her neck instead, and as the hair is lifted from her face, as he catches a glimpse of the flesh underneath, he recoils slightly and curses involuntarily. Her right eye is blackened and the cheek under it is heavily bruised.

Once again, the mood swings violently.

Kelly's excitement is dampened, but he feels more confused and concerned than anything else.

Margaret Malone is distraught. A look of fury flashes across her face. There are tears in her eyes. Of anger. Of frustration. She breaks away from him and hurries into the cottage, past the whining greyhound, who senses but can't understand her distress. But she doesn't close the front door behind her.

Kelly considers the situation for a few moments, and then follows her. He's never been inside the cottage before and is unfamiliar with the layout, but he eventually finds her in the front room to the left, sitting on the settee in front of the television, crying quietly. She's removed the fleece-lined jacket and dropped it untidily on the floor. He stands beside it, awkwardly, uncertain what to do.

'What happened to you, Margaret?' he asks.

She covers her eyes with her hands, shaking her head, not answering.

'You didn't fall, did you?' Kelly asks, eliminating all the possible excuses himself. 'And you didn't run into any doors. That's for sure.

Someone hit you, didn't they? Who was it? Was it himself? It was, wasn't it? It was the old tyrant.'

She looks up at him then, her hand still covering her mouth, her eyes filled with tears.

'Jesus!' Kelly says in disgust.

He sits down beside the shaking woman. He puts his arm around her shoulders to comfort her. She tilts her head towards him, resting it on his chest. The shared emotion makes them tender towards each other again. Through the warmth of their touching bodies, the mood slips back towards intimacy.

Kelly feels sexually excited once more. He wonders if it's still appropriate. But Margaret Malone is already ahead of him, crushing her wet lips against his, probing inside his mouth with her tongue, stroking his erection under his constricting trousers. Then suddenly, maddeningly, she pulls away again and turns her face from him.

'You don't want to see me like this, Pat,' she says, drawing her hair across the ugly bruises on her face.

'I don't mind, Margaret,' he protests. Reaching out for her again, urgently, getting frustrated now, beyond the point of self-control.

She rises from the settee, slipping out of his reach, and paces the floor. 'Wouldn't you like to see me at my best?' she asks.

He says, 'Yes, obviously, but—'

'Do you want to?' she wonders.

He's baffled. 'How do you mean?'

And instantly she's sharp and impatient again, stamping her foot, intolerant. 'Do you *want* to?'

He stares upwards at her. She's breathing heavily and clearly excited. He can't help responding to that. But he also senses danger. This is a dark and unfamiliar place for him. He's never been here with any woman before. He has no idea what he might be agreeing to. But he finds that apprehension only heightens his arousal. 'Yes,' he says hoarsely, 'I want to.'

She picks up a remote control for the VCR and presses the play button. There's a tape already in the machine. As it starts, flickering into focus on the television screen, she discards the remote control and kneels in front of him, looking hungrily upwards into his face.

The video is a home movie, but not like anything Kelly had ever viewed before. It features Margaret Malone, at a time when her hair was dyed auburn, long before she was given the black eye. She's dressed in a nurse's uniform. It's unbuttoned at her breasts, the skirt is far too short, and she wears black stockings and a suspender belt under the starched white linen. She vamps to the camera, striking a number of suggestive and receptive poses, over and around some leather upholstery, before settling into a sexy striptease.

'Do you like it?' Margaret Malone asks.

'Yes,' Kelly confirms drily.

She unzips his fly, the noise synchronizing perfectly with the sound of another zip being unfastened on the video. His erection is caught and bent in the bunched folds of his underpants. She frees it and takes it out. She breathes on it while she talks. 'How much do you like it?' she asks.

He moans. But it's not enough, this inarticulate response. She squeezes on his cock, painfully. 'How *much* do you like it?' she insists. His praise grows more absurd, more colourful, because she takes him in her mouth when he exaggerates and abandons him again when he becomes so lost in his own pleasure that he forgets to appreciate her. At one stage, the greyhound outside springs to life again and starts barking frantically. As if someone else is approaching.

'Himself,' Kelly remembers then. 'What if he comes home? What if . . . ?'

But he's too far gone really to care. The spice of danger has become mixed with the thrill of letting go so completely, with the excitement of indulging himself in such perversity. The cocktail is heady. And weird. Even as he ejaculates into Margaret Malone's mouth, he notices a photograph of her on top of the television, above the image of her masturbating on the screen, above her actual face buried between his legs. Three tiers of her image. Like a wedding cake, it occurs to him.

She's younger in the photograph. She has black hair and seems to be in her late twenties. What interests Kelly most, though, is the man who is standing beside her, with his arm around her. He recognizes this individual, of course. The old tyrant. The man with no name, he jokes to himself. When he asks her about it afterwards, she merely shrugs and curses bitterly.

'How long have you been stuck with him?' he teases. 'That must be five or six years ago.'

'Eight,' she admits.

'You should get away from him, girl,' he advises. 'You shouldn't have to put up with that kind of treatment.'

He's far more comfortable now. Not only physically, however. Mentally also.

The woman's vibrant sexuality has rather shocked him, he admits. He knows, if he continues this affair, that things will become more rather than less perverse. More extreme. More dangerous. But he's also confident that he can manage to fit this into his life, that he can somehow juggle self-destruction and domesticity. Even though it's well past eight o'clock in the evening when he finally leaves, after another two, but less intense orgasms, and he already has considerable ground to make up on the stories he must spin his wife.

From the cottage doorway, Margaret Malone watches him trudge back across the snow to the Mercedes. There's a thin layer of ice on the car's windows and he has to use a spray to dissolve it. He already looks nervous about the journey. It's pitch dark and even in decent weather the narrow roads and lanes in these parts of the mountains can be treacherous at night. There's nothing she can do to help him, however, so she doesn't even wait for him to finish manoeuvring the Mercedes outside the cottage. She watches him sit in behind the wheel, but as soon as he starts the engine she turns away and closes her front door.

Although the short-term forecast is for milder conditions, it doesn't thaw that night. By twelve o'clock it's down to minus five and still dropping. Margaret Malone doesn't feel it. For the first time in weeks, she sleeps properly that Sunday night. When the alarm wakes her at seven in the morning, she's fresh and rested. She's also aware of an appetite. She has a substantial breakfast, of muesli, toast and coffee, and a little after eight, she takes the small Fiat from the barn and heads for work.

This week, it's her responsibility to open the dental surgery in Tallaght in the south suburbs of Dublin and to receive and settle the early patients. The roads are iced, particularly in the mountains close to the cottage, but the little car is well equipped, with chains on its tyres, and she's an experienced driver. She descends slowly, along the unsurfaced track. The narrow approach road to Donard has already been gritted by the local authority, however, and she makes better progress from there. Passing through the village, she notices that Patrick Kelly's shop is not yet open. This is unusual. Maybe he's sleeping it off, she jokes to herself. Maybe, she thinks, his wife wanted sex when he finally got home.

Margaret Malone's good humour lasts through the morning, surprising her employers and patients, who know her as efficient and kind-hearted rather than lively and vivacious. Because nothing seems to be weighing on her heavily, it also lends credibility to her story that she accidentally bruised her face while working on the outhouse over the weekend.

At lunchtime, however, when the surgery closes and she leaves with two other nurses to eat in a nearby café, she is suddenly overwhelmed, while sitting at a table, by the sense that someone is following her, that someone, right now, is watching her. Her mood darkens immediately. Although she enjoys being looked at and appreciated, although she will even act out fantasies to attract favourable attention, she hates it when she is not in control of how the observer sees her. She hates the thought that someone might be furtively spying on her. It makes her feel anxious, and self-conscious, and slightly grubby. She drops out of the conversation with the others and looks openly around the cafe. She doesn't recognize any of the faces. A few look back, but only idly, for an instant. No one tries to conceal their interest or avoid her eyes. And yet she's convinced that someone, somewhere, is secretly watching her.

The sensation clings to her throughout lunch and on the walk back to the surgery, but it lifts again while she's working indoors during the afternoon. Proof, she decides, that the threat is real, and not just inside her own mind. It's dark when she finishes at five o'clock and it's also snowing once more. The normal rush-hour noise is muffled by the snow that's lying on the ground and by the fact that there are so few people about. The silence is eerie, and slightly menacing. Margaret Malone walks by herself from the surgery to the car park. It takes her less than ten paces to know that someone *is* following her. She slows a little, preparing to stop. She resists the urge to look around. She wonders if she should double back, surprising the stalker, but decides that this might be too dangerous. Up ahead, she notices a laughing young couple approaching their car, close to where she has parked, and she quickens her pace, hurrying to reach the Fiat around the same time as them. Once she's inside the car, with the doors locked and the engine idling, she watches for any sign of suspicious activity. There isn't any. She feels, again, the same release from immediate threat that she felt in the afternoon.

Nevertheless, she decides to take an alternative route home. Although she starts out as usual, by travelling south along the carriageway, she then overshoots her normal turn and doubles back beyond it. She needs to be absolutely certain before approaching the dirt track to her isolated cottage that no one is watching her.

Ten kilometres south of Dublin, before she reaches Blessington, she pulls over to the hard shoulder and stops. Through the rear-view mirrors she checks that none of the vehicles behind follows her over to the side. She watches the traffic overtaking her. A few of the drivers glance curiously across. None seems to have any real interest in her. South of Blessington, at Pollaphuca Dam, and again beyond the turn off to Donard, she repeats this manoeuvre, both times with the same result.

The elaborate detour, through Keadeen Mountain and the Glen of Imaal and back to Corriebracks, adds almost twenty kilometres to her journey. And at the end of it, there's a bitter-sweet surprise for her. As she approaches the cottage, her headlights pick out the shape of the four-wheel drive that's already parked outside. The old tyrant, as Patrick Kelly calls him, is finally back.

Margaret Malone doesn't know whether to feel relief or resentment. It depends on whether he's alone or not, she decides. The previous week – the cause of their violent quarrel – he'd dragged a prostitute back with him and had her stay in the cottage overnight.

She finds him sitting on the settee in the front room, flicking through the television channels. He hasn't been there for very long. His face is still raw from exposure to the cold and flecks of thawing snow cling to his hair and eyebrows. A tall man, he is casually dressed in a black woollen polo-neck sweater and white chinos. He's lean and has soft features and short greying hair. At sixty-two years old, he looks more like a youthful grandfather than the popular notion of a tyrant. But this evening, his humour is obviously still dark.

'They claim that people who live together come to resemble each other,' he says. 'The idea is plainly rubbish. I'm hungry. There's no dinner prepared.'

Margaret Malone doesn't bother pointing out that he couldn't have been expected. She stands in the open doorway, jingling the car keys in her hand, a habit that she knows annoys him. 'Is somebody with you?' she asks.

He glares at her. 'A spirit, perhaps?' he wonders sarcastically. 'A presence? A metaphysical cat burglar?'

She leaves and checks the rest of the cottage. The kitchen. The bedrooms. The bathroom. All of them are empty. When she returns he's still sitting on the settee, still mindlessly hopping through the television channels.

'Were you in Tallaght today?' she asks.

He doesn't look up. 'Why?' he grunts.

'Where I work,' she clarifies. 'Around by the surgery and the car park.'

'I don't need a rudimentary geography lesson,' he says acidly. 'What I need, I ask for. I asked you why you wanted to know if I was in Tallaght today.'

'Because if you weren't,' she tells him, 'someone was following me.'

Finally, he looks up at her and smiles. But his expression is menacing rather than reassuring. 'Come here,' he says. When she doesn't move, he lowers his voice, darkening it with an unspoken threat. 'Come here.'

She walks across and stands beside him. Her body is tensed and shivering slightly.

'Take off your panties,' he says.

She reaches under the skirt of her white uniform and hooks her thumbs under the waistband of her panties. She pulls the garment down and steps away from it when it drops to the floor by her feet. He draws her closer to him. He lifts his right hand under her skirt, between her naked thighs, and finds her clitoris, holding it between his thumb and forefinger. At first he caresses it, exciting her despite herself, but as soon as she is moist he pinches it savagely, making her cry out with pain.

'Every woman, Margaret,' he says dismissively then, 'now routinely derives her power and her purpose from presenting herself as a victim. It may fool the legislators. It may fool the educationalists. And it undoubtedly fools the incompetents who administer our criminal justice system. But I'm afraid it cuts no ice with me.'

Unable to compete with him, either in strength or in argument, she turns away from him and leaves again. She goes to the smaller of the two bedrooms and locks the door behind her. What she feels at his return, she decides, as she lies on her back on the bed, staring at the ceiling, is not merely resentment. This is too mild. She feels a frustration so intense that she knows she must do something about it. She thinks of Patrick Kelly. She remembers his sexual excitement, his attraction to the perverse, his quick addiction to the forbidden. Underneath her the previous evening, handcuffed to the same bed that she is lying on now while she rode him savagely, he had gasped, 'What if he comes home now and catches us, Margaret?'

'Then you'll have to kill him, won't you, Pat?' she had encouraged him.

Their eyes had met. For an instant, they were locked together as accomplices. Then he had wriggled away with a joke. 'Not with these fucking bracelets on my hands, I won't.'

Margaret Malone sighs and stretches on the bed, feeling more warm and comfortable. Thinking of Patrick Kelly's helpless ecstasy, she slips her hand through the opened buttons of her uniform and begins to stroke herself. She closes her eyes, the easier to see how she might persuade her neighbour to kill.

The Investigation

There's an over-reliance on procedure in the guards that can be very restricting. Every time you make a move on the job there's a rule governing what you should do, a piece of paper you should fill out before you start and another piece of paper you need to fill out afterwards, explaining everything that happened, including the proper completion of the first piece of paper. In a way, this is only natural. Without a book of rules, all you have is chaos. And you know that it's necessary, because the chances are that the business you're doing will end up in a court someday. On the other hand, though, the people you're dealing with on a day-to-day basis are all over the place. Most of them have very little control over their lives. If it's a junkie, he has no allegiance to anything except his drugs and no notion of a future beyond organizing his next fix. Even if they're not on anything, the vast majority of criminals are opportunists, living from one moment to the next, and the only time the past bothers them is when they're caught.

The paperwork we have to do is the black and white world where the politicians and the authorities live. The field work is every shade of grey you could possibly imagine. Some guards never manage to reconcile the two. They're usually the rules and regulation men, not able to move their bowels without a clearance docket, and they're the type you never want on a detective unit. Occasionally you get the opposite type, a guard who wants to bypass the system, who sees the unexpected in everything and whose head is always crowded with ideas, although most of them are completely off the wall. Left to himself he'll burn out very quickly and it can be dangerous to put too much trust in him, but in a tightly run unit he can be a pure inspiration at times.

In our case, the maverick was Jimmy Coyne. Early in the new year, Jimmy picked up on my theory about the vodka and decided to run with it, straight through the bad feeling between the pathologist's office and the unit, until he was well out of sight. We didn't see him for a couple of days. I suppose the sergeant knew where he was, but he didn't mention anything about it to the rest of us. Early on Wednesday morning, I think – in the middle of the second week in January anyway – when we'd just clocked in and were hanging around checking our assignments for the day, Jimmy made his reappearance.

We all fell quiet for his big entrance, as if he was a scout coming back with vital information after a night behind enemy lines. It was a big let-down, though. Jimmy was unusually quiet and sheepish and down in the dumps, so whatever novelty he'd been chasing obviously hadn't worked out for him. Even the sergeant, who'd taken to positive reinforcement after a recent training seminar, was particularly short with him. Definitely not a prodigal son scenario.

Anyway, we sat down, as we did every morning by that stage of the investigation, to pool information and discuss possible leads. About halfway through the session, which he clearly hadn't been paying attention to, Jimmy suddenly piped in with, 'You know what I've done?'

The sergeant gave him a black look and obviously turned over a few other responses in his head before he finally asked, 'What?'

'I've kind of promised old Powlson a look at the files,' Jimmy admitted.

As I've said before, I was too young ever to have worked with Dr Powlson, but I knew that he was a very controversial figure. He was supposed to have been a brilliant forensic pathologist and college lecturer. Everyone told the same racy stories about his career and his private life, but the stories always diverged when it came to explaining how and why he had suddenly fallen out of favour. Some said that he believed so completely in his own infallibility that he got careless and was responsible for losing a major case. There were rumours that he had a homosexual affair with a government minister. Others claimed that he'd started turning himself into a personality, a sort of celebrity pathologist who did TV profiles and dragged on corpses for ghoulish entertainment. In any case, there was an almighty row between himself and the Minister for Justice at the time, after which he resigned from police work. That had been five years earlier, when I was twenty-three, still in uniform and dreaming about the glamour of detective work. Shortly after his resignation, Powlson had also retired from academic work and disappeared from view. Because of our frustrations, people kept suggesting bringing him in as a consultant, but actually, no one was really certain whether he was even alive or not.

Well, he was, as Jimmy Coyne explained. All too alive.

Early one morning, about a week after Jimmy's initiative, Powlson turned up at headquarters to address us in the conference room. Those of us who had never met him before could see immediately why he might rub the authorities up the wrong way. Everything about him was flamboyant, larger than life. I think he was almost seventy years old by then, but he dressed like a young peacock, all in greens and purples. He had a shock of thick white hair and wore a pair of heavy glasses low down on his nose. Looking at us over the rims, he was like a professor taking a tutorial, insisting on all the students being still and attentive before he started.

'I decided to come in,' he explained, 'because there are some uncertainties I'm worried about and I wanted to discuss them face to face instead of relying on written reports. I also enjoy an audience, of course. I'm not as familiar as I used to be with the personnel in here, although things can't have improved that much, with one exception.'

He stared at me so obviously when he said this that I actually blushed. True to form, the rest of the lads made it worse by overreacting. The Doc was obviously a practised charmer as well as everything else. I wondered if the stories about him being gay were accurate. I wondered if he'd ever had a partner, man or woman. It must have been a very patient person.

'I've been following the reports of the various cases in the newspapers,' he told us then. 'Casually, in any case. Until I read the files, I didn't realize that they were so closely linked. Tell me, there's a handwritten note attached to Mary Corbett's file ... *Could be overdose of sedative cleared from system. Midazzlem? Diazepam?* Who wrote that?'

'That was Dennison,' someone remembered. 'Why?'

'The spelling of midazolam is incorrect,' Powlson said.

The sergeant, who'd developed a fierce loyalty to the memory of Dennison, wouldn't hear a bad word said about the man. 'If it is,' he insisted, 'he got it from a medical source.'

Powlson ignored this. 'I was once involved in a case in England,' he recalled, 'where a young woman was diagnosed as having died of heart failure while making love with her boyfriend, and it was only when the later crimes of the boyfriend came to light – he raped and sexually assaulted other women while they were in a drug-induced state – that he admitted using midazolam to subdue his victims. Midazolam is a sedative administered for minor operations. If the dosage is too large, it causes temporary paralysis and memory loss. An overdose will kill, typically by respiratory suppression. Which is what happened with our boy friend. The first time he used midazolam to render his victim helpless, he overestimated the amount required, with fatal consequences.'

'Are you suggesting that it was used in these murders?' the sergeant asked.

'Look,' Powlson said, 'for all your understandable frustrations, there is nothing lacking in any of the post-mortem reports. The bodies were in advanced stages of decomposition when discovered. I'm not suggesting anything, therefore. But I have a question. Was the possible use of midazolam investigated and eliminated from your enquiries?'

The sergeant shook his head. 'It was never followed up at all.'

'Then I'd recommend it as a line of enquiry.'

'But it never showed up in any toxicology report.'

'It wouldn't. It has a half-life of only two to three hours.'

'Meaning what?'

'Meaning that after three hours only half the amount administered remains in the system, after six only a quarter, and so on. Unless the corpse is examined shortly after death, midazolam is almost undetectable.'

'How is it administered?'

'Routinely, by injection. This may or may not be an option here. There are no apparent puncture marks on the body of Matthew Rushford, for instance. Midazolam can also be taken orally, however. Mixed with a strong beverage, such as coffee or alcohol, it is undetectable. In the case in England, it was disguised in brandy.'

'Or vodka?'

'Why vodka?'

'The stomach contents of three of the victims.'

'I see.'

'And it would be consistent with the known circumstances of each abduction,' the sergeant added. 'A young woman, already drunk, is abandoned in a storm in the mountains and then picked up by an apparent Samaritan. "Here, have a slug of this to keep yourself warm, love." But then, the killer would have to be travelling with the mixture already prepared, wouldn't they?'

'Apparently so,' Powlson agreed. 'But a word of caution here. You're not going to make yourselves popular with your superiors if you try to enlist me as an expert witness.'

'We're not thinking that far just yet,' the sergeant told him. 'We're thinking of catching, not convicting.'

'In that case,' Powlson said, 'if you want to follow through on this idea, I suggest that you check out Accident and Emergency departments, where midazolam is almost exclusively stored and used. Also, any reported thefts of the drug in recent years would be significant. The distribution and usage are very tightly controlled, as you can imagine, so you should notice even minor discrepancies.'

For the first time, we not only had a possible explanation for what had happened to the four people who had been killed, but we had a rational one as well. It's impossible to overestimate the value of logic in situations like these. We think we're technologically advanced, well in control of the world, but the fact is, until we have reasonable explanations for things that are troubling us, we're as primitive as cave people, full of weird fears and superstitions. What Powlson had achieved in less than an hour, and it shouldn't be played down, was to give us back our self-belief.

There were a lot of other avenues in the investigation still to be explored and exhausted, of course, but after this meeting with Dr Powlson the sergeant dedicated about half the unit, along with some extra reinforcements, to working on the midazolam angle. It was very time-consuming and very tedious work, and by the end of it the real job was only beginning. We had a long list of the names of those people who had access to midazolam and the know-how to use it. All of them had to be interviewed separately. When we came back together one morning to divide this huge workload, about a week after the conference with Powlson, our initial enthusiasm had kind of drained away from us again. You looked at the thousands of names on the list and you reminded yourself that the midazolam thing was only a theory anyway, and your heart sank.

There wasn't any point trying to deny the size of the task, and the sergeant didn't bother. 'But let's be sensible about it,' he advised. 'Someone with an address in north County Dublin working in a hospital over there is less likely than someone living and working in Wicklow. We're not ignoring anyone on the list. We're just separating them into groups, on a sliding scale of suspicion, and taking the top group for interviews first.'

'Talking about groups,' someone put in, 'are we concentrating on men or women here?'

'We can't make that call,' the sergeant told him. 'Both. Let's say it's not an issue yet. What is an issue, though, is that we are not mentioning midazolam to anyone. The word midazolam does not pass anybody's lips. Is that clear?'

The worst thing about extensive enquiries in a murder investigation is that you have no interest in the people you're talking to unless they make your skin crawl a bit. I had responsibility for the hospitals and dental surgeries along a strip of the east coast and I'm sure I must have met loads of fascinating characters while I was working through the interviews, but the only one I can remember now is a particular orderly. He was a very nervous young fella, twenty-four years old, who claimed that his real talent was writing TV crime drama. I didn't believe him, mainly because he had no curiosity. He never asked me anything about my job as a detective. It was possible, of course, that he was jittery about something other than the Wicklow Mountains murders. He'd once been charged with possession of cannabis, for instance, although he hadn't been convicted. There was nothing irregular in the records of the hospital where he worked. All the drug supplies were impeccably accounted for. But a couple of disturbing things still came out of my conversation with the orderly, enough to put him on the secondary list of those recommended for a follow-up interview. For one thing, he knew so many people working in other hospitals in the region that the group looked to me like a small network. For another, he let slip that he travelled extensively around County Wicklow, scouting locations for his stories, as he put it.

I remember all this, not because the orderly featured again in the investigation – he didn't – but because his was the last interview I did that day and when I got back to the office there was a note waiting for me on my desk. A fella called Bill Keane wanted me to ring him back. I had no idea who he was, but I took the shortest route to finding out by returning his call immediately. He turned out to be the owner of a garage in Carlow, the main town in the next county south of Wicklow. He reminded me that we'd met back in November, when I was making enquiries about car sales, and he said that he had something he'd like to talk to me about. I covered the mouthpiece and shouted across to the sergeant to clear this idea, and then made an appointment with Bill Keane for the following morning.

He was a main dealer for Subaru, a big, broad-shouldered, middle-aged man who looked and dressed like a bouncer in a nightclub. We were joined in his office at the garage by a thin young fella who was introduced as Clive Belton, a junior salesman. Keane explained that he'd been away the previous three weeks, mostly on business, partly on a short break, and that the story to be told was really Belton's, who had passed it on to his boss only because he was worried a customer might complain about his treatment of her.

It seemed that a blonde woman had driven an Impreza on to the garage forecourt a couple of weeks back and enquired about newer models. Belton had escorted her around the showroom, fed her all the spiel, all the literature and all the best deals he could offer her, while in the meantime a mechanic had taken a quick look at the Impreza to evaluate it for a trade-in. The car was only eighteen months old, but it had a substantial distance on the clock. Nothing to worry about, Belton explained, if the owner was a sales representative, say, or a trades person making house calls, but the woman let slip in conversation that while she needed something for rough terrain, she only drove a short distance from home to her work in Tallaght, in Dublin, with the occasional day trip at weekends. According to Belton, the woman went ballistic when he mentioned the trade-in value of her present car. She tore strips off him, he said. And completely out of the blue. He had never seen anyone switch so suddenly from being a pleasant customer to behaving like a scalded cat. Even though he admitted that he'd made a mistake and apologized for it – she only wanted to buy a new car, he accepted, not trade the old one – she just hissed at him a bit more before driving off in a fury.

I got a description of the woman from him. He couldn't give me the registration number of the Impreza she was driving, because he had no reason to take a note of it at the time. And the garage had no CCTV, so I couldn't get an image of the woman to support his description.

I still had about fifty leads from the earlier enquiries into car sales that no one had found the time to follow up properly, and the sergeant wanted to know why I was so eager to put this one to the head of the queue, particularly as he'd have to draft in a replacement to cover the hospitals and dental surgeries on my patch. I don't think he took much convincing, to be honest. He was already aware of the possibilities and probably only wanted me to clarify them for myself.

'If the woman works in Tallaght,' I said, 'and drives a short distance from home over rough terrain, she can only be living in the mountains to the south of Dublin. And Carlow was more than eighty kilometres from the capital. Why drive that far? Why not use a local dealer?'

The sergeant gave me a week to devote myself to finding the woman, if I also committed myself to clearing up the other outstanding leads in the process. He gave me a couple of short cuts as well. His guess – and it showed the value of experience in these things, because it hadn't occurred to me – was that the woman wouldn't drive the Impreza into another garage. If she wanted to buy a new car, she'd arrive on foot or get dropped off by a friend. On the other hand, if she was going to off-load the older model, she was more likely to do it privately or through one of the smaller, shadier dealers. Of course, she'd only behave like this if she had something to hide. If she was a law-abiding woman with a very bad temper and, say, a teenage daughter who took the car a lot without permission, she wouldn't.

I had the make, the model and the year of the car. So my first task was to find out what dealers had imported Imprezas that year and who had bought them. While I was waiting for the manufacturer's import agents to come back to me on this, I drew up an information sheet, including a description of the blonde woman, and circulated copies of it to every dealer and garage in the region, from County Carlow in the south to north County Dublin. And while I was waiting for responses to that, I checked the For Sale columns in all the relevant newspapers and car magazines for the previous months.

After three days, when the sum total of my findings amounted to absolutely nothing, the sergeant, who was probably sick of looking at me, suggested I should go out and get acquainted with the rougher end of the trade: the back lane dealers, the scrap merchants, the guys who made a living out of old bangers. I thought there'd be far too many of these dealers, but when I checked the information I already had from government departments, I found that they were few enough. The country's recent prosperity had driven a lot of them out of business. People didn't buy so many old cars any more, they didn't need so many spare parts, and they traded in junk to government scrappage schemes rather than privately.

Whether the woman was telling the truth about her workplace or not, I made up my mind to start with Tallaght as my centre and draw an arc thirty kilometres south of it, an area that included all the burial and abduction sites that we knew of. And the only reason I decided to begin on the east rather than the west of this arc was because I was already familiar with the area from checking the hospitals and dental surgeries there. That was a piece of luck. And it probably saved me two to three days of legwork.

The morning after the sergeant pushed me out of the office, on about the fifth call I'd made that day, I was talking to an old man with oil-stained overalls and a blackened face, who was sitting like a gnome on top of a pile of shattered car shells in a yard off the main road out of the village of Rathnew. Yeah, he told me, he'd seen the car I was talking about. And the woman, too. 'What did she do?' he wanted to know.

There I stood, looking up at him on his perch, my heart pounding and my insides churning like clothes in a washing machine, calmly telling him that she hadn't done anything, as far as we knew, but that the car had been dirty before she bought it.

'Maybe she knew that,' the old man fenced.

'Maybe she did,' I said.

'That would explain a lot of things,' he hinted.

'Like what?' I asked.

'Not everything, mind,' he hedged. 'But a lot.'

This dance went on for an awful long time. In the end, along with the vital bits, it included his own life story, his reasons for drifting into the motor racket, a calculation of the number of black people living in Ireland, and dire warnings about the consequences if the figure ever went over a certain percentage of the population. He'd particularly noticed the Impreza, he explained finally, because you never get two-year-old cars being offered for sale as scrap. 'Unless there's something drastically wrong with them, either mechanically or legally.'

In fact, that was his big mistake the day the blonde woman brought the Subaru in to him, two weeks earlier. 'What's wrong with it?' he'd asked. That was the only thing he said, apart from 'Hello!' and 'It looks like we'll have snow before the month is out!' But for the blonde woman it was one question too many. 'A nasty little piece of work,' the old man called her, 'with language out of her that'd make a sailor blush.'

The old man had remembered most of the car's registration. The year, because it was the first thing he noticed. The letter identifying the licensing authority, because he'd have to deal with them if he took the car. And the rest, the unique five-digit number, because he was annoyed at the way the woman verbally abused him and he was half-dreaming of tracking her down and teaching her manners. The only thing that hadn't stuck in his mind was the final digit. 'But it can only be one of nine, anyway,' he consoled me.

It turned out to be the tenth, a zero. The numbers one to nine in the same sequence had been allocated to other makes of cars.

Back in the office, it took me all of fifteen minutes to establish that its owner was Margaret Malone, a woman with an address in Tralee, County Kerry, a town on the opposite side of the country, and only a little longer to locate the details from her driving licence, where the address was given as the same. Although this address was consistent with the licensing authority which had issued the registration plate, it struck me as an odd starting point for someone who ended up visiting garages in County Wicklow, two hundred and fifty kilometres away.

The driving licence was a standard ten-year type, issued six years earlier. The photograph attached to it showed a good-looking, but very serious young woman, with long black hair. Her date of birth made her thirty-four now, twenty-eight when the photograph was taken.

One of the things that's drummed into you on seminars and training courses these days is to make sure that you keep cross-referencing and cross-checking all the open lists during an investigation. The instructors keep reminding you of all the major enquiries that failed or were fatally delayed because this wasn't done, particularly the Yorkshire Ripper case in England, where the killer's name was on three separate lists of suspects drawn up by three different forces and nobody noticed it until it was all over. You're told that this sort of thing is what computers are good at. The job that used to take ten officers a whole month to get through with card files can now be done by a computer in a matter of hours.

When I fed Margaret Malone's name into our database, I did it as routine. I was really thinking at the time about how to handle the address in Kerry, whether to leave it to the local guards to check out or whether to push my luck and ask the sergeant to approve a trip down there. I hit the Enter key after typing the full name and then I looked down the office towards the sergeant, who was talking to a couple of the lads about their returns from the interviews they were conducting. Three minutes later I got the surprise of my life. There were five matches for the name Margaret Malone. Three of them referred to an older woman from Rathfarnham, close to the housing estate where Michael Elwood lived, who had been interviewed as part of the house-to-house enquiries in the area. The fourth listed a Margaret Malone as one of the hundreds of people who had bought a Subaru Impreza from a dealer over the last four years. But the fifth was on that long list we had drawn up after the conference with Dr Powlson of all the people who had access to midazolam and the know-how to use it. Margaret Malone was a dental nurse working in a surgery in Tallaght, in south County Dublin.

Looking at this, my eyes suddenly filled up with water and went completely misty. Isn't that an odd reaction, when the thing you really want to do is to see clearly and to make sure that you've read the information correctly? Instead, I was actually blinded for a few seconds. Does it happen because the mind wants to shut down all the other systems while it's processing the shock? I don't know. I felt dizzy and light-headed. I could feel a rush, which was probably adrenaline pumping through my body. I got caught a little short of oxygen and had to take a couple of deep breaths and close my eyes.

Older fellas on the job will tell you that these queer moments of elation never happen, or if they do then they only come when a court conviction is secured against someone you've been chasing for a long time, that the satisfaction is in the result and never in the process of getting there. I'd have to disagree with them on that. I really would.

In any case, after fumbling with a paper hankie and rubbing the moisture from my eyes, I managed to calm down by reminding myself that if there were two Margaret Malones on the database, then there was no logical reason why there shouldn't be three of them. It mightn't necessarily be the same woman at all. With this in mind, I took another few deep breaths and opened my eyes. And then I called for help. 'Sarge?' I said. I must have sounded frightened, or weird in some way, as if I'd accidentally erased the entire database, because he came running over immediately, and the lads who were with him came along too.

I like to think that it was only their greater experience, rather than the fact that they were men, which made them more confident and decisive than I was, because it was immediately obvious that none of them had anything near the same reservations about the findings as I had myself. As soon as I showed them what I had, every one of them, at some stage or other, said, 'Jesus, Galetti!' To tell you the truth, I was so confused, it sounded like irritation to me. And it was only afterwards that I realized it was really a compliment of sorts.

I don't think it makes any difference whether you're a police officer, a teenager or a businessman, whether what's on your mind is a murder enquiry, a first date or a corporate merger, everybody reacts the same way to personal worries. I couldn't eat and I couldn't sleep that night. I went to a film with Fergal in the evening and I can't remember what was slowing, who was in it or what it was about. We had a drink afterwards and went home and made love. I must have made a good job of pretending to be there. Fergal fell asleep with his arms around me, convinced that I was dozing off contentedly too. Anything but. I was like a car skidding in mud, with its engine roaring and its wheels going nowhere. My body was trapped under Fergal, but my mind kept spinning furiously, going over and over all the events of the day, all the hundreds of possible outcomes. The worst thing about worry is not that you can't do anything. It's that you can solve the problem a thousand times in your mind, and still be left with it.

I remember looking at the clock for the last time at 5.17 in the morning. I'd say I managed two hours of sleep. And it showed. Fergal didn't see me, because he left before me in the morning, but when I got to the office the rest of the fellas, as fellas do, thought I'd been out on the town. 'Jesus, Galetti!' they said. 'What were you celebrating?' The funny thing is, it's better not to admit, even to colleagues, that you're concerned about the job. 'Boyfriend won a bit of money,' I croaked.

The sergeant was getting a team ready to send to the surgery in Tallaght to interview Margaret Malone when I put a suggestion to him. It was the only thing I could still remember from all the plans and all the fantasies I'd dreamed up in the night. After he gave me the go-ahead I spent an hour with an artist, scanning photographs into the computer and retouching them, before I set off in search of Gary Gaynor, the man who'd last seen Michael Elwood leaving Johnnie Fox's pub with an unknown woman.

Gary was out of work, as it happened. He'd recently broken his fibula playing soccer and he was lying at home on the couch with his right leg in plaster, watching weird sports like tractor-pulling and in-line skating on the Eurosport channel. I don't think his wife appreciated having him for company all day. She was rude, even before I explained who I was, and she left me to find my own way around the house after turning her back on me in the hallway.

When I finally discovered where he was, I questioned Gary Gaynor again about that night, more than a year ago now, when he'd seen Michael Elwood in the pub and I got him to describe for me once more the woman he'd noticed at the bar. Then I showed him the photographs I'd prepared. Some were mug shots from our files. Two were of vaguely recognizable actresses who played minor roles in television soaps. The last was the photograph Margaret Malone had submitted for her driving licence. All of them featured women in their early-thirties and all had been touched up to give the subjects glasses and pinned-back auburn hair.

I'd have to say, they all looked pretty similar. I wasn't that confident of getting a conclusive result from the exercise. There are too many variables in these things. Some witnesses are more perceptive than others. Some people are better at describing what they see. Memories fade over a long period. And the connection between a photograph and a real face, particularly one you've only seen on a single occasion, can be difficult to make.

I was more than happy with what I ended up with, though. Gary Gaynor picked out three of the photographs that he thought might resemble the woman he'd seen in the pub. I was pleased that he didn't try to be more definite than that, because I wouldn't have trusted him if he was claiming a positive identification. One of the photographs was of a shoplifter, one was of an actress. On the night in question the previous March, the first had been in jail and the second had been on location in England. The third photograph was of Margaret Malone. Nothing you could bring into court and convince anyone in there to accept, but I was pretty certain that at last we had found the woman who had led Michael Elwood to his death.

I had the right suspect, as I quickly confirmed. But I had the wrong word. The trouble with Margaret Malone was that no one *could* find her.

She wasn't at her work place in Tallaght. The last anyone there had heard from her was a Tuesday morning three weeks earlier when she'd called in sick, complaining that she was suffering from influenza. At the time, she anticipated being out for one or two weeks and the surgery had organized a temporary replacement. When the fortnight went by, they contacted the telephone number they had for Margaret Malone. There was no response, so they left a message.

They were struggling without her, the senior dentist claimed. She was an excellent nurse, reliable in emergencies, always willing to pitch in with more than her share. She'd been with the practice for five years and nobody had any complaints about her. A model employee. But this reputation came under a bit of strain when the dentist put two and two together after the lads asked if she had any responsibility for ordering, storing or administering drugs and then requested details of their records covering the last five years, as well as the telephone number and address on Margaret Malone's personnel file.

Actually, there were two addresses on her file. One was in County Kerry, which we already knew about. The other was in Dublin city. This turned out to be a small apartment, only five minutes' walk from our own headquarters. But even before anybody reached it, we all knew that she wasn't going to be there, either.

Still, it was important not to go bursting in there. 'We've been patient for a year and a half,' the sergeant said. 'We can be patient another few days.' First, he wanted to establish who owned the apartment and what agency was responsible for selling or letting the accommodation in the block. He wanted to know how the rent or the mortgage for Margaret Malone's apartment was paid, whether it was in arrears or not, and what contact she had with other owners or tenants and with the service staff. Particularly, he wanted to find out what her neighbours knew of Margaret Malone. Precious little, was the answer to the last question. Most had never seen her. One young executive thought he'd met her in the lift one morning, but couldn't be sure. He'd seen someone like her get on from her floor as he was coming down, someone who looked like the woman in the photographs we showed him, except that her hair was different.

While the sergeant was organizing a court order for search and entry, he put surveillance on the apartment. Just in case. But nothing happened. Nobody came. Nobody went.

Once you got to look inside, this didn't in the least surprise you.

The apartment had never really been lived in. For all the world, it looked like a showroom apartment, with shiny wooden floors, spotless rugs, sparkling worktops, fresh linen and shop-window furniture. Not that much of any of these things, really. Just enough to take the bare look off the place.

There was nobody there, of course. At the same time, you could tell that *somebody* had been in and out. The wear on the front door lock wasn't consistent with the apartment's age, but it showed evidence of regular use. As well as that, the only post on the mat inside was an advertising brochure from the Electricity Supply Board that had been delivered to every home in the country over the previous fortnight. If the apartment had been unvisited for long periods, there would have been more. More flyers. Newsletters from the local residents' association. Junk mail. Somebody collected the stuff and binned it on a frequent basis.

The telephone and electricity accounts were in Margaret Malone's name, as was the lease. All were paid by direct debit through her bank account. The address on the bank account was that of the apartment. Neat little circles.

There were only two messages on the telephone answering machine. Both were from the surgery in Tallaght. Get well soon, Margaret. We miss you.

After a quick look, the sergeant decided to clear us out and ask in the Technical Bureau. To the naked eye, there didn't seem to be much that could be collected from this bare scene. There were no clothes, no personal effects, no newspapers or books or magazines. But whoever checked in on a regular basis was sure to have left a great many traces, without being even aware of it. Ideally, what you'd hope for would be something decisive. Hair, for instance, to match the two samples we already had, from Karen Stokes's grave and Matthew Rushford's cottage.

It's funny, how suddenly things can change, how quickly hope can fade away. While we'd once had three addresses where we might find Margaret Malone, now we had none. We already knew, because we'd asked the local station, that she wasn't at the family home in Tralee, County Kerry. The word was, she hadn't been down for a visit since Christmas.

What we did get from the local guards, though, was a personal history of Margaret Malone. It made for interesting reading. She'd had a troubled childhood. There were a couple of convictions by a juvenile court, for stealing from clothes shops, when she was twelve years old. The Probation Act had been applied. The temper, and the mood swings, that the Wicklow car dealer had mentioned to me had always been a feature of her personality, leading to constant difficulties with teachers. Probably for that reason, she'd skipped school a lot. Finally, she'd run away from home at fourteen, nobody knew to where, and only came back, two months later, when her father also disappeared. Her father had never been heard from again, but apart from a brief spell the following summer running with kids who were dealing dope, she seemed to have settled down in his absence. Academically, she was fairly bright. She got good results in school examinations and had an excellent record as a student before qualifying as a dental nurse. She'd worked in England for a few years, emigrated to America in 1994 and finally come back home to join the practice in Tallaght. She was an only child. Although she visited her mother on a regular basis, at least four times each year, she'd broken all other contacts with her home town and never called on anyone else when she was in Tralee.

'Do you fancy going down there, Kris?' the sergeant asked me.

A five-hour drive, an overnight stay in some hotel that hadn't seen a tourist for at least a month, one more indulgence from Fergal for re-arranging plans, and a cast-iron guarantee that Margaret Malone wouldn't be anywhere within fifty kilometres of the place? 'Sure,' I said.

'Who do you want to take for company?' he asked.

A five-hour drive? An overnight stay? When the chips are down, I suppose chauvinism is really a self-defence mechanism.

There was another young woman detective who'd joined the unit before Christmas. 'How about Melanie?' I suggested. 'You know, good experience for her.'

To be honest, I expected the visit to Mrs Malone to be nothing more than a routine interview. We'd pick up a little background colour, I thought, one or two pointers as to where the daughter might hang out, and maybe something that could be useful in understanding why she was implicated in such gruesome crimes, although the little we knew of her childhood already hinted at an answer to that.

As I'd planned, the long journey down to County Kerry was really a breeze. Melanie Carey was the same age as myself and had exactly the same experience of male guards in the force. We passed the time swapping stories about crude pickups and sexist comments. It was a relief, when we stopped for lunch, not to have to make it clear that we were *only* stopping for lunch. Even the most decent of men will always be thinking of sex, and five hours in a car with them will keep you so much on your toes that you'll be flaked out at the end of the journey.

Then again, a man would always insist on driving the whole way on a trip like that. He wouldn't share. He wouldn't say anything about it, so you'd be left to decide whether he thought you were too weak, too thick, too incompetent or too valuable to put behind a wheel. Either way, whether he was saving you or saving himself, he'd be telling you that he was better. If you accepted it, you felt bad about yourself. If you didn't, you had a row. I can tell you, those were the kind of complications I genuinely missed on the trip down to Kerry with Melanie.

At the local station in Tralee we met up with the community guard, who was detailed to bring us to the Malone home and introduce us to the mother, whose name was Bridget. There was no easy way to explain our interest in the woman's daughter, so the story we'd agreed on was that, although Margaret wasn't officially listed as a missing person, her colleagues and friends hadn't been able to contact her the past week. The likelihood, we'd say, was that she'd just taken a break somewhere. All we were doing was looking for suggestions about the location.

The terraced house was very small and very cramped, typical of the local authority dwellings built for working people back in the 1950s. Great workmanship inside and solid red brick on the outside, but with tiny rooms. As a guard working in Dublin, you get to visit hundreds of the same type. Before you got there, you would've been confident of closing your eyes and predicting its contents, from the type of furniture to the china ornaments, from the family photographs to the old sports trophies.

I had no idea how accurate I could have been if I'd put my mind to this game, because I swear, stepping into that house was like walking on to the set of a film you've seen a hundred times or walking straight into a scene that keeps recurring in your nightmares. It was that familiar. I was so affected by it that I was speechless for a while and Melanie, who didn't understand what was happening to me, had to take up the conversation with Bridget Malone.

On a glass cabinet, for instance, in the little front room where we were invited in to talk, there were a number of old wooden trophies with brass greyhounds perched on top of them. These were the first things that caught my eye. I immediately went across to take a closer look at them, as Melanie, after a bit of early confusion, settled fairly smoothly into the formalities. I stooped to read the inscriptions that were etched on little silver plates attached to the bases. I never managed it, though. I couldn't tell you a word or a date from any of them. My eyes were distracted. Further down, inside the cabinet itself, across the upper shelf, there was an untidy row of crime novels. Agatha Christie. Margery Allingham. All the old English classics. But no sooner had I noticed these than my eyes travelled down again, to the lower shelf. And that's what took my breath away. Because there, propped up, with its cover facing outwards, was a black, leather-bound stamp album.

The cabinet was locked. I tested it discreetly. Afterwards, I stood in front of it for a while, my hands itching to reach past the glass, my mind racing with wild thoughts. I felt dizzy. I went back and sat down in the old armchair Bridget Malone had offered me when we'd come into the room, but even then, like a child with a packet of sweets that's just out of reach, I kept looking hungrily across at the stamp album.

'Who raced the greyhounds?' I asked finally.

Bridget Malone was only sixty-two years old, still in good shape and not suffering from anything more serious than the usual colds, but she was one of those really gloomy people who gave the impression that things had never been so bad and would only get worse. It didn't matter what you were talking about. You could ask how the weather had been in Kerry and she'd moan as if she was in agony and tell you how many people had ended up in the morgue during the last cold snap, whose cat had drowned in the recent floods, and the names of three notorious sunbathers who were dying of skin cancer. I suppose, since she'd been abandoned at forty-two and had reared a fairly disturbed only child, she had some genuine cause for misery. But you'd also think that she'd have pulled herself out of it by now. Whenever she mentioned her husband, she actually had tears in her eyes. 'That was Christy's father kept the dogs,' she explained.

I was surprised. 'Your *husband*'s father?'

'Margaret's grandfather. Francie. We had to put them all down when he died, God rest him.'

'When was that?'

'His heart was broken when Christy went missing. He never got over it. There wasn't a day passed when he didn't mention it. It was the last thing he said on his deathbed. If only Christy was here, he said, I'd go easier. He'd be dead fifteen years now this September. That's a picture of him there. And that's Christy with him, when he was only eighteen.'

She showed us photographs then, some of them already hanging on the walls, some from albums she brought out for us to inspect. When she left the room to dig up even more photographs, frantically I pointed out the stamp album to Melanie, forgetting that she was too recently on the job to understand its significance. I started to explain, but Bridget Malone bustled back in with an armful of paper wallets stuffed with family snapshots.

'Brian McCartan,' she said. 'One of Christy's friends. He was always mad about cameras, even when he was small. He took a lot of them.'

The real Christy Malone – at least in the few years before his disappearance, according to the local guards – had been considered odd by his neighbours. They had nothing bad to say about him. He was just unsociable. Although he worked as a labourer in the local bacon factory, along with his father and most of the other men in the community, he never drank with his workmates and rarely took part in any group activity. His pastimes were solitary.

In the first sequence of photographs – the ones that were already either hanging on the walls of the front room or inserted into albums – Christy had come across as pretty much the average young man of his time, posing with his workmates on seaside holidays, standing with his father at greyhound meetings and sitting with his sister and both his parents at the family home. All of them had been taken between his sixteenth birthday in 1958 and the year before his marriage a decade later. The longer you looked at the rest of the collection, though, the more you noticed that he seemed to have deserted his family long before he actually disappeared. Apart from the conventional photographs of his wedding, he no longer featured in the shots. His wife cradled or fed or played with their young daughter, but always by herself. His father shared the frames only with the greyhounds now. And when his workmates gathered, they seemed to leave a space for the absent Christy.

'Was your husband away during the early years of your marriage?' I asked.

'No, he was never away.'

And yet, one particular batch of photographs, about thirty in all, had been taken in New York. All were of well-known buildings. None had any recognizable human figures. But still . . . 'When were you in America?' I wondered.

'Me?' Bridget Malone asked, obviously astonished by the idea. 'I was never in America.'

I showed her the photographs.

'That must have been Christy himself,' she explained. 'He came home from New York to marry me when we found out . . . When we had a date for the wedding.'

'How long was he over there?'

'He wasn't long. He was only there about a month. That time. He was over before that, too. Another time.'

'What was he doing over there?'

'I couldn't tell you that now, to be honest. It was that long ago.'

'You don't know any American people named Kleisner, do you, Mrs Malone?'

'Kleisner?'

'Sarah Kleisner. Or Robert Kleisner.'

'I don't know any Americans at all, girl.'

'This one,' I said, handing her another photograph. 'I know it's probably just one he picked up somewhere. But that's Berkeley University, isn't it? In the States. When they were having riots there in nineteen sixty-eight.'

'I wouldn't know, love. We never had a university in Kerry.'

'When your husband disappeared, Mrs Malone, did anyone think of America?'

'They did, I suppose, but what good would it have done?'

'Why not?'

'I knew Christy wasn't still alive, God rest him. I always knew he wasn't alive. If he had been, he would've been in touch with myself and Margaret, no matter where he was. He's lying out there stretched in some bog or wood and he'll never be found now. I never liked to say it when his father was still with us. It would have finished poor Francie. And then, you'd have people saying I was only doing it for the widow's pension. No, Christy would've let us know if he was still alive. He went looking for Margaret, you see, that time she gave us all a fright and ran away for a few days. Something happened to him then. He never took his passport or anything with him. He left everything behind him. He never planned to be away more than the few days.'

All the time, even as we were talking about her vanished husband, she kept feeding me new batches of photographs and I kept flicking through the snapshots. Most of them I put back in the wallets that they'd come from. Some I put to one side, on the arm rest of the chair I was sitting on. I got no impression from Bridget Malone that she was anxious or nervous in any way about my inspection. There was an uneasiness to her, but it didn't seem to have anything to do with the photographs. I guessed that it was her unexpected pregnancy in 1967 that had brought Christy Malone back from America and that Margaret's birth the following year had kept him in Ireland. But once she got over her initial embarrassment about this, it didn't seem to bother her any more.

All in all, I'd have to say that the photographs were affecting me a lot more than they were her. When we'd finally worked our way through all the wallets, for instance, and I picked up the little pile I'd set aside, the photograph on top was that of a fat man in a blood-soaked apron grinning at the camera and holding up the corpse of a dead greyhound as if it was a hunter's trophy.

'Who's that?' I asked.

'That's Brian,' she told me. 'Brian McCartan. Who had the cameras. Christy's friend.'

'Was he a butcher?'

'I think he had a place of his own.'

'A place of his own?'

'A slaughterhouse. I think he had.'

'Do you know where he lives?'

'He's dead now, God rest him.'

Creepy enough. But another set of photographs that I was particularly interested in showed Margaret Malone as a child, from infancy to early teens, in the company of two rough-looking country men, sometimes on her own, sometimes with her mother.

'They're my brothers,' Bridget Malone explained. 'Margaret's uncles. Bob and Ted.'

As soon as you knew the relationship, of course, you could immediately spot the facial resemblance. 'Did they keep greyhounds?' I wondered.

She laughed, the only time I heard the sound from her through the entire interview. 'No, they never had dogs. They hated dogs. They had a little farm outside town, where we were all born.'

'A crop farm?'

'A bit of this and a bit of that. Crops. The odd livestock. But chickens, mostly. They bred chickens all their lives. They're dead too now, God rest them. They were always older than I was.'

'What about that other photograph album?' I asked then, trying to keep everything casual and my voice as steady as possible. 'The one in the little glass cabinet there. Anything interesting in that?'

Immediately, she got all flustered. Things dropped from her hands to the floor. Her face went red. 'No, that's not a photograph album,' she said.

'No?' I persisted. And I got up to have a closer look at it again. 'What is it?'

'Stamps,' she said. 'It's a stamp album.'

'Was it Margaret's?'

She didn't answer this. She tried to change the subject. 'Them aul' books on the shelf above it, now. They were Christy's. You wouldn't believe how long they've been sitting there. Margaret used to read them as well when she was small.'

When this didn't work, I kept returning to the stamp album, no matter what diversion she tried. She turned on the tears, wailing that her daughter was probably dead or disappeared and we wouldn't tell her, and what was she going to do now, the only person she had left in the whole world . . .

I took a chance and decided to play along with this. 'To tell you the truth, Mrs Malone,' I said, 'we *are* worried about your daughter's disappearance.'

'But you only said—'

'I didn't want to alarm you too much earlier. The fact is, I've been instructed to return with photographs, which you've kindly offered, and to ask about a stamp album which Margaret keeps referring to in her diaries.'

It took a lot more persuasion and a lot more pressure than that, and the whole thing ruined the good humour of the interview and did away with the hope of any further revelations, but in the end I got what I wanted. She agreed to let me have the stamp album when I was going. She still tried to out-manoeuvre me as I was leaving, creating a big diversion that involved her grief, her health and the community guard, and conveniently forgetting, until I had to remind her, about that stamp album that was still in the cabinet. Then, of course, she couldn't find the key to the cabinet. She searched and searched, turning over everything else in the house, and all in vain, until Melanie suggested that she could easily pick such a simple lock without damaging it. *Then* the key was found.

I put the album and the photographs into an unsealed evidence bag and waited until Melanie had driven back to the local station to drop the community guard and we were out on the main road to Castleisland, where we were staying overnight, before examining it.

I don't think I'm easily shocked any more. My time in the guards has hardened me up. But certain things, because of the combination of being offensive in themselves and the context in which you look at them, can really disturb you. For me, that stamp album was one of those things.

As described in the narratives, it contained only Irish stamps. It didn't have all of these that were ever issued – that would make it extremely valuable – but it had all the definitive issues and all the commemorative issues from 1952 to 1981, and those from the first half of 1982. My guess was, that Christy Malone started collecting them as a twelve-year-old boy in 1952 and kept at it until his disappearance. An extraordinary level of persistence and devotion and care that he didn't seem to give to anything else in his life.

The chances were, then, that it wasn't Christy himself who had obscenely defaced some of the stamps. It was hardly his wife, although she obviously knew about it. So perhaps it was their fourteen-year-old daughter, when she'd come back home following her father's disappearance after being on the run for a few months?

There was a simple pattern to the destruction. It involved only the stamps that were issued for Christmas each year, and even then, only the stamps that depicted the traditional Christian Holy Family of Joseph, Mary and the Infant. Stamps that showed only the Madonna and Child were untouched. It started with the Flight into Egypt of 1960, where Mary is cradling the infant Jesus and rides on a donkey led by Joseph. It included another Flight into Egypt of 1973, this one after a sixteenth-century Flemish painting, the Nativity of 1976, the Holy Family of 1977, another Nativity of 1980, based on a child's winning entry in an art competition, and it ended with a final Nativity of 1981, which used a painting by Frederico Barocci.

I didn't have all this information, of course, the first time I looked at the stamps. I'm not that bright. I swotted it up afterwards.

It wouldn't have made any difference to my reaction, one way or the other.

Although I'm not religious any more, I was brought up Catholic as a child, so obviously there was a personal element to the disgust I felt. But I think it's the glimpse inside a very damaged mind that affects you the most.

All the male figures of Joseph in each of the stamps I've mentioned had been given a huge erect penis, drawn with a fine black marker. But possibly most disturbing of all was that the erect penises weren't directed towards the woman on the stamps; they were attempting to penetrate the figure of the little child.

The morning after we came back from Kerry with the stamp album and the photographs, it was decided to treat the search for Margaret Malone as a missing person's enquiry. It's a normal enough tactic and can be very useful. You'd make sure you had more than the usual publicity, with a lot more coverage in the media, more photographs released, and possibly even a reconstruction on television, but otherwise it looked the same as any other missing person's enquiry, even to the extent of directing informants to their local Garda station instead of to the unit investigating the murders.

The address given on the press release sheet was that of the apartment in Dublin, although it was obvious that Margaret Malone must be living somewhere else, and possibly with others. It was felt at one stage that she might already be out of the country, so passenger lists on flights and ferry sailings were rigorously checked. The search for the Subaru she had tried to sell to the dealer in County Wicklow was broadened and intensified, an area I still had overall responsibility for. Every patient who ever received treatment in the dental surgery in Tallaght where she'd worked was traced and interviewed, a long and tedious business that was made even more vital when it was discovered that there were major discrepancies in the records at the practice. Not only midazolam but other drugs as well were missing and unaccounted for.

When I had a bit of spare time, I went back over the TV news footage I had of the crowds at the earlier grave sites, looking for Margaret Malone's face. I imagined I saw her once or twice, but I suppose I was only fooling myself. No one else, and most of them were using equipment a lot more sensitive than my eyes, could see anything better than blurs.

I thought a lot too about Bridget Malone in her little house down in Tralee in County Kerry. The woman puzzled me. You'd have to wonder why she kept that stamp album all those years, particularly in such a prominent place, where she could see it every day. She knew what was inside it. That much was obvious from the way she'd reacted when I asked to have a look at it.

It's probably a sad reflection on the bleakness of my life at the time, but whenever I had fantasies, I dreamed of talking to Bridget Malone again and getting her to tell me exactly what had happened in that little family of hers, exactly what circumstances her husband had left in, and exactly what had been said and done when their fourteen-year-old daughter returned home within days of her father's departure.

Everybody has dreams. That's my only defence.

And while we are dreaming them, the world invariably takes an unexpected turn.

It seems unfair, of course, that the private description of a desirable future is now called fantasy. Like most private functions, it doesn't enjoy a decent reputation. Since the word is derived from the Greek for appearance and since appearance has traditionally been opposed to reality, from the fourteenth century onwards fantasy has denoted delusive imagination and baseless supposition. Not really the sort of things to be caught indulging in. On the other hand, the *public* description of a desirable fantasy is known by many names, and all of them are dignified. Sometimes it is called political philosophy, sometimes prophecy, and sometimes a Programme for Economic and Social Progress.

However.

Four days after Margaret Malone was officially listed as a missing person, a man walked into the small Garda station in the village of Donard in County Wicklow. Already well known to the guard who was on duty at the time, he was listened to with considerable attention and respect. The man explained that he had come in with information concerning the apparently elusive Margaret Malone. He could not, he said, be absolutely certain where the woman actually was, but he could, nevertheless, offer an educated guess, since the authorities had the wrong address for her. The impression he gave was that he was treating the entire affair as a joke, and one that must be shared with his country friends, including the local police officers. Only the incompetents in the city, he suggested, would think of looking everywhere for a woman, with the notable exception of her own home.

This man's name was Patrick Kelly.

Margaret Malone, he insisted, did not have an apartment in Dublin. That must be another woman, of exactly the same name. This Margaret Malone, the one in the photographs released by the police, copies of which he had seen for the first time less than an hour before, lived with her partner in their cottage up at Corriebracks, in the mountains above the village.

Partner? repeated one of the city incompetents who came out to interview him later that day.

A bit of a tyrant, Patrick Kelly confided.

What's his name?

I'm not sure. I've only really seen him. I've never talked to him.

How did you come to know the woman, then? the investigators asked.

Well, I have a bit of a business concern in the village, a shop ...

Do you know her because she was a customer in your shop?

Not exactly, no ...

Does she have an account with you?

No, not at all.

None of the other business people in the village seem to know her, you see. In fact, nobody in the village, including the local guards, ever remember seeing her.

Well, she wouldn't have to pass through the village to reach her home, you see. She could get there on the back roads.

So how do you know where she lives, then?

By all accounts, this was when Patrick Kelly suddenly relinquished his hold on the humorous side of things and began to reconsider his commitment to the public good. He had come in voluntarily, after all, out of the goodness of his heart, as he stressed, with the sole intention of increasing the average IQ of the police force. And now he found himself being treated as a suspect. He had, of course, the usual reaction. He was outraged. Now look here! he shouted. And inevitably, he was not only a personal friend of the local superintendent, but also a trusted ally of the most powerful politician in the county.

It did not, however, take very much to quieten him. A whispered hint that he might be safer calling in his solicitor at this stage, which he did, followed by a whispered lecture from his solicitor, after the man was made nervous by a briefing from the police, was sufficient to achieve it.

Then the investigators were treated to Patrick Kelly's story.

Late in August, Kelly had been hunting or hill walking – it varied from one telling to another – up in Corriebracks when he chanced on the remote cottage where Margaret Malone lived. As luck would have it, she happened to be outdoors at the time, sunbathing in front of the cottage. He watched her through binoculars from the woods and, as he expressed it himself, took a shine to her. (Perhaps, since she was naked at the time, this was a euphemism for masturbating.) But so much of a shine, in any case, that he took to spying on her whenever he got the chance, which wasn't very often, unfortunately, only the occasional Sunday afternoon, because he was a very busy man, with a very sharp-eyed wife.

One afternoon, however, while he was in Carlow on business, he noticed a Subaru Impreza parked on the street with Margaret Malone sitting behind its steering wheel and he immediately seized what he took to be an opportunity to charm and impress her. She was rather rude to him. In fact, she almost completely ignored him. Shortly afterwards, an older man, who seemed to be in his sixties, came striding from a newsagent's and sat in the car beside her.

He was even more unfriendly, Kelly grumbled. Possessive, I suppose. Those old fellas get like that.

Did the woman refer to him? the investigators wanted to know.

No, he never said anything.

Did the *woman* say anything? Did she give him a title, for instance? My friend. My husband. Did she mention where they were going?

No, they just drove off.

To Kelly, the subsequent chase was perhaps no more than a boyish adventure, a bit of frivolous, if slightly questionable relief from a hectic business schedule and a tight-reined marriage. In any case, for one reason or another, despite the rebuffs, he indulged himself by persisting with it. And not without success, for having now established that Margaret Malone did the bulk of her shopping in Carlow, he managed to bump into her again on a number of occasions.

She was grand while her partner wasn't there, Kelly claimed, but a different woman altogether when he showed up.

One Sunday, perhaps because he found himself with some unexpected free time, perhaps because he believed he had chanced on a clever method of establishing social contact with the couple, he drove up to the peak of Corriebracks in heavy snow. Having already noticed the greyhound kennelled to the side of the cottage, he imagined that it might be a profitable idea to pretend that he was interested in buying some dogs.

The old man was away at the time, though, he told the investigators, and Margaret was alone in the cottage.

And? they prompted him.

And that was the last time I saw her, he said.

Did you go back? they asked him.

Kelly shook his head. No, I haven't seen her since. That was the last time I saw her.

Why not? they wondered.

What do you mean?

But surely, the meaning of the question was obvious. Why *hadn't* he gone back? What kept him away? What else did he know? What exactly had happened that Sunday afternoon? Why had he suddenly lost interest in Margaret Malone?

The hole Patrick Kelly now found himself standing in was only made deeper by his increasingly frantic efforts to dig himself out of it. From his safer position on the rim, this was something his solicitor finally made plain to him. And eventually, after a great deal of coaxing, after he had paled and weakened, Patrick Kelly confessed that he and Margaret Malone had had sex that Sunday he called to her cottage. Quite bizarre sex, he claimed, that involved copulating with various images of Margaret Malone as much as with Margaret Malone himself. At the time – in the moment, as they say – the strange experience had excited him and terrified him in more or less equal measures. The more he thought about it afterwards, however, the more his excitement died, and the more his terror increased. Like all penitents, of course, he was confusing distance with conscience. The woman was dangerous, he decided. Too extreme for his own milder tastes. Having looked into the depths of her devilish eyes, he had seen that he was just an ordinary man, attracted only by the permissible lapses of infidelity, but not by anything more permanent or more complicated, and certainly not by risk.

Being only human, of course – as the technicolour memories of what he had done and of the pleasures he had endured returned to challenge him in moments of tedium over the next few weeks – he had felt the

218

occasional tug in the direction of Corriebracks. But he had never given in to this temptation. And he had never gone anywhere near the cottage again. Margaret Malone had not contacted him. He hadn't seen her in Carlow, although he had been in there on business quite frequently. And neither had he seen the older man who was living with her in the cottage.

It was already dark, and quite late in the evening, before Patrick Kelly had finished his account. The delay was partly caused by the long wait for the solicitor he had requested, and partly by his own whimpers and evasions. By then, Sergeant Mullery and Superintendent Mullane, along with other members of the unit, had joined the interview team at the small station in the village. Despite the shared root of their surnames – *maol* is the Irish for servant and also, ironically, forms the basis of Malone as well as Mullery and Mullane (although confusingly *maol* is also the Irish for chief) – despite this, however, the two men were at loggerheads. The sergeant insisted on immediately assaulting Corriebracks with search warrants. The superintendent overruled him. It would be impossible to take the narrow path up the mountains without headlights to show the way, the superintendent argued, and the occupants, given a few minutes' warning of an impending raid, might well manage to escape the net. They could not be aware that the police had already located them. If they left, therefore, for unrelated reasons, they would do so by car, down the track and on to the road. To counter this, a squad car, manned by two uniformed guards, was positioned near the exit overnight.

The pair were still there at dawn the following morning, when the convoy of detectives passed them, two thin young men whose glazed expressions and frozen extremities were testimony to the fact that nothing had happened during the night.

First impressions of the cottage, however, seen through the morning mist at the end of the rough track when the convoy emerged from the woods, were extremely disappointing. It seemed deserted. There were no cars outside. There were no signs of life around it. And most depressing of all, there was no barking from the greyhound that Patrick Kelly had promised would resent their approach.

The cottage was whitewashed, but not so brightly or so recently that it stood out in any way against the landscape. The barn beside was of corrugated iron and painted a dull green that also did its best to blend with the surroundings. Between the barn and the cottage a gate had been erected and on the other side a small outhouse was in the early stages of construction.

All this was quickly noted and absorbed as the convoy broke from the woods and hurried on, each member of the unit braced for their separate task, with some detailed to check the barn, some to secure the rear exits of the cottage, some to handle the dog if it started giving trouble. All in all, an impressive display of speed and co-ordination, if anyone had been watching. But in the absence of an audience, perhaps it didn't even raise itself to the level of an illusion.

Sergeant Mullery knocked on the front door. Receiving no response, he instructed the others to force an entry and they immediately poured past him, their weapons at the ready, and fanned out through the building, working to the plan of the interior already supplied to them by Patrick Kelly. Some bundled into the front room, sweeping the space with their revolvers, the blood pounding so violently in their heads that they could hardly hear their own voices calling out – Clear! – and hardly catch the faint echoes of their own calls from the other rooms. Clear! Clear! The house was empty.

It was probably only then, of course, as the disappointment sank in and the adrenaline receded, that the detectives started noticing the framed prints that decorated the walls and furniture in the cottage. These weren't photographs. They were computer-generated images. Margaret Malone featured in most of them, but she had a different companion in each. Always a man, of course, but never the same one twice.

It was during this confused suspension of operations, as the others were puzzling over the tantalizing images, that Jimmy Coyne came bustling through the front door, badly out of breath after running across from the barn. He was looking for the sergeant.

Have you got a body? they asked him.

He shook his head. No. Cars!

They found the sergeant in the smaller of the two bedrooms. Although the white sheets on the unmade bed inside the room were heavily bloodstained, the sergeant wasn't looking at these. He was standing in front of the dressing table, staring down at the framed print that was placed there in front of the mirror. This one showed Margaret Malone standing on a beach between two men, who had their arms around her back and who were straining to caress her breast on the other side, although, quite impossibly, the figure to her left had the wizened face of

Matthew Rushford and the groper to her right was Thomas Dennison. A mere trick, of course. An idle invention, simply produced by scanning a number of photographs into a computer and abandoning all except surprise in the mix. The time-worn technique of a million crime novels, in other words. Effective, nonetheless. Crude. But startling.

We need you in the barn, Jimmy Coyne told the sergeant quietly.

Okay, the sergeant said. But he didn't turn around for quite a long time. And when he did, his face was still tense. Where's Patrick Kelly, by the way? he asked.

Nobody knew, other than the fact that he wasn't in custody. Most guessed that he was either still in bed or preparing to open his shop.

Get a uniform down there to make contact with him, the sergeant ordered. I want him to stay with Kelly until I come down to see him.

Is he under arrest? they asked.

No, the sergeant said. He's under protection.

He did not explain the reasons for this, only gestured to Jimmy Coyne and then silently followed him to the barn, where three cars, parked in a neat triangle, were awaiting his inspection. And perhaps his response, if he still had reserves of energy after his ordeal in the bedroom. One of the cars was the blue Opel Astra belonging to Michael Elwood that he had driven away from Johnnie Fox's pub on his final journey. Another was the Mondeo that Karen Stokes had parked between two white vans on the night of her disappearance. And the third was the Subaru Impreza that Margaret Malone had twice tried to get rid of over the previous few months.

The sergeant ordered a small team to check the boots and interiors of all three cars, but once these were found to be empty, he instructed the area to be cordoned off and left for the Technical Bureau to examine, for although all the vehicles looked immaculately clean, as if they had just been valeted, they would, of course, still contain many unseen traces of hair and skin and fibres.

Since the interior of the cottage had also been preserved as a crime scene, members of the investigating unit now regrouped in front of the building, close to the abandoned shell of the outhouse. The situation was analysed, the case re-examined, and certain conclusions reached and agreed on. As one detective rather colourfully put it, it was clear that the monster they had been hunting for the past year and a half had two heads, not merely one. Although no one, including the psychological experts, had anticipated or mentioned this, it was quite obvious that a couple had been involved in the abduction, killing, mutilation and burial of at least four individuals. The man's strength to transport and bury the bodies. The woman's guile to attract and dupe the victims.

Hindsight is a wonderful perspective. Enlightened by it, one could imagine Mary Corbett, drunk and abandoned during a storm in the mountains, quite gratefully accepting a lift from a rather beautiful young woman and her older companion, who happened to be passing. One could understand how the retiring Michael Elwood had been persuaded, again by a rather beautiful, if vulnerable, young woman, to rescue her by offering her a lift. And one could see how Karen Stokes had also been trapped by her own charity, helping an old man who seemed to be bewildered and lost.

A MARRIAGE MADE IN HELL, one of the headlines from the tabloids screamed over the following days. Although others, it has to be said, preferred the more musical LOVE AND CARNAGE. BAND OF GORE was undoubtedly a failure. RIPPER AND JILL was too allusive for a mass audience, although it had possibilities. And the rest were predictable. DEADLY DUO. KILLING FOR LOVE. SICKHEARTS.

It was thought by the police, one female correspondent claimed, that the evil couple may have experimented with drugging and raping young women before they carried out their heinous plans to abduct and murder their selected victims after stalking them for long periods.

No such thoughts, of course, ever crossed the minds of the detectives attached to the investigating unit. The weakness in the theory that the couple conceived and executed a series of masterly campaigns was the presence of Margaret Malone in Johnnie Fox's pub on the night of Michael Elwood's disappearance. This extremely public location was a mere ten kilometres from her workplace in Tallaght. It was entirely possible that some of the surgery's patients, who knew her, were also regulars in the popular public house. Although she had lightly disguised herself, wearing glasses and unfamiliar clothes, as well as dyeing her hair, she ran a considerable risk of being recognized.

This episode in Johnnie Fox's started out as no more than what might be called a dry run, therefore, a test of what might be achieved, and almost inadvertently developed into an actual murder. Accordingly, the detectives' understanding of the sequence of killings was correctly revised as follows. Mary Corbett was not stalked. Neither was she pre-selected as a victim. Although the couple may have been ready to kill at this stage, the choice of Mary Corbett was entirely accidental, an opportunity that presented itself rather than one that was in any way planned. Once the couple had decided, within the unique terms of their private world, that a middle-aged man had been responsible for the death of Mary Corbett, it was decided to test how easily a middle-aged man could be lured into offering himself as the culprit. All too easily, was the answer, as Margaret Malone demonstrated in Johnnie Fox's pub, an ease that was responsible for accelerating events beyond the preferred pace of the couple. The remaining victims, Karen Stokes and Matthew Rushford, were more carefully selected and monitored and trapped, if more hurriedly disposed of.

The second major conclusion agreed by the detectives gathered around the outhouse early that morning was that at least one other body was buried in the vicinity of the cottage. Opinion was sharply divided as to the identity of the corpse, however. Or corpses, for that matter. A couple who have co-operated in the abduction and killing of four others will have developed, not only a very special kind of bond, based on a shared world, a profusion of mutual encouragement and reinforcement, a sense of superiority and a siege mentality, but also a rather unique, and rather volatile, type of trust. You fall asleep each night knowing that the partner beside you, who may be still awake, is a multiple killer. You lose consciousness, all too aware that your partner, who may still be dressed for outdoors, has sufficient evidence to send you to jail for life. The moment this unique trust is fractured, in other words, what begins to dominate is mutual fear and mutual suspicion, intense hatred, and the slow circling of one killer around the other, searching for the most vulnerable spots.

It is impossible to end this type of relationship in any normal manner. There are, in fact, only two possible exits. One of the partners decides to barter their knowledge in return for a reduced prison sentence and walks into the nearest Garda station. Or one of the partners silences the storyteller before they can even begin.

The bruised face that Margaret Malone had shown Patrick Kelly and that he had described to the police, the psychologists informed the investigating detectives, was the first symptom of such a breakdown of trust. And the fact that Margaret Malone had seduced Patrick Kelly, presumably as an act of rebellion, was confirmation of this. And surely

Sergeant Mullery had been right, after all, to worry about the safety of Patrick Kelly. Kelly, who had been admitted to the interior of the couple's bizarre world and might have stumbled on something vital, was surely a threat to the surviving killer. Or killers.

For several days, once the Technical Bureau had finished examining the various scenes, teams of detectives and uniformed guards lifted up floorboards inside the cottage, dismantled the interior of the barn and dug the surrounding land, including the nearby woods, in a frantic search for further graves. When nothing was found, the search was broadened, to include more distant woods, more improbable hiding places. A common error, this confusion of territory with progress, of expansion with achievement. How much space does a nation require? How much ground does a body need?

At lunchtime one chilly afternoon, detectives in boiler suits and wellington boots were sitting on the layer of cemented breeze blocks that formed the low, unfinished walls of the abandoned outhouse to the side of the cottage, drinking tea and coffee from flasks, eating sandwiches of ham and beef and salad. How old is this thing? one of them suddenly asked. It must have been Jimmy Coyne, the youngest, the brightest, the sharpest of them all. How do you mean? they wondered. When was it built? Jimmy Coyne elaborated. What stage was it at when Patrick Kelly was up here? How much work has been done on it since then? Who did the work? How quickly morbid thoughts transmit themselves! Uneasily, the detectives stood up and stepped away, neglecting their food. As if the cold bricks could touch their hearts. As if their postures were disrespectful.

Sergeant Mullery was instantly summoned and he himself wasted no time in dispatching a squad car, down the narrow track, down through Blackpits, and into the village of Donard, to collect and come back with Patrick Kelly. Kelly's account was inconclusive, but disturbing. When he was up here, that Sunday afternoon, Margaret Malone was covering the exposed foundations with tarpaulin. At that time, there was no concrete floor to the outhouse, no row of bricks that marked the beginnings of the walls.

Drills and mechanical diggers, shovels, sledgehammers, pickaxes and chisels were all requisitioned. The existing bricks were numbered and removed and put aside. As soon as the concrete floor was tested, however, it revealed itself as fragile. Unusually thin, and supported only by a layer of weak wooden laths, it shattered immediately under the drills. Beneath it, there was a chamber, hollowed out of the ground. A burial chamber, for inside it, lying face upwards, was the corpse they had all been searching for. It was, as anticipated, entirely naked, although, in a radical departure from the treatment of the previous victims, the woman's face bore the evidence of a fatal blow. Beside her right hand, almost as if this was what the hand itself was reaching for, lay a bundle of papers, a narrative, lightly wrapped in a single sheet of cellophane, its text, at least on the first page, plainly legible beyond the transparent material. *My name*, it began. An autobiographical effort. But hardly voluntary. A confession, then. If not admissible in court, because produced under duress, then at least acceptable to us, who must press on, regardless of legitimacy, to the end.

Was it worth all the loss that the woman had endured?

What is the proper exchange rate between words and humans?

One life, let us say, for every worthy manuscript? Does that strike you as fair? Or a life for every *entertaining* fantasy, perhaps? Is that fairer? Then what of James Joyce, who drove his own children to madness and suicide, while he scribbled furiously, blindly, for seventeen years? What of W. B. Yeats, with his pompous declaration that one could achieve perfection of the life or perfection of the art, as if granting himself a licence to condemn everyone to suffering, if that was the price of his dreams? And what of Marx and Engels, Rousseau, Tolstoy and Shelley? For, ironically, it is when our fantasies are most magnificent, contemplating utopias of universal peace and prosperity, that they are also most inhuman. And what of my mother, whose inventions granted her life and brought others death? Were they not all murderers, Joyce, Marx, my mother, through neglect, through heartlessness, through lies? Through words.

What did Sergeant Mullery say, as he looked down on the woman's body lying among the foundations of the outhouse and as he read, through the thin film of cellophane, her already outdated account of herself? *My name is Kristina Galetti. I'm twenty-seven years old, of distant Italian descent, 170cm in height, medium build, with black hair and hazel-brown eyes, most frequently seen wearing denim jeans and dark shirts. You might guess, I was trained as a detective.* Did he cry out? Did he express his rage or despair? Did he murmur a prayer? Did he curse and rail against fate or his God? Did he swear revenge, or retribution?

Or perhaps, being an experienced detective, he had already prepared himself for this moment, this discovery. Perhaps, once he had learned of the mysterious disappearance of Kristina Galetti in the days after Margaret Malone was officially listed as a missing person, he had accepted that she was already dead and had grieved in private. Perhaps he was silent, then, at her grave. As silent as my father.

Perhaps the narrative overwhelmed him. For once it was released, after a minute, but fruitless examination by the forensic science laboratory, that narrative discovered in the grave of Kristina Galetti was found to be rather substantial, and rather cyclical, opening, as I've said, with *My name is Kristina Galetti*, rambling through her account of her involvement with the investigating unit, and closing with the doubts about what, if anything, Sergeant Mullery had said, as he looked down on his slain colleague lying among the foundations of the outhouse and as he read, through the thin film of cellophane, her already outdated account of herself? *My name is Kristina Galetti. I'm twenty-seven years old, of distant Italian descent, 170cm in height, medium build, with black hair and hazel-brown eyes, most frequently seen wearing denim jeans and dark shirts. You might guess, I was trained as a detective.*

A loop, in other words. A circuit. A ring. An orb, if one insists on being poetic. In many ancient mythologies, and indeed still in popular superstition, the circle is a symbol of perfection, of a closed and protected world, of fertility and immortality. Like most ancient beliefs, it is utter nonsense, promoted to soften the harshness of life. Even those of us whose exposure to depth is limited to the Hollywood western will know that an encircled wagon train is actually in danger of extinction and that hope, and promise, are offered only by a long thin line of wagons receding through a cloud of dust over a distant horizon, fading from our static perspective, leaving us behind to draw nooses, or coronets, or garlands, or haloes, or some other consolation, in the dirt.

The greyhound didn't bark.

Do you remember that Sherlock Holmes adventure in which Holmes refers to the curious incident of the dog in the night-time and, on being reminded that the dog did nothing in the night-time, explains that this was the curious incident? Well, the silence on Corriebracks that February morning was equally significant.

When I woke, after a late night and little more than three hours' sleep, it was already eight o'clock. The house, as they say, was as silent as the grave. Margaret, who invariably disturbed me while preparing to leave for work, seemed either to have overslept or furtively departed. And our greyhound could not be heard. Rosie, who always greeted the dawn, and then two or three of the following hours, with sustained barking.

I was regaining consciousness in the front room, of course, rather than in either of the bedrooms, but as an explanation for the eerie stillness, this was clearly irrelevant. I was still lying on the settee, where I had fallen asleep, exhausted from overwork, a few hours earlier. At the workstation to my left, around the computer and its printer, the fruits of my night's labours, so to speak, were untidily scattered. And on the floor in front of me, her head wound almost married to the carpet by the blood that had flowed from it and then congealed, lay the body of Kristina Galetti.

Yes, I know. In the previous section, the body of Kristina Galetti, along with the narrative that described her fatal journey, were both exhumed from a makeshift grave beneath the outhouse at Corriebracks. But that, I'm afraid, was merely how it should have ended. How it was meant to end. If it had to end. Not, in other words, with a neat resolution. Not with the outlaw's belated apprehension and the restoration of complacency to the prosperous suburbs at the foot of the Wicklow Mountains, but with the guards' discovery of their colleague's body and its accompanying narrative and with the reader's queasy suspicion that all their sympathies, all their outrage, their horror and their curiosity, had been guided by a predator. As Michael Elwood was guided. And Mary Corbett. Karen Stokes. Matthew Rushford. And Kristina Galetti.

Guided.

It allows for the involvement, as well as the submission, of the victim. Don't you agree? It's true that the innocent always expect to be treated fairly. On accepting a lift from strangers, for instance. On offering a lift to strangers. On first opening the pages of a new book. It's true. But the expectation is also naive. Scepticism is an undervalued virtue, if it is even numbered among the virtues. And why should we expect openness, when we disdain the transparency of other creatures? If humans had tails, most of us would wag them while preparing to bite. Some day, some diligent ornithologist may finally discover a complete joker of a bird who gives a warning signal to his own species just for the fun of it, when there is no danger, like the boy who cried wolf in the fable. Then we may have some real competition on this planet. But for the moment, we are its only liars. For our own purposes, we mislead each other. But perhaps we enjoy misleading ourselves most of all. Or perhaps we would go mad if we couldn't believe in the existence of trust. Once every four years or so, hordes of well-dressed men and women descend on the rest of us with outrageous promises. They look us steadily in the eye. They shake our hands vigorously. And you'll never catch one of them lounging or slinking about. They're called politicians, they control a large part of our lives, and they're voted into power by the rest of us.

Still dressed in chinos and a black sweater, because I had fallen asleep before undressing, I got up from the settee, stepped over Galetti's body and walked across to the front window to look out. On the track below, edging out of the pine woods at Blackpits, a convoy of vehicles was slowly climbing towards the cottage.

Margaret! I called.

There was no answer.

Rosie! I shouted.

And there was no response.

I snatched the binoculars from the sideboard. Through them, I brought the occupants of the lead car into focus and immediately, schooled by Galetti's superb description from the previous day, recognized the figure of Sergeant Mullery in the front passenger seat.

Although I could see the bonnet of the Subaru Impreza through the open doors of the barn, I knew that there was no prospect of escaping by car. Merely by approaching, the convoy was blocking the only exit. If they had come to arrest me, and there could be no other interpretation of their visit, they would, no doubt, have posted sentries to cut off other retreats. But perhaps, I thought, they might not have the capacity to cover all sectors of the mountain simultaneously and perhaps my greater familiarity with the terrain might prove a decisive advantage.

Pausing only to toss the binoculars aside, to gather the wallet with my money in it and to place the appropriate pages of printed text on Galetti's corpse, I hurried to the back door. To the south, along the exposed ridge of the mountain, I saw a pair of uniformed guards trudging wearily towards their positions. They hadn't yet reached the woods, where, presumably, they were destined to join with others and form an unbroken line. If I could clear

228

the open ground behind the cottage without being spotted, I thought I stood a reasonable chance of exploiting the small gap that still existed in the cordon.

Such is the perversity of human nature, however, that I almost hesitated. The prospect of leaving as a fugitive, as a malleable character, let us say, in someone else's narrative, while not entirely inconsistent, struck me as inappropriate, an unsatisfactory development, an unacceptable conclusion. But the instinct for self-survival seems, in the end, more powerful than the need for artifice. If one can make a distinction between survival and artifice. In any case, I stooped as I ran, trusting, quite correctly as it turned out, not to my own speed or cunning, but to the inept co-ordination of the various police units. Their convoy had moved off too early, before all the other officers were in place. There were no alarms, therefore, before I made it to the cover of the woods. No summons. No pursuit.

Coming out on the lane at the back of the woods, however, I heard voices to my right and I was forced to take another sharp, unpleasant detour, along the banks of Trether Brook and through Leeragh's Bog, from which I emerged wet and muddied, but still free. The back gardens of a number of houses now confronted me. In one of these, where the occupants of the house seemed to be away, perhaps on holiday, there was an old Ford Escort conveniently parked. I'm not particularly skilled at mechanics, but breaking into and hot-wiring a car, especially a model as dated as this one, is not one of life's greater challenges.

I drove north, for the excellent reason that the lane terminated in a cul-de-sac in the opposite direction, and eventually came to a T-junction, where I was offered a choice between Hollywood to the west and Laragh to the east. I chose east. I thought if I could get to Laragh, I'd abandon the car and catch a bus to Dublin, from where escape, while not easy, would be much more likely.

Laragh was a mere fifteen kilometres away. But halfway there, in the valley between the peaks of Tonelagee and Camaderry, beside two parking bays for idling tourists, I encountered a rather make-shift roadblock. Two uniformed guards and a mud-spattered patrol car. Disappointing.

I had no intention of alerting them by panicking, however. Confident that I could demonstrate the value of their time and the scandal of wasting it on myself, I drove on at a steady pace.

The guard who signalled me to stop, and who then came to the driver's *window to talk, was very young, very fresh-faced, and extremely cold. Good morning, sir, he said.*

Good morning, I responded.

Where are you coming from, sir? he asked.

Hollywood, I said. For who but a native, or a madman, would claim such an absurd origin?

And where are you going? he asked.

Laragh, I said. I have to collect my mother and take her to hospital. She's not at all well.

I'm sorry, he sympathized.

Cancer, I explained.

Unnerved, by the prospect of even gorier detail or even moister intimacy, the young guard stood upright. And was on the point of waving me on. When he suddenly had second thoughts.

Excuse me, sir, he said, stooping again to address me. Do you know that your tax disc is out of date?

The irony. And not even the expected irony. Too preoccupied with cursing my luck and with reassessing my options, I failed even to consider the possibility that he was lying. Scepticism is indeed an undervalued virtue, even among its own enthusiasts. The disc wasn't out of date at all. For some reason, the young guard suspected that the car wasn't mine and was testing my familiarity with the vehicle.

It occurred to me afterwards, of course, that I could simply have plucked the disc from the plastic wallet that was adhered to the inside of the windscreen. Having checked its expiry date, I could have waved it triumphantly in the young guard's embarrassed face. But I didn't do this. I trusted instead to my own guile. I invented plausible excuses for not renewing the road tax and offered convincing promises that the oversight would be rectified within twenty-four hours.

It was a performance, although brilliant of its kind, that succeeded only in rescuing the guard from the difficulty of keeping me talking while reinforcements arrived. He must have signalled to his partner at some early stage of our renewed encounter. Within minutes, while I was still patiently pleading my case, we were surrounded by other police cars, all spewing on to the tarmac a clutch of eager officers. I was pulled from behind the steering wheel by two muscular detectives and unceremoniously thrown to the ground, where I was pinned and roughly searched. They found nothing, apart from the wallet containing my cash, because I had left the cottage with nothing other than the money. When this was confiscated, and I was formally arrested, I was forced into the back seat of an unmarked police car, where Sergeant Mullery, wearing a grim expression, was already waiting for me.

Are you William Tracy? the sergeant asked me.

William? I repeated.

Tracy, the sergeant said. Margaret Malone says that you are William Tracy.

Then she is telling you lies, I advised him.

That's not who you are?

She is merely preparing her own defence, I explained. Whether it will succeed or not, however, depends entirely on whether she was apprehended in flight or surrendered voluntarily.

Never mind that now, the sergeant insisted. Just tell me what your name is.

A clarification first, I suggested.

What?

How did the young guard know that I wasn't the owner of the car? I wondered. From the smudges of printer ink on my fingers, perhaps? Did he have a description of me? Or did he see it in my eyes?

I have a particular interest, of course, in the mysteries of perception. We all know the person who reluctantly offers a dead hand when introduced and then leaves it hanging limply in your own like a dead fish, and we accept this as a sign of coldness, perhaps of sneakiness, just as we accept that the complete stranger who crushes your knuckles and dislocates your shoulder while pumping your hand in hearty greeting is open and warm and sincere. The conviction that those who look you straight in the eye are invariably sincere and trustworthy is common and deep-seated and has no less a popular authority on its side than Charles Dickens. And whatever the medical benefits of an erect posture, morally it still characterizes an upright individual.

But how do we get beyond such received simplicities? Rarely, perhaps? And always, do we have to say, when it is already far too late?

There had been a moment, of course, with each of the five subjects, an extraordinary moment, suspended between the realization that they had been drugged and their inevitable loss of consciousness, when they simultaneously groped for light and resisted darkness, when there was no longer any distinction between appearance and reality, when their faces paled with perception.

After leaving Johnnie Fox's pub and turning into the parking bay at the foot of Djouce Mountain, Michael Elwood abandoned his reserve, confided his troubles to Margaret, and finally, to hide his tears, and perhaps to dull his pain, accepted a drink from her. Perhaps he imagined that they were about to become lovers. Perhaps he anticipated pleasure and forgetfulness in her arms. Although he found, I'm afraid, only the latter, and never quite made it to her arms.

On a country road, off the south-bound carriageway, Karen Stokes braked sharply when the old man in her front passenger seat suddenly cried out that he had spotted his fugitive dog cowering in a nearby field. She waited patiently, her engine idling, after he had hurried from her car and clambered over a low wall. When he didn't return, she worried so much about his safety that she decided to follow him. Cold, wet from a fall into shallow puddles after losing her footing on the muddy ground, and carrying a ruined shoe that had been sucked from her toes, she was naturally a little irritated when they came together again, in darkness, in the middle of a field. So she accepted his tentative offer of bracing alcohol with a curious mixture of gratitude and resentment.

Mary Corbett and Matthew Rushford were the least challenging, the least interesting. One was already drunk, the other was desperate to become so.

And Kristina Galetti? For a number of reasons, she was, of course, unique. Her involvement was uninvited. Her inclusion therefore demanded a startling innovation. She was a police officer. Warped by the distortions of novels and films, by the seductions of policiér and thriller, most detectives are now persuaded that they are, by definition, hard-bitten and cynical, obsessed and alienated, driven by despair and fuelled by drugs and alcohol, and still far more perceptive than anyone else. The awareness of the danger she was in lasted so much longer than with any of the others, allowing a greater complexity in our relationship. And finally, once the dénouement was forced on me, she offered, not the egregious explanations that trivialise the absurdly misnamed mystery story, but a genuinely mysterious end to the series, and the serial.

Most of us, after all, soon tire of recurring patterns, no matter how perfect they are. In fact, the fewer defects there are in any given sequence, the fewer variations, the more quickly it seems to bore us. Verbal patterns. The tics and habits of a careless mind, the clockwork shrieks that grate along the nerves, *like the dripping of a leaking tap, when you have lived with someone for longer than a year. Don't you know, as Margaret always said. And if you like. And at the end of the day. But not only verbal patterns, of course. Sexual patterns, too. And structural patterns. Narrative and profile and investigation. Narrative and profile and investigation. Narrative ... Intensity is always lost in repetition. The novelty that excited us yesterday, leaving us gasping for breath with its freshness, provokes only an irritated sigh of recognition today. Familiarity, let us say, restores our restlessness, our appetite for flight.*

Led, flanked and followed by motorcycle outriders, our convoy, with its sirens screaming impressively, weaved its way through the untidy jam at the Wicklow Gap, where I had been apprehended, and hastened towards Wicklow town in the east, where I was to be formally interviewed.

Is that your name? the sergeant persisted as we travelled. William Tracy? Do you know a woman named Margaret Malone.

Margaret.

It didn't surprise me, of course, that she had ended up in the comforting arms of the authorities. For several days, aware that she was listed as a missing person and that the guards were searching for her, she had been brooding on her options. She claimed that no one knew of her residence at Corriebracks, that the only address they had for her was the apartment in central Dublin. That this was a lie is not really relevant. Long before we argued over the prostitute at Corriebracks, long before she attempted to even the score with Patrick Kelly and the police identified her through her amateurish efforts to offload the Subaru Impreza, I had anticipated her betrayal. After the death of the old man, Matthew Rushford, after the removal of his ears, we had difficulty justifying the episode. Or rather, I had difficulty. I had tired of the pattern and I found the sexual excesses dull. Routine. Unexciting. I observed the motions, of course. But dutifully. Abstractedly. Margaret, as always, was swamped by the passion and failed to notice my dullness, no doubt because it had no physical expression and I remained, stimulated by memory and by dream, as erect as duty demanded.

That great dialectic between security and risk, between familiarity and the unknown, between stability and progress, the tension that makes sense of human life, never had the least attraction for Margaret. Perhaps had no meaning at all for her. She was a deeply conservative woman, sustained, and handicapped, by a religious temperament. Left in sole charge of our enterprise, she would have turned the hunt and its climax into a solemn ritual, governed by a precise catechism of gesture, a breviary of accepted spells and responses, a rite of charms and incantations. She hated deviation. And even the palest novelty, the smallest improvisation, made her extremely nervous and suspicious.

The truth is, therefore, that long before the lacklustre sex after the death of Matthew Rushford, we were already drifting apart. For me, the passion had withered. And the attraction, too. There was nothing left but regret. And the regret was so intense that it had turned into a tendency to reinvent what had happened, into a desire to escape from a monotonous sequence. Into lies on one side. And sullen silences on the other.

Are you a student of western culture? I asked the sergeant.

He stared at me, ironically bewildered. Having already failed, with both encouragement and provocation, to make me talk, he clearly wondered what internal process had finally loosened my tongue. Student? he repeated.

Of western culture, I said. Of its literary and popular novels, its films, and its TV soaps and dramas.

I go to the cinema, he admitted warily.

Then you will understand, I said, that this is the real tragedy, this enforced separation of the passionate lovers, just as the initial romantic spark is surely the real purpose of life. This is what touches the heart. Not the incineration of millions, but the fading of love's eternal flame. Young Lovers Thwarted By Iceberg; Ship And Several Passengers Also Lost. Did you see that film? I forget its title and remember only the plot and the publicity tag. Or the other. Sneak Attack Destroys Promising Relationship At American Naval Base. Did you see that?

What I mean is this.

Several times during the convalescence of Matthew Rushford, I suggested employing the old man as an audience, a helpless voyeur. Perhaps I no longer wanted him to die. Perhaps I struggled to prolong his life by finding new uses for him. Perhaps I had simply wearied of the whole business. Margaret was appalled, however, and flatly rejected the request. When I brought the prostitute to the cottage on Corriebracks, it was therefore a gesture more of desperation than rejection, a last invitation to variety. This was refused. Instead, Margaret childishly retaliated by displaying the bruises from that argument to Patrick Kelly and by luring him inside the cottage. I left because we could no longer sleep while both of us were in the same house. I returned because I could not rest elsewhere either, knowing that she was capable of betraying me. And you are right. The previous narrative, which I wrote while

I was away and carried back with me – Between Trooperstown Hill and Laragh, where the road bridges the Avonmore River, there is a parking bay and picnic site for tourists – *was intended as Margaret's confession, to be found in her shallow grave. The final episode in the series. The completion of the loop.*

This chaffing relationship, however, when the stories we launch catch an unexpected current and drift back, edging too close to the life we want to escape, has always been an irritant. As my mother once discovered, it is the great problem with invention. Inherent. Unavoidable. Kristina Galetti called to the cottage on a routine visit. While waiting for the missing person's alert to bear fruit, the guards had decided to check on remote houses within a short driving distance of the dental surgery in Tallaght, and Galetti had drawn the addresses in our area. Seeing her, though, Margaret mistook her for another of my prostitutes. Refusing to heed my warnings to stay out of sight, she accused me of perpetrating yet another seedy manoeuvre in the deadly endgame we were already engaged in, and then insisted on vacuuming the front room, where Galetti was perched on the settee, slightly bored by now, and more than eager to leave.

Perhaps all stories terminate in farce.

Galetti immediately recognized Margaret, of course. She tried desperately to conceal her surprise, and her excitement, and her fear. But she failed, quite dismally. And her transparency left me with no option but to subdue her and to prevent her from summoning assistance with her radio.

Would you believe that, initially, I also had no intention of killing her? I saw no point to it. My ambition was flight. A new life. A new serial, perhaps. But irony of ironies, Galetti was a talker. Voluble. Loquacious. As natural a storyteller as my mother, with all that this implies. Her tongue was loosened by fear at first, no doubt. But it remained quite fluent once the shock had worn off. Quite voluntary. Almost relaxed. And irresistibly autobiographical. Confessional. And curiously, the more detail she confided, the closer she drifted at times, although unconsciously, I'm sure, to both the style and the content of the narratives from the graves. This was when it first occurred to me. This was when that perfect ending first formed in my imagination, of her colleagues simultaneously exhuming her narrative and her naked corpse from beneath the shell of the outhouse on Corriebracks, the perfection that I could not resist imposing on the story, even though it never came to pass. A scruple that would never have troubled my mother, of course. And therefore a clue to our diverging fates.

Naturally, I started taking notes while Galetti talked. When I saw that this inhibited her, I abandoned it, but installed a concealed tape recorder instead. I felt elated. Absorbed. Privileged.

Unfortunately, Margaret then became violently jealous. She persisted in disrupting our conversations, ironically with a succession of noisy domestic chores. She was nervous, of course. We hadn't yet finalized our arrangements for flight and it was clear that others would soon come looking for Galetti. But she was also spiteful.

Kristina Galetti was an ordinary young woman, an unexceptional detective. Neither plodding nor intuitive, neither enthralling nor off-putting, her qualities can best be encapsulated by the most agreeable adjective in the English language: nice. Although the details came from her own account, although Dennison actually killed himself and the others crumbled pathetically under the pressures of the work, she would have been appalled, for instance, by my depiction of her colleagues as the neurotic failures they undoubtedly are. Consequently, therefore, hers were the standard queries, the conventional questions. What was my name? Why did I kill? Why did I sever the ears of my victims? Why had I written things to leave in their graves? In exchange for her own absorbing story, she would have been content with the standard responses, the conventional lies. My name is William Tracy. I kill for the pleasures of power, for the thrill of being able to do whatever I want to another. I write for precisely the same reason. And I keep the ears as trophies.

Tell her the truth, Margaret suddenly interjected.

Galetti was sitting in an armchair. Her hands and feet were bound. I was standing across from her, close to the television. Margaret had come from her bedroom and was sprawled on the settee, dressed only in an unbuttoned white blouse and a short black skirt, neither of which concealed the fact that she wore no underwear.

Tell her the truth, Margaret insisted. You told all the others the truth.

The implication was clear. The truth was a death sentence. And Margaret jealously feared that I was unwilling to pass it on Galetti.

Perhaps she was right.

Tell her the truth, she mocked. You'll feel better for it.

Better for it.

As if the truth was a portion of contaminated food I had inadvertently swallowed. As if I was Raskolnikov in Dostoyevsky's Crime and Punishment, made feverish by guilt and saintly again by confession. As if we were not all born manipulative and acquired innocence only as we age. As if children didn't lie routinely. As if the truth existed. As if every man wasn't the aggregate of his own lies. And every woman, too.

Margaret laughed as she caught the look of contempt on my face. She stood up and sauntered across to me, provocatively swaying her hips. She took my right hand and placed it between her thighs, lifting it under her skirt until it touched her moist clitoris, perversely, if I'm allowed the adverb, granting me my earlier wish to employ another as an audience, a helpless voyeur. She looked at Galetti, however.

Tell me, detective, she said. Are you repelled by the practice of incest? Or are you one of those who understands that society's taboo, imposed to keep deformities from the genes, is no longer relevant in this age of mass contraception and personal emptiness?

Galetti, of course, not only immediately recognized this passage from the narratives, but immediately understood its significance also. Her face paled. Her eyes widened as she stared at us. She started trembling uncontrollably. And then she looked frantically around the room, an irrational movement that I first interpreted as a renewed urgency to escape, but that I later came to accept as a desperate search for corroborative evidence, a copy, for instance, of one of the photographs she had already inspected in County Kerry. In the end, of course, she didn't need a snapshot. She recalled the image of a young man posing with his workmates on seaside holidays and then imagined the process of its ageing over forty years, until she eventually arrived at the face that was staring back at her.

You're Christy Malone, she whispered finally.

Margaret laughed again, triumphantly, and pulled away from me, leaving my damp hand suspended in mid-air and slowly closing into a fist. Perhaps I should have been merely disappointed. I was enraged instead. After all my subtle evasions, my endless reinventions and fluid dislocations, here we stood, with all our complexities behind us, faced with the prospect of a trite biography.

What would you think, Margaret scoffed, of a young fella whose only ambition was to get away from the place where he'd been born, away from the sweaty bacon factory where he worked, away from all the stupid drinking sessions and the mangy greyhounds and the coarse men and women, a fella who read every book he could find and saved all his wages for five years and then, when he'd finally got his chance, came back to it all after only a month as a student in America when he got a letter telling him that he'd made a girl friend pregnant back in Ireland? Would you say he did the honourable thing? Even if I told you that he always blamed the child that was born for ruining his life? Even if I told you that he made her pay for it every day, first by telling her he wished she'd never been born, then by beating her, and finally by fucking her, when she was ten years old? Would you still think that he did the honourable thing? But you don't know the whole story yet. You know what the funniest thing was? The girl in Ireland was lying when she wrote to him that she was pregnant. She didn't get pregnant until after they were married, after he spent all his money on a wedding and a house, after his chance in America had gone up in smoke. He didn't even realize it until six or seven months into the marriage. Always the last one to know, as they say. The husband.

I lunged at Margaret several times, but she always managed to evade me. When I did catch up with her, she slipped through the open doorway. I chased her to her bedroom, managing to lodge my foot across her threshold before she could slam the door in my face. We argued bitterly, and at considerable length, loosening and embroidering the recriminations of a lifetime. We fought not only with words, of course, but with fists and with objects too.

All of this might have been insignificant. The argument. The revelations.

But I will never, so to speak, be the woman that my mother was, that my wife still is. Essentially, I am an innocent, as deeply in thrall to the colourful shifts of storytelling as any wide-eyed child. What I had failed to understand was that Galetti's chronicle concealed a deeper motive. While I was being distracted, she was planning her escape. During the row between myself and Margaret, she seized her chance, casting off the rope she had already loosened around her wrists and ankles and scurrying through the front door of the cottage.

In other circumstances, she would have made it. It was dark by then. Once she was out in the open, it would have been impossible to know which direction she had taken.

Unluckily for her, though, there was a dog on the premises.

As soon as I heard Rosie's furious barking, I pulled away from Margaret and hurried outside, through the now empty front room, and into the night. I immediately released the greyhound, and the bitch quickly picked up the scent and tracked Galetti to the open ground behind the cottage. When I caught up with them, I pleaded with Galetti to return and complete her account. Had I fallen for the young detective, I wonder. Or for her story, perhaps? In any case, she refused my request. She swung a rotting branch. I caught a glancing blow to my head that deflected me. But only temporarily. Rosie snarled and lunged at Galetti. I grabbed the makeshift weapon. In the ensuing struggle, as we slithered to and fro, Galetti slipped and knocked her head against a jagged rock, sustaining the injury to her right temple that left her lifeless.

I carried her body back to the cottage. I laid it on the floor in the front room. Mournfully, I have to say. The open wound to her temple was extremely ugly. It was foreign to my scheme, like a crude contrivance in an otherwise absorbing tale. Nevertheless, I had a project to complete. Ignoring Margaret's pleas to abandon the cottage and take flight, I worked feverishly at the computer through the night, typing the narrative that would lie beside the otherwise silent detective in her grave. My name is Kristina Galetti. I'm twenty-seven years old, of distant Italian descent, 170cm in height, medium build, with black hair and hazel brown eyes, most frequently seen wearing denim jeans and dark shirts. Afterwards, I rested on the settee while the pages were printing, estimating that I had at least two clear days before Galetti's colleagues retraced her movements and arrived at the cottage. But I fell asleep, from sheer exhaustion. When I woke, the greyhound wasn't barking. And Margaret had deserted me, to search among the head shrinks for understanding and forgiveness.

She hasn't changed, you see, my Margaret. She obsessively dyes her hair, from black to blonde and back again, sometimes within the same twenty-four hours, but she doesn't change. In essence, she is the same now, an entire lifetime afterwards, as she was the first time she left me, when she ran away from home as a fourteen-year-old. She still imagines that she can stimulate compassion merely by her absence. How little she has learned from her paternal grandmother, or inherited from her mother. How promptly either would have told her that only lies can stimulate compassion, only the tricks of the storyteller.

But then, perhaps only the barren, who need them most, can fully appreciate the comfort of lies. Having strangled my voice and my feelings as a child, having bolted my meals to escape as quickly as possible from the violent tension between my parents, I claim an insider's knowledge.

Was Margaret's childhood all that brutalized by comparison with my own, therefore? I doubt it. When she ran away from home at fourteen, for instance, she did so, not to escape what the sanctimonious like to call abuse, but to arouse my concern, to strengthen my attachment to her, to encourage my lustful pursuit. It was the wrong move, as I've explained, the least effective form of persuasion. But I doubt if any other would have succeeded. The truth is, I had already tired of exacting my revenge on Margaret. A month earlier, and this was the real reason for Margaret's desperate flight, I had met a young American woman, an academic, who was visiting Ireland while researching a thesis on the humorist Flann O'Brien. The more perceptive will have guessed already that her name was Sarah, just as the more knowledgeable will have noted that William Tracy, an eminent writer of Western romances who once delivered his wife of a middle-aged Spaniard, is a minor character in O'Brien's novel At Swim-Two-Birds.

It was Sarah who financed my disappearance, my forged identity papers, my fictional history, my passage to America, and my enrolment in a university. We spent twelve years together in the city of Trenton, New Jersey. Twelve years. Until a Friday afternoon in mid-August, when I was weeding in our back garden and waiting for Sarah to return from shopping. A little after six o'clock, I heard her unlock the street door and close it again behind her after entering. Through the large kitchen window I watched her reading her post. It was only when she suddenly swivelled from this, looking upwards after turning, that I realized that she wasn't alone and that her companion, a slim dark-haired young woman, finally came into view, stepping forward to plant a kiss on Sarah's cheek. Instantly recognizing my abandoned daughter, despite not seeing her since her early teens, I felt as if an abrasive cord was sharply tightened around my stomach. Like Adam cowering from his displeased God in the biblical myth, I desperately tried to shrink out of sight, even though I was already crouched behind the only decent cover in the garden.

She had known of my affair with Sarah back in Ireland, of course. Such was our cloying intimacy, our mutual paranoia, that we could hide nothing from each other for longer than an hour. Following her bitter return to the family home, she had doggedly worked her way through secondary school, through nursing school, and into employment in England and the States. And here she was, waving at me like Nemesis through our large glass window.

The rest, I'm afraid, is as tiresomely predictable as the dénouement of any policiér.

Within a month of Margaret's intrusion, Sarah had died of heart failure, brought on, her doctors apologized, by what was clearly an existing, if undiagnosed, condition. They misinterpreted my ironic laughter as mild hysteria. And so, before the coffin was even concealed in its grave, we danced again, my daughter and I, more wretchedly than ever before, her heart in my cold hand and mine in hers, from Trenton down to Washington, and from there across the Atlantic to the hills of County Wicklow, where my new prosperity bought us a cottage and the means to travel the mountain roads without detection, until . . .

The key was no longer in the ignition, it suddenly occurred to me.

Isn't that why the young guard held me at the checkpoint, I said to the sergeant. There was no key in the ignition. And he deduced, correctly, that the car was probably stolen.

The sergeant looked at me gloomily, without responding. He had been dull and taciturn for some time now, since we had entered and departed from Laragh and settled into the final leg of our journey. The excitement of the chase had obviously faded. The adrenaline had subsided. And I could see that he was mourning the death of Galetti, the loss of a colleague, perhaps of a friend. I wondered if he had already read the narrative I had left back at the cottage. But surely not. Surely he would have hurried on without pausing after establishing that the cottage was emptied of the living. And surely the printed pages would have been sealed in an evidence bag and taken away for forensic analysis.

I hope I have brought her to life, I confided to him.

He stared at me, rather blankly. What? he asked.

I hope, I said, that I have brought her to life. Kristina Galetti. As I hope that I brought all the others to life.

Shut up, the sergeant said wearily.

He didn't mean it, of course. My silence was the last thing the investigation needed just then.

All this was . . . Well, some time ago now. I no longer travel the lanes and back roads of the Wicklow Mountains, not with Margaret, not even with squads of heavily armed and nervous detectives any more, and certainly not by myself. For the moment, I live in a small, but rather comfortable cell, deep in the extensive grounds of an institution known as the Central Mental Hospital, where the criminally insane, as we are called, are incarcerated.

The authorities refuse to allow me the usual writing materials. Perhaps they are terrified that I will transform the pens and pencils into deadly weapons and the sheets of typing paper into tanks and fighter planes. On the other hand, they are desperate, as they say, to encourage me to express myself. They have given me, therefore, a small laptop computer. It has no connection to the outside world, of course, so I am immune to viruses. Every morning, I switch it on and miraculously re-enter my own past, adding a little more to my own history with every visit. Every evening, a young detective downloads the computer's data on to floppy discs and then removes the material for analysis the following day. I have no access, of course, either to the Galetti narrative I wrote during that last night in the cottage or to the other narratives found in the Wicklow Mountains graves. These have all been confiscated. What I do have, however, is an excellent memory, along with near-perfect recall. When I choose. Inevitably, however, there will be slight differences between the narratives I am re-writing and the ones already held by the police, fascinating variations that may keep scholars and psychiatrists occupied and remunerated for decades to come, thus fulfilling at least the secondary function of all stories in our contemporary world, even if, ultimately, this confession fails to prove that all you need is love.

I am here, incidentally, in the Central Mental Hospital, rather than in a standard, high-security prison, because my lawyer, an energetic young woman appointed by the court, has persuaded the judge, who may simply want to fuck her, that this is where I belong while undergoing psychiatric tests. No doubt she is preparing a defence of insanity, or temporary insanity, or unfitness to plead, if such a legal phrase exists. It is a strategy that has been more or less forced upon her, I imagine, largely by Margaret's enthusiastic, but imaginative co-operation with the police and the prosecutors.

I am told that Margaret has reinvented herself as an abused woman, formerly an abused child, an image that generates astonishing sympathy in our little society. In other circumstances, apparently, with a normal father, followed by a normal husband, she would have been a normal wife, lost in the weekly visit to The Rocky Horror Show, the annual viewing of Some Like It Hot on television, and the constant re-reading of some classic of unrequited love. Such cynical abuse of cliché should not be confused, of course, with her mother's pure invention. Margaret reads from another's text and is merely parroting the phrases she has learned. While the male's aggression inflicts untold carnage on the world, she recites, expressing itself in wars and tribal conflicts, rapes and homicidal driving, the female sadly picks up the shattered pieces and lovingly knits them together again, never the assailant but often the victim, driven to violence, in extreme cases, only by the need to protect herself and her children.

So, there are very few costumes left over for myself.

When you're older, Christy, my mother used to say to me, you can be whatever you want to be. You can be a famous scientist, a wealthy art dealer, even a successful artist. All you have to do is imagine it. And keep working hard in school. Otherwise you'll end up like your father, smelling of pig's blood and stale Guinness and incapable of holding his head up, even in his own house.

I know that she saw through my apparent disappearance and recognized it as the stratagem it really was. I know this because it was she who encouraged my flight, she who always insisted that utopia was not only possible, but necessary. Appalled by my teenage rebellion against the restrictions of school and my decision to embrace the man's world of the bacon factory she so deeply detested, she worked tirelessly to undermine my contentment. And she succeeded. I read, initially at least, to please her, but then became enthralled by imaginations that were even more powerful than hers. She blossomed, apparently, when I deserted both my family and the bacon factory, a cheerful response to my disappearance that was inexplicable to everyone else. I would have liked to have shown her what I achieved in America. She would have appreciated the irony of William Tracy, a fictional character who delivered a son who was old enough to be his father. But among the many evils that Margaret brought to Trenton was the news that old age had finally overtaken my mother. She was losing everything to it, including her gift for narrative, and we, her creatures, were already beginning to fade as we drifted further and further from our only source of light.

I won't stand at her graveside in the laboratory coat of a famous scientist or in the stained smock of a successful artist. There are very few costumes, as I've said, left over for me now. Either monster or maniac, it seems. And my lawyer, wisely perhaps, has chosen the motley of the fool. In this regard, she stresses that, in particular, my behaviour during the police interviews had a decisive influence on the decision to transfer me to an asylum, and she clearly implies that, if I am lucid enough to understand her point, then I should continue to behave irrationally. I admire her respect for fakes, but she misrepresents me, I think. I had no calculated behaviour at the interviews.

Tell us a little bit about yourself, William, the guards persisted in their neighbourly way, long before Margaret, with impeccable timing, finally demonstrated the redemptive powers of therapy and remembered that I was her father. Anything at all that you can think of.

Would you believe, I said, that while serving with the American Marines in Vietnam in 1968, I wore a chain around my helmet containing the right ears of eighteen gooks I had killed, the highest body count in our unit, although it's true that Woolrich, who, for some perverse reason, preferred the penis to the ear as a trophy, displayed an even score of severed phalluses around his neck.

You know we can check this stuff, William, don't you? they insisted. We know all the William Tracys that were born in this country. We can check these things. Just tell us a little about yourself.

My Uncle Charles, I said, whose mission was to save the world, announced his intention of addressing the meeting that had been called to agitate for the legalization of cannabis. In the Garden of Eden, he began, relieved of the encumbrance of clothing, Man was touched by the consciousness of his own perfection. With his eyes fixed on the audience, his fingers found and loosened the buttons on the first of his cardigans. He led by example. Words, useful in the groundwork, he did not trust to carry the full impact of his message.

Tell us the truth, William.

The enemy is at the gate, I said. A bearded young man, dressed in combat fatigues and carrying a Kalashnikov rifle, interrupted my sleep to bring me this curious phrase. I don't remember his name. Perhaps he woke me with the news that we were already surrounded as a final effort to extract the few words of recognition I had always denied him. If so, he had understood nothing. I don't deride his ignorance, however ...

Would you agree, they persisted, that you show more interest in the characters you create than in real people? This is an important point, William. Margaret Malone says that you treat people like characters. We don't agree. We think you have far more regard for the characters. What do you think?

When they had exhausted their questions, I reminded them of Kafka's parable, The Silence of the Sirens, in which he pointed out that although it was possible that someone might have escaped from the singing of the sirens, no one could have escaped their silence. They had no interest in Kafka, of course. Kafka had committed no indictable crimes in their jurisdiction. They had no interest in myself, either. They were concerned only with creating a culpable identity for me. Any identity, really. An explanation for my existence, consistent with the crude parameters of clinical psychology. A confirmation that I was different from them, and that they were different from me. But the study of psychology is a debilitating condition, for which the only known antidotes – faith and cynicism, lies and silence – have crippling side effects. And I refuse to offer my interrogators the reassurance that they are innocent. The Germans wonder why the rest of the world remains obsessed with the Holocaust, when the essential thing is to move on, to leave the beast behind. But the answer is simple. The Germans already know what they are capable of. The Germans have known for more than half a century what they are capable of. And we are still uncertain.

I'm almost finished now, you see. Except for a final turn.

Consistent with the internal conventions of the piece, this confession, concluding with the current narrative, will be discovered on the body of its author. Tonight I will hang myself. We are forbidden potentially damaging materials, of course, and the guards are particularly vigilant in this respect. Nonetheless, an opportunity occasionally presents itself. Every Saturday afternoon, a team of male nurses plays a soccer match against local opposition on the pitch at the rear perimeter of the hospital's grounds. Some of us, under heavy escort, are allowed on the sidelines as spectators. It seems to be part of our therapy. Perhaps they hope we will gain in self-confidence by comparing ourselves with the lunatics on the pitch. In any case, if one dares to be unsporting and refuses to keep one's eye on the ball, useful distractions may arise during a particularly exciting passage of play. A length of rope, for instance, used as a draw string to close a net of footballs. With this, I will hang myself tonight, although, for practical reasons, I must remain clothed, to place the laptop computer in a pocket, and I will hardly manage, post-mortem, to make trophies of my own ears.

The police, of course, will be surprised once more, challenged once more, and baffled once more, although the attentive reader will have already anticipated my suicide, and the later discovery of this confession on my corpse, as not merely satisfying, but also inevitable.

To you, therefore, and to all who have ears, I now must say, goodbye.